ANNA'S BOOK

A Dark-Adapted Eye
A Fatal Inversion
The House of Stairs
Gallowglass
King Solomon's Carpet

ANNA'S BOOK

RUTH RENDELL WRITING AS
BARBARA VINE

HARMONY BOOKS · NEW YORK

Published by Harmony Books, a division of Crown Publishers, Inc., 201 East 50th Street, New York, New York 10022. Member of the Crown Publishing Group.

Random House, Inc. New York, Toronto, London, Sydney, Auckland

Published in Great Britain by Penguin Books Ltd.

HARMONY and colophon are trademarks of Crown Publishers, Inc.

Manufactured in the United States of America

Library of Congress Cataloging-in-Publication Data
Vine, Barbara
Anna's book / Ruth Rendell, writing as Barbara Vine.—1st ed.
I. Title.
PR6068.E63A87 1993
823'.914—dc20   92-34309

ISBN 0-517-58796-3

10 9 8 7 6 5 4 3 2

ANNA'S BOOK

My grandmother was a novelist without knowing it. She knew nothing about how to become a novelist and if she had, it would never have occurred to her as feasible. The alternative path she took is now well known.

This is a collection of papers and memories: my grandmother's diaries, an account of a crime and a transcript of a trial, letters and documents and the things I remember. It is a double detective story, a quest for an identity and a quest for a lost child. At the same time it is a voyage of discovery and a witness to the triumph of chance.

At first I thought I must include the diaries in their entirety. It was impossible; I would have had a volume of a million words. Besides, most of my readers, if the sales figures are anything to go by, will already have read *Anna.* It seems to me sometimes that the whole world has read it. You may possess parts I to IV and have them on your shelves, at least in the paperback editions. You will know that the passages I include are extracts only and if you want to put them in context you have simply to consult your own copies. I have been obliged to choose the relevant passages—relevant, that is, to Swanny's story and to Edith's.

As to those few who have only heard of the diaries, heard them read on audio cassettes or seen the television adaptations, I would remind them that the notebooks themselves span sixty-two years, that those from 1905 to 1944 have already filled four fat volumes and that there are more to come.

It is the fashion to make films about how a film was made and television documentaries about producing documentaries. This book is about discovering a diary and about the long arm, nearly a century long, of artfulness and well-intentioned deceit.

Ann Eastbrook
Hampstead
1991

1

JUNE 26, 1905

Idag til formiddag da jeg gik i Byen var den en kone, som spurgte mig om der gik Isbjórne paa Gaderne i Kóbenhavn.

When I went out this morning a woman asked me if there were polar bears in the streets of Copenhagen. She is one of our neighbors and she stands behind her gate waiting for people to go by so that she can catch them and gossip. She thinks I must be a savage and half-witted too because I'm not English and I don't speak English well and stumble over words.

Most people here feel like that about us. It is not that there are no foreigners (as they see us), they are used to people from all over Europe but they don't like us, any of us. They say we live like animals and take away their jobs. What must it be like for little Mogens at school? He doesn't tell me and I haven't asked, I don't want to know. I'd rather not know any more bad things. I'd like to know some good things but it's a puzzle to find them, as hard as finding a flower in these long gray streets. I close my eyes and remember Hortensiavej, the birch trees and the snowberries.

This morning, in the great heat and sun—sunshine is never nice in a city—I went to the stationers at the corner of Richmond Road and bought this notebook. I practiced what I would say, the words

I'd use and I must have got it right because instead of grinning and leaning over me with his hand cupping his ear, the man in the shop just nodded and offered me two kinds, a thick one with a stiff black cover for sixpence and a cheaper one with a paper cover and lined pages. I had to take the cheap one for I daren't spend money on things like this. When Rasmus comes he will expect me to account for every penny I have spent, in spite of being the worst man in the world with money himself.

I haven't kept a diary since I was married, though I did when I was a girl. The last words in the last one I wrote two days before my wedding and then, the next day, I came to a decision and burned all my diaries. This was because I had made up my mind there would be no place for writing in my new life. A good wife must devote herself to her husband and to making his home. That's what everyone told me and what I suppose I thought myself. I even thought there would be some pleasure about it. I was only seventeen and that's my excuse.

Eight years have gone by and I feel differently about a lot of things. There's no use moaning and no one to hear me if I do, still less to care, so what complaining I do I shall have to do in these pages. The funny thing is that once I had bought the notebook I felt a lot better. For no reason at all I felt hopeful. I was still all by myself in Lavender Grove with no one to talk to but Hansine—for what that's worth—with two little boys and a dead one to think about and another coming. That wasn't changed. Nor was the fact that I haven't seen my husband for five months and haven't heard from him for two. The notebook couldn't take away the heavy weight of this child I carry, swinging on the front of me like a great sack of flour. It was my loneliness it changed, which is one of the worst things I have to bear in this horrible foreign country. In a strange sort of way it seemed to take the edge off my loneliness. I thought, I'll have something to do this evening when Mogens and Knud are asleep. I'll have someone to talk to. Instead of brooding about Rasmus, about how you can dislike someone and not want him yet be jealous of him, instead of worrying about the boys and what's happening with this baby inside me, I'll be able to write again. I'll be able to write it all down.

And that's what I'm doing now. Hansine has been in and brought me the newspaper. I told her I was writing letters and not to turn down the gas, which is what she usually does, all in the great cause of saving his money. It would still be light in Copenhagen at ten but it gets dark half an hour earlier here. Hansine has pointed this out three times since Midsummer Day, just as she tells me with peasant regularity that the days have started getting shorter. She asked me if I had heard from "Mr. Westerby." She always asks, though she knows the postman comes next door on both sides but never here. Why does she care? I believe she feels worse about him than I do, if possible. Probably she thinks that if he doesn't come back we three will end in the workhouse and she will lose her place.

The second time she came she wanted to make tea for me but I told her to go to bed. Soon, if no money comes, we shall all have to eat less and perhaps she will get thinner. Poor thing, she's so fat and getting fatter. I wonder if it's due to the white bread. None of us had ever tasted white bread before we came to England. The boys loved it and ate so much of it that they were sick. Now we have put the rye bread cutter Tante Frederikke gave me for a wedding present away in a cupboard. I don't think we'll ever use it again. Yesterday I opened the cupboard and looked at it, it has become a symbol to me of our old life and I felt my eyes burn with tears. But I won't cry. That was the last time I cried, when Mads died, and I never will again.

This room where I'm sitting, the "drawing room," would be tiny if I didn't keep the folding doors to the dining room open. All the landlord's furniture is ugly but for the mirror, which is just a little bit less ugly than the rest of it, an oblong glass in a mahogany frame with carved mahogany leaves and flowers twining about the top of it. A branch with carved leaves on it actually comes across the glass, something I expect the carver thought very clever. I can see myself in this mirror, sitting at the circular table with its marble top and iron legs. It is like the tables I see in public houses when I pass their open doors. I am sitting in a chair that is covered up with a bit of brown and red tapestry to hide the worn patches where the horsehair is coming through.

The curtains are not drawn. Sometimes a carriage goes by, or more likely a cart in this dreary place, and sometimes I hear a horse stumble on the pitted road. If I look to the right I can see the garden outside the French windows, a tiny yard with bushes covered with blackish green leaves that are the same winter and summer. This house is very small but the same number of rooms are crowded into it as in a proper size house. It's rundown and shabby round here, but pretentious, and that's what makes me angry.

In the mirror, in the pale gaslight, I can see just the upper half of myself, my thin face and my reddish hair that is coming loose from its pins and hanging beside my cheeks in wisps. I have the bluest eyes Rasmus ever saw, he told me before we were married, before I knew about the five thousand kroner. But perhaps anyway it wasn't a compliment. Blue eyes aren't necessarily beautiful and I'm sure mine aren't. They are too blue, too bright, the kind of color that is better on a peacock or a kingfisher. In fact, they are exactly the color of the butterfly's wing in the brooch I had from Tante Frederikke for my sixteenth birthday.

Not that it matters what color they are. No one looks at an old woman's eyes and I feel like an old woman, though I'm not quite twenty-five. That has reminded me to put the brooch on tomorrow. I like to wear it, not because it's pretty—it isn't—or because it flatters me—it doesn't—but, well, maybe out of what Rasmus calls my perversity and waywardness. I wear it to make people think, does that woman know that brooch is exactly the color of her eyes? And, that woman ought to know better than to show up the ugly color of her eyes. I like that. It's the kind of thing I enjoy, speculating about what people think of me.

The intolerable sun went down half an hour ago, dusk has come and it's quite dark outside now and very quiet. The street lamps are lit but it is still warm and close. I haven't recorded much on my first day of writing my new diary and I must record something, so I'll write down what I read in the paper about an awful accident to a

Danish cadet training ship. I only read it because the *Georg Stage* is Danish and the accident happened near Copenhagen. A British steamer rammed into it in the dark and twenty-two young boys on board were killed. They were very young, from fourteen to sixteen. Still, I don't suppose I knew any of them or their parents.

JUNE 28, 1905

My baby is due on July 31. Now, whenever she comes, it will be written down that July 31 is the day she was expected. I've put "she." Hansine would say that's tempting Providence. Luckily for me, she can't read. She gossips with people she meets when she goes out shopping, her English is awful but fluent and she doesn't mind making a fool of herself. I do and that's probably why my progress is so slow. But she can't read any language. If she could I wouldn't dare write in Danish which means not writing at all as I'm incapable of producing a line of English. "She"—I want a girl. There's no one I dare tell that to and anyway no one here who would care. Imagine saying something like that to the woman who asked me about the polar bears!

I wanted a girl last time, insofar as I wanted a baby at all, and instead it was poor little Mads who came along. He was dead within a month. So there, I have recorded that too. I do want this baby and I do want my daughter. Even if Rasmus never comes back, even if the worst happens and we have to make our way to Kórsór and throw ourselves upon the mercy of Tante Frederikke and Farbro Holger, I want my daughter.

But I wish she would move. I know babies don't shift about so much in the last weeks. I should know, I've had three. I wish I could remember how it was with Mads. Did he go on moving about right up to the end? Did the others? Are girls different and might her stillness be a sign she's a girl? Next time, and I expect there will be a next time, for that's woman's lot, I'll know. I won't need to remember, I'll have my diary and it makes me feel better to write these things down.

JULY 2, 1905

I don't write in this book every day. This is partly to keep it a secret from Hansine—she would try to guess what I was doing and think of something grotesque, letters to a lover perhaps. Imagine it!—and partly because it's not only a record of what I do but also of what I think. And it's about people. It's stories too, I've always liked stories, telling them to myself, true and made up, and now of course I tell them to my boys. I tell them to myself as a way of getting to sleep, for instance, and in the daytime to get away from reality, which isn't too pleasant to say the least.

When I was a girl and kept a diary I put stories in but I always had to be a bit careful about what I wrote in case Mother or Father found it. There is no place to hide anything where you can be absolutely sure it's safe from other people's eyes. But a foreign language makes things safe because it's like a code. It seems funny to call Danish a foreign language but that's what it is to everybody here. Well, not quite everybody. There must be Danes living here, our ambassador and consul and people like that and maybe professors at Oxford, and of course the Queen is Danish, and sometimes I read about Denmark in the papers.

Our Danish prince may become the first king of Norway, for instance, and there's been more about the *Georg Stage*. They've held an inquiry in Copenhagen but they say the President of the Court was biased and forgot to be impartial. The captain of the British ship broke down but still says he wasn't responsible for the deaths of those twenty-three boys. Another had died since. King Edward has sent his sympathies!

A much more important item is about a Russian ship called the *Kniaz Potemkin*. I wish I could understand better but there are so many long words. The people of Odessa, for some reason, wouldn't let the ship come ashore and take on provisions, or that's what I think happened, and so the ship turned its guns on the city and started shelling it. Those Russians are savages, worse than the Germans!

I saw a Cook's tour to Denmark advertised. If only I could go on it! We buy Danish bacon and there's a Danish firm makes something to spread on your bread called Butterine. They're called Monsted and the very name makes me homesick, so Danish, so *familiar.* But no Dane is likely to come to this house. Hansine can't read, Mogens and Knud haven't learned yet and I don't even know where Rasmus is. I could even put improper stories in only I don't know any.

If it was only a record of what I do this diary would be nothing but repetition. My days are all the same. I get up early because I wake up early and if I lie there all I do is brood about things and worry that the child inside me is sitting too high up. The boys are awake by the time I'm up and I wash their hands and faces and dress them and we go down to the breakfast Hansine has made. Coffee, of course, and the white bread Mr. Spenner the baker brings and the boys love. A Dane needs coffee more than food and I drink three cups. I can be careful with money in almost every way but I can't give up a single cup of my coffee.

Hansine has begun talking to the boys in English. Mogens is better at it than she is, children of his age seem to pick up a language very fast, and he laughs at her mistakes which she doesn't mind a bit but laughs with him and clowns about. And then Knud tries to speak it and they all make fools of themselves but seem to think it the best joke in the world. I hate it because I can't join in. I am jealous and that's the truth. I'm jealous because she's a woman and they're men, after all, aren't they? Somehow I know that if I had a girl she'd be with me, she'd be on my side.

JULY 5, 1905

I've thought of forbidding Hansine to speak English in the house and I think she'd obey me. She still respects me and is a bit afraid of me, though not half so afraid as she is of Rasmus. But I won't forbid it because I know I have to do the best I can for Mogens and Knud. They have to learn English, because they have to live here and do so perhaps for the rest of their lives.

Hansine takes Mogens to the school which is two streets away in Gayhurst Road. He wants to go alone and soon I'll let him but not quite yet. She grumbles under her breath because when her visitor is in the house she gets fearful pains in her stomach. I stay at home with Knud and take him on my lap and tell him a story. It used to be Hans Andersen for both the boys but when I left Denmark I left Andersen behind too. I suddenly realized how cruel some of his stories were. "The Girl Who Trod on the Loaf," about Little Inge who had to spend all her life in the Bogwife's kitchen underground just because she was proud of her new shoes, that was my mother's favorite but it revolted me. "The Tinderbox" was horrible too and "The Little Match Girl," so I've started telling the boys stories I make up myself. At the moment it's a serial about a little boy called Jeppe with a magic friend who can do anything. This morning we got to the bit where the magic friend polishes all the green verdigris off the copper roofs in Copenhagen one night and when Jeppe wakes up in the morning they are bright shining red-gold.

When Hansine gets back I go out. I put on my hat and then the smock that covers my great belly and a cape to cover that and hope people can't see I'm expecting but I know they can. Then I walk. I just walk. I walk all the way down Lavender Grove and Wilman Grove to London Fields and over to Victoria Park, sometimes up to Hackney Downs or down to de Beauvoir Town, all these places whose names I can't even pronounce. Along the streets mostly, looking at the houses, the churches, the great buildings, but sometimes I walk on the grass of the marshes or by the canal. It's too hot to wear a cape but if I didn't I'd feel too ashamed of the shape of me to go out at all.

Hansine makes *smorrebród* for luncheon but it's not the same without rye bread. I'd as soon not eat but I force myself for her sake, the baby's. If I don't go out walking again in the afternoon, and sometimes I do, I sit in the drawing room by the bay window. Our house in Lavender Grove is one in a row of nine, all joined together. It's not very pretty, in fact it's one of the ugliest I've ever seen, not as tall as it should be and built of gray bricks with clumsy stonework and wooden windows. There's a funny little stone face wearing a crown over the front porch and two more faces just the same over each of the upper windows. I wonder who they are or who they were meant to be, those girls with crowns on. But the house does have this bay window and a bit of garden in front with a hedge. I won't have net curtains, whatever Hansine says, because if I did I couldn't see out when I sit here and do my sewing.

Mother taught me to sew long before I went to school and I hated it. I hated the thimble—I remember I specially hated being given a thimble for a birthday present!—but I hated the needle going into my finger worse. Still, now I'm glad I learned. It's something I'm better at than Hansine who gapes at my tiny stitches and my careful darning of the boys' clothes.

Sometimes she fetches Mogens from school and sometimes I do. It was she who went today, on her way back from Mare Street where she got some thread for me from the draper's. She and Mogens came in talking English together. She had quite a tale to tell. An adventure had happened to her. Walking along by London Fields, she saw an old man ahead of her come out of the public house and stagger from side to side of the pavement. All that was important to her was to avoid cannoning into him but as she stepped to one side, he crashed into the wall and fell down unconscious.

It was a great shock for her and she was kneeling there beside him, trying to find his pulse for a sign of life, when a crowd began to gather. Of course there was no policeman or doctor. There never is when you want them. She was sure he was dead. Then a young woman came up and gave a great scream when she saw him. She said she was a servant in the house where he was a lodger. Everyone became very excited, as you'd expect, and some said it was the heat but the young woman said, no, it was the spirits he drank had got to him at last. Hansine said she would stay with her until help came, which she did, making her late getting to the school.

"I hope you didn't talk about all that to little Mogens," I said. "Old drunken men falling down in the street." "Of course not," she said, "as if I would," but I'm not sure I believe her. To women of that class such an incident is the most delightful and exciting in the world and they can't keep a word of it to themselves.

I said I didn't want to hear about it but she went on just the same, coming out with all the details in front of the boys. "That's quite enough," I said and I put my hands over my ears. "It'll be in the newspapers," she said, playing into my hands. "Well," I said, "that wouldn't be much use to you, would it, even if it was in Danish?" She went red as a geranium and held her hands over her stomach which is nearly as big as mine, she hates anybody talking about her illiteracy, but I just turned away. I don't care. I don't care any more about anyone but myself—oh, and my daughter that's coming, of course.

JULY 6, 1905

My birthday. I am twenty-five years old today. Not that anyone knows that. You can't expect a servant to know and the boys are too young but I confess I did expect my husband to remember. I ought to know him by now but I don't. Hope is a horrible thing, I don't know why these church people call it a virtue, it is horrible because it's so often disappointed. When you get old I'm sure you expect your birthday to be forgotten, you might not even want it remembered, but it's not like that at twenty-five.

All day I dreamed about how I'd have liked to celebrate my quarter of a century. I dreamed of a husband who'd give me a present, a fur coat or a diamond ring, and a grand dinner in the evening. Reality, as usual, was rather different. *Frikadeller* for supper again. Meatballs and potatoes have become our staple diet. We have *rødkaal* sometimes, done with vinegar and sugar, but Hansine has trouble finding red cabbages in the market. I long for *rullepølse* but we can't find the right kind of beef here and no good fish at all. Sausages are only 9d. a pound, so we have those. At least there is milk for the boys at 2d. a pint and I try not to worry about tuberculosis. Stonor's Dairy invites its customers to come and inspect the lairs where the cows live and Mogens and Knud are dying to go but we haven't been yet.

Hansine puts the boys to bed and then I go up and tell some more about Jeppe and the magic friend. Mogens said, "English boys aren't called Jeppe." "You're not English," was all I could think of to say to him. Then he said he would be if we were going to go on living here and could he call himself by another name? "What other name?" I said. "All the children laugh at my name," he said. "I want to be called Jack."

That made me laugh. Or I pretended it did. Really, I wanted to cry, I was so afraid, but I never do cry. I was afraid of everyone becoming English and slipping away from me and I'd be left alone, the only Dane in England. This evening I've been more homesick than ever I've been since we left Copenhagen. I've been sitting at this table in the fading light but not seeing the room or what's outside the window, only seeing pictures from the past. The green roofs of my city and the twisted spire of the Frelsers Kirke, the beech forests of Sjaelland, tea on the lawn at Tante Frederikke's. Why do the English never eat their meals outdoors in their gardens? Their climate is better than ours, a little bit better, yet they shut themselves up indoors while we take every chance we have to be in the sunlight and the open air.

I wonder tonight if I was wrong in what I said to Rasmus. But we have moved about so much, and always I think when I was in the family way, always in quest of some business advantage for him, some opportunity to make his fortune. From Copenhagen to Stockholm, where Knud was born, from Stockholm back to Copenhagen and the best place, my little white house in Hortensiavej. But I had to leave it and come here, London was the place, London was the center of the world; only when we had been here a month, just one month, he was all for being off again and trying America. That was when I said no, I put my foot down. "The worm has turned," I said. "You've crushed me for the last time."

Not that I was ever much of a worm. At least, I've always stood up to him wherever I can, I've given back as good as I've got. Except for the children, of course. He can punish me with many children but I can't punish him in the same way, can I? I said if he went to America he'd go alone, I was going home, and he could have the boys if he wanted. Instead, it was he who went home, attending he said to some "pressing business need" and I was left here alone. I knew by then I'd fallen for another baby.

Not a very enjoyable birthday!

JULY 12, 1905

I hate it here but somehow I know it's my fate. It will be better when I have my daughter. Not long to wait now, maybe no more than two weeks. I felt a little faint movement tonight, not much but enough to reassure me, though she is still high up and not standing on her head as she should be by this time, ready for escape. I think of it, her escape from me, as a hard swim against great breakers that keep her struggling, pushing her back. And that's how they come out at last, babies, swimming, thrusting against the tide, and opening their lungs to cry with relief when at last they reach the shore.

I must press on, I must be strong, come what may. Sometimes I think of Karoline that my father left on the streets of Copenhagen to find her own way to his house. She told me the story herself, for my mother never would, it was too improper for me to hear, and I am sure my father had forgotten all about it. But Karoline herself could never forget, the experience lurked there always in her mind like a goblin and she dreamed of it.

My father came to Copenhagen from a place near Aarhus in the north of Jutland. He married my mother, who was half Swedish, and did quite well, owning property and buying and selling furniture, and the time came when he thought my mother should have a maid to help her in the house, so he sent home to the farm for one of his nieces. They were so poor and there were so many children that you can be sure they were delighted to get rid of one of them. Karoline came. She was fifteen and she had to cross the Store Baeldt and the Lille Baeldt by ferry and take the train and do these things all by herself. She had never been anywhere, she couldn't read or write. She was like an animal, a farm animal.

My father met her at the railway station. It was a long walk to our house, several miles, and the poor girl was just an animal. When she needed to relieve herself she did what she had done in the country, moved a little aside—in this case to the gutter—lifted up her skirts, and squatted down and made water in the street. My father was so shocked and so angry he took to his heels and ran away from her. He had forgotten or made himself forget that this was how they behaved where he came from, he was nearly a gentleman now, so he ran away home, not looking back, running through the twisting streets and by the back alleys.

Karoline had to get there as best she could. She knew no one. She spoke with a coarse accent many couldn't even understand, she didn't know the address, only that the name was Kastrup, and she had never been in a city before, not even Aarhus. But she found her way, she had to. It took her till midnight but she found our house. I've never known how. "I asked a hundred people," she said to me. "I asked everyone I saw." At least when she got there my father didn't turn her away.

She was with us as our maid for many years. When I was sixteen and my mother died, Karoline too died of a monstrous cancer that grew out of her back. She can't have been more than thirty-two or three. She was already ill when she told me the story and it's been an example to me, something to think of and keep me going when I'm close to despair. I say to myself, Karoline made it and so will I. I'll get through and come out the other side.

JULY 14, 1905

I have heard from Rasmus and he has sent me money. Hansine was covered in smiles, her fat face all red and nearly split in two, when she brought me the letter this morning. I've said she can't read but she can recognize his handwriting and a Danish stamp.

"Dearest Anna," he calls me, and later on, "my dear wife," which is not at all the way he speaks to me, I can tell you. (What do I mean "you"? Have I begun talking to the diary?) Never mind. There is money, just when we were beginning to think even *frikadeller* were beyond our means and we'd be reduced to broken biscuits and Butterine.

It was a money order for seven hundred kroner which comes out at nearly forty pounds, the most you're allowed to send. I took it to the Post office in Lansdowne Road and they cashed it, making no trouble, asking no questions and not even smiling at my accent.

Now, at any rate, I shall be able to buy material to make baby clothes and have indeed done so already, white lawn and nun's veiling and white wool to knit from Matthew Rose's big department store in Mare Street. I shall be able to pay the doctor if I have to send for him when the baby comes. But I hope I don't have to. The others came fast, especially poor little Mads, without difficulties though with much pain. We shall call the doctor if there are problems but Hansine will be here to help me, as she did with Mads. She knows about making the afterbirth come out and how to deal with the cord. (It's a good thing I'm writing in Danish. Just think of someone reading that!)

Rasmus is back in Aarhus and has given me an address to write to, though he says he doesn't expect to be there long. I can't imagine what he's doing. He's an engineer, so-called, and I don't know what else to call him. The fact is I don't exactly know what it is he does. He's been a blacksmith, at any rate he can shoe a horse, and he can do anything with animals. He boasts that the most savage dog is quiet when he speaks to it and the funny thing is it's true. He makes animals love him. It's a pity he isn't as good with a wife.

Another thing he can do is make things out of wood. He could earn a living as a cabinetmaker but he won't. He despises that sort of thing. Motors are what he likes. He once told me—he hardly ever tells me things or talks to me much but he did tell me this—that he wanted to "bring motorcars to England." I thought there were motorcars here already, in fact I've often seen them, you see a few every day even in this place, but he means motorcars for everyone. Imagine a day when every man has his own motorcar!

What would happen to the horses, I said, and the trains and omnibuses come to that, but he didn't answer. He never answers the questions I ask.

One thing is certain and that's that there are no motorcars in Aarhus. I wonder if he's there to try and borrow money? He's supposed to have a rich uncle in Hjórring at the ends of the earth, though I only half-believe in this man's existence. I suppose I should be thankful Rasmus isn't a Mahometan, otherwise I'm sure he'd be finding another wife up there to marry for five thousand kroner.

JULY 18, 1905

This evening Hansine came into the drawing room and stood there twisting her apron in her fingers. It must have been the money making me feel good, or better than I have been, for I told her to sit down for a bit and talk to me. When I was a child I read a book translated into Danish from the English about a man stranded on a desert island, I can't remember what it was called. But this man was very lonely and when another man came along he was so happy to have someone, anyone, to talk to and be with at last that he didn't mind its being a negro savage. I feel a bit like that with Hansine. I have no one else to talk to except a seven-year-old child and a five year old and even the conversation of an illiterate servant is preferable sometimes to their nonsense and their everlasting questions.

I had the impression Hansine was trying to tell me something. She kept stuttering and turning her head about to avoid looking at me. Our Karoline was stupid and ignorant but I sometimes think she was a genius compared to this one. At last I said, "Come on, out with it, what is it you want to tell me?" I was thinking by this time that she'd broken something, not that we have anything valuable to break, or else it was about the sweetheart she had in Copenhagen, but it was only this old man that fell down in the street.

She is now firm friends with the servant from the lodging house who she calls "Miss Fisher." Apparently, she found out where the house is, in Navarino Road, north of London Fields, and went there, if you please, "to ask about the poor old gentleman." It turned out he was dead on arrival at the German Hospital. I suppose she was interested because he was a foreigner too. "Like us," she said, only he was a Pole called Dzerjinski. What's more likely is that she was just curious.

The people "Miss Fisher" is in service with are a man and his wife and two children, and an old mother-in-law, but no more lodgers now Dzerjinski is gone. Fisher said her master had given her notice but "her mistress, Mrs. Hyde" had "taken that back as there was plenty for her to do," minding the baby, cleaning the house and cooking for all of them.

I began to wonder what all this was leading up to, if anything, but it turned out just to be her way of asking if she could have this Fisher for tea here in the kitchen on her afternoon off. I couldn't help thinking how lucky she was to have found a friend while I know no one, but I said I'd no objection, provided she didn't neglect her own work and remembered it wouldn't be long before I'm confined.

It helps her with her English, having a friend who can't speak anything else. "I'll soon be chattering away better than you, ma'am," says she with a stupid grin and another blush.

I sent her to bed and then I wrote all this down. The baby sits heavy and unmoving and I have the strange feeling, almost certainly nonsense, that her head is caught up in my ribs. It's time she turned over. But at least I know what will happen next week or the week after when she begins her escape. I knew nothing when I was expecting Mogens, less than nothing. For one thing, I thought he would come out through my navel. I reasoned—not understanding about the afterbirth and how a baby feeds inside you—that the navel must have some use and what use could it have but to open and let the baby out? It was a great shock, I can tell you, when Mogens started coming out the other way. My mother told me Adam had no navel and, more to the point, neither did Eve. They weren't born but made by God. But the strange thing was that I never made the connection.

I'm tired and I'm going to bed.

JULY 21, 1905

It has been insufferably hot and it's like this all over Europe and America, according to the papers. (I make myself read the paper every day to help my English.) People are falling down dead from sunstroke in New York and here, which is more to the point, children have been poisoned by ice cream. I have forbidden Hansine to buy any for the boys.

A tremendous fuss is going on between England and Germany and Denmark and Sweden, all to do with who's going to be the King of Norway, Prince Charles of Denmark or Bernadotte. Or I think so, I could follow it better in Danish. The Emperor William is involved, as might be expected.

I've written a long letter to my husband which is why I haven't felt like writing this diary for three days. I wrote pages and pages of what I think are called "home truths," how horrible it is living here in this dreary street, how hostile everyone is with their stupid questions, the polar bear woman Mrs. Gibbons, for instance, and about the heat and my fear of war. It would be even worse for foreigners here if there was war with Denmark and Sweden was involved. How could he leave us here alone for months and months in a foreign country?

I told him something else I read in the paper, that the Princess of Wales has had a son, born on July 13. I am not so fortunate. I asked him if he'd forgotten I was expecting his child which may be born any day. Am I to bear it alone here? Suppose I die? Hundreds of women die in childbirth every day, though not Princesses of Wales. Hansine came back from fetching Mogens from school and told me of a woman who died this morning after her twins were born. She got it from another friend of hers, a very low class of person, a slum-dweller in those hovels off Wells Street. There are five other children, all under seven, and the father is sick and out of work. I screamed at her to be quiet, not to tell me these things, is she mad, has she no feelings? But I put the story in the letter to Rasmus. Let him hear it. Why should I bear it alone? It's his child too and his fault it exists.

Of course I don't suppose the letter will ever reach him. He will have moved on somewhere else in search of money or a loan or something to do with motor cars. Anyway, I didn't call him "my dearest husband" or anything like that. I believe in honesty. I wrote "Dear Rasmus" and ended it "your Anna," more to be polite than anything else.

JULY 26, 1905

Today I went out for a long walk. I took it slowly, carrying my great burden before me, and walked for many miles, returning by way of Ritson Road and Dalston Lane. I wanted to have a look at the Lutheran church, though it is German, not Scandinavian, and then I made a little detour to see the house where Hansine's friend lives.

If only Rasmus had taken such a house for us! It's not grand, it couldn't be in this part of London, but it's big, on four floors and you can see it's seen better days. There are steps up to the front door which has two big pillars holding up a portico, nice railings along the front of a real front garden and lots of trees around. Navarino Road isn't wide like Lavender Grove but narrow and shady and that always gives a better look to a street.

I was standing there looking at it, thinking the rent couldn't be more than £10 more than the £36 a year Rasmus pays for Lavender Grove, when a woman came out with a little girl. She was dressed very showily with a big feathery hat, but I had eyes only for the baby. That was all she was, though she could walk. She was so pretty and fair and dainty, like a fairy. I swear my baby moved when I was thinking this, put out a hand perhaps to greet this other child from inside there.

Fanciful nonsense, I know that. But it cheered me up and saw me safely home, like the great awkward ship that I am, rocking and swaying into harbor. Mogens and Knud were outside on the pavement playing with the hoops I bought them out of the money my dear generous husband sent us. If I don't need to pay a doctor when my daughter comes I shall spend some more and buy little Knud a spinning top. The boy next door has one so why shouldn't my boy?

As I entered the house a strong pain took hold of me and doubled me up. For a little while I thought, this is it. I didn't want Hansine fussing, starting to get water boiling and hanging sheets over my bedroom door, so I went upstairs to take my hat off and stayed there in my bedroom, not sitting down but standing and holding on to the bedpost. Another pain came but fainter than the first. I stood there, watching the boys and thinking how Knud too would be starting school in September and not knowing whether I was glad or sorry.

Then it came to me that I'd have my daughter by that time. She would more than a month old and I should be glad to have the boys out of the way. Perhaps she'd be born tonight, I thought. But though I stood there and finally sat down on the bed with my hands pressed to the great heavy lump, there were no more pains and I realized the same thing had happened as when I was expecting Mads. These are false pains some women have hours or even days before a real labor begins. Probably there is a scientific name for them but I don't know what it is. Last year, in February, I had them on the Wednesday and Mads was born on the Friday. Poor little boy, I didn't want him and I didn't know how much I loved him till after he was dead.

Suppose this one, my daughter, suppose she . . . But, no, I won't write it. I won't even think it. Or will writing it down be a kind of insurance and make sure it can't happen? I don't believe in things like that. I'm not superstitious and I don't believe in God. I won't give him a capital letter, I'll cross that out, it's ridiculous honoring something you don't believe in. He's just god, a god I know doesn't exist. I think I first knew that when I had a baby coming out of the wrong place that I thought was going to split me into two bits. I shan't be going to the Lutheran church, German or Danish or any other kind. And I won't be churched after the birth, as if there was something dirty about having a baby.

I won't have the doctor unless I must. Hansine can see to things. If there are complications she can run and fetch him. If only there were women doctors! I wouldn't think twice if it was a woman coming into my bedroom in a trim black dress with a stethoscope hanging round her like a smart necklace. But I shake with disgust at having a man there, seeing me so exposed, so vulnerable, my body open and indecent. And I believe men think it funny, doctors or not. You can see that little half-smile on their faces, the way they cover it with a discreet hand. Women are so absurd, they seem to be saying, so weak and foolish, letting this happen to them! How ugly they look and how stupid!

I went downstairs at last. Hansine was calling the boys in for their supper. My appetite has gone and I couldn't eat a mouthful. It was the same with all my babies. A few days beforehand I just stop eating. The boys were on the subject of names again. A friend Mogens has made at school told Knud his name is really Canute like a king who sat on the seashore and commanded the waves to stop or the tide to turn or something. He said he would call Knud Canute and all the others at school would and then the boys in the street started singing "Canute, Canute, like an old boot." So now, as if it wasn't enough Mogens wanting to be Jack, Knud wants to be Kenneth. Apparently, there are four boys in Mogens' class called Kenneth. I said they must ask their father, which is a sure way of postponing things for months.

1988

2

In our society, the extended family fast disappearing, one sees one's cousins only at funerals and then very likely fails to recognize them. The man who came and sat beside me in the church I knew only because he came into the front pew. Only a nephew of the dead woman would do that, so this must be John Westerby. Or his brother Charles?

I'd seen neither of them since my own mother's funeral over twenty years before and then only briefly. Business affairs called and both had had to rush away. This man looked smaller than I remembered. He also looked a great deal like Rasmus Westerby, whom I had called Morfar. He enlightened me by whispering, "Here's John coming now." It must be Charles.

My other cousin—I only have two—had come with the full panoply of family. The pew was just big enough to hold us all, Charles, John, John's wife, son, daughter, son-in-law and could it be a grandchild? I was temporarily distracted by trying to remember the names of that son and daughter but had reached no conclusion by the time a voluntary began and six men came in slowly, carrying Swanny's coffin.

There must have been a hundred people in the church. They sang up, they all knew the hymn. I hadn't been able to decide what to have, as far as I knew Swanny had no favorite hymn, but Mrs. Elkins had been able to name one. She said that in those last terrible months when she "wasn't herself," when she was "that other one," Swanny had gone about humming "Abide with Me." So that was what we sang, at full throttle, to the backing of a tape, because organists are hard to find these days.

I left first. There is a recognized protocol about these things, and John's son, who seemed to know all about it, deserted his family to walk with me. I murmured that he was very kind and he dipped his head in a formal kind of way. It was no use, I had no memory of his name, still less of what he did or where he lived.

The tears I hadn't quite cried seemed to dry up in my eyes. I felt choked. If I remembered her shuffling about that house, humming and mumbling, I was afraid of crying aloud. Instead, as we crowded round the graveside and the coffin was lowered, I made myself think how different it would have been if she had died ten years before. She might easily have done, she was over seventy then.

But for the diaries all these people wouldn't have been there. Swanny Kjaer (always mispronounced by the media) would have lived and died in obscurity. Who would have been at that woman's funeral, the woman she might have been? I, certainly, John or Charles but not both, Mr. Webber her solicitor and one or two Willow Road neighbors. Harry Duke's daughter and perhaps *her* daughter. That's all. As it is, we had the media *and* the press. Yes, there is a difference. The media's representatives would call themselves her friends and perhaps they were, those publishers' editors and publishers' publicity people, a crowd from the BBC, a producer and a head of features from the independent television company which made the series. The press were there with recording devices and cameras to put it all in the papers.

How would it have been if they could have seen her in her last days? What a story within a story that would have been. If they could have seen her divided into two by some strange illness of the mind, less and less herself as the other one took over. As it was, some of the young ones had tended to confuse her with her mother. The year 1905 was as far in the distant past to them as 1880 was. To them she was more the author than the editor of the diaries.

Their pale unmarked faces glazed with boredom as we processed across the damp grass to the grave someone had hygienically lined with Astroturf. After the coffin was lowered one of the Danish cousins, come here all the way from Roskilde, threw in a handful of earth. I identified the woman who followed suit as Margaret Hammond's daughter, but who the rest were, soiling their sleek gloves with damp London clay, I had no idea. A good many of the women were dressed more for a wedding than a funeral. Their high heels sank into the mushy turf. As we left the graveside it began to rain on their hats.

I took Mr. Webber back to Willow Road in my car and the rest followed—those that were invited, that is. I'd asked her agent and her publisher and the producer but I couldn't face giving wine and sandwiches to that mob of publicity girls and secretaries, all of them longing to see the inside of the house where Swanny Kjaer had lived.

It's a nice house, I'd always liked it, but I'd never seen anything remarkable about it until Torben told me it was looked on as one of the best examples of thirties' architecture in London. They moved into it when it was new, a few years before I was born. Now, as I unlocked the front door and stepped over the threshold, I caught Mr. Webber's eye. Or, rather, as I tried to catch his, he avoided mine. His face seemed more than usually impassive. I thought, do solicitors really read wills after funerals or is that something that only happens in detective stories?

Mrs. Elkins had prepared food and Sandra, who had been Swanny's secretary, had appeared from somewhere and was organizing the drinks. Smoked salmon, white wine and sparkling water—it is always the same wherever you go. I spotted the two nurses, Carol and Clare, and then the relative whose name I couldn't remember was at my side, telling me he remembered seeing Swanny at his own grandfather's funeral and how impressed he'd been by the look of her, her height and her beauty.

"I couldn't believe that was a great-aunt. I was only twelve but I could see how elegant she was and how much better dressed than the other women."

"She was different from the rest of the family."

"In more ways than one," he said.

I knew then that he didn't know. His father hadn't told him because *his* father hadn't told *him*. Ken, I remembered, had never believed a word of it. He said suddenly, surprising me, "You'd have thought, wouldn't you, that Anna and Rasmus having all those children, they'd have a great many descendants by now but there's only us. There's only *me* to carry the name on. Aunt Swanny didn't have any children, Charles hasn't—and you haven't, have you?"

"I've never been married," I said.

"Oh, sorry," he blushed a fine rose red.

That reminded me of how young he must be, that and saying he was only twelve when Ken died. He looked young, of course he did, but his clothes weren't a young man's. Until now I'd never seen anyone under fifty in a stranglehold stiff collar and a dark overcoat with a waist. His hair was neatly parted and cut short at back and sides. The blush mantled his face for a good half-minute and by the time it faded Mr. Webber was back by my side. He seemed to have constituted himself my protector.

He stayed until everyone else had gone. I didn't really notice until they *had* gone and he was still there. A woman in a big black hat, on her way to the door, had asked me if there were any more diaries to come and would I be editing them, and another in a gray fur hat, less well informed, wanted to know (flatteringly, I suppose) if I was Swanny's granddaughter.

Mr. Webber and I were left alone among Swanny's things. He said, with great and unexpected sensitivity, articulate as ever, "When someone famous dies people tend to forget that those left behind may well feel the same degree of sorrow as, in a like situation, do the nearest and dearest of some obscure person."

I said he put it very well.

"They suppose," he said, "that the wellsprings of grief have been desiccated by the fierce light that beats upon the high shore of the world."

I smiled uncertainly at him, for that wasn't at all the way I had thought of Swanny, though many may have. Then we sat down and he took some papers out of his briefcase and told me she had left me everything she had.

Though the will had yet to be proved, I could have stayed there. Who was there to object? Instead, I went home. To have remained after the news I had had would have overwhelmed me. I should have entered I think one of those strange nervous crises in which it is impossible to keep still, one must wander from room to room, twisting one's hands, pacing, needing someone to tell it all to but not knowing who that someone might be.

At home was better. I sat down quietly. I asked myself why I had never thought of this but had supposed I should get a small legacy and all the rest would go to the Roskilde relatives. There had been a message from Swanny for me in the will. Mr. Webber had read it: ". . . my niece Ann Eastbrook because she is Anna Westerby's granddaughter in the female line and the only living woman descended from her." He hadn't commented on this and neither had I. All it said for me then was that Swanny had loved her mother, which I knew already, and that John and his children were excluded because their descent was through Uncle Ken.

I should be rich. An authors' researcher, which is what I am, leads an interesting life but doesn't make much money. I could, if I wished, go and live in Willow Road. I could give up work if I chose, though I didn't think I would so choose. I would have money and stock to the extent of about half a million. There would be royalties for years to come. I would possess the four-poster that perhaps, or perhaps not, had belonged to Pauline Bonaparte, the black oak table carved with oak leaves, the Head of a Girl, the ormolu clock, the Bing and Grøndahl Christmas wallplates, each one different and each one dated, from 1899 to 1986, though excluding the most valuable, the first one of 1898.

Indeed, I possessed them already. They had been mine since Swanny's death. Already I owned the limited edition of three differently shaped vases, all white and embossed with crowns and the Royal Arms of Denmark, created for the coronation of Christian X and presented to Torben's parents on their marriage. The Flora Danica dinner service was mine now and so was the Karl Larsson that hung in Swanny's drawing room of the parents and children having tea under the birch trees.

The diaries were mine too, published and unpublished, printed and still in manuscript, translated and untranslated. Those, I'm sure, are what most people in my position would have thought of first. And if I'd stayed in Swanny's house I expect I should have been tempted to look for them. Not knowing where Swanny kept the originals, I should have had to find them and do what I had never yet done, look on them alone and touch them.

Of course, if I'd done that after Mormor died or even fifteen years ago, it would have meant nothing to me. They would just have been an old woman's jottings, an old woman with no pretensions to being a writer beyond a fondness for telling stories. Since then they had undergone a metamorphosis, not only their contents but the materials of which the notebooks are made too, their physical substance, so that this has somehow been hallowed and taken on the quality of a First Folio or a copy of the Vulgate. Thinking of them made me want to see them. I did the next best thing and went to look at the dollhouse.

The place I was living in had an exterior room separate from those which comprised the flat. A flight of steps and two landings were between my front door and the door of this room which had its own Banham lock and key. The previous owner told me with commendable honesty that he had found it quite useless. You couldn't give it to a guest because in order to reach the bathroom he or she would have to put on a dressing gown and slippers, let themselves out of one front door, climb a flight of stairs and let themselves into another front door. I said I should find a use for it. It would be somewhere to keep the dollhouse.

Two or three months had passed since I had last looked at it. Feeling guilty over this neglect, I took a duster down with me, unlocked the door and let myself in. It was early spring and quite dark. I put the light on and closed the door, not wanting to be seen by other tenants passing up the stairs.

It was stuffy in there because the windows had been kept shut and the blinds down. There was a little black gritty dust on the windowsills but none on the dollhouse. I thought of Swanny, a girl of ten when Morfar began to make it, I thought of her watching him work after my mother had gone to bed and I wondered, by no means for the first time, what she had thought. Had she minded? Had she felt rejected? Or did she consider herself at her age too old for such things and the little sister welcome to it?

The first page of the first diary had been started a decade before but from then on the diary-writing never stopped for very long, so Mormor must have been setting everything down in her notebook at the time Morfar was carving miniature wood paneling and sculpting tiny stone fireplaces and laying bits of velvet for carpets. I opened the back of the dollhouse and looked into the drawing room where I knew the only books were. The ones in the two bookcases with mica fronts that looked like glass were simply rows of spines painted onto card, but a real book lay on the console table, a tiny object half the size of a postage stamp which nevertheless had real pages and a real leather cover. It was very ingenious but if you look at it you can see how he has done it, how he cut a quarter-inch square from the thickness of a notebook—one of hers?—and bound it with a strip of kid glove. Perhaps that was one of hers too. Remembering them, I could imagine her berating him. She never had any time for the dollhouse.

For all that, the diaries, notebook one or two or five, come to that, should have lain on that table. The tiny pages of his book were blank. Morfar had not been a literary man. I was standing there, thinking about Swanny witnessing all this craftsmanship and wondering if I could get a kind of micro-version of the diaries made for the dollhouse, if it was worth it or if it would be silly, when the phone started ringing in the flat upstairs.

The answering machine was on but still I went up. By the time I had closed the rear of the dollhouse, switched off the light and locked the door behind me, the ringing had stopped, I could here my own voice saying I wasn't available and then a woman's unfamiliar voice.

She had wasted no time, whoever she was, the features editor of a magazine I had only vaguely heard of. She was interested in the future of the diaries now Swanny Kjaer was dead. Having heard that there were not only diaries yet untranslated but that extracts from the early diaries had been suppressed, she wanted to know if I as their new possessor would be publishing them. However, she would call me back next day.

I switched off the machine and the phone rang immediately. It was Mrs. Elkins. She had been at the funeral but we had scarcely exchanged a word. Would I want her to continue cleaning the house in Willow Road? I said, yes, please, and resisted uttering a panicky cry: Don't leave me! The nurses, presumably, would know their services were no longer required and sometime or other a huge bill would arrive. Thinking of them brought back in a too-vivid picture Swanny's deathbed and I wondered how long it would take to erase that from my memory, the sight of her rearing up in bed and crying, "Nobody, nobody . . ."

I banished it, temporarily, by concentrating on my plans for her memorial stone. I sat down and drew a gravestone, though I can't draw, and wrote on it a line from Eliot: "There is no end, but addition," her dates, 1905–1988, and her name as Swanny Kjaer. Her name in full no one ever used except occasionally Torben. I was grown-up before I knew what it was.

Another ringing from the phone interrupted me. For a moment I couldn't place the plummy voice and the name Gordon meant nothing. But when he said we'd talked a couple of hours before I knew it was the young man with the rich full blush and the black overcoat. As soon as I heard his name I remembered his sister's: Gail. They were Gordon and Gail.

"My second cousin," I said.

He wouldn't have that. He spoke gravely, as if it was of serious importance. "No, no, your first cousin once removed. You see, my father was your first cousin."

"Right. And your child, when you have one, will be my first cousin *twice* removed."

"Oh, I shan't have any children. I'm gay."

For one who blushed so easily, he said it with a calm unembarrassed casualness, as if he had been saying he was cold or English or a cricketer. Good. If this was the new way, I was glad.

"What can I do for you, Gordon?"

"I'm a genealogist. That is I'm an amateur genealogist. By profession I'm a banker. And, just for the record, it's pronounced gee-nee-a-logist, not gee-nee-o-logist. I always tell people because otherwise they get it wrong. I do family trees for people. I charge a thousand pounds a time."

I said faintly that I didn't want a family tree.

"No, no, I don't suppose you do. I'm doing one for me. My father's side, the male line. I thought you might give me some help. I wouldn't take up much of your time, I promise you. I shall be going to Denmark for my summer holiday to trace our forebears there but I shall need a little information—" he hesitated, "—from someone on the spot. And I thought perhaps you'd let me have a look at the diaries."

"Three volumes are published. They're published up to 1934."

"I meant the originals. I believe in going back to sources."

"They're in Danish."

"I've a Danish dictionary. Perhaps sometime I could come and just take a look?"

"Yes, well, sometime," I said.

To avoid more enquiries, instead of switching the machine on to the answer mode, I unplugged the phone and the extension. The quite irrational idea came into my head that this was just the night for someone to break into the house in Willow Road and steal the diaries. I had scarcely given them a thought while Swanny was alive. If anyone had wanted to steal them they might easily have done so, she and the night nurse were alone in that big house and couldn't have stopped them. Now she was dead they were becoming a worry to me. They seemed both enormously valuable and enormously vulnerable. I began to wish I had stayed in Willow Road to keep an eye on things. I wondered if I should sleep.

Then, made uncharacteristically nervous, I became convinced I had left the light on in the room on the mezzanine floor. I had left the light on and not locked the door after me. I went down and found, of course, that the door was locked. I had to open it to check that the light was off. Padanaram, the dollhouse, sat there, looking handsome, owning the room, testifying to bygone skills and old-fashioned arrogance.

Someday, I would have to find someone to give it to. As I walked back up the stairs I wondered if the little girl who was Ken's great-granddaughter and Gordon's niece would like to have it.

The journalist called back next day. I told her no extracts from the diaries had been suppressed. I'd no plans for their future and suggested she give me a call next year. With that she had to be content, though I don't suppose she was.

By lunchtime there had been two more calls, one from a magazine specializing in domestic interiors, which wanted to do a feature on the house in Willow Road, and another from the editor of a Sunday supplement suggesting I might be interviewed for their series on people with famous grandparents. They easily found my phone number. The nature of my work requires that I advertise my services in *The Author.*

I said no to both and departed for the newspaper library, to continue with my research of Kensington in 1890 for a client who wrote a series of historical detective stories. Of course I left the machine on. I have to. I need the business—or do I? I asked myself that, coming back on the bus. Did I need it anymore, now I had Swanny's house and Swanny's money?

However, for that day at any rate, such reflections came too late. The *Hampstead and Highgate Express* had left a message and so had Cary Oliver.

"It's Cary, Cary Oliver. Don't hang up on me, don't switch the thing off. I know I've got an awful cheek but please please can we let bygones be bygones? I'll explain what I want—yes, of course I want something—I'll phone you. It's about the diaries, but you've guessed that. I'll get my nerve together and phone you. But in case, in the highly unlikely event of you feeling like phoning me, I'll give you my number."

She gave it, she gave it twice, but I didn't write it down.

3

My mother gave me the dollhouse when I was seven. It was a birthday present and yet it was not. The dollhouse had always been there, occupying a spare bedroom in our house almost to the exclusion of everything else. I was accustomed to it, allowed to look at it but not to play with it. That was reserved for my attainment of the age of reason.

I knew I'd get the dollhouse on my birthday and with it unlimited license to use it as I wished. Still, if it had been the only present from my mother I think I'd have been disappointed. The ice skates were what I had longed for and exulted in. Hope deferred may make the heart sick at first; later it leads only to boredom. By the time the dollhouse was mine I was fed up with waiting for it.

Pleasure came later. Enquiring about its provenance came much later. Then I knew only that the dollhouse had been made by my grandfather, a man said by those who had known him to have been capable of making or constructing anything. It was a facsimile of his own house, or rather, the best and biggest of his houses, and the one they lived in longest. Padanaram was its name and this was also what we called the dollhouse. Indeed, we *always* called the dollhouse Padanaram, whereas I suppose the original was sometimes referred to as "our house" or "Far's house." For a long time I thought it was a Danish name, a name of sentimental association given to the house by my grandparents to remind them of something or somewhere they had loved in the country they had left. It was my Aunt Swanny who set me right when, some five years afterwards, I asked her and my mother what it meant.

"Why did you think it was Danish?"

"Well, they were," I said. "I just guessed it must be. It's not English, is it?"

Swanny and my mother laughed a lot and began trying to pronounce Padanaram in a Danish way, giving the *d* a *th* sound and placing a sighing stress on the final syllable.

"What does it mean then?" I said.

They didn't know. Why must it mean anything?

"The house was called that when Far bought it," Swanny said. "The people who sold it to him would have given it that name."

No curiosity had impelled any of them to try to find out. In a dictionary of place names I was looking through for quite some other purpose I found Padanaram. A village in Scotland. The name comes from Genesis and means "the plain of Syria." Did it arise from a Nonconformist chapel sited there? My job was discovering such things and it gave me pleasure to tell my aunt. Swanny took it unenthusiastically.

"Those people who had it first must have been Scottish" was all she said. She tried to remember their name but couldn't.

My Padanaram, that had been my mother's before me, made for my mother, was about the size of a small dining table, and it was on a dining table whose top was a very little larger than its own area that it stood. The original, in Highgate, to the east of the Archway Road, I'd often seen, walking past or from the top of a bus, though of course I'd never been inside it. But according to Swanny and my mother, my Padanaram was a faithful reproduction. The outside certainly looked the same, of stucco and brick, with two large gables, many latticed windows, an imposing front door inside a portico with curved roof showing a Dutch influence. Thousands of such houses were built in the nineties in the suburbs of English cities for a prosperous bourgeoisie.

Morfar had papered the walls with wallpaper he had painted to look like the originals. The stairs he'd made from real oak and

French-polished them, according to Swanny. She could remember him sitting there, using bits of cottonwool wrapped in lint to dip in the polish and making painstaking figures of eight, on and on for hours, to bring a deep shine to the wood. The carpets on the floors he made from tapestry cut-offs. He had painted in the brickwork on the outside with rose madder oil paint and Chinese white, and had made the stained glass for interior and exterior windows from pieces of Venetian glass.

"Mor had a set of twelve Hock glasses," Swanny said, "and one of them got broken. I suppose Hansine broke it."

"Hansine was always breaking things and if Mor broke anything she put the blame on her because Far was such a martinet."

"I'd ask her, only she'll say she's forgotten. You know what she's like, Marie. Anyway, whoever broke it, it was broken and Mor said the set was spoiled. I wouldn't have thought it was. When were they ever going to have more than ten people all drinking German wine at once? But she must have thought the set was spoiled or she'd have made more fuss when Far broke three more to make the stained glass windows for Padanaram."

"He broke wineglasses to make stained glass windows?" I said.

"Don't ask me, I don't remember," my mother said.

"You weren't allowed to see, Marie. It was his big secret. He'd do it after you'd been put to bed."

"I know. I had to go to bed early for two years."

"Well, it took him that time. Mor made the furniture and the curtains and he built the house. First of all he made the drawings. Mor said he drew like Leonardo, which was amazing for her, she never has a good word for him. He meant to build the house to scale but in the end he abandoned that idea. It was too difficult and it wasn't necessary. He used to spend whole days hunting for the things he needed, those tapestries, for instance. He plundered Mor's things shamefully. I remember a necklace she was very fond of, it was only paste though it looked like diamonds, probably it was very good paste. He took it to bits to make a chandelier. And the thing was, she wasn't even interested. They had terrible rows over it. Do you remember how they fought, Marie?"

"I hated it," my mother said.

"He broke a red Hock glass and a green one and he meant to break a yellow one, only Mor got so angry she threw it at him and it broke that way. Mor said it was ridiculous making a dollhouse for a five year old to spoil. She called it a 'palace for a princess' and she said an old packing case would have done just as well."

I was about twelve when this conversation took place and Padanaram, a serious plaything of mine for three or four years, had recently taken on the status of a museum piece or exhibit in my life. For some time I had ceased to move dolls in and out of it, have them encounter each other in the various rooms, get up, go to bed, entertain. The adventures they had there, mostly enacted inside my own mind in a stream of mental activity, had dwindled and lost their enchantment. Now I kept Padanaram exquisitely clean, and having repaired the depredations of the past careless years, darned the tapestries and titivated the upholstery with dry-cleaning fluid, displayed the dollhouse to visiting friends who, if highly favored, were led into the room where it still stood and permitted to see the hinged fronts opened, though never to touch.

It was then, probably in the middle of this phase, at its height, that I asked the question. Asking it, I wondered why I had never thought of it before. How could I have possessed Padanaram so long and yet never asked? I had brought a friend home from school to tea, and her wonder at the sight of Padanaram, her almost reverential awe, was particularly gratifying. I saw her off, going down to our front gate with her, and came back into our sitting room where my mother was with Swanny, who regularly came to spend Wednesday afternoons.

They were speaking in Danish. They always did, to each other, to Mormor and, on the rare occasions when they met, to my Uncle Ken. Yet neither of them had been born in Denmark, as Ken had, but in England, in the house before Padanaram or, in Swanny's case, in Lavender Grove, Hackney. Still, Danish was their first language, truly learned at their mother's knee.

At my entry, again as always, Swanny switched to English in

mid-speech, and the soft, monotonous, glottal, elided sentence ended in a graceful falling pentameter.

"Why did Morfar make Padanaram for Mummy and not for you?" I said.

As I said it, as I was uttering the very words, I had a momentary feeling of making a mistake, a faux pas. I shouldn't have asked. The question would cause embarrassment. They would be upset by it. But I was wrong. I knew at once I'd said nothing tactless, hurt no feelings. There was no frisson. No half-glance of warning or concealment passed between them. My mother shrugged and smiled. Swanny looked merely amused. But she was prepared to explain. She always appeared frank and open, as all three women did, expansively ready to speak of anything, to air their emotions and open their hearts. This is the insidious kind of frankness, more deceptive and finally maddening than true transparency, the apparent artlessness that seems impulsive and spontaneous, yet masks an ingrained passion for privacy.

Swanny spoke plainly, even cheerfully. "He didn't like me."

Immediate protest from my mother. "Now that's not true, Swan!"

"You mean you don't like it being true."

"Of course I don't like it, but that isn't the point. When you were little, Far and Mor weren't living in the sort of house you'd copy for a dollhouse. They were living in Stamford Hill. I was born there. No one would make a dollhouse to look like that place in Ravensdale Road."

"And since when," said Swanny, "does a dollhouse-maker have to copy his own house? He can copy someone else's, can't he, or make one up out of his own head? If I can admit it, why can't you? He never liked me, he scarcely took any notice of me. You were the daughter he was waiting for." She gave my mother a sidelong look, a charming almost coquettish look. "After all, Mor loved me best." Nothing was said. "Still does. Always will." She started laughing.

"Thank goodness," my mother said.

· · ·

Scandinavians have solved that question of what to call one's grandparents. Not for them the decision as to which grandmother shall be called Grandma and which Granny, which grandfather Grandpa and which Grandad, nor the awkward habit of speaking of "Grandpa Smith" and "Grandpa Jones." One's mother's mother is simply that, Mormor, and one's mother's father Morfar. Similarly, the other side would be Farmor and Farfar. I called my mother's mother Mormor from the start because my Mormor had called her grandmother that and I never questioned it until I went to school and the other children laughed or mocked.

After that I learned to refer to "my grandmother" and, in relation to Padanaram, "my grandfather." The old names were kept for family use and, in Mormor's case, direct address. I shall sometimes call them Mormor and Morfar in this narrative but more often refer to them by their Christian names, Anna and Rasmus, for this is only occasionally my story, I am only the watcher and the recorder, the notetaker, the privileged insider. Mormor and Morfar do not figure in it as my grandparents but as themselves, as Anna and Rasmus Westerby, Danish immigrants to an insular and xenophobic country at an inauspicious time, the dollhouse-maker and his wife, the diarist and her husband.

Still, it's not their story either, though they play important parts in it. Nor the story of my mother, for whom the dollhouse was made, nor of Jack and Ken, born Mogens and Knud, nor of Hansine Fink's descendants. It is the story of Swanny herself, my grandparents' elder daughter, Swanhild Anna Vibeke Kjaer, born Westerby.

Or perhaps born something else.

My parents had to get married. This was quite a disgraceful procedure in 1940, though the alternative was worse. My mother never made a secret of it but told me the tale with Westerby openness. She was married in August and I was born in December. In the meantime, my father, a fighter pilot eight years her junior, was burned to death in his blazing Spitfire over Kent. It was on one of the last days of the Battle of Britain. Mormor and Swanny also, from time to time, told me the tale of the hasty marriage. Only Morfar had been enraged, disgusted, appalled (his words, apparently) and all for disowning his favorite child. Absurdly, he had threatened to take the dollhouse back. Padanaram, made for her, owned by no one but her, the child's unique property, the errant woman was to forfeit.

Socially one of the elite, my father had come down the scale a step or two in marrying Marie Westerby. His own father was a small Somerset squire and his mother an Honorable. But this pale gray pair, thin, gentle and unfailingly courteous, welcomed their son's widow as if, instead of a waitress in the officers' mess, she had been the daughter of some neighboring landowner. Once a year we spent a week with them in their small manor house near Taunton. Away from them, I recalled only their low voices, an almost extravagant gentleness and an absentmindedness, particularly marked in Grandpa Eastbrook, so apparent as to make me ask my mother if he was talking in his sleep.

Very different were the grandparents who lived close at hand. East London was where they had come to in 1905 and, to use a phrase that would have meant nothing to them, "upwardly mobile," they had moved northwards into a bigger and better house. The original Padanaram was the summit of their upward mobility in the area of home buying. During the depression of the early thirties, when Morfar's business failed, they were forced to move to a shabby double-fronted villa in a road off Crouch Hill, to be known in the family from its street number, as was the family's way, always as "Ninety-eight."

It may be only hindsight, but now it seems to me that I always saw them as slightly disreputable. It must be hindsight when I say they were like hippies grown old, since in the fifties no hippie had yet come into being. Unlike my Eastbrook forebears, they weren't stalwart reliable people, but retained into old age something child-like and capricious. Morfar was a violent old man, without wisdom, constantly looking back to regret lost opportunity and blaming everyone but himself for that loss.

A tall and handsome figure, who always wore a beard (according to his wife, to hide a weak chin), he came regularly to our house on a Sunday afternoon for conversation with my mother's "fiancé." My mother had a number of these "fiancés," in series of course, none of whom she married nor even perhaps had any intention of marrying. No doubt they were her lovers but if they were, she acted in their company with a quite uncharacteristic discretion and none of them ever stayed overnight. Morfar took a great fancy to one of them, whether the first or the second I don't remember, and passed a good two hours of a Sunday telling this man the story of his life.

His English never became good. It was fluent, of course, but grammatically appalling, each phrase studded with errors. Nine out of every ten words he mispronounced. He was especially bad with ultimate ds, w sounds and the letter b which in his rendering changed to v. Reading this, I see how merciless it looks, how unsympathetic towards an old man's ineptitude, yet no one who had known Morfar could have seen him in that light. He was so self-assured, so confident of his general superiority to all, so insensitive, so certain of his linguistic mastery, that he would often boast of being equally proficient in Danish, English and German, to the extent of having to pause and think before he could be sure which language he was speaking.

Seated in our living room, drinking sweet tea, he would inflict on my mother's fiancé a stream of doleful or indignant reminiscence, sometimes growing heated and thumping a large gnarled fist on our coffee table. Everyone, it seemed, that he had ever been associated with in his business ventures had swindled him, a word frequently on his lips and rendered as "shvinded." "It schoothe not have veen," was what he said when he meant something shouldn't have happened, which was almost every transaction of his commercial life.

Casual clothes were unknown to him, even the formal casual clothes of the period, sports jackets and flannel trousers. He always wore a suit, a shirt with a stiff white collar and a dark tie, in winter a gray trilby hat and in summer a straw boater. And he invariably arrived, in one of his ancient cars of course, the Morris ten or the huge unwieldy Fiat, alone.

He and Mormor seldom went anywhere together. Until I read the diaries I had only a distorted idea of what their married life must have been. They had stayed together, but most people did, however incompatible. Mormor sometimes said, with a harsh laugh, that she had to live in a big house "to get away from my husband." Even to me, he was always referred to as her husband, never "Morfar" or "your grandfather" or "Rasmus." Ninety-eight was scarcely big enough to allow of this freedom, though there were four bedrooms. Looking back, it astonishes me that until he died they continued to share a bedroom and a bed.

She went out on her own. When she came to us it was on her own. A small thin woman with elaborately coiffed white hair, she was the last person you would have thought of as a walker. But she walked, she always had, roving apparently purposelessly the streets near her home, stopping to stare at houses, peer over garden fences, sit on seats and mutter to herself, walk again. She dressed until she died at ninety-four in the fashions of the twenties, her prime and when she had been at her richest. Photographs of her in these clothes show a tweed coat by Chantal, a Lelong dress, a rubberized raincoat and flyer's helmet by Schiaparelli. For a few years, Morfar had made money selling his Cadillacs and was not yet the prey of swindlers.

But mostly I remember her in waistless black or dark blue "frocks" with embroidered insertions in their V-necks, high-heeled shoes with double instep straps. She went for her long walks in those shoes, grinding the heels down. For going out in the evenings and for funerals she had a black satin coat in a crossover style that fastened with a single jet button, and a pancake-shaped black satin hat. The first time I saw this hat was when she wore it in our house at a family gathering after Morfar was dead.

Never one to beat about the bush, she came straight to the point.

"Now I must decide which one of you three I am to live with."

She spoke as if such a decision must lie entirely with her. Had any widowed parent since Lear dared to put it so bluntly? Mormor was a reader but it was Dickens she read, not Shakespeare. She had Lear's choice of making her home with one of three children, though one of them was male. John, Charles and I sat silent, possibly aware this was a momentous meeting.

Swanny and my mother were no Goneril and Regan. Still, no one spoke. Mormor surveyed her son and her younger daughter with that mild malice, tempered with amusement, a twitchy smile, that was so characteristic of her. I doubt if she had ever seriously thought of Ken's large dark mansion flat near Baker Street as a possible home for herself, nor of the stout dull headmaster's daughter he had married as a possible companion. But she would keep them on the hook for a few minutes longer, savoring Maureen's efforts and her failure to look warm and sympathetic, before turning away and leveling her gaze on my mother.

"I shouldn't take up much room, Marie."

While almost everyone who knew my mother had anglicized her name into Mari or gallicized it into Maree, Mormor and Swanny continued to pronounce it in the Danish way, roughly as Maria with the *r* coming from the throat. As she spoke, Mormor seemed to swallow her *r* even more than usual.

My mother said, rather feebly, that we really didn't have any room, and it was true that our house was small. But we had three bedrooms and if some solution could have been found to the problem of where to put Padanaram, the third could have accommodated Mormor. My mother and I lived on the income my father had left her, having inherited from his own grandmother the capital it derived from, plus her widow's pension and the considerable allowance my Eastbrook grandfather made her, an allowance which continued under his will. We were quite well-off.

Both she and Swanny would have thought it demeaning for a married woman or a widow to work, an almost direct reversal of the attitude prevailing today. I never heard my mother mention the possibility of taking a job. She had no hobbies, no apparent interests beyond reading women's magazines and very light popular fiction. She kept our house clean and cooked very nicely. As far as I know she was serenely happy. She looked it. She was even-tempered, sweet, pretty and kind. I never once saw her in tears. A large part of her time she spent in caring for her clothes and looking after her appearance. Shopping she enjoyed and going to the hairdresser. After I came home from school she would change her clothes, do her hair and make up her face in the heavy elaborate way that was then fashionable, and one of the fiancés would come or else we would go out, usually to the cinema. For years we went to the pictures twice a week.

What did she and the fiancé do? Talk, as far as I know, sometimes put on a record and dance. I never saw a kiss or a touch, apart from the dancing. Two of them had cars and would take us out for drives. I was always included in these trips and on long Saturday or Sunday outings, but once a week, until I was old enough to be left by myself, my mother would go out alone and Swanny would come to be with me. I have since supposed that it was on these occasions that she and the current fiancé went somewhere to make love but I may be wrong.

Into this pleasant innocent existence my mother had no intention of allowing Mormor to intrude. I remembered how when I had enquired about the dollhouse, Swanny had said simply that Mormor loved her best. And perhaps we all understood, within moments of her selection beginning, that it was to be Swanny with whom Mormor would choose to live until she died.

But she wasn't prepared to put the rest of us out of our suspense just yet. When she wanted to use an endearment to her daughters or to me she would prefix our names with the adjective *lille*. In Danish this of course means "little" but it can carry in its sense, far more than the English word, a suggestion of "dear," of affection, of tenderness. Swanny received it most often—"*lille* Swanny." Now it was my mother's turn, a fairly rare instance.

"I could have your guest room, *lille* Marie. You could put that old dollhouse in your garage."

"You'd have to ask Ann about that. It's hers, remember."

"What does a big girl of fourteen want with a baby's toy?" said Mormor rather grandly. Her bright blue eyes, a hard, almost ugly turquoise blue, snapped with their kingfisher flash. She proceeded to shock everyone, as she always could. "My husband's dead. He won't get to know about it where he's gone to."

A month later she moved in with Swanny and Torben. But first she put Ninety-eight on the market and sold it within days. If she had ever had the chance she would probably have turned out to be much better at business than Morfar. No one would have "schvinded" her. She drove a hard bargain and, refusing offers, stuck out for the five-thousand pounds she had asked for the house. Today it would fetch forty times that but it was a good price in 1954.

The four-poster that had possibly belonged to Pauline Bonaparte was one of only two pieces of any size she kept and took with her to Hampstead. There had been valuable furniture, for Mormor's own father had owned property in Copenhagen and when his tenants defaulted on the rent he took their tables and chairs from them in lieu of the money. Quite a lot of this Morfar had managed to get his hands on. But everything went and, apart from the bed, a big black carved table and her ancient couturier-designed clothes, all Mormor took with her were her albums of photographs, her complete works of Dickens in Danish translation, and the notebooks, by then forty-nine of them, in which she had been writing down her life since she was a young girl.

Now that the diaries have been published, now that *Anna* and its sequels are bestsellers and it is fashionable to say how wonderful they are or what rubbish they are, it seems strange that none of us was in the least interested in what Mormor wrote or had even noticed that she wrote anything particular at all.

Open about matters most women of her age are anxious to keep dark, she was secretive about that one thing. When she was writing and someone came into the room, the notebook was quickly slipped away. Sometimes, I believe, she sat on it. So when I say that the notebooks arrived along with the bed, the complete works of Dickens and the photograph albums, when Mormor moved in with Swanny, I don't mean that any sort of parade of them was made. I only know that they must have arrived with her because Swanny found them when Mormor died nearly twenty years years later.

The fashion for "granny annexes" had hardly arrived in the

fifties. Swanny's house was quite large, big enough for a flat to have been contrived in it, but Mormor lived *en famille* with her daughter and son-in-law. They had no children and she was with them as much as if she were their child. That is, I think, she was with them when it suited her. She ate all her meals with them, sat with them in the evenings and was determined always to be there when they entertained. But she never went out with Swanny, she never came to us at the same time as Swanny came. She went out alone or, as often as not, with Uncle Harry, and was gone for hours, just as she spent long hours alone upstairs.

Mormor was a very old woman by this time and it was inevitable she repeated herself. The interesting thing was how seldom she did so when telling her stories. Some, of course, had passed into a family mythology, the one about her own parents' maid Karoline from Jutland, for instance, and the one about the drunk but otherwise puritanical uncle who disapproved of Morfar's brother being divorced and threw a bottle at him in a bar in Nyhavn. But she was always coming out with new ones. She could always surprise us.

My mother and I were with her in Swanny's house when she recounted one none of us had heard before. Mormor had been living there for about a year by then and her seventy-fifth birthday wasn't far off. Out of courtesy to me, for my Danish was never good, she spoke in English, a heavily accented drawled English, though immeasurably better than Morfar's had been.

"My husband married me to get my dowry. Oh, yes. Not very nice to think of, is it? But I'm used to it, I have had to live with it."

She didn't look as if it particularly distressed her. She looked as she habitually did, astute, calculating, rather pleased with herself.

"That's the first I've heard of that," Swanny said.

"No, well, I haven't told you everything. Some things I have kept back." She gave me one of her hard intense smiles. Age had not made her face sag but tightened it so that there was not much flesh left, only a mask of bones and deeply lined skin with those bright harsh blue eyes staring out of it. "It's good for old people to have some new things left to tell. Otherwise they might become very boring to their poor children."

My mother asked, "What dowry?"

"Five thousand kroner," said Mormor, rather triumphantly, I thought.

"It doesn't seem much." It was about two hundred and fifty pounds.

"Not to you perhaps, *lille* Swanny, you with your rich husband and lovely house. It was a lot to *him*. He came to Copenhagen and heard about old Kastrup's daughter who would have five thousand kroner when she married and the next thing he was coming round to our house and making eyes at *lille* Anna."

It sounded like something out of Ibsen. Mormor's utterances often did. It also sounded fairly unlikely. I could see from their expressions that neither Swanny nor my mother believed a word of it. Mormor shrugged her shoulders, leveled her blue gaze at each of us in turn in the way she had.

"What did I know? He was tall, he was good-looking. He had a weak chin but he wore that brown beard to cover it up." Something made her laugh. She laughed harshly. "He was a clever engineer, he could make anything, everyone said. He could make a silly girl fall in love with him. For a little while."

It wasn't much of a revelation after all. Much of it was probably in her imagination. It seemed unlikely to me that any man would marry a girl for the sake of two hundred and fifty pounds. I thought the story on a par with one we had heard before and which she now proceeded to retell, about how when she was pregnant for the first time, she thought the baby would come out through her navel.

"Imagine my surprise when he was born the usual way."

All this is in the diaries of course, but we knew nothing of that then. It saddens me sometimes to think that my mother never knew, that she died before the diaries were found. Some of Anna's stories could be disproved. The anecdote about Hansine, asking as she cleared the dinner table when guests were present, "Are we gentlefolk or do we stack?," I later found out had originated in a *Punch* cartoon from the twenties or thirties. The birth of Mogens coming as a surprise to his mother was perhaps another fantasy that had found its way into her mythology. A lot of her stories were funny, some bizarre or grotesque. The biggest one from her past she might never have told but for a malicious intervention, and then she did no more than put up a kind of defense.

It was good for old people to have something left to tell, as Mormor herself had said, for otherwise they might become boring to their poor children.

4

Igaar var der Solformórkelse. Vi Havde fortalt Drengene at det vilde blive mórkt—Laererne giver dem ikke altid de rigtige Oplysninger—saa de var meget skuffede over at det var bare Tusmórke og at det ikke varede laenge.

Yesterday there was an eclipse of the sun. The boys had been told it would get dark—these teachers don't always give accurate information—and were very disappointed when it only became twilight and that not for very long.

Things are getting worse in Russia and now they are having riots against the Jews. There is cholera in Berlin. I haven't heard from my husband since he sent the money and that was before Swanhild was born. But I don't care. We're all right on our own, the boys and the baby and Hansine and me. In fact we're a lot better without him and but for the money, which we'll soon need, I'd as soon he never came back.

For one thing, he won't like the baby's name. He'll say it's a Norwegian name and it is, but so what? Just because he has a lot of stupid prejudices and despises the Norwegians. I expect he will want her called Vibeke after his ugly old mother. Even if he makes me have her christened Vibeke or Dagmar I'll still call her Swanhild. And when I cuddle her and put her to the breast I'll call her Swanny. There's no one can stop another person calling someone what she wants.

I've loved the name since I was a young girl and read the *Volsunga Saga*. Svanhild was the daughter of Gudrun and Sigurd Fafnersbane. When Gudrun killed her second husband Atle she tries to drown herself but the waves take her to a land where King Jonakr rules. She marries him and Svanhild grows up at his court and is later wooed by the mighty King Jormunrek.

He sends his son Randver to ask for her hand in marriage, she accepts and follows him home on his ship. But Bikke, the evil servant, tries to persuade her to take him for her husband instead and when she refuses tells Jormunrek she has been unfaithful.

Jormunrek hangs his son and sentences Svanhild to be trampled to death by wild horses but the horses cannot touch her so long as they can see her beautiful eyes. Bikke blindfolds her and then nothing can stop the horses. There are more terrible revenges and Wotan comes into it all somewhere. I was romantic when I was young and I liked the idea of beauty taming wild beasts. It's all so ancient too, lost in the mists of antiquity, as Onkel Holger says, a favorite phrase of his.

SEPTEMBER 1, 1905

We weighed Swanhild on the kitchen scales this morning, Hansine and I. They belong to the man who owns this house and they weigh in pounds and ounces, not kilograms. It sounds strange to me, nine pounds, two ounces, it doesn't mean anything much, but it must be all right because it's a lot more than when she was weighed at the chemist's a month ago. I'm proud of her. I love her. I like writing that down because a few weeks ago, if anyone had asked me and asked me to be really honest, I'd have said I don't love anyone in the world.

I'm only twenty-five and I could honestly have said I felt love for no one. I thought I'd love my husband when I married him but that didn't last five minutes. In fact, it was over that first night when he hurt me so and I thought he was a madman who was trying to kill me. I get worried about the boys if they're ill or I can't find them in the street but I don't care about being with them. The truth is, they bore me. You can't call that loving. As for my father and Tante Frederikke they're just old people who heaved sighs of relief when I was safely married and out of the way.

The friends I had at school have all disappeared. Well, they got married too. When women get married they've no time for friendship. A woman I talked to before I came to this country told me her husband was her best friend. I ask you! So I'd come to the conclusion I didn't love anyone and it frightened me a bit, thinking like that. It seemed wrong, it seemed wicked, even though I couldn't help it. It wasn't anything I'd *done* but just something which *was.*

As I wrote that last word Swanhild started crying upstairs. She always cries at the right time, when my breasts are getting uncomfortable and too heavy with milk.

I'm coming!

OCTOBER 15, 1905

The trial has begun of the man who murdered his wife in Navarino Road. Hansine is fascinated by all of it. She has begged me to read the account of it to her from the Hackney and Kingsland *Gazette* but of course I won't. I didn't know these people and I don't want to read about them. The next thing was that I came upon her asking Mogens to read it to her. He can read anything, both in Danish and English, I think he's going to be a bright boy, but naturally I said no, on no account. I've told her not to mention anything about that trial or those people in this house. I was so fierce I frightened her. Anyway, she was quiet.

Rasmus might murder me if he knew everything about me, if he knew everything that goes on in my heart. For that's where I'm free, free to be myself, to do as I like, to think as I wish and not pretend. There are no noisy schoolboys there and no screaming baby—not that I'm complaining about Swanny, she's the best thing in my life—no chattering thick-headed maid and no absent wandering husband who may be anywhere.

I know he's all right, though. More money has come, another five hundred kroner, so we're safe and can pay the rent and eat plenty of good food. We shall have a fat goose for Christmas and a *kransekage*. As soon as the money was in my hand I went to Matthew Rose's store and bought material to make clothes for Swanny. I haven't written in this diary for days because I've been sewing, doing drawn thread work and making fine tucks on her long gowns.

This afternoon Mrs. Gibbons called to see me. I think she only comes here to find out if I've really got a husband, she's always asking about him. First she wanted to know when Swanny was going to be christened. She's very religious (though that doesn't stop her laughing at my accent) and she's always hobnobbing with the curate at St. Philip's. I said, never, I didn't believe in god. (See how I write it with a small g.) "I don't believe in god," I said, "or any of that. It's all the invention of ministers and vicars."

"Oh, my dear," she says, "you shock me, you really do."

She didn't look shocked, she looked greedy for more. So I gave it to her.

"You people talk about god being a loving father," I said, "but even a bad father wouldn't kill his daughter's babies."

She gave me a funny look because I had Swanny on my lap. My right hand was under her head and my left hand lying lightly on her chest and I could see Mrs. Gibbons start looking at my hand. She's so plain you really want to laugh. For one thing she's very stout and the way her corsets push up the top half of her and push down the lower part makes her look like a parcel that's tied up in the middle with too tight a string. What makes it worse is that her dress is just like brown paper, creased the way brown paper is, and pleated like a parcel where you fold in the edges.

She lifted her eyes and then looked very pointedly back at my hand.

"You don't wear a wedding ring, Mrs. Westerby."

I hate the way she pronounces my name, but they all do it that way here, so I suppose I must get used to it. I drew out my other hand from under Swanny's soft furry head and held it out to her the way you might hold out your hand for some man to kiss. Not that I know any men who would.

"That's on your right hand," she said. "Is it your mother's?"

"We wear our wedding rings on our right hand in Denmark," I said very coldly.

She wasn't put out, she wouldn't be. "I'd change it over if I were you. If you don't want people talking."

It's too big for that finger. One's right hand is always a bit bigger than one's left, I suppose. Anyway, I've changed it over even if it does slither up and down. I wouldn't care if it was just me but I have to think of the children and it's not fair on them if people think I'm not respectable.

Reading over what I've written I can see there's a line that really shouldn't be there. But who's going to read it? It's in Danish and Danish might as well be Hottentot for all the people round here understand a word of it.

OCTOBER 23, 1905

Autumn has come and all the leaves are turning. I love the trees with leaves that are five-fingered and bright gold and the fruit that hangs on them like apples with spikes, though I miss the beeches. I haven't seen a beech tree since I came to England.

Another visit from Mrs. Gibbons with more nosiness and impertinent questions. If we were Danish how did it happen we had an English name?

"It's not English," I said. "It's pronounced Vest-er-bew."

She gave a funny little laugh to indicate she didn't believe me. It is odd the way the same letters can be pronounced so differently. When I first came here I kept saying to myself that I wanted to see Hootha Park, and was I surprised when I found out how they pronounce Hyde here! I'm glad I never said Hootha aloud.

The sky was a very pale blue yesterday but today the fog has come back. The fog is thick and yellow and I'm not surprised the people here call it a pea-souper. Still, it reminded me of pea soup, the kind made with a hambone and yellow split peas we used to have when we lived in Sweden, so I got Hansine to make some and we all had it for supper. Well, not all, not Swanny, who still just has me and thrives.

OCTOBER 25, 1905

A letter yesterday from Tante Frederikke, the first for more than two months. The Thorvaldsens had a memorial service for Oluf which, I agree with her, seems very affected for a boy aged fifteen. They never recovered his body from the sea. There were lots on the *Georg Stage* that were never found. I can't imagine how that would feel, to know you have a child and next day you haven't any more, you've nothing, not even a dead body. It doesn't seem right, though I know few people would agree with me, this training children to fight at sea, for that is what it amounts to, training fourteen and fifteen year olds to be soldiers on ships. It's even worse than training girls of sixteen to be wives.

I've discovered that if you don't want to dream of something the best way to stop it is to think about it very hard before you go to sleep at night. You'd think that was the way to make you dream of it but the reverse is true. So I made myself think of Swanny being taken away from me and hidden somewhere and me having nothing of her, not even a picture. It won't happen, it can't happen but it made my pillow wet with my tears. Still, it worked and I dreamed of Rasmus coming back and saying we all had to go to Australia and me agreeing like a good little lamb. Well, dreams don't have much relation to reality, I must say.

Coal fires have started. I expect the smoke from so many of them makes the fog worse but I like the red coals and the bright flames in my grate in the drawing room at night. It's not really cold, not the way it was in Stockholm. I wonder what Mrs. Gibbons would say if I told her how the wolves used to come down from the hills there when the snow was deep. They were starving and howling for food and one night they ate my washing off the clothesline. I suppose she wouldn't believe me or else she'd ask if the polar bears came too.

NOVEMBER 2, 1905

I am writing this upstairs in the boys' room with the door locked. It's bitterly cold and I've got mittens on and my feet in a foot-warmer Tante Frederikke made for me about a hundred years ago. I could ask Hansine to light a fire in the grate but she would only start on how there's a wonderful fire already in the drawing room and it's as warm as toast downstairs et cetera.

The secrecy will have to start now, I suppose. Well, I *know*. It amuses me when I think about it, how elaborately I will have to keep my best and favorite activity a dark secret the way other women hide a clandestine love affair. I only have love affairs with a notebook! But I want him to know about it as little as some other woman would want her husband to know about the men she spent her time with. They are her passion, this is mine. We can't all be the same, can we?

Swanny is lying in my lap, wrapped up in shawls, but although I feel cold my body is warm to the touch and that's what keeps her warm. She's fast asleep, clean and sweet and full of good milk. Her hair is the same gold as my wedding ring. People say a baby's cheek is like a rose leaf but that's not what they really think, that's what they get out of books. A baby's cheek is like a plum, firm as fruit, soft and hard at the same time, as smooth and as cool.

Last evening I was sitting in the drawing room, not writing in my diary, but mending Knud's sailor suit. His trouser pockets were full of the cigarette cards they are both mad about collecting. "Look at this, Knud," I said, "suppose they'd gone into the tub when Mrs. Clegg comes round on Monday to do our washing." He wouldn't answer me, he wouldn't even look round. He says he won't answer unless I call him Ken. If you don't answer me you'll get a smack you won't forget, I said, so we are at loggerheads, Knud not speaking to me unless I call him Ken and I adamantly refusing to do any such thing.

What he needs is a father's discipline. I was just thinking this—not to mention how Rasmus would give them an inexhaustible supply of cigarette cards, he smokes so much—when there came a smart double knock at the front door. Hansine went to answer it and I heard her give a great scream. What a charming parlormaid she makes! Anyway, the drawing room door flew open and in walked my husband.

I got up and the sewing fell on the floor. Not a word of warning, not a letter for weeks, and then he just walks in one night.

"Well, here I am," he said.

"At last," I said.

"You don't seem very pleased to see me." He looked me up and down. "You might at least give a fellow a kiss."

I put up my face and he kissed me and I kissed him back. What else could I do in the circumstances? He certainly is good-looking. I'd half-forgotten that, I'd forgotten the feeling of a little shiver inside me. It's not love, it's more like being hungry and I don't know what to call it.

"Come and see what I've brought," he said, and I'm such a fool, I never learn, I really thought for a moment he meant presents for us, toys maybe for Mogens and Knud. And I never get over my longing for a fur coat, though I'm sure I'll never get one. Just at that moment I honestly thought he might have brought me a fur coat.

So I went out into the hall with him but there was nothing there. He threw open the front door and pointed out into the street. There's a lamp right outside our house, so I could make it out all right. Besides, he'd already stuck an oil lamp on the road next to it so that it wouldn't get bumped into by a cart.

A motorcar. A big one with spokes on its wheels like a bicycle, only four of them. "She's a Hammel," he said, "made in Denmark. Isn't she beautiful?"

It was freezing out there, so we went back indoors and he was talking motors before he'd even got his coat off. What he really wants is to get hold of the kind called an Oldsmobile, an American machine. He said they made five thousand of them last year, which made me laugh because it's so absurd. He always exaggerates everything. Five thousand, I said, you wouldn't be able to move along the roads. Automobiles, he said, that's what they call them over there, and he gave them a lot of other names, oleo locomotive and motoring and diamote among others, with a look of adoration on his face that he's never had for me.

I thought he'd soon be back with that old idea that we all decamp and set off for America, land of the three-horsepower curved-dash automobile, so when I'd listened to a whole lot more of this stuff and rubbish about the Duryea Brothers and someone called James Ward Packard, I asked him if he'd like to see his daughter.

"I daresay I'd better," was what he said. Charming!

She was asleep. But she woke up when we came in and he saw her open her beautiful dark blue eyes.

"Very nice," he said, and, "where does she get that color hair from?"

"All Danes are fair," I said.

"Except you and me," he said with a funny sort of laugh.

I can always tell when he really means something or when he's just what he calls "joking." He was joking then, he didn't seriously mean to imply anything.

"Her name is Swanhild," I said, pronouncing it the English way, knowing how he likes anything English.

"Thanks very much," he said, "for making up your mind without consulting me."

I said he hadn't been here to be consulted and we quarreled a bit the way we invariably do. But he didn't say any more about her not looking like us. If I know him he knows me and he knows I'd never be unfaithful to him, he knows I'd see that as just about the worst thing a woman can do. We women don't have to be brave and strong or good at earning money like men and if we are it doesn't matter, it doesn't count. We have to be chaste. That's the only word

I can think of that expresses what I mean. That's where our honor is, in being chaste, pure in our behavior and faithful to our husbands. I must say it would be easier if one had a nice loving husband but that's life!

NOVEMBER 6, 1905

When I first started writing this diary I told myself I'd write down only the absolute truth. Now I understand that's not possible. It wouldn't be possible for anyone, not just me. All I can do is be honest about what I feel, I can do that, what I feel and what I believe in. Total openness about facts I can't manage and I've given up arguing with myself about it. I needn't tell lies but I can't tell the whole truth.

Yesterday was Guy Fawkes Day. They just as often call it Bonfire Day and when I heard that I thought it must be the way they celebrate St. Nicholas, though that's a month away. But the English always do things differently from everyone else and I shouldn't really have been surprised to hear (from the vicar) that November the fifth is all about some man who tried to blow up the King of England and got hanged for it. Now, for some unaccountable reason, they make a big doll and burn it on the anniversary of the day. Why not hang it? I suppose burning is more exciting.

Rasmus bought fireworks for the boys and we had a bonfire, though we didn't have a Guy Fawkes. I promised to make one for them next year. They are all over Rasmus, they love him for his cigarette cards and the motorcar, he is all in all to them, and poor Mor is nowhere.

NOVEMBER 21, 1905

Hooray! Prince Charles of Denmark has been elected King of Norway.

For two days I've thought I was in the family way again but it was a false alarm, thank goodness. No man can know what that's like, the waiting and the hoping and the despair from hour to hour, from minute to minute, and the relief when you're unwell. It's only been a bit delayed. I suppose there's nothing else that can happen to you that's quite like it. Knowing you're going to have a baby can be the worst thing in the world for some women and the best thing for others, an enormous joy or the most appalling blow, and there's no middle way. I've never come across a woman who said she was rather pleased to be having a baby or rather sorry. No, it's bliss or horror but more often horror.

Rasmus' birthday tomorrow. I meant to pretend I'd forgotten but now all is well I shall give him his present after all. Fancy giving a husband a present because he hasn't made you *enceinte!*

5

One of Mormor's favorite stories was of Swanny's courtship. She called it a romance and talked about it with great pride, for though both her daughters had made what she called "good marriages," my father had spoiled my mother's by dying young.

In spite of speaking Danish like natives, neither Swanny nor my mother went to Denmark until they were grown up. Swanny, at nineteen, had never got over the death of her favorite brother in the First World War. Mormor sent her to stay with her own cousins, the Holbechs, the son and daughter-in-law of her aunt Frederikke, in Copenhagen. This was Padanaram time, when they were living in some style, and there was money.

As in the song, Torben Kjaer saw a stranger across a crowded room. He was a young diplomat, home on leave from a posting in South America where he was second secretary. Swanny was a bridesmaid at the wedding of a girl called Dorte, and Torben was one of the guests. Apparently, he fell in love with her at first sight. He asked her to marry him two days later and accompany him back to wherever it was, Quito or Asuncion.

Mormor would tell this story to anyone who happened to be there and was willing to listen. She told it in front of Swanny and Torben, by then a distinguished-looking gray-haired attaché at the Danish Embassy. He remained impassive, trained to show nothing much. All those years ago, a blue-eyed blond boy of twenty-two, he

had returned alone to Ecuador or wherever it was because Swanny
had been too astounded by his proposal to take it seriously and
didn't want to go to South America anyway.

"But he never forgot my daughter Swanhild," Mormor would
say, "and for years he wrote her these wonderful love letters which
I know are wonderful, though of course I have never seen them.
One doesn't show such letters to one's mother. When he came to
a post here they were married. Imagine it, ten years had passed, but
to him he said it was no more than a day. What a romance!"

Looking at Torben and Swanny now, one could hardly believe
it. They were both so suave, so calm, so well-dressed, so *middle-
aged.* My mother, though only six years younger, was like a child
beside dignified Swanny. There was no resemblance between them
and none between Swanny and Uncle Ken or Swanny and Mormor.
Still, they were a family of disparate appearance, none looked very
much like any of the others. My mother was much prettier than her
mother, though of the same sort of build. Ken looked a bit like one
of the uncles in the old photographs, short and burly but with
rather handsome pointed features, and his younger son is like him
though much taller. They all had reddish or dark brown hair and
eyes ranging from cat's green to a bright blue, they all were inclined
to freckles and sunburn.

But Swanny—Swanny was the perfect Danish type. Or the
Nordic type, perhaps I should say. She was taller than any of them,
even Morfar, and she was a dazzling blonde. In sunshine she went
brown, not freckled. Her eyes were a dark sea blue. Even in the days
I'm talking about, Willow Road in its heyday, Hampstead in the
sixties, when she was in her late fifties, she still had that look of a
goddess out of Wagner, with hair silver instead of gold and a profile
like an empress on an ancient coin.

She and Torben gave a lot of parties. I didn't know and still don't
if he was obliged to give them as a diplomat or if they just liked
parties. A bit of both, I expect. I used to go to them, or some of
them, because I was at college just over the hill, and because there
was a man who was one of Torben's assistants and was always

roped in to help with drinks and conversation that I was keen on. Later on he became keen on me too but that is another story.

Mormor loved those parties. My mother, who occasionally came with the current fiancé, used to say to me she expected Swanny and Torben would have preferred Mormor to keep out of it, to stay in her own room or at least leave early, but didn't know how to tell her without hurting her feelings. For "hurting her feelings" I privately substituted "making her furious," as I never saw Mormor as vulnerable or sensitive. But in fact I think Swanny and Torben liked her being there. After all, she wasn't the usual old granny, infirm and bumbling, sitting in the corner and complaining about her ailments to anyone who would listen. I think, if they were wise and they were, they saw her as an attraction, a star turn. Some of those people came to their parties because they knew Swanny's mother would be there and Swanny's mother was *fun*.

I've since thought how they must look back, remembering it was Anna Westerby of *Anna* they met in the house in Willow Road and who told them those stories, many of which appeared in the diaries. If they had known would they have paid more attention, been more polite, more deferential? Perhaps not. I never saw signs of Mormor being neglected. It was rather the reverse. She was always one of an animated group and it seemed to me she always dominated it.

Why didn't she get tired, like old ladies of eighty are supposed to? Why did she never say at nine o'clock that she must be off to bed? She never mentioned tiredness, never seemed to flag. An enormous energy possessed her. She was tiny, her body too small for her rather large head. I suppose her body had shrunk and her head hadn't. Her face, by then only a little less white than her hair, was copiously powdered but otherwise without makeup. She smelt strongly of Coty's L'Aimant as if her clothes were steeped in it. She often wore one of those brooches that must make conservationists wince, a piece of blue butterfly's wing mounted in mica and gold. It brought out the color of her eyes, which were the same sort of blue, but in fact it needed no bringing out, being sharp and brilliant enough, and the combination of eyes and brooch, instead of flattering, was somehow embarrassing.

A curious thing about her was that she never sat down. Of course she must have sat down and if I think specifically about occasions when we were together, I can place her in a certain chair at a certain time but still my overall memory of her is that she was always on her feet or else reclining as in the picture of Mme. Recamier. Certainly, at those parties, she stood the whole time. People knew better than to offer her a chair.

"Why? Are you tired of standing up talking to me?" she said sharply to some hapless young man who was new there.

To the Danes among the company she spoke Danish. It was by then as heavily accented as her English was, one of these people told me. Her accent gave a curious piquancy to the stories she told, at least to my ears. Although I've read most of them in the diaries since then, she seldom repeated herself in reality. Before I read it I only once heard the story about Karoline, the girl who peed in the street, and only once the story about the big dinner party in Copenhagen in the twenties at which she and Morfar were the one couple who had never been divorced.

It was at a Willow Road party that I heard her tell the one about her cousin accidentally killing her lover with poisonous fungi and on that same occasion the one about some relative going to an orphanage in Odense to pick out a child for adoption. This story has some relevance to what happened later. I suppose I ought to say now that I never knew how much of these stories was true and how much exaggeration and embroidery. Mormor, as I've said, was a true novelist, only her novels were the diaries she wrote over a period of sixty years. I don't really know it but I'd guess that the truth with its disappointing complexities and its failed dramas, the sort of damp squib properties it often has, dissatisfied her. She made it better. She gave it a beginning, a middle and an end. With her it always had a climax.

Mormor had no brothers or sisters. This was supposed to have happened to a wealthy cousin, one of the Swedish lot. The woman was happily married but childless and eventually she and her husband decided to adopt, a simple enough business at that time. According to Mormor, you picked the child you wanted and took it home with you.

Sigrid's husband took her to an orphanage in Odense on the island of Fyn, native place of Mormor's mother's favorite Hans Andersen. (Mormor digressed here to say how she hated Andersen and give a reminder to her audience that he was, nevertheless, "the world's greatest children's writer.") The submissive Sigrid was led by the matron to a particular child, a little boy whose beauty and pretty ways immediately won her heart. He was about a year old, according to Mormor.

"My cousin loved him at once," she said. "She took him home with her and they adopted him and then the husband told her the truth. This was his child by another woman, a girl he had met on business trips to Odense." She added with relish, "His mistress." It was a word which, to her, carried many undertones of glamour and vice. "He had arranged the whole thing. Sigrid forgave him and kept the boy and he must be quite an old man by now." Here Mormor fixed a fierce and brilliant blue eye on one of the men in her audience. "I wouldn't have. The very idea! That boy would have gone straight back to where he came from."

Of course a discussion ensued on the ethics of all this and people said what they would have done in Sigrid's position and her husband's position.

"You might have loved him by then," a woman suggested.

"I wouldn't have," Mormor said. "Knowing whose he was and how I'd been deceived would have finished that." And then, devastatingly, "I don't love people easily." Her eyes roved the faces, the distant reaches of the room. "Most of this talk of love is bosh!"

It was one of her favorite words. Sentimentality and tenderness, sensitivity and diffidence, it was all bosh. Drama was what she liked, vitality and power. Many of her stories featured violent death. After the great market crash of 1929 another cousin, the brother of this Sigrid, had shot himself, leaving his widow and four children bereft. A distant relative emigrated to the United States in the 1880s and never knew until he was an old man returned to Denmark that the house he had lived in with his wife and children in Chicago was on North Clark Street next door to where the St. Valentine's Day Massacre would take place.

Mormor, by day, wandered Hampstead and the Heath. She walked up and down Heath Street and in and out of the shops, "just looking." She talked to people and what they said to her she put in her diaries but she made no friends. Hers was the journalist's way of being in touch with others. She interviewed them. My mother told me she had no women friends, she could never remember her mother having a single close "chum." Morfar had his old business associates from the distant Chelsea days and Mormor knew their wives. She had acquaintances among the neighbors at Padanaram and at Ninety-eight. There was only one person who called her by her Christian name and whom she called by his and that was Harry Duke.

Like so much associated with Mormor, he was something of a surprise. Though I seldom saw him, I'd known of him since I was born and accepted him as I accepted members of the family. He was Uncle Harry to me, as he was to my mother, to Swanny, and for all I can tell to Uncle Ken too. Most of what I know of him I know from my mother. He had retired in 1948 but before that he'd been a clerk with Thames Water or the Metropolitan Water Board as it was then called. His home was in Leyton. He liked watching Leyton Orient playing at home and going to dog racing, but he was a reader too and fond of the theatre. Mormor was a snob but not where Uncle Harry was concerned. No one was allowed to say a word against him in her hearing.

He took her to the dogs once, though she drew the line at football matches. His wife died a few years before Morfar and after that Swanny and my mother called him "Mor's boyfriend." He was kind and nice, not commonplace but sharp and funny, and he adored Mormor. They drove about in his car, went to museums and exhibitions together and shared large meals. They both loved eating and drinking. Harry Duke was a fine-looking, tall and handsome man who still had his own teeth and most of his hair the last time

I saw him, which was at Morfar's funeral. There was one far more remarkable thing about him and that was that he had the VC. He had won it in the First World War for rescuing, among others of the wounded and dying in no-man's-land, Private "Jack" Westerby.

Compared with him, Hansine, who had been their maid-of-all-work and household slave until she married in 1920, remained a mere acquaintance. Hansine died the same year as Morfar, and Mormor apparently had no contact at all with her daughter. Swanny told me she and Torben wanted Hansine and her husband Samuel Cropper invited to Mormor and Morfar's Golden Wedding party in 1947, but Mormor wouldn't hear of it.

"If I asked her," she said incredibly, "it would be to help out, but the caterers are going to see to all that."

Swanny said Mormor seemed almost glad when Hansine died seven years later. It was a kind of relief. Perhaps only because here was someone else who might be a nuisance out of the way, someone else to cross off the slate. Weeks went by without Mormor's even seeing Harry or speaking to him on the phone. Mormor was almost chillingly self-sufficient.

This changed very little as she grew older. One day, in Swanny's house, she told me she hadn't cried since she was twenty-three and her baby, the one called Mads, died when he was a month old. It was another of her stories, but not one to be told in public. They expected his death and she was with him when he died, sitting by the side of his cot, holding him in her arms. This was in a house they had in the Hortensiavej in Copenhagen. She came downstairs to where Morfar was, told him the baby was dead and began to cry. He stared at her for a while and then left the room. She resolved after that that she would never cry again and she never did, not even in solitude, not even when the telegram came to tell her Mogens had been killed.

On the other hand, she laughed a good deal, a harsh tinkly laugh, or a wise knowing one, or a dry giggle. She might laugh at other people's discomfiture but she also did so at her own. It was one of the endearing things about her. She even uttered that harsh cackle after she had told me the story of Mads' death and her own unregarded tears. I would have thought her the soul of discretion, capable of any restraints, with no longer any need to confide, if she had ever had such a need, her past and her emotions under an iron control. Mischief I knew her to be capable of but not malice. She may have taken advantage of Swanny's love for her and her unselfishness, but she loved her dearly and was inordinately proud of her.

If she had belonged in a later generation her pride would have been prompted by different things. Because she was born in 1880 she was destined to be proud of a son for his prowess as a soldier or his professional success, of a daughter for her beauty and social achievements. If one of her daughters had become Mistress of Girton or a live peer but hadn't married, I think Anna would have been rather ashamed of her. As it was, Swanny was all she dreamed of and more. Swanny getting her photograph in the *Tatler* marked the culmination of Anna's social ambitions. When she showed the copy of the magazine to Uncle Harry, Swanny said, she swelled with pride so that with her rather large head and spindly legs she had the look of a cocky little pigeon.

The photograph in question had been taken while the Queen of Denmark (or it may have been the King of Denmark and his Queen) were on a state visit to London and posed with some of the embassy staff at a dinner party. Torben was looking very grand and aristocratic in a white tie and tails and Swanny magnificent in a long pale lacy gown and strings of pearls round her neck. Their names were in the caption underneath along with the royals and the ambassador and a Danish woman historian who was being given some sort of honor.

I believe, and always have, that this picture was the cause of all Swanny's subsequent troubles. Swanny wouldn't have it and nor would my mother but why else had the writer of the letter waited so long before imparting his or her piece of news? Surely it would be too great a coincidence for the only photograph of Swanny that had ever appeared in a national magazine to be there one week and the letter to arrive the next?

Either the photograph sparked off a sudden explosion of envy and resentment in the letter writer or else it was the final straw in a back-breaking load of lifelong bitterness. I inclined toward the latter view. I felt very strongly that whoever it was had kept an eye and an ear on Swanny from a distance for years, learning from various sources the progress of her life, perhaps coming once or twice to Willow Road to look at her house and even watch its handsome chatelaine come and go. The picture in the *Tatler* pressed a button that signaled: now is the time, write now!

It was the day of a luncheon party, all women. Two women came in to cook and another to wait at table, so Swanny had very little to do, but for some reason it was quite late in the morning before she opened her post.

Mormor had already come down, had her coffee and gone into the kitchen to see what food was being prepared. Always fond of her food, she remained essentially faithful to Danish cuisine. Nothing in her estimation quite came up to pork with red cabbage, roast goose, fruit soups, *sildesalat* and *Krustader,* though she was fond too of a hearty steak and kidney pudding. If the meal Swanny had ordered for the ten visiting ladies hadn't included some item of smoked fish or meat she wouldn't have been pleased and she'd have said so, at the table as likely as not.

Swanny never used Torben's study in those days. It was his, it was sacrosanct. She took her letters upstairs and opened them in her bedroom where she had a small escritoire. It was something she often did, as much as anything to be away from Mormor's devouring curiosity. ("Who's that from, *lille* Swanny? I know that writing. Is that a Danish stamp I see?") This time Mormor was safely out of the way, lifting saucepan lids and sniffing smoked salmon. Swanny told my mother and me that the letter was the last she opened. Her name and address were printed and she didn't much like the look of any of it. What she expected was a request for money, a begging letter. She and Torben occasionally had those.

When she had read it she said she grew hot all over. She could see her face in the mirror and it had turned dark red. She felt as if she was suffocating. One of the windows was open and she put her head out and breathed deeply. Then she read it again.

There was no address, no date and no salutation. *You think yourself very high and mighty but your airs and graces are quite a joke when you know you are really nobody. You are not your mother's child or your father's. They got you from somewhere when their own one died. Off a rubbish heap, for all you know. It's time you knew the truth.*

It was printed, in ink and with a fountain pen, on Basildon Bond writing paper, blue, the octavo size. The envelope matched it and the postmark was Swanny's own district, London NW3.

The second time she read it Swanny began to shake. She sat on the little chair by the escritoire and her whole body shook. Her teeth chattered. After a little while she got up, went into the bathroom and drew herself a glass of water. It was twelve-fifteen and her guests were due to begin arriving at half-past. She told herself the only thing to do with the letter was tear it up and put it and its contents entirely out of her mind.

This she couldn't do—the tearing up part, that is. She found herself physically unable to do it. Touching the letter was bad enough. She had to approach it with a tremulous hand as someone might attempt daringly to touch the object of a phobia, extending one finger and immediately drawing it back. Her head bent, not looking, she scrabbled up the sheet of paper and stuffed it into her handbag. It was gone, she breathed a little more freely, but what she had read remained in her mind.

Before the first guest arrives she is downstairs in the drawing room and Mormor is with her. Mormor is in one of those fringed black numbers, the blue brooch pinned on somewhere, her white hair cunningly woven and puffed under a fine net with brilliants on it, and talking animatedly about the *snaps* they are to drink with their first course, a particularly good brand she thinks it is that Torben has got in. And she begins to tell a story about her own mother that she calls "your Mormor," about how she never touched any alcohol but *snaps* for which she had this remarkable capacity, but all Swanny hears is this woman being described as her grandmother which she may not be, which if the letter is true, she cannot be.

The guests come. They congregate in the drawing room, having pre-lunch drinks and smoking cigarettes. These are the sixties, so nobody thinks twice about driving home over the limit or "under the influence," as it was called then. Everyone drinks several sherries or gin and tonics and inhales on high-tar king-size. Nobody minds that Swanny's pretty drawing room fills with smoke so that the Karl Larsson on the wall disappears in a fog.

Swanny moves among her guests in a daze, trying to be a good hostess, speaking to each one in turn. She finds it hard to keep her eyes off her mother. She is drawn to gaze at her mother as a lover can't keep from gazing at his love. It is as if she is fascinated by her mother.

Mormor is part of a group and she is holding forth. Her high "Louis" heels raise her up and she is no longer tiny, she is a commanding figure, a force to be reckoned with. Everyone seems to want to hear what she has to say, including the professor of maritime history, Mrs. Jórgensen, Aase Jórgensen, who is the guest of honor at this party. And Mormor is talking about all the things that were happening in the world while she was a young woman in Hackney: the fuss over who would be King of Norway, the American airship disaster, the *Potemkin* in Odessa Harbor.

Someone says, "The Battleship *Potemkin,* do you mean?"

They have seen the film, but Mormor, who has never even heard of the film, says, "A ship, yes, it was a ship. That was in nineteen hundred and five, in the hot summer," and she is going to say more but Swanny touches her arm and whispers, can she have a word?

At this particular moment? She said she could wait no longer, she was in anguish, she was stifling. She has heard all this about the Battleship *Potemkin* but now there is no one in the room but her mother, she can literally see no one else. But what can she hope for? An explanation? A dismissal of what she has read as nonsense, not worth thinking of for another moment? She doesn't know. She only knows she must get her mother away and ask her.

Why? Why not wait until the party is over? Mormor thinks that, for she tells her impatiently that whatever it is can wait, she is talking, she is telling Mrs. Jórgensen about the shelling of Odessa.

And she embarrasses Swanny by saying loudly, "My petticoat isn't showing, is it? Is that what's the matter?"

Swanny can't move her. She goes out to the kitchen, ostensibly to find out if lunch can be served in ten minutes. All is well, there is nothing to do. She does something quite alien to her, something she swears she has never done before, takes a swig of *snaps*, splashing it into a sherry glass and tossing it down.

She must, of course, go back into the drawing room. Her mother is no longer there, no longer even in the room. She walks about, looking for her. But there are, after all, only eleven people including herself. Perhaps her mother is out in the hall, looking for her, having relented, but before she can leave the room the waitress has appeared to announce luncheon and she must lead her guests into the dining room. Mormor is already there with Mrs. Jórgensen, showing her the Royal Copenhagen china in the limited editions and talking about some woman porcelain collector who married a man called Erik Holst, himself a naval officer and onetime cadet on the doomed training ship *Georg Stage*.

If she had been able to get her mother alone in those moments she would have asked her. She would have been able to ask her. As it was, when the party was over, some inhibition crushed her and tied her tongue. That first *snaps* and the rest she had drunk stunned her, all she wanted was to lie down, sleep, find forgetfulness or hope that she would feel differently when she woke up.

The evening passed. Torben was spending a rare few hours away from home. Mormor reclined on the sofa reading *The Old Curiosity Shop* and went up to her bedroom early, saying she had had a tiring day. She needed, no doubt, a couple of hours' solitude in which to write her diary. Swanny had a racking headache. She hadn't looked at the letter again. It was in her handbag and her handbag was with her in the drawing room, as it always was wherever she might be, on the floor beside her chair or on a sofa cushion. She said she kept looking at it and thinking of the thing inside it. It was as if a bag of vomit or some dead decaying thing had been thrust into her handbag and sometime or other she was going to have to clean it out.

Long before Torben got home she took two aspirins and went to bed. Although they shared a room, she and Torben had never shared a bed. She woke up very early in the morning, at five or earlier, and she nearly went up to the next floor to wake her mother, to say to her, read this and tell me if it's true. Is it true? Tell me it isn't true. I must know.

But she didn't. Not then.

6

By chance I happened to be at home when Swanny came round to tell us about the letter. It was a usual Wednesday afternoon. Swanny had even taken care not to arrange a special time. Although it had been a Friday when the letter came, she still waited until the following Wednesday to tell anyone. She made herself wait. As she said, she didn't "want to make a thing of it." She hadn't shown the letter to Torben or said anything to Mormor. Nor had she phoned my mother to warn her she had something she particularly wanted to talk about. Of course the truth was she didn't want to talk about it, she wanted to forget it, but couldn't. Who could forget a thing like that?

Her bright silver hair was always beautifully cut. Strangely, this made it look not as if it were naturally that color but as if it had been artificially made that way. The effect of dark red lipstick against that lightly tanned skin was arresting. Torben's rings on her left hand were platinum and diamonds, large bright diamonds, and she wore diamond earrings that Nancy Mitford said somewhere were just the thing for an aging face. I used to think that I'd like to look like her when I was her age, but I'm only ten years off it now and I don't. Not at all. It would be surprising if I did.

She took the letter out of her bag with the very tips of her fingers. She made her fingers into tongs, yet it wasn't a theatrical or affected gesture but a natural expression of disgust. My mother tried to make light of it.

"I've never seen one of these before."

"Don't mock, Marie, please don't. I can't bear it."

"Swanny," said my mother, "you don't mean you believe this rubbish?"

Swanny's eyes went rather helplessly from my mother to me. She put her hands down and clasped them together as if without that clutch they might fly apart and spring up again. "Why would this person say it if it wasn't true? Whoever it is, they wouldn't just make it up."

"Of course they would. It's someone who's envious of you."

"It's someone who saw your picture in the *Tatler*," I said.

"Oh, surely not. How would they know where I lived? How could they know anything about me?"

"Honestly, Swan, you tell me not to mock but actually I could just burst out laughing. No one but you would give it a moment's credence. I mean, if it was me I'd just have burned it."

Swanny said very quietly, and that was when we knew how seriously she took it, how she must have been thinking about it, "It wouldn't have come to you, would it? You look just like Mor."

Then my mother did laugh, if a bit hollowly. "The obvious thing is to ask her. If you really take this seriously, ask her."

"I know."

"I can't think why you haven't already. If it was me I'd have asked her straightaway."

"Don't keep saying if it was you, Marie."

"All right. Sorry. Just ask her. You should have asked her last Friday but ask her now."

Swanny made a movement of her head, a tiny shake. She said very quietly, "I was afraid."

"Oh, but you must ask her. You must. Is this really worrying you?"

"What do you think?"

"Of course you must ask her. Now. As soon as you get home.

Show her the letter. It'll turn out that this anonymous *beast,* this pig, this totally mad person, meant something quite different."

Swanny said simply, looking from one to the other of us, "Like what?"

"Well, I don't know. How should I know? But it's obviously nonsense. You're Mor's favorite, you've said so yourself, you know you are. She's always saying it, she doesn't care whose feelings she hurts. I mean, is it likely she adopted you? Why would she? Look at it like that, why can't you? She could have kids of her own, she was always having them, even now she often moans about the number of kids she had and blames it on Far."

"You'll have to ask her," I said.

"I know."

"D'you want me to ask her?" my mother said.

Swanny lifted her shoulders, shook her head.

"I don't mind asking her. I'll come back with you and ask her if you like."

Of course Swanny wasn't going to have that. My mother would have done it. If it had been she who got the letter, she would have asked her straight out, on the spot. I loved my mother and remember her with affection, she was a good mother to me and she was unusually unselfish, but it's no use pretending she was sensitive or had much imagination. Swanny had the sensitivity, the reticence, was the imaginative diffident one. Curiously, though, all these traits were present in Anna, who was sensitive and insensitive, gentle and hard, tough and vulnerable, aggressive and shy—the writer of fiction and nonfiction.

My mother couldn't understand the kind of fear Swanny had. She could only be indignant, sense that some outrage was being perpetrated, be aware of a great injustice looming. She wanted to set things right by having it out with her mother now, before another night had passed.

Swanny said, "I'll ask her. You've shown me I have to ask her." She sighed. Her face had taken on that haunted look we were often to see now. "I don't like to make a thing of my age, I'm not old yet, fifty-eight's not old, but I'm too old to have this happen to me.

You hear of teenagers finding out they were adopted. Not people of fifty-eight, for God's sake. It's not just horrible, it's grotesque." Although her tone didn't change nor her expression, incredulous and attempting a faint ironical amusement, her words made her at last pathetic. "I can't have been adopted, can I, Marie? Can I, Ann? It has to be that the letter writer's lying. Oh, if only I hadn't opened it!"

You would have expected my mother and me to have discussed all this after she had gone but we didn't. My mother said only that the letter writer probably thought it was true—why did we assume it was a woman?—but that the story probably derived from an invention of Anna's. You could imagine Anna romancing on about foundlings, several of her stories were about that very subject, and some listeners actually took them seriously. She said it lightly enough, trivializing the whole thing, to make further serious conversation about it impossible. The subject was changed. The fiancé, he who was to be the last of them, the final lover that she was going to marry "one day" to make it all respectable perhaps, he arrived and shortly afterwards I left. Not another word was said about Swanny and quite a long time went by before I heard the outcome.

If this had been one of Anna's stories it would have involved a tremendous scene with a climax, an opening of the heart and ultimately some sort of confession. But it wasn't, it was life itself which she so loved to embroider. Swanny told my mother that after another two days' delay she came out with it and asked Anna. When it came to it she was actually trembling, she felt sick. The night before, repeatedly telling herself this would be the last night before she knew, she had hardly slept.

Then, in the morning, she nearly fell into further procrastination. Wasn't anything better than to know? But could she bear to go on not knowing? She and her mother were alone in the house. The "daily" woman didn't come every day. Swanny pursued her usual tasks, those aspects of housework she enjoyed, polishing certain pieces of furniture, tidying up to improve the look of one of the large reception rooms, taking a delivery of flowers and putting them into her Chinese vases. It was high summer but not at all warm. The grass was bright green and the trees in rich full leaf and the garden full of flowers, but the sky was leaden gray and it was cool.

Anna was still upstairs in her room on the third floor. She often didn't appear till coffee time but always by then, invariably to come out with some remark about the impossibility of a Dane's existing without coffee. Fantasies flowed through Swanny's mind, one after another. Anna had gone away and married Uncle Harry. Anna had died up there. Anna was lying there dead. She thought, not that she would grieve or miss her, but that then she would never know the truth of it.

As the time approached eleven she grew even more sick with tension. It was all stupid, she knew that. Here she was, a woman in late middle age, going out of her mind with anxiety because a week before a poison pen letter had told her she wasn't her parents' child. The letter itself she had read and reread, had quite got over comparing it to a bag of vomit or a dead rat, had become entirely familiar with it, had long known the words by heart.

Anna came down at two minutes to eleven, her white hair netted, her face well powdered, dressed in dark blue ("a dark blue walking costume") with the butterfly wing brooch holding a navy blue scarf in place. Her butterfly wing eyes were so bright that on some days the beam from them itself looked blue, a shaft of colored light.

She only ever said two things at this point, so it must have been one or other of them: the remark about the indispensability of coffee to Danes or, "Do I smell the good coffee?"

Swanny brought the coffee in. It was soon to be Anna's eighty-third birthday and she intended to have what she called a chocolate party. That is, Swanny was to have a chocolate party for her. I had once been to one of these and very good it was. No one would give a feast like this today, for the drink was sweet hot chocolate into which you put a huge dollop of whipped cream and the food was *kransekage,* a wonderful cake made of an almond paste mixture and shaped like a multilayered crown. Anna was talking about this, whom they should invite and so on, what other food should be served. Swanny interrupted her to say she had something she

wanted to ask her, speaking so breathlessly that even Anna could
tell something was wrong. She asked her what was wrong.

Then Swanny came out with it. She said it was the hardest thing
she'd ever had to ask anyone. She said she thought it would kill her.
Her blood pressure rose and her head drummed. The words came
out hoarsely.

Anna was silent. She had a look on her face, Swanny said
afterwards, of someone who has been caught out in a forbidden act,
a how-can-I-get-out-of-this-one look, a child taking one of mother's
chocolates. Her eyes moved, the blue gaze cast up, then shifting to
the right, to the left. She looked appalled, she looked trapped,
Swanny said, and then she burst out laughing.

"Oh, don't laugh," Swanny cried out. "Please don't. I've been in
such a state. I've lain awake nights. But if it's a lie you can laugh.
Is it a lie?"

Anna, of course, said the worst thing she could. She often did.
"If you want it to be, *lille* Swanny. If that makes you happy it can
be a lie. What is truth anyway?"

"Moder," said Swanny, and she hardly ever called Anna by the
more formal word, "I have a right to know, I must know. Please
look at this letter."

Anna took it and looked at it. Of course she couldn't see it
without her glasses and these had to be groped for in her handbag,
taken out of their case, perched on her nose. She read the letter and
then she did what seemed an awful thing to Swanny. Before
Swanny could stop her she had torn it in two, in four, across again,
reduced it to tiny pieces.

Swanny gave a cry and tried to take the pieces of paper from her,
but Anna, just like a child in the school playground, like a teasing
crowing child, held up the paper scraps high above her head,
shaking the hand that clutched them like someone waving freneti-
cally. She waved the scraps in the air, uttering a high-pitched
amused, "No, no, no, no!"

"Why did you do that? Please give me those pieces. I must have
that letter. I must put it together again."

Before she could stop her, Anna had picked up a lighter and set fire to the pieces in an ashtray. She looked defiantly at Swanny and brushed her hands against each other as if the paper had laid a coating of dust on them.

"Oh, this is so silly, Swanny. At your age! Don't you know what to do with anonymous letters? You burn them. Everyone knows that."

"Why did you burn it? How could you?"

"Because burning is the best thing for it."

"How could you, how could you?"

Mormor wasn't in the least embarrassed. She wasn't upset or remorseful. Swanny said she had the curious feeling that her mother had no emotions left, they were all used up, nothing mattered anymore except the things you suppose old women don't care about: having a good time, dressing up, eating and drinking, having a man friend to go about with.

She made one of those dismissive gestures of hers, a turning of her head one way, a wave of her hand in the opposite direction, the implication that this was all too trivial, too time-wasting. Swanny hadn't touched her coffee but Anna drank hers. She could always drink coffee and tea scalding hot, though one of her favorite stories was about some relation who had burned a hole in his esophagus doing just that.

"Mother," said Swanny, "you must tell me. Is it true?"

"I don't know why you mind so much. Haven't I been a good mother to you? Haven't I loved you best? Aren't I here with you now? What's wrong with you, digging up what's all past and gone?"

Of course Swanny asked her again and this time, she said, a cunning look passed across her mother's face. It was just the same as the look Anna put on when lying to them as children. They always knew. In the evening when she and their father appeared all dressed up: "Are you going out?" "Of course not. Why would I go out?" Or when their parents embarked upon a particularly vicious quarrel, with insults and reproaches flying, "Do you really wish you hadn't married Far?" "Don't be silly, of course not."

"Of course it isn't true, *lille* Swanny."

"Then why? I mean, why did someone write it?"

"Am I God? Am I a psychiatrist? How should I know why mad people do what they do. You should be thankful someone here has a little sense and knows that the right thing is to burn dirty evil letters. You should appreciate your good mother who cares for you."

Anna was going out. She had had her coffee, brought her hat downstairs with her and now she was going out. She never said where she was going or when she'd be back. While she was out she would buy some cards to send out for her chocolate party.

Left alone, Swanny told herself she must believe. Believe and forget. Of the existence of the diaries she had no idea at that time. They were just books Mor had brought with her. More photograph albums, she thought, if she thought about them at all. Had she known, she told me years later, she'd have gone through the lot that day while Anna was out. I must believe, she said aloud in that empty room, talking to the flowers and the coffee cups.

Anna wasn't like an old woman, not like an old mother with her daughter. Instead, Swanny was the mother and Anna her adolescent daughter whom she suspected of some terrible act the girl had no intention of admitting. The girl, as a girl might be in such a situation, was in control. Swanny was powerless.

That evening, in front of Torben, after dinner but still at the table, Anna announced that she had something to tell them. She might be going to die. It might happen quite soon. In the nature of things she couldn't live long, but as it happened she suspected she had cancer.

They were all concern, all sympathy and enquiry. As it turned out, all the tests subsequently done on Anna were negative, she didn't have cancer, there was nothing wrong with her. Perhaps she suspected there was, perhaps on the other hand it was all done for effect, because she so much enjoyed making dramas. But that evening she went up to bed early for her and asked Swanny to come to her bedroom when she was undressed.

This was a most unusual, an unprecedented, request. Swanny expected when she got there to have symptoms recounted which her mother might think unfit for Torben's ears, though it would

have been unlike Anna to have such qualms. Instead, she told her
what she had prevaricated about that morning. She had always
meant to tell Swanny before she died. To die with something like
that on her conscience wouldn't be right.

She didn't look guilty, Swanny said, she looked pleased with
herself. She wasn't in bed but sitting by the bed, wrapped in a bright
kingfisher blue silk robe Uncle Ken's wife had given her for Christmas and which Swanny never remembered seeing her wear before,
she had said so vehemently how she disliked it. Her eyes were like
buttons covered with the same material.

"You may as well know it all," she said. "You're not mine. I
mean, I didn't give birth to you. I adopted you when you were a
few days old."

It took a while for the shock to strike. It always does. Perhaps
it was because Swanny was stunned that she could speak, and speak
calmly.

"Like the people in that story of yours?" she said. "The one
about the couple who went to the orphanage in Odense. Was that
you and Far?"

Anna didn't hesitate. "Yes."

Even then Swanny knew of course that it couldn't have been.
The dates were wrong. Her mother was living in London when she
was born, she was born there, it was on her birth certificate, while
her father was somewhere in Denmark. But she wanted so desperately to believe. This way, though he had never loved her, she could
have Rasmus Westerby for her father.

"Why didn't you tell me when I was young?"

Anna shrugged. "You were mine. I thought of you as mine. I
forgot you were someone else's."

"Was Far my father?"

"There wasn't much to be said for my husband, *lille* Swanny, but
he wouldn't have betrayed his own wife. He wasn't as bad as that.
I'm surprised you can suggest it."

Swanny said she screamed. She screamed out and covered her
mouth. "You're surprised! You're surprised! You tell me these
things and you're surprised at what I say."

Anna was quite cool and calm. "Of course I'm surprised when you speak like that to your mother."

"You're not my mother, you've just said so. Is it true?"

Again that strange look, Swanny said, an indifferent smile, a half-acknowledgment of naughtiness committed. Anyone who knew Anna recognized it at once from her description.

"Am I a criminal, *lille* Swanny? Are you a policeman?"

Swanny said, like the child she had been at the time, "He didn't make the dollhouse for me."

"You're just a big baby. Come and give me a kiss."

She beckoned, she lifted her cheek. Swanny said she felt like taking hold of this little old woman and shaking her, seizing her by the throat, torturing the truth out of her—tell me, tell me. She kissed her meekly and went away to cry.

Torben found her crying in their bedroom and he took her in his arms to comfort her. He thought she was crying because her mother hadn't long to live. But Anna wasn't dying. She would live another eleven years.

7

How those eleven years passed, in that particular aspect of them, she told me in that time when we became close, after my mother was dead. I mean, of course, that she didn't tell me everything, for no one ever does, but she told me what she chose I should know.

After that first confrontation with Anna over the coffee cups, after the second that night in Anna's room, it was a long while before she said anything to Torben. My mother was her confidante but forbidden, for the time being, to discuss any of it with Anna herself. So why was Torben kept in the dark? Everyone said theirs was a good marriage, they seemed devoted to each other, inseparable. The story of his long ardent courtship was well known. It was possible when with them to see the occasional conspiratorial glance which passed from him to her, the half-smile she gave him covertly in return. At home they spoke Danish together, their private language, their personal code. But she didn't tell him what her mother had confessed to her.

When my mother saw her she was often distraught, with dark rings round her eyes from lack of sleep. She even got tranquilizers from the doctor. Didn't Torben see? Didn't he notice these changes? Or did she lie to him and attribute these effects to some other cause?

After he was dead and Anna was dead Swanny told me she was

afraid of what he would think of her. Apparently, his family were upper class, he may even have been a scion of a minor aristocracy. Imagine being afraid her own husband might despise her for possibly lowly origins after thirty years of marriage! The worst thing, she said, was not knowing who she was, for by then, by the time she told him, she had made her mother state categorically that she was no more Rasmus' child than she was Anna's. Hadn't Anna herself said, when telling the tale of the orphanage, that if she'd been the finally enlightened wife she wouldn't have kept the boy but "sent him right back where he came from"?

That his wife had received an anonymous letter shocked Torben. The fact of it being an anonymous letter seems to have angered him more than its contents. Of course he had never seen it.

"Mother burned it."

"You mean Mother imagined it."

"No, I got it, it was sent me and when I let Mother read it she burned it."

Torben dismissed the whole thing as nonsense. I don't mean he did this peremptorily, he wasn't that sort of man, but after listening attentively and by then doubtless seeing how distraught it was making her, after considering it and thinking about it, he told her his conclusion was that her mother had made it up.

"But the letter, Torben."

"Ah, yes, that wonderful letter."

It was a dry look he gave her. He smiled ruefully, he cast up his eyes a very little. She said she knew what he meant, what he was thinking but would never say. She could tell who he thought had sent the letter. He put it all reasonably. Anna was old, Anna was senile. Now, certainly in the last decade of her life, she looked back on a dull existence and wished to invest it with an excitement it never had. So that she might feel she hadn't wasted it, so that she could show she had lived. She projected her secret desires on to a life gone by that no one now alive could prove had been different.

The next thing, he said, she would be saying Swanny was her child but not Rasmus', hers by a lover. There was a certain kind of woman who did this, it was a well-known fact. Curiously, this did comfort Swanny for a while. She even said to my mother that she wished she'd been sensible and told Torben long before.

However, Anna never did say Swanny was her child by a lover. Torben had perhaps overlooked the fact that she belonged in a generation to whom a married woman's having a lover wasn't only unethical, but almost criminal. The diaries show plainly enough what she thought of women who "sinned" in this way and what she thought a woman's "honor" was. By this time, anyway, she had managed to put the whole business of Swanny's origins into the past, to bury it. Impatient with discussing it, bored and irritated by it, she made it plain to Swanny that this was the last thing she ever wanted to talk about again.

"Let's forget it, *lille* Swanny," was her most frequent rejoinder to Swanny's reiterated questions, or, with exasperation, "What a lot of bosh it all is!"

In those years that went by after her confession, she simply dismissed the whole subject as fast as she could. What relevance did something which happened sixty years before have today?

"I love you, I chose you, you've had a good life and you've got a good husband—" Anna couldn't resist adding that this was more than she had had "—and you're comfortable, you want for nothing, so what's wrong with you, going on like this?"

"I've a right to know who I really am, Mother."

"I've told you. We adopted you, your father and I. We wanted a girl because we only had boys until Marie came along. We picked you out in an orphanage—there, does that satisfy you? I don't know what's the matter with you, *lille* Swanny, I'm the one who should be moaning, I'm the one who lost those babies, one dying after another—but do I complain? Never! I make the best of things, I *get through.*"

You have to understand that Swanny now found herself quite alone. She told me that she felt an outcast in many ways. Her mother, for all her vaunted love, was no longer her mother, had never been her mother. Her sister and brother were not her sister and brother but only the people she had been brought up with. It struck her forcibly at about this time, a year or so after the disclosure, that she was most likely not even Danish. Her Danishness had been important to her in ways she hadn't fully appreciated until it had been shown not to exist. For a while a curious thing happened and Danish, her cradle tongue, grew stiff on her lips and when she spoke it she felt like an impostor, uttering a language to which she had no right. She had no language, for she had no nationality. And all this was compounded by the ridiculousness of it at her age. What had happened to her, though inevitably an evil, more *suitably* happened to children or adolescents.

One of the worst things was that her husband, who had always been her support, a rock that she could cling to, was no comfort to her here because he simply refused to take it seriously. He wasn't irritable but he was incredulous. Many times he told her that it was beyond him, an intelligent sensible woman like herself, swallowing any amount of nonsense her senile mother chose to tell her. For his part, he had never believed it, had never doubted, and he claimed to be able to see strong resemblances between his wife and various personages in Mormor's photographs of ancestors.

Then why had Mor said it? She got it out of Dickens, Torben said, with some triumph at finding this ingenious solution. It was true that Mormor seldom read anything but Dickens and read him all the time, true too that children turning out not to be who and whose they seem figure prominently in his plots. Look at Estella, look at Esther Summerson, said Torben, himself no mean reader. Anna was senile and she confused fiction with reality, fantasy with fact. Swanny realized something she had never noticed before, that Torben disliked her mother.

Anna's cancer was something she had imagined or invented or thought up as a useful ploy. For a woman of her advanced age, she was exceptionally strong and healthy. It was my mother who had cancer and died of it.

She had been going to be married. I don't mean simply that she was engaged, she had been engaged several times, but this time it was serious, George the last fiancé was serious, and they were to be married in Hampstead registry office in August. The cancer she had is called carcinomatosis, a kind of total malignancy that consumes the sufferer very swiftly. She was dead three weeks after diagnosis.

The funeral was at Golders Green and Anna came. Swanny discouraged her but she came, dressed in her funerary uniform, the crossover black silk coat and the pancake hat. After the service, as we were looking at the wreaths laid out in the crematorium garden, she made, very loudly and clearly, one of her devastating remarks.

"My children are always dying."

It was true. First the baby Mads, then, presumably, the baby Swanny had replaced, Mogens on the Somme, now her daughter Marie. Since Swanny was not hers, Knud, my uncle Ken, was the only living child that remained to her.

Swanny said faintly, "Oh, Mor . . ."

"It's not so bad as it used to be, I can tell you. You get hard when you get old, these things don't mean very much. I've no feelings left." And Anna, to everyone's shocked astonishment, picked up a large bouquet of roses from the ground, sniffed them and removed the card attached to their stems. "I think I'll take these home, *lille* Swanny. I like red roses. You often forget to put flowers in my room."

She did take them home, remarking that they were no use to Marie now and that it would have been better if Peter and Sheila (whoever they were) had given her flowers while she was alive.

I went back to Swanny's house with George and his son Daniel, a very handsome rather quiet man of about my own age, who was a psychiatrist. These days Swanny could have had counseling for her problems of identity and loss but not in the 1960s. Even to go to a psychiatrist seemed a daring step to take. But it crossed my mind to suggest this, to him or to her, as we arrived in Willow Road. He seemed pleasant, not watchful of one's every move as they sometimes are, not superior or remote.

At the funeral he had asked me who Anna was and shown interest in her in a rather unusual way. He spoke the way men do when admiring some beautiful young woman they want to know better.

"Who's *that?*"

"My grandmother."

"She looks remarkable. It's hardly suitable to say it here but she looks as if she knows how to enjoy life."

I said, and I meant it, "I don't know."

"I'm very sorry about your mother." He'd said that before, perhaps he had forgotten. "I'd have liked her for a stepmother."

Someone must have introduced him to Anna, for I came upon them in Swanny's drawing room, deep in talk. She was telling him the story of the man her cousin knew in Sweden who murdered his mistress to get their child for his wife. I wondered if Swanny had also speculated about any relevance this story might have to her own origins, though hardly casting Far in the killer's role.

In the event, I did nothing about getting Swanny to a psychiatrist, Daniel Blain or anyone else. My mother's death affected her deeply but it distracted her from her own troubles. It also drew her closer to me or me to her. Her sister Marie had been her closest woman friend, she had no child of her own. It was only natural that I should become, at least in her own eyes, her daughter.

She mourned. She grieved for her sister. She drew closer once more to Torben who shared her sorrow, who sympathized utterly. He had loved my mother as a sister but I hope I don't wrong him in saying that as far as he was concerned, if she had to die, there was no better time for her to have done it. Her death restored his wife to him and banished from her mind—as far as he could tell—all that introspective brooding over her origins.

He had never, of course, been as bad as Uncle Ken, an insensitive brash man who, in any woman between the ages of thirty-five and sixty, blamed every divergence from the strictest convention on "her time of life." Before my mother died, before my mother was even ill, Swanny had gone to him with her desperate enquiry. He, after all, had been *there.* He had been, not an infant, but a child of five at the time, a child of school age.

She could remember herself at five. She recalled the death of Edward VII in the May of that year and her father saying the Danish Queen was a widow now. She even remembered one of the scandalous stories so dear to the heart of Anna who repeated the rumor that Queen Alexandra wore collars of diamonds to hide the scars on her neck where the King had tried to strangle her. Surely Ken could remember Anna giving birth to a daughter, his being shown the child, the nurse or doctor or both in the house. At that time she was passing through one of those semihopeful phases, in which she went along with Torben and tried not to believe any of it.

Ken couldn't remember. He said, quite proudly, according to Swanny, that he remembered absolutely nothing of what had happened before he was six. He could barely remember the house in Lavender Grove which they had moved out of when he was six and a half. She, Swanny, had always been there in his life.

"It's her age," he said to Torben, basely repeating to her husband everything Swanny had asked him. "They go a bit mad, I've noticed it time and time again. And it takes them all of seven years to get over it. At the very least."

I've since wondered if Ken couldn't remember because (as Daniel might have said) he blocked off that early childhood, if trauma excised those years which were too painful for recall to be allowed. They must have been bad years, with the continual shifting from place to place and country to country, his parents' vicious quarrels, the death of a baby brother, the move to England and a new language and his father's apparent desertion. No doubt, that would have been enough to blot out the past. Things got better soon afterwards, the year of Swanny's birth was the family's lowest ebb.

On the other hand, he may have remembered but been too bolshie to tell. That again would have been typical. Women shouldn't be indulged in their fancies, women were "strange beasts." He often said how glad he was never to have had a daughter. But I don't believe he knew any more than he told. The facts of conception, pregnancy, birth, were carefully kept from children when he was a child. Mor went to bed and someone brought her a baby. She says so in her diary.

Maybe it was true.

. . .

Mormor wasn't a woman who loved nature or even seemed to know it was there. A garden to her was a place you sat in when the sun was shining and ate in under an arbor. In fact, one of her contentions with Torben and Swanny was that they had never made proper provision for eating out in their garden. There was no table under a tree with chairs round it, no garden furniture with sunshade to be brought out each spring and arranged in some suitable corner as a breakfast nook or tea place. This she lamented often, citing Padanaram where it had been so "cozy" (a favorite word) to have tea under the mulberry tree. A photograph testified to this: Anna pouring tea from a great silver pot, Swanny beside her, my mother on Morfar's knee, the boys in Norfolk jackets and Hansine standing behind and beaming, got up in a maid's uniform and cap for the occasion. Torben disliked eating in the open air and earned her incredulity by saying so.

Because it was impossible to sit there, except on a hard teak bench, Mormor seldom went into the Willow Road garden. There were flowers but not the sort she liked. Her preference was for florist's rosebuds and scented waxen exotics out of hothouses. Swanny and Torben employed a gardener who came two or three times a week. Even then, in the sixties, I'm sure he wasn't supposed to have bonfires; even then, London and its suburbs were called a smokeless zone. Still, he did occasionally have them to burn autumn leaves and path sweepings and, according to Swanny, was very surprised one afternoon to see "the old lady" come down the path and make off with his wheelbarrow. If he asked her what she wanted it for Mormor probably played deaf, as she sometimes did when she didn't want to answer, though her hearing was as good as mine. Off she went with the wheelbarrow, at a run, the gardener said, marveling at her vigor.

Swanny was out having her hair done. When she returned the gardener was just leaving. He told her "the old lady" had come back with the wheelbarrow full of books and papers but by then he had put his bonfire out and was treading out the wood ash. She asked him if he'd be having another fire the following week but he said, no, not till next year.

Swanny asked Mormor about it and got, as she put it, a dusty answer.

"It was private, *lille* Swanny. Why do you think I chose to do it while you were out unless it was private?"

"If you've something you want to burn, Mor, it can go in the kitchen stove."

"I changed my mind."

No change in her was obvious after the diary writing stopped. If it stopped, as I believe it did and as the diaries themselves bear witness, in the autumn of 1967. She continued to walk, to attend Swanny and Torben's parties, to tell stories, to read her Dickens and, when she did so in company, to read aloud long passages she found specially astute or insightful, regardless of whether her companions wanted to listen or not. Her favorite characters were those as unlike herself as could be found: Amy Dorrit, Lizzie Hexham, Sidney Carton, Esther Summerson.

I don't believe I ever entered the room she had up there on the third floor. She had chosen it herself and refused to be moved, refused to listen to all Swanny's protestations that the stairs were too many for her to manage. And when Swanny asked what she thought people would think of a daughter who allowed her mother in her late eighties to climb three flights of stairs to reach her room, Mormor replied with a rather grim smile.

"Haven't you learned by your age, *lille* Swanny, that it's no use worrying about what people will think? They will think something whatever we do and they usually think quite wrong."

Up there she kept her Dickens, her photographs, her clothes and had once kept the diaries. The other things were fairly obviously displayed, Swanny said, even the clothes, as she left her wardrobe door open all the time "to let the air in," but not the diaries.

The diaries were lying low, waiting.

8

JUNE 29, 1910

*Jeg voksede op med Had til Tyskerne—eller Prósjerne og Os-
tigerne som vi dengang Kaldte dem. Krigen mellem dem og
Danmark eller skulde jeg sige Besaettelsen af Danmark var forbi
i 1864, laenge fór jeg blev fódt, men jeg skal aldrig glemme, hvad
min Fader fortalte mig, hvordan vi maatte give Afkald paa en
Del af vores Faedreland, det hele af Slesvig og Holsten, til Prójsen.*

I grew up hating the Germans—or Prussians and Austrians as we
called them then. The war between them and Denmark, or their
invasion of Denmark, I should say, was over in 1864, long before
I was born, but I can never forget what my father told me, how we
had to give up part of our country to Prussia, the whole of Schleswig and Holstein. He had an uncle and aunt living in Schleswig. But
the worst thing was my own grandfather, my mother's father, who
had fought in that war and had a terrible wound. He had a permanent gangrene in his foot and one day the pain got so bad that he
went out into a outhouse where they lived and hanged himself. My
mother found him hanging from a beam. She was only sixteen.

So I hate all Teutons. They are always trying to take other
people's countries away from them. Last year it was Bosnia-
Herzegovina and they tore up the Treaty of Berlin, on which the

peace of Europe was founded. Or so Rasmus and his friend and business partner Mr. Housman were saying this evening. They talked for hours about my least favorite subject, war. I suppose it makes a change from motorcars. I said that if it does come to war, we won't be involved and nor will Denmark.

"Women," said Rasmus charmingly, "what would you know?"

I could see Mr. Housman trying not to smile. He covers up his mouth with his hand when Rasmus says words beginning with a *w*. Vimmin and var and "voothe" for "would."

"Europe is preparing for var, you'll see," Rasmus said. "Not just Austria-Hungary but France and Russia too. You mark my vorthes."

I shouldn't laugh. My own English is far from perfect. I admire and envy the children who speak it so well, all three of them. There'll be a fourth next year. I'm almost sure and for once I'm happy about it!

The one I conceived soon after my husband came back from Denmark that first time, I lost three months later and I was sorry. I felt too bad and bitter even to put it down in my diary. Some things go too deep even for writing down. Then, for some reason—I can't say what, for there was plenty of "love"—I haven't fallen again until now. It's a mystery, what goes on inside a woman, and I suppose no one ever will quite understand it.

FEBRUARY 11, 1911

Another girl. If I have to have babies, and it appears I do, I much prefer girls. I haven't written in this diary for months, I've been so afraid of having another boy.

She was born yesterday morning. It wasn't a difficult birth but short and sharp, a swift affair with one terrible pain at the end, like a sword cutting me in two, and there she was. After I'd had a sleep and a good meal I sat up in bed and thought about the contrast between this birth and the last one. Things have certainly changed for the Westerby family.

Quite a nice house, for one thing, and a girl to help Hansine with the "rough." Enough money not to go short of anything. When Swanny was born Hansine brought me a great plate of sausages and potatoes which she slapped down on the bed in front of me. This time it was salmon in *Krustader* and roast fowl to follow. I'm wearing a new white silk nightgown and the ring on my finger my husband has seen fit to give me because I've made him so happy! His words.

We are going to call her Marie. For once we are in agreement about something, if for different reasons. I just happen to like the name, it's my second-favorite girl's name after Swanhild, it has such a pretty sound. Rasmus, of course, likes it because it can be English and all things English he adores. "The English can pronounce it," he says, by which he means they pronounce it "Maar-rie," as in Marie Lloyd whom we've seen on the stage. "The French can pronounce it too," I said in my way, "for what that's worth," but he doesn't mind what I say at the moment. I am perfect because I've given him a daughter. Anyone would think she was his first!

MARCH 3, 1911

Today I went out for the first time since Marie's birth. I'm a "lady" so I'm supposed to spend weeks in bed after being confined, though there's nothing wrong with me. Lower-class women never do that, they're up and about next day, they have to be. I've known cases of servants secretly delivering their babies in back kitchens and outhouses and returning to their work the same day.

It was good to be out, even though Rasmus insisted on my being driven about in the horseless carriage by him. Not that I'm allowed to call it that in his hearing. It has to be the "motor" or even the "automobile," and this one was one of the American electrics. It goes so slowly you could walk as fast—well, run.

Luckily, I get my figure back within days of being delivered. In fact, I've never needed corsets, though of course I have to wear them. Rasmus has become nearly as fond of fashion as he is of motorcars—I tell him that when these "autos" go out of favor, as they must do, he'll be able to sell frocks—and wants to see me dressed up. I suspect he thinks it good for business to have a handsome wife about when customers come to the house. Not that I'm handsome but these days I do look smart.

Out in the motor this morning I wore my cream pongee coat with green linen revers and my hat with a whole bird on it, I don't know what kind but with black and green feathers. I had a green motoring veil and a white fox muff and I was freezing cold all the time we were out.

Rasmus could see me shivering and said what I'd never dared hope to hear from him. "I'll tell you what, old girl, I'm going to buy you a fur coat."

It's a promise I'm going to hold him to. He's been buying me this new magazine from America that's called *Vogue* and I've seen a fur coat in it which is the one I want. It's Persian lamb trimmed with white fox, very showy and enough to make people stare, but that's what I like. I suppose I don't really care for clothes the way some women do, I just like dressing-up and being looked at, people thinking what a lot my clothes must have cost and wondering how I dare wear such outrageous things.

My ring has an emerald, deep set in 22-carat gold with tiny diamonds in the "shoulders." He says it cost five hundred pounds but he always exaggerates. I love it but I'd give it up if by doing so I could make him love my little Swanny. I'd throw it in the River Lea or give it to Hansine, only I know you can't buy things that way in this life.

It's worse since Marie was born or it seems worse. He never took much notice of the boys when they were little, he was proud of having sons but that was all, but he holds Marie in his arms and carries her about. He takes her out into the yard and shows her the motors standing there. She's three weeks old and she's supposed to understand when he talks to her about battery power and detachable cylinder heads.

I don't mind him loving her, I'm glad he does, it's a real change to see him love anyone. He actually loves me at the moment, though it can no more last than Ford motors can and I expect they'll go on longer. He's all right with the boys, I mean he's not unkind or anything, but he'll never play cricket or football with them, which they'd love. Anyway, Mogens at thirteen is nearly as tall as he is and growing whiskers on his chin, so I expect it doesn't much matter. But Swanny's only six and she's such a sweet gentle little thing. She's the best looking of our children too. Marie will never come up to her, I can say that without a doubt though she's such a tiny baby still.

He doesn't like the way Swanny looks. I don't know why. I can't imagine why. I've asked him, I made myself ask him, and first of all he said that was nonsense, where did I get these ideas from. But I persisted. There's this beautiful little girl, tall for her age, really straight and upright, a credit to my good meals and care, lovely skin as white as milk and hair the color of a guinea, the true bright gold, eyes that are a soft sea-blue, not the harsh color mine are, and he doesn't like the look of her! He admitted it at last.

"She looks so Danish," he said.

"What's wrong with that?" I said.

He just gave one of his silly laughs. I knew he meant he wants to be English and all his "possessions" (which is how he describes us) English too. The funny thing is that no one who heard him talk could for one moment mistake him for anything but a foreigner. I know I've got an accent and I always will have but at least I don't say "schooth" for "should" and "tree" for "three."

Of course it wasn't long before he was telling me he loved all his children equally, they were all the same to him, but that's only what he thinks he ought to say. It cuts no ice with me, as the Americans say. But I feel like killing him when I see her go up to him, lay her little hand on his knee and ask him something, and all he does is brush her away as he might a dog. In fact, he takes a lot more notice of Bjórn, our Great Dane puppy, than he does of her.

What is it about her he really doesn't like? I get frightened when I think of it like that, so I try not to.

JULY 28, 1911

Little Swanny's birthday. She was six today. We gave her a doll the size of a real baby and with real human hair. I write "we" but of course I chose it and bought it and smuggled it into the house without her seeing. Rasmus just had his name on the card: love from Mor and Far.

I've been meaning to write something about Rasmus in this diary for a long time. I'd like to say he's a peculiar man but how would I know? I've only lived with one man, been married to one man, and a girl never really knows what her own father is like. Usually she sees the best side of him or the side he wants her to see. It may be that Rasmus is no stranger than any other man.

There is a shed or outbuilding at the end of our garden and this he has turned into a workshop. It is big enough to get a motorcar inside and it's in there that he tinkers with engines. He spends hours and hours in there taking motor engines apart and putting them together again. When he comes back into the house he smells of oil no matter how much he washes. The oil has a very strange smell, bitter and like you'd imagine metal might smell if it were melted to liquid, and if you smelled it long enough it would make you feel dizzy.

He also has a workbench and a lot of tools and has made Björn a kennel with a window in the side and a sloping roof with real tiles on. I couldn't help admiring it and showing my admiration, though as a rule I try not to show anything like that because it goes to his head. All the time he's thinking of new things he wants to make and do. Glass-blowing is the latest and I expect sculpture will come next. While we were out in the motor today, supposed to be taking little Swanny for a birthday ride, I with Marie fidgeting about on my lap, he stopped by a yard where a monumental mason was working and we must have been there an hour while he watched this man chipping away at a gravestone, of all things. And all this down at South Mill Field, the most slummy desolate place in the neighborhood.

Rasmus is hardly ever in the house. There seems to be some sort of rule that women are indoors and men outside. It's funny because we all get very shocked and on our high horses about women kept in the harems of the east but I can't see that it's so very different here. I live in the house and Rasmus lives outside it. Of course I go out, I go out for walks, I escape, but that's what it is, an escape, and if Rasmus ever talks about it that's how he treats it. "You were out a long time," is what he says, or, "Haven't you got anything to do in the house?"

When he'd finished making Björn's kennel he wanted to make a Noah's Ark for the boys. It was the idea of carving all those little animals that appealed to him, I expect. If I want to speak to him between the hours of, say, eight in the morning and nine at night, I have to interrupt one of his business deals or else take myself down to the workshop. I went down there yesterday morning and asked him if he knew how old his sons were.

"Have you come disturbing me to ask me a fool question like that?" That's his charming way of talking to me.

"I thought I'd ask," I said, "before you waste your time making baby toys. Because, in case you've forgotten, Mogens is thirteen and Knud is eleven."

He never likes being told anything, so he changed the subject to ask me why I didn't call them Jack and Ken. He's so madly in love with England that everything has to be English for him.

"If you want to make something," I said, "why don't you make Swanny a dollhouse?"

He didn't answer. "Haven't you got anything to do indoors?" he said.

Those are our conversations. I've only just noticed it. We both ask questions and neither of us supply answers.

MARCH 5, 1912

Hansine has a man courting her. I never thought that would happen, though, when I come to think of it, she'd had one before in Copenhagen. This morning she asked if she might speak to me and when I asked her what it was about, said could she have a friend of hers to tea in the kitchen.

Naturally I thought she meant a woman, another servant like herself. There have been a few friends of that sort over the years. But when I said, "Is she in service in our street, Hansine?" she looked very shifty and blushed up and twisted her apron in her hands the way they do.

"It's not a she, it's a he," she said.

I couldn't help laughing, at the way she put it really, which sounds very funny in Danish. But of course she thought I was laughing at her, I was so astonished or something, and she looked as if she was going to cry.

"Oh, don't be so silly," I said. "I didn't mean that, it's just that it was a surprise. Of course you can have him to tea. What's his name?"

"Sam Cropper," she said, "and he's on the railway."

That may not sound funny to English ears, it may sound quite normal, but it sounded hilarious to me. I did my best to keep a straight face but she could see my lips twitching. She thinks me very unkind. I know she does because little Swanny told me so a few weeks back.

She calls me *lille mor* which is very sweet. *"Lille Mor,"* she said, "Hansine said to me, your mother can be very unkind sometimes, and I said, well, she's not unkind to me, because you're not, are you, not ever?"

"I hope not, my darling," I said but I was seething inside.

I felt like sending for Hansine and asking her how dare she say things like that to my daughter, that I was the mistress of this house, and she could take her notice if she was going to talk like that. But of course I couldn't quite do that. Not in the circumstances. We've known each other a long time now, Hansine and I, we've been through a lot together. So if she thinks me unkind she must think it. I am sometimes. People haven't been very kind to me and you give back what you get.

I couldn't help wondering what sort of a man would find her attractive, though. Her face is heavy and flat and reminds me of a big piece of mutton, the cut they call the saddle. When you say a woman is blond and blue-eyed you give people—especially men—the idea she's beautiful. They want to meet her. But features are more important in my opinion. Hansine's got the fair hair and the blue eyes and she's also got a mouth like a sauceboat and a nose like a spoon. She's what the English call a strapping wench. I read that in a novel, not a very good one that I bought, so I'm going to join the public library to get good books out.

She fetched Swanny from school and brought tea for me and the girls at four o'clock. We have to have it in the dining room with a piece of drugget covering the carpet because little Marie throws food out of her high chair all over the place, laughing and waving a spoon about. I can't stand too much of it and usually have to ring the bell for Emily to take her away and feed her somewhere else. But today I carried her outside myself.

There was no sign of Emily. Hansine and a tall handsome man were sitting at the kitchen table, drinking tea and eating far nicer-looking cakes than the ones sent into the dining room. Hansine had a silk blouse on, one of mine that I'd given her, and she'd hidden her apron away somewhere. It's a strange thing, you'd think hand-some men would want handsome girls but they almost never do. They seem to prefer the plain ones which is a bit of a waste really. This Cropper looks like a photograph I've seen of a famous lawyer called Edward Marshall Hall and far too upright and distinguished for a common working man. I wonder what he does on the railway. If he's a porter all the women must want him to carry their luggage.

They looked quite put out at the sight of me, as well they might. Hansine went even redder than her normal color.

"Where's Emily?" I said in English and Hansine said a stifled, "In there, ma'am," pointing a thumb.

Poor Emily had been relegated to the scullery where she was sitting all on her own with a cup of tea and a hunk of bread and jam. I dumped little Marie in her lap and sailed back through the kitchen. They were staring like cats and as silent as rabbits.

JUNE 2, 1913

A letter this morning from my cousin Ejnar, the one who's an
officer in the Danish Army, saying Tante Frederikke is dead. I think
he might have telegraphed me, not that I would have gone all that
way to the funeral. It's nine years since I saw Tante and time dims
things. If I tell Rasmus he may insist I go into mourning and I don't
want to wear black in the summertime, so I don't think I'll tell him.

Ejnar says Tante Frederikke wanted me to have her collection of
the works of Charles Dickens translated into Danish. I shan't say
no. I can read English well, of course I can after eight years, I'm sure
I read it better than a lot of English people, Emily for instance, but
it will never be like my own language to me. We have no books in
this house, I've noticed that for the first time. No one reads but me.

Mourning is all humbug unless you loved the person. I didn't
love Tante, though she said she loved me, she said I was the
daughter she never had. Love hasn't much chance of survival in a
relationship where one person is always telling the other one what
to do and bullying and preaching. I don't suppose I ever saw Tante
without her criticizing me, my looks, my manners, my way of
talking, my clothes, my tastes, not to mention my morals. Though
I hadn't got any morals, I didn't know what they were, I was good
because I had no chance to be bad and because I was afraid.

I shall make myself sad if I go on like this. Besides, as Tante used
to say so monotonously, it doesn't do to be always thinking about
oneself. "Come out of yourself, Anna," she was always saying. I'll
be glad to have the books, they are all I want of what was hers.

So I'll write about Hansine instead. She is walking out with
Cropper now. She meets him regularly on her afternoon off and I'm
sure he comes here more often than I know. Even Rasmus, who
never notices what people do or even if people are *there*, even
Rasmus has seen him about. There was a very funny thing which
I must write down. I wasn't going to at first because I was thinking
it's wrong to laugh on the day I heard of Tante's death. But that's
about as silly as can be. If I was going to be serious I should have

done that two weeks ago when she actually died, not today. Anyway, I need all the laughing I can get.

Rasmus didn't say a word till he'd seen Cropper hanging about the house three times. Then he put on his preacher face, the one that makes him look like the Lutheran pastor at the church when we lived in Hackney.

"Who is your friend, Anna?" he said to me.

"What friend?" I said.

"The tall gentleman I saw in the garden yesterday."

I knew then. I guessed. But I led him on, I pretended I didn't know what he meant, I even looked guilty. Then at last I said, as if light had suddenly dawned, "Oh, I know who you mean. That was no gentleman, Rasmus, that was Hansine's suitor."

He went a fiery red. For one thing, he doesn't want me to think he could ever be jealous, not a clever, busy, important engineer like him. And for another, he knows he ought to be able to tell a working man from a gentleman, like any Englishman could. Of course, apart from his clothes, Cropper doesn't look like a working man. I expect Rasmus thought I was following in the footsteps of Mrs. Roper—only he's never heard of her, and just as well.

JULY 6, 1913

My birthday once again. I am thirty-three today and soon to be middle-aged, if middle-age begins at thirty-five, as my father used to say.

Rasmus forgot, as usual. My next-door neighbor, Mrs. Evans, told me she doesn't give her husband a chance to forget her birthday or their wedding anniversary but reminds him every day for two weeks beforehand. "Now you know what Friday week is, don't you, dear?" she says to him and "You know what next Thursday is, you know what tomorrow is?" I wouldn't lower myself to do that. If he doesn't care enough to remember I'd rather he forgot. Presents are dust and ashes when they come from duty.

I expect Hansine jogged the children's memories. She wouldn't dare remind Rasmus. Anyway, they all gave me presents: a tiny pair of scissors in a pigskin purse from Mogens, two handkerchiefs initialed *A* in a silver box from Knud and a thimble from Marie because I'd made a hole in my old one with the point of a bodkin. I've left Swanny's till last to write about it separately because it was the only homemade one, the only one I like to think of as made with love. It was a pen wiper she sewed herself, very beautiful small hemstitches round the border of a lovely piece of violet-colored felt with a red rose embroidered on it—she knows red roses are my favorite flowers—and "Mor" in pink chainstitch. I shan't use that for wiping any pens. I'll keep it forever.

Just before supper Rasmus came in, holding an instrument. I'd never seen one before though I'd seen pictures. "There you are," he said, "a telephone. How d'you like that?"

"Is that my birthday present?" I said.

I could see him thinking. "Of course it is."

"Who's going to use it, then?"

"I need it for business, naturally," he said. "But you can use it too."

I saw this line printed on the screen at the moving pictures last week and I've been dying to use it ever since. "Thanks a million," I said.

He sulked for the next hour. I pity the poor children if one of them says anything to him when he's in that mood. Except of course for Marie, who can do no wrong. She's the naughtiest child I've had, never still, always tearing about and playing tricks. This afternoon she did an awful thing, went to Hansine and said, "Mor's fallen down on the floor and her eyes are closed and she can't speak."

Hansine came running up the stairs in a terrible state and found me quietly sitting in my bedroom, writing this diary. Well, she didn't find me writing it, I'd quickly put it in the drawer, but she found me sitting calmly, looking out of the window. Marie had done it to get attention, I suppose. I've found that little children don't like it when you're writing or reading. They feel shut out by these activities which they can't do and can't even comprehend.

Still, she mustn't be allowed to tell lies and get away with it. I gave her a hard smack and I told Rasmus what his little favorite had done. But all he said was how clever she must be to know how to do that at only two years and five months. I wonder why he loves her best. She looks exactly like I did at that age, she's going to look just like me when she grows up. She's even got my peacock blue eyes, my high cheekbones and thin lips, and her hair is the color of wet sand.

So, another birthday gone by!

SEPTEMBER 20, 1913

We are going to move.

My dear husband informed me of that fact this morning. I am sure there must be marriages in which the husband and wife *do things together,* though I don't really know about other marriages, I only know what I observe from watching couples arm-in-arm or when we go, as we very occasionally do, to the homes of people who buy motorcars from Rasmus. Perhaps those women's husbands don't consult them about anything either. But I can't believe it's normal for a man to say to the woman he's been married to for sixteen years that he's bought a house and you'll all be moving in next month.

As a matter of fact, I don't mind because I'd love to move. I like moving, I like the change, the upheaval, the packing and especially the first night in the new house. It's an adventure. But I would like to have some say in choosing the house I'm to live in, I'd like not to be treated like a child or a lunatic.

"Where is it?" I said.

"Highgate."

Immediately I thought of the old village and the horrible old houses round the green or down the West Hill. Nor would I want to live next door to a cemetery. But, no, for once it sounds as if he has got it right.

It's a big modern house in Shepherds Hill called Padanaram.

9

I first knew Cary Oliver when we were both working at the BBC in the late sixties. She stole my lover from me and married him.

That sounds very bold and dramatic. I think Cary herself would agree that it's true. There is really no other way of putting it. I and Daniel Blain, the psychiatrist, son of my mother's last fiancé, lived together for about five years. It would be an exaggeration to call him the only man I've ever loved, though he came close to being that. Cary set her sights on him and took him away.

I know all the arguments. No one can be taken from someone else, they have to want to go. People are not things to be snatched and borrowed and taken and abandoned. People have free will. If he had really loved me . . . Well, perhaps he didn't. It was I who moved out. I didn't leave him, it was more what they used to call constructive desertion.

Later on Daniel and Cary got married and still later divorced. He disappeared to America. From time to time I heard of her. More often I saw her name in the credits that follow television productions on screen. She had become quite a successful producer of drama. But until it came over on the answering machine I hadn't heard her voice for fifteen years, not in fact since the evening she communicated her feelings to me in an ecstatic gasp:

"He's so good-looking!"

I didn't call her back. It was she who had phoned me and I

admired her nerve. Fifteen years are nothing, an evening gone, in these matters. If I'm honest I must say I wondered what she could possibly want. The diaries had long been adapted and dramatized for television, not to mention read aloud as *A Book at Bedtime,* and a proposal had just come in to put them on audio cassette. But I thought I could live quite contentedly without ever finding out.

A huge pile of letters of condolence had come, had been coming since Swanny's death nearly two weeks before. Up until a year before she died Swanny had had a secretary who came in three days a week. This woman had dealt efficiently with her correspondence, which of course was enormous, but she had left when Swanny had her first stroke and became incapacitated. Swanny could scarcely have signed a letter, still less taken in the sense of it. Besides, in whose name would she have signed at that stage? Along with the other personality she put on, would she have produced that other persona's signature?

So there was no one but me to reply to the letters and I set about working through them. Swanny hadn't known many people, that is she had few personal friends, but she had had thousands of fans, or her mother had, and she had represented her mother to them. I'd written my surely hundredth card to a reader thanking her— they were nearly all women—for her letter and assuring her publication of the diaries wouldn't stop, when Cary phoned.

She still had her breathless discursive manner. "You got my message and you hate me, you've been besieged and you're going to put the phone down, but please, please don't."

My mouth had dried. I sounded hoarse to myself. "Cary, I won't put the phone down."

"You'll talk?"

"I am talking." I was thinking, what's this about being besieged? Had I been besieged? I'd been out and the answering machine had been switched off. I said carefully, "It's a very long time since we talked at all."

She didn't speak at the other end but she wasn't silent.

"You could get a job in one of your own productions," I said, "as a heavy breather. You're very good."

"Oh, Ann, have you forgiven me?"

"Suppose you tell me what you want. Let's get that straight first. You do want something, don't you?"

"Of course I do. I said I did. But I'm like a child, I know you think I'm like a child. I want you to tell me everything's all right first. I want to be forgiven and things made right. I want to start again with a sort of—well, a clean slate."

I thought, Daniel should hear you now, but I didn't say it, I didn't want to mention his name. "Okay, I forgive you, Cary. Is that all right?"

"But do you really, Ann?"

"I really do. Now tell me what you want. Surprise me."

She did, rather. She waited awhile, as if luxuriating in the catharsis of being pardoned, as if it were a warm bath to soak in. The sigh she gave had a purring sound. Then she said, "First tell me if you're putting a total embargo on anyone even taking a peek at the unpublished diaries."

"What?"

"There's a bit missing from the first diary, as you must know. Are you letting anyone look at it?"

"Is there a bit missing? I hadn't noticed."

"You haven't?"

"I don't even know what you mean, a bit missing. Entries that ought to be there and aren't or what?"

"If you don't know, I'll breathe again, I'll know there's a chance for me."

The most improbable reason for the request that was to come was that she might be interested in Swanny's origins. After all, Swanny might have become a well-known figure, broadcasting, and going on television, being interviewed by magazines and so on, but even while she was alive that she was or was not Anna's natural daughter would have been only of minor interest. It was Anna who interested people. Swanny was only her go-between, in a way her mouthpiece, her interpreter. And now she was dead, public concern was not for her but for the future of the unpublished diaries she might or might not have edited. Still, I immediately jumped to the conclusion that what Cary wanted to know about was Swanny's birth. I must have been very involved with it myself, more than I was aware of.

"I'm sure there's nothing about my aunt's babyhood that hasn't already appeared in print."

"Your aunt's babyhood? Ann, who's your aunt? I don't even know who your aunt is."

"Swanny Kjaer."

"Oh God, yes. I'm sorry, I knew she was some relative, it hadn't really registered she was your aunt. What about her babyhood? You surely haven't had the paparazzi pestering you about that?"

I asked her, if it wasn't that, what was it?

"Ann, could we meet? Would you? Could you bear it?"

I thought for a moment and decided I could. Of course I could. "But you can tell me what for?"

"Roper," she said. "I want to do a series on Roper."

I said, truthfully, that I didn't know what she was talking about.

"In volume one, in *Anna*, the very first entries, there's a bit about what's she called, the maid . . ."

"Hansine."

"Yes, Hansine, coming home and saying she'd made friends with the maid in a lodging house in the next street or a street nearby."

That was probably the first instance of someone approaching me and taking it for granted I had all the diaries' contents, word for word, off by heart. Soon there were to be many. "I suppose so."

"And she goes on to say more later, about the woman coming to tea with Hansine and the people she works for. Well, the people she worked for were Roper and his wife and mother-in-law. There! D'you mean you really didn't know?"

The name meant nothing to me. I wonder now that I didn't ask to be enlightened but I didn't and just made a date with Cary to meet her in two days' time. The beginnings of curiosity came when I'd put the phone down. I found my own copy of *Anna* and read those first entries. There was no mention of anyone called Roper. I found the references to the old man falling down in the street, to Hansine's friend and the people she worked for. They were a man and his wife and the wife's mother. The maid spoke of "her mistress, Mrs. Hyde," not Mrs. Roper. Later on, Anna wrote how she went to the street where these people lived, looked at their house and saw a woman come out with a child.

That was in the entry for July 26, 1905, two days before Swanny's birth. There were no more entries until August 30, something I'd never noticed before and which rather surprised me, though it did no more than that at the time. Gaps did occur in the diaries, Anna hadn't written in her notebooks every day, nor for that matter every week. Later on I found a reference on October 15 to "the man who murdered his wife in Navarino Road," but again no name was given. That was all. No explanation, no details. Anna evidently wasn't much concerned. Nor was I—then.

Of much more interest was the next letter I opened. It was from someone called Paul Sellway.

Here was a name that meant something to me but I wasn't sure what. I thought about it for a moment before reading what he had to say. Sellway, Sellway. Had some relative of Maureen's, Ken's wife, married a Sellway? I got no further. I read it.

He wanted me to know how he sympathized with me in the death of my aunt. He just remembered her, having met her once when he was a boy and soon after his grandmother died. The letter was several paragraphs long but it wasn't until the last one that he explained who he was. The son of Joan (née Cropper) and Ronald Sellway, born in 1943, and therefore the grandson of Hansine Fink. His letter was headed: Dr. R. G. Sellway, with an address in London E8.

I found myself, for some reason, imagining how Anna would have reacted. She had been a snob and, like most snobs, with no justification for such an attitude. To learn that Paul Sellway was a doctor (a calling she deeply respected though rather disliked) would have made her incredulous. What, the grandson of illiterate Hansine, a doctor! The descendant of that Fink, that peasant, like the wretched Karoline, no better than a farm animal! That Morfar himself came out of the same sort of stable (in more senses than one) affected this view not at all. She herself had the dubious distinction of being two generations, instead of one, away from clogs.

Swanny had felt very differently. Pursuing her search for her own origins, she had gone to Hansine's daughter. This was about two years after my mother's death. She had adjusted to her younger sister's dying, was used to the fact of it, had learned to use her Wednesdays in other ways and accustom herself to the absence of that daily phone call. Into that empty space, in much the same way as nature abhors a vacuum, returned her anxieties about her own provenance.

Hansine herself, though two or three years younger than Anna, had died in the early fifties. That death, or its aftermath, must have been the occasion of Swanny's encounter with Paul Sellway. I've a vague memory, not of Swanny's going to Hansine's funeral— neither she nor my mother nor Anna did that—but of her calling on the daughter some days or weeks later for a purpose now forgotten. Perhaps Hansine asked Joan Sellway to give Swanny something of hers for a keepsake. Swanny had been her favorite among the Westerby children, as she was Anna's.

Now Swanny went to see her again, though it wasn't quite as simple as that. For one thing, Joan Sellway had moved. Swanny phoned the old number and got a stranger who had no idea where the Sellways now were. You have to understand that Swanny both wanted to find her and did not want to find her. She wanted to know the truth and she was at the same time afraid to know it. She was once more working herself up into a state.

I was to trace her. Swanny wasn't the first person to treat me, because of my profession, like a private detective. I would know how to go about it, I would run her to earth. In fact, anyone could have done it, there was no difficulty. Joan Sellway or Ronald Sellway her husband weren't in the London phone book because they had moved outside the range of its area. I found her in Borehamwood in the local directory.

And now I must be careful what I say about Joan Sellway. I never knew her, I can't speak from experience and it would be wrong in me, particularly in me, to report on her character from hearsay. In any case, she was no more than cold to Swanny and she seemed simply not to understand.

She was a tall fair-haired woman, big-boned and gaunt, what Swanny called "a certain Danish type," with large blue eyes and strong capable hands. Her response to Swanny's questions was to say, "I don't know what you're talking about," and "I don't know what you mean." At last, as if by a great effort to take the ravings of madness seriously, she came out triumphantly with, "Why don't you ask your mother?"

Swanny said she had and explained the result of asking.

"I'd rather you talked to my son," Mrs. Sellway kept saying.

This, of course, was the Paul of the letter. She very much wanted Swanny to refer all this to her son, evidently the rock she leaned on after her husband had left her, and Swanny's asking how would he know, he wasn't there, had very little effect.

"*I* wasn't there," Joan Sellway said.

Swanny could see no resemblance in her to Hansine. Anna's maid-of-all-work had been a jolly smiling woman, motherly where Anna wasn't, caring and dependable. Or that was how she remembered her.

"I just thought your mother might have said something to you about that time. I mean about the time she was with my mother."

"She didn't."

And then Swanny understood from Joan Sellway's manner, a kind of retreat even further into herself, a terrible anger totally repressed, that she had never wanted to know about her mother's life before her marriage, had perhaps asked her not to speak of it in front of her husband, her son. Her mother had been in service. Her mother had been in a menial position in the employ of this woman's mother. And what had *she* done that she should be subjected to these mean enquiries from a woman who was no better than she, she with her nice house in Borehamwood, her son about to be a doctor? Probably the woman had only come there, was only asking, to mock her, to taunt her with her mother's humble, even shameful, origins. Swanny knew she must not press it but knew too that Joan Sellway had nothing to tell, knew nothing, was as ignorant as she was but with no desire to end that ignorance, no motive for ending it.

Swanny was humbled. She saw, or thought she saw, that she was making a fool of herself, but she couldn't help it, she couldn't stop. She was worse than before my mother died. And all the time she was afraid that Anna herself would soon be beyond disclosing the truth. Even if she were willing to do so, Anna herself would have declined too far into senility to remember or to speak coherently of her memories. In fact, there were no signs as far as I could see, at that time, when Anna was in her ninth decade, that she was anything other than she had always been, capricious, stubborn, self-absorbed, outrageous and curiously charming.

It was Torben who had put the idea of her approaching senility into Swanny's head. Anna's senility, in his view, was responsible for what he called "this whole sad business." Swanny wanted to think her senile because that might mean the "sad business" was what Torben thought it was, a lot of nonsense. But if Anna was senile would she ever be able to tell her daughter the truth, always supposing she wanted to?

She went to Uncle Harry. He was younger than Anna by two or three years but had worn less well. Who hadn't? He still lived alone but was looked after by his bevy of daughters, all married and all but one living nearby in Leyton.

Anna used to say how much he loved Swanny, how he'd taken to her when first they met when she was only fourteen. He called on Anna at Padanaram to give her a firsthand account of her son's death. It was quite the usual thing, something survivors of war did, went to bereaved parents to comfort them with the story of the dead child's last hours, his courage, his fortitude in suffering and his glorious—it always had to be that—his glorious, noble, courageous death. Emily had answered the door to him but it was Swanny he found when she showed him into the drawing room and Swanny he spoke to during the ten minutes they waited for Anna to come down.

"Your brother," he said to her, "told me he'd got a dear little sister but he never said she was a beauty."

When she went over to Leyton, to Essex Road where he lived in half a big terraced Edwardian house, she found him alone, the daughter from the flat upstairs having just cleared away his lunch things, made up the fire and brought him the newspaper. When young he had apparently been as fine and tall a man as Paul Sellway's grandfather Sam Cropper, only fair where Sam was dark, but age had shrunk and bent him. His face had taken on the pinkish-whitishness of a child that feels the cold. He had Parkinson's and his hands shook constantly, but he was still funny and gallant and cheerful.

He took Swanny's hand and kissed it. No one knew where he had acquired this un-English habit, which so endeared him to Anna. He always kissed *her* hand and she loved it. Swanny told him everything. He was easy to talk to and a good listener. He had had to be, going about with Anna as he did.

At last he said, "She's never said a word to me."

Swanny wailed, "She won't tell me! Could she have made it all up? Could she?"

"I'll tell you something, dear, for what it's worth. I've heard all my life about it's a wise child knows its own father but that's rot, isn't it? You can always see parents in a child and a child in its parents. It's harder to tell with your own because you don't really know what you look like yourself, you don't see yourself straight in mirrors. But with others, when you know the parents and the children, you can always see. And when you can't that means trouble."

"You knew my father," Swanny said. She corrected herself. "You knew Rasmus Westerby, you know Anna. Can you see them in my face? Can you see either of them?"

"Dear," he said, "have you got to ask me that?"

She said she had to ask him that, she had to.

He was quiet for a minute. He held her hand. "Then the answer's no. No, I can't. I never have and it's been a puzzle to me. That's why I'm not surprised by what you've asked me, not a bit. You see, after we got to know each other well, your mother and me, after we got to be friends, I waited for her to tell me. I thought, the day's going to come when Anna'll tell me that girl's not hers, that little beauty's not hers, she adopted her. But it never did. I love your dear mother, there's no harm saying that now, but you were too lovely-looking to be their child."

He kissed her when she left, very tenderly. He promised, unasked, to ask Anna himself. If he did Anna told him nothing or nothing that found its way back to Swanny. Anna wasn't at all pleased that Swanny had been questioning him.

"The poor old man, plaguing the life out of him like that," she said. "He had tears in his eyes when he told me what you'd said."

"I simply asked him if he knew you'd adopted me."

"It was a shock for a poor old man with a bad heart. And of course the only result has been to make him think you're a crazy woman, *lille* Swanny. As if you could be anything but my own child and my husband's!"

"But I'm not, Mor, you've told me I'm not."

"That doesn't mean I want all the world to know it, does it? Have a bit of sense, please. Why ask him, anyway? You were fourteen before I met him. What would he know?"

"He's your closest friend, that's why."

A rather proud dreamy look came over Mormor's face then, Swanny said.

"It's been a lonely life for him. He never remarried. I don't suppose I've ever told you this, but he asked me to marry him. Oh, a long time ago now."

Swanny was so exasperated by her mother at this point that she really wished Mormor had married Harry because if she had she'd be living in Leyton now and looking after him. "Why didn't you?"

The sweeping glance in one direction, the wave of the hand in the other. "Oh, really, it wouldn't have been suitable. It's all right for you with your nice husband and your fine house but I didn't much like it the first time round. Why risk it again? People change when they get married, let me tell you. I'd rather have a friend than a husband."

Harry died a few weeks later. But he knew nothing, he had nothing to tell.

The years went by. Swanny told me she made the utmost efforts to stop herself asking Anna again to tell her the truth, but she couldn't stop herself. She nagged Anna to tell her and Anna rejoined in various ways. She would say it didn't matter, it wasn't important, or else that she had forgotten or that Swanny should stop worrying about something which would only be significant if her adoptive mother had not loved her. She, Anna, plainly did love her, had always loved her best of her children, so why was she being so foolish?

Then Anna played her trump card, or she may have simply been tired of being nagged and playing games didn't come into it. She was sitting down more by this time, though usually on the edge of the chair in a restless way. Not tense, though, she was never that. She put her head back and turned up her eyes, in the way the exasperated do. It is supposed to be a hangover from a time when people looked to heaven and asked God to grant them patience.

"Suppose I said it wasn't true, I made it all up?"

Swanny began to tremble. This was a more and more frequent reaction to her mother's comments on the question of her origins. She would shake and sometimes her teeth would chatter. She looked at Anna, trembling, and Anna said, "Let's say that, shall we, *lille* Swanny? I made it all up because I'm a bad old woman who likes to tease. That's what happened and now we'll say no more about it, let there be an end to it."

"And I suppose you wrote the letter?" Swanny said scathingly.

One of those light shrugs, a sidelong look, a smile. "If you like. If it makes you happy."

Swanny had made up her mind to do a daring and dreadful thing, a thing which at first she could hardly contemplate without shame. It was sometime after Anna's death before she brought herself to tell me. While she spoke, in a low voice, she looked away. She intended to take the first opportunity that presented itself to search Anna's room and go through her things.

Her chance came when Anna went to stay with Ken and Maureen. This visit was unprecedented. Anna didn't much like Ken, she used to say she'd never got over her irritation with him for changing his name. But Mogens had also called himself something else and she seems not to have objected to that. The truth probably was that she had never wanted Ken in the first place, she had wanted a girl. The son she had been fondest of was Mads, the baby who died. Swanny, in a rare fit of exasperation, once said that if *he* had lived he would certainly have changed his name and this, incongruously, made Anna laugh.

Ken and Maureen had often invited her to stay but she always refused. They had moved from the Baker Street flat when Ken retired and were living in Twickenham. Anna said she didn't like suburbs. Hampstead was different, she wouldn't call Hampstead a suburb, except the bit that was a Garden Suburb which wasn't Hampstead at all to her way of thinking but Finchley. Always an explorer and observer, she had watched it being built. Ken and Maureen pressed their case again when Torben went into hospital.

He'd had a heart attack and had made a very good recovery. Swanny spent a large part of every day in the hospital with him. When Ken heard about this he told Anna she must be lonely in that big house on her own and he told Swanny it would "be a bit of a rest" for her to have their mother off her hands for a couple of weeks. Anna, of course, wasn't really on her hands, she wasn't at all a typical ninety year old, needing care and attention. She was independent, she had all her faculties.

Swanny longed for her to go, she told me, so that she could have unhindered access to that room. She suspected her brother of some ulterior motive, though what she couldn't guess, Anna had nothing to give and not much money to leave. Not, at any rate, what he'd call "real money." Swanny's miseries and the perpetual doubt she lived in had made her mean spirited, she said. Probably Ken and Maureen were just being kind. Anyway, she didn't care, she wanted Anna to go but knew better than to encourage her. It was Anna herself who surprised her by suddenly saying that she had never been to Kew Gardens. If she went to Twickenham, to the part where Ken lived, she could walk to Kew Gardens.

Not that she was interested in nature. She knew a rose from other flowers and somewhere in the diaries there's a bit about beech trees, but also a line that makes it plain she couldn't identify a horse chestnut. Kew was inviting because she wanted to see what bananas looked like, growing in the hothouse. After she had gone off in Ken and Maureen's car Swanny went straight upstairs to Anna's room on the third floor. She said she was compelled to it, as secret drinkers are to their tipple when at last alone, as others may be to masturbation or some fetish, though those words are mine, not hers. But the compulsion made her breathless and rather sick. She was addicted to finding out who she was.

Anna's room was large, two rooms in fact, divided by double doors which were always open. She had her own bathroom. You could really say she had the whole third floor, for no one used the boxroom and she could have done so if she chose. I have said I never saw it and I never did until after Swanny herself was dead. Anna didn't invite people into her domain. She was interested in them but she had no need of them. I never saw it until fourteen years after its occupant quitted it but of course I saw photographs of it in magazines and Sunday supplements, as everyone did who bothers to read features like that. This was the last home of the author of the diaries and therefore—at least, every time a new volume of diaries came out—very much in the news.

It was comfortably, indeed luxuriously, furnished, as was every room in Swanny's house, but to me it looked bare, it didn't look lived-in, and Swanny assured me she had changed nothing, added nothing and taken nothing away. Anna hadn't been a hoarder, she was concerned with life, not the memorabilia of existence. The furniture in the room, the ornaments, were Swanny's and they had been there before Anna came to live in Willow Road. All that was Anna's was the Napoleonic bed and the dark polished table with the fruit and leaf carvings, the books, the photograph albums and a number of framed photographs, not standing on furniture in the usual way but hung on the walls: a gloomy sepia photograph of Padanaram, apparently taken on a dull day, several portraits of Swanny, my parents' wedding photo and Swanny's, a studio portrait of herself when young with a Copenhagen photographer's name across the bottom right-hand corner and "Anna" scrawled on the left like a pop star's autograph.

Swanny had already been through Anna's desk, or perhaps I should say the desk Anna used. If she used the desk. Swanny didn't know. There was writing paper in the drawers and envelopes, an unused notebook, a surprising number of cheap ballpoint pens. Of course she told me all this with hindsight, she had no idea then of the existence of the diaries. She had no idea that the thick bound notebook lying in the top drawer was the last diary, the one Anna had abandoned two or three years before, had written in it the last line she was ever to write and finally closed it on the evening of September 9, 1967. Nor did it register with her till long afterwards that September 9, 1967, was the day after Harry Duke's funeral.

Naturally, Swanny looked inside it. She was bitterly ashamed of herself but she neglected nothing, she scrutinized everything she could find. The writing was in Danish, which she could read but didn't bother to when she saw dates in 1966 and '67. Some years before this, a relative of Torben's had died and left a diary she had written while living in St. Petersburg in 1913. Her husband had been a clerk with the Great Northern Telegraph Company and they had lived there for a year in an hotel. When he heard about it Torben had great hopes of this diary, at last managed to get hold of it and was anticipating a picture of life before the Revolution with all kinds of fascinating political and social comment. It was certainly social. What he had got was nothing more than a pedestrian record of a young woman's engagements, the parties she went to and the clothes she bought, with a daily commentary on the weather. Swanny remembered this when she had her mother's last diary in her hands. She read a passage about a bad storm and a tree falling down in the garden next door, and put the book back in the desk.

The wardrobe doors were open as usual, to let the air circulate. There was nothing in there, she had looked before. Still, she looked again. Wincing at what she was doing, she felt in the pockets of coats Anna hadn't worn for years, delved into ancient handbags.

But Anna kept nothing, she didn't even allow rubbish to accumulate in her handbags as most women do. It wasn't that she was fastidious or particularly tidy. She didn't want to be cluttered with the paraphernalia of living.

Swanny's principal goal was the locked cupboard. The key wasn't in the lock, so presumably Anna had taken it with her or hidden it somewhere. But this presented no particular problem. There were several lockable cupboards in the house and Swanny was right when she guessed that a key to one would be a key to all. She said she hated what she was doing but at the same time she savored being alone in the house and knowing no one could interrupt her. I think she was nearly as nervous of Torben discovering her as of Anna. Her husband was a high-principled man, a bit of a stuffed shirt though his niceness counteracted this, and he would have been as deeply shocked to find her searching her mother's room as if he had come upon her watching a pornographic film.

But poor Torben couldn't interrupt her. Though recovering and soon to be home again, he was still in hospital. Anna was miles away, heading for Twickenham. Swanny opened the cupboard and found it full of clothes.

As far as she could tell these were much the same sort of clothes as in the wardrobe, only older. They smelled powerfully of camphor. Since Anna didn't hoard and seemed to be without a trace of sentimentality, Swanny concluded she must have kept them in the hope of their returning to fashion one day. In fact, they would have done so, for in the year of Anna's death ankle-length skirts came in. These dresses and "costumes" dated from the Great War and earlier and there were one or two beaded confections from the twenties. Swanny was deeply disappointed. As it happened she was wrong about Anna's motives. She intended to sell the contents of the cupboard and actually did so a few months later, having found a shop in St. John's Wood High Street that specialized in satisfying the new passion for antique clothes. She sold them and made a tidy sum, once more demonstrating her gifts as a woman of business.

Swanny found nothing more, no letters, no documents. She said she went into her own bedroom after that and contemplated her birth certificate. This wasn't, of course, the first time she had looked at it since the arrival of the letter. It was more like the hundredth time. But she looked at it now and saw once again that her birth had been registered on August 21, 1905, at 55 Sandringham Road, Dalston, the Registrar's Office for the Southwest Hackney District. Her name was there as Swanhild (the other names, Rasmus' choice, had not yet been added), her father given as Rasmus Peter Westerby, engineer, aged thirty-one, and her mother as Anna Birgit Westerby, née Kastrup, aged twenty-five. The registrar had signed the certificate as Edward Malby.

It was all beyond her understanding.

10

The day before I was due to meet Cary and take her to look at the diaries I went up to Willow Road to see for myself. It was years since I had seen for myself, fourteen years in fact since Swanny showed me the originals.

I wasn't able to park the car anywhere near the house but had to drive round and round before resigning myself to leaving the car on what seemed the only vacant place in Hampstead, half a mile away in Pond Street. I don't think I would have recognized Gordon Westerby among the crowd of commuters coming out from Hampstead Heath Station. I wouldn't have given him a second glance if he hadn't hailed me so enthusiastically.

The weather was much warmer than on that dreary April day when we had first met at Swanny's funeral and he had made his own concessions to it. But these were in the direction of lightness, not informality. Although it wasn't raining, rain wasn't forecast and there had been none for a week, he was wearing a raincoat, the kind of thing you see on detective inspectors in television police procedurals. His collar was as high as at the funeral but less stiff and evidently part of a blue and white striped shirt that matched a plain blue tie. Also matching each other were his glossy black shoes and briefcase.

"I hoped I'd run into you," he said. He spoke very earnestly as if a chance encounter was the only means open to us of getting together. The posts didn't exist, the telephone hadn't been invented. "I'm very glad to see you."

"But what are you doing here?" I said, half-amused, half-puzzled. Was he on his way to Willow Road?

"I live here." He seemed a little worried by my surprise. "I have a half-share in a flat in Roderick Road. Did you think I lived with my parents?"

I hadn't thought about it at all. I'd scarcely thought about him. Evidently he didn't expect an answer but said confidentially, inclining his head closer, "When I came out of the closet it was naturally an embarrassment to them. The kindest thing was to move out. We're on extremely good terms, you mustn't think otherwise."

I assured him I wouldn't but I did wonder why, living where he did, he'd never been to see his great-aunt.

"That family tree I mentioned to you, I had this rather brilliant idea. There are going to be more diaries published, aren't there?"

Yes, certainly, I said. Next year or the year after.

"Only when I've done my tree, it could go in. Go in the book, I mean. And when they reissue past editions it could go in those too. What do you think?"

He leveled at me an earnest, intense, scrutinizing stare. His eyes were Anna's, but the shade was paler, faintly diluted. If hers were oil his were watercolor.

"I've bought the diaries in paperback. I've never read them, you see. It will be a weekend treat for me. My friend that I share with and I, we very much like reading aloud to each other."

I asked him if he needed help with the tree. By no means all the details of Anna's and Rasmus' forebears and connections were to be found in the diaries but I thought I could fill in the gaps.

"I've been relying on you," he said. "I was sure you'd say that. My father knows nothing. I've noticed how women are interested in families and men not at all. I'm always coming across that when I'm in pursuit of my hobby." For the first time he smiled, showing a double row of large Bertie Wooster–like teeth. "We'll get together," he said, remarked that it had been nice meeting me and set off rapidly in the direction of Gospel Oak.

Swanny's house, for I still thought of it like that, seemed pecu-
liarly silent but it was warm and fresh smelling. That gleaming
quality it had always held for me was still there, the sensation a
little like walking into a jewel box. Swanny and Torben had had so
much silver and brass, so much glass in ornaments and on chande-
liers, that the rooms never seemed still but always filled with tiny
moving lights. At all times of the day and night that glitter in
various forms was present, the moon-shaped shine on the curve of
a vase, the burnish on bowl and cup, the flash on the facet of a
prism, the bright running spot made by the reflection from cut
glass. In the absence of sunshine all this gleam and glitter was
muted. It had become subtle and expectant as if it waited for the
dark to lift.

Torben had always kept a room downstairs as his study. I don't
know what he studied there, or read or wrote, come to that, he
must have had plenty of room for that kind of thing at his embassy,
but men of his kind always did have studies while women had
sewing rooms. After his death it remained empty until Swanny took
it over for her own purposes. She always called it her room, with
a slight emphasis on the second word. It was in there that she was
photographed when the Sunday *Times* made her the subject of one
of their "A Day in the Life Of" series.

I'd often been in the study and I knew Anna's notebooks weren't
there. Swanny had added a word processor and a photocopier to
Torben's rather austere appointments, his fountain pen and blotter
and Crown Derby inkwell. The house contained a lot of books,
several thousands probably, and most of them were in the study
that was very nearly a book-lined room. The three volumes published as *Anna, A Live Thing in a Dead Room* and *Bright Young
Middle-Age* Swanny had rather self-consciously displayed on shelves
in all the languages into which they had been translated, Icelandic
being the most recent of these. Hanging up on the wall in a frame
of pale polished wood was the (much enlarged) facsimile page from
the first notebook.

Swanny had hobnobbed with publishers and met eminent writers at parties, been an honored guest at her agent's and been on

promotional tours, but she had never quite attained the true book person's attitude to books, a total familiarity with them, an indifference to their exteriors and commitment to what lies between the covers. She never lost that certain reverence she had for a published book. So a first edition of *Anna* boxed in a presentation case stood propped up on her desk, partly propped in fact by the Gyldendal limited edition in D format and lavishly illustrated, while bound but uncorrected proof copies, even those numbered one in the run, were relegated to the lowest tier of the bookshelves that filled the wall facing the desk.

I've said that the notebooks, the originals of the diaries, weren't there. What I meant was that the notebooks weren't, and had never been, anywhere visible. I looked through the desk drawers, on the off-chance, having the shadow of that feeling Swanny had when she raided and riffled through Anna's room. Swanny, however, hadn't gone as Anna had to see a relative in Twickenham. Swanny was dead. A pang assailed me, I closed the drawers and sat there unseeing of limited editions and presentation copies, thinking of her frantic efforts and of the peculiar predicament of the seeker after truth who is aware that the one person who knows what it is will never be made to divulge it.

Torben had had another heart attack six months later and died of it. With his death Swanny entered the nadir of her life, perhaps indeed her only really low ebb, for as she said to me after the tide had turned for her and for a while washed away much of her misery, she had been a happy woman, a sheltered, protected, indulged and loved woman. Apart from feeling so deeply the death of her brother Mogens when she was eleven, she had known no sorrow.

It had always meant much to her that she was openly declared to be her mother's favorite child. Torben's passion and his enduring devotion had placed her in a position of privilege. She told me that she lived daily with the certain knowledge of her husband's worship, that when he came home to her each evening it was with a young lover's breathless excitement, hurrying the last few yards to be there a fraction sooner, that when he and she were in a room full of people the faces of those others were always faint or vague to him, while hers shone with clarity. He told her all this.

Neither of them had much wanted children and when no children came he told her was glad because he would have been jealous. But it wasn't jealousy that made him dislike her mother. The cause was quite other. What he called her senility, but couldn't understand or allow for, had led her to make Swanny unhappy with her lies and fictions. That he could never overlook.

He loved Swanny with the hungry desire he first felt at the age of twenty-two when he saw her across that room in Copenhagen. In one of those letters that Anna had never seen but boasted about at parties, he had told Swanny that if she wouldn't finally agree to marry him he would die a virgin. Apparently, he had never made love to a woman and never would unless it was to her, had "saved himself" for her, to be as "pure" as she, talking of it in the way people presumably did then and which seems so ridiculous to us now. There was something Wagnerian about Torben Kjaer, and not only in his height and his Nordic appearance.

Swanny got out those letters and reread them over and over, staining them, she said, with many tears. The tears were as much from guilt as grief, she confessed to me, for she felt she had never fully appreciated Torben while he was alive. She had never loved him as he loved her. But this may be true of any relationship in which one party loves as passionately and as wholly as that. Human beings, it appears, are capable of almost limitless ardor but not of a matching level of response. Swanny used to say in her misery that it's better to be the one that kisses than the one that turns the cheek. It's always better to be the active than the passive, the doer than the done to. She had sometimes been impatient with Torben's transports.

But now she grieved. She even said she realized only now he was gone how much she had really loved him. She was unwise enough to say this to her mother—but who else, after all, had she to talk to for most of the time?—and Anna was derisive. Of course she had loved him: was she mad? What woman wouldn't love a man who gave her so much, was so good to her, wrote such letters, was handsome, generous and kind, she herself should have had such a man, and so on, and so on.

I began paying a regular weekly visit to Willow Road at this time, usually to have an evening meal with Swanny. As well as her grief, she had an increase of arthritis to bear (another cause of wonder and near-disbelief in Anna) and had begun on a series of painful gold injections. Her knees always hurt her now, the joints of her fingers had begun to show swelling. She had lost weight and grown gaunt. No one who saw her then, on those Wednesday or Thursday evenings, when she would cook for me but herself barely eat, would for a moment have foreseen the woman she would become in the eighth decade of her life.

I visited regularly but until Swanny's last illness, I seldom went upstairs. Mounting the stairs now, on that dull and rainy morning, I asked myself where to start. I knew only that Swanny's bedroom was the big one in the front over the drawing room but I couldn't imagine her keeping the notebooks in there. In Anna's own room, then? As I climbed the two higher flights I wondered again at her choice of the third floor and asked myself how a woman of ninety had managed those stairs several times each day while I, more than forty years younger, found it arduous to climb them once. No doubt, she had enjoyed being isolated up here. Like most writers she alternated extreme gregariousness with a powerful physical need for solitude.

The diaries weren't there.

That isn't strictly true. The last one was there, the incomplete diary for 1967 that stopped on September 9. It lay where Swanny had found it, on the desk. The photograph albums were there too, rather consciously "arranged," one of them, for instance, propped upright on the black oak table and open at the picture of Mogens and Knud in sailor suits and their hair in long curls, the name of the photographer just showing at the foot: H. J. Barby, Gamle Kongevej 178. It had been taken just before they came to England. Two more albums were on a console table, a vase of dried flowers beside them.

I recalled the feature in the *Observer* magazine and the color plates of this room. Swanny must have arranged things like this and kept them so for the journalists who came and the editors of magazines concerned with domestic interiors. It was a little like a shrine but not intended to house the sixty-two remaining diaries. I pulled open the carved flange in the oak table Swanny had once told me was a secret drawer. Sewing things were inside, needles and a pincushion and a silver thimble, and, incongruously, in a modern plastic zip-bag, the red and purple felt pen wiper Swanny had made for her mother's thirty-third birthday.

There was one more floor. I went up and found rooms no one seemed ever to have lived in, rooms containing trunks, boxes and suitcases, all extremely tidy and well cared for. In the first was a hatbox in a large linen bag of the kind called "Holland," and a leather traveling wardrobe, stamped in gold with the initials of Torben's mother, M.S.K. I opened it and found the polished wood hangers still inside on their rail. There were other cases as well and a trunk but all were empty.

I began to sense, as I entered the second of these rooms, something dramatic about to happen, some revelation or some disquieting find. But I had forgotten Swanny, what she was like. I had forgotten her dislike of the sensational, her quiet ways, her prudence. She had suffered more from discovering, at nearly sixty, that she was not her parents' child than an excitable or romantic woman might have. That went out of my head and I expected, here at the end of her life, and the end of her house, some final shocking gesture.

The cardboard crates in this room contained books, but they were stacked so that the spine of each one could be seen. Most of them were Swedish, publications of Bonniers and Hugo Geber, in those old paperback editions with flimsy light fawn covers. In among them, with a label on it in Torben's handwriting was that diary kept by his aunt or cousin while she was living in St. Petersburg in 1913. I took it out, looked at it and thought once again how the handwriting of every European before, say, 1920 looks the same, forward-sloping, looped, pleasing to look at but not easy to read. I could read none of it and put it back where it had come from.

One room remained. I was making the drama myself, for none

derived from the physical evidence. Furniture stood about, chairs stacked seat-to-seat and legs-to-back, a table and two more chairs in the art deco or moderne style that obviously would have been unsuitable downstairs. The mahogany cupboard with the double doors was the last place in the house where the diaries might be and there they were.

It seemed to me that I had found them at the end of the world. I had been searching for three hours. Yet I immediately saw what a sensible place this was: because heat rises this was the warmest part of the house, away from the ministrations of cleaners, among other stored, cared-for but seldom-used possessions, far enough away from the habitually lived-in parts of the house to avoid some visitor coming upon them and indulging his or her curiosity, to avoid in fact some journalist's serendipity.

Each volume was in a plastic bag and each group of ten contained in a larger bag. These were secured with two rubber bands. It was possible to see through the double layer of plastic that each volume was labeled with its year and through the single layer each batch labeled with the dates it encompassed. There was nothing to show that some of the notebooks had been translated, edited and published.

I felt a certain awe. Then I reminded myself that the diaries were mine now, insofar as they were anyone's, the copyright being Swanny's still and for many years to come. I took out the first parcel, the one on the left at the top, that was labeled 1905–1914. This constituted *Anna,* and these were the diaries Cary Oliver wanted to see. Specifically, it was the first notebook she wanted to see.

A smell came off the page, not Coty L'Aimant but the sweetish dusty smell of early decay. The mold spots, the size of a small coin, had faded to a pale coffee color. But I could read what was written. Knowing as I did, as thousands of ardent readers must do, the first lines by heart, I could read them in Danish and in Anna's deeply sloping but quite legible hand:

When I went out this morning a woman asked me if there were polar bears in the streets of Copenhagen . . .

Reading the original brought me a little shiver. I turned the pages, wondering now how Cary meant to deal with the language problem. I could show her the translation but she didn't want that. Anyone could read the translation in the published diaries—or could they? Was she implying that not only the diaries themselves but the original translation might contain revelations omitted in the published text? Perhaps.

July 18, July 21, July 26 . . . Not all the writing was easily legible to me, much of the Danish was incomprehensible. I turned that page and deciphered the piece about the boys changing their names, the point where Anna abruptly comes to a stop: "there are four boys in Mogens' class called Kenneth. I said they must ask their father, which is a sure way of postponing things for months." It's easy enough to read a familiar foreign language when you know what to expect.

I expected no more until August 30. In the published diaries Swanny's birth was written about as imminent, then five weeks later, as having satisfactorily taken place. I had assumed, as I suppose all her readers had, that Anna had been too occupied or even too unwell to make diary entries during those weeks.

But it was not so.

Some five or six pages from the notebook had been torn out. These were the pages that came between July 26 and August 30 and including, it seemed, a few more sentences after "postponing things for months." I have said "five or six" but now I counted them, I counted the stubs. There were precisely five; ten, if you take into account that Anna wrote on both sides of the page; getting on for two thousand words when you calculate that she wrote between ten and twelve words to a line and there were twenty-five lines to each page.

Swanny must have torn those pages out. But perhaps she had done so only after the translation had been made. As I've said, I was in the United States at the time she found the diaries, but this had its advantages for me now. She had written to me, at length and often, and I had kept her letters. I didn't have to rely on my own memory. Somewhere in those letters there might be a mention of lost pages, though I couldn't recall it. I certainly couldn't recall her making any great revelation at that time, beyond the finding of the diaries and the realization of their worth.

At any rate I could look at the translation now. There might be no mystery or only a small one. This could be discretion on Swanny's part, not secrecy. I put the 1905–1914 diaries back in the cabinet, with the exception of the first one, and took it downstairs to compare it with the translation.

Swanny's neatness and method made all these investigations easier than they might have been. The translations in typescript were in the bottom drawer, the deepest one, of the desk in the study that had been Torben's. They had been placed there in chronological order, each in its own cardboard folder, untitled but with the dates and the translator's name.

I opened the first one.

> When I went out this morning a woman asked me if there were polar bears in the streets of Copenhagen . . .

July 18, July 21, July 26, and those lines that marked the end of that day's entry:

> . . . there are four boys in Mogens' class called Kenneth. I said they must ask their father, which is a sure way of postponing things for months.

The next entry was August 30.

Cary was already there when I got to our meeting place, the Hollybush on Holly Mount. She had lost weight and was looking smart in High Street jeans and a pink tweed jacket from someone grand, probably Ralph Lauren. Cary's hair is always a different color. She told me, not then but the next time we met, that she had forgotten what its natural color was and now, when she scrutinized her part, she saw that it was white. On this evening her hair was the color Anna called "plain" and later generations call "dark" chocolate.

Before the rift we'd been in the habit of kissing. I've never been a hand shaker. We looked at each other, assessing what time had done.

"You're looking well."

"So are you."

"Would you think it awful if I said we could each have a glass of champagne?"

We had it. "You're going to be disappointed," I said, "or I think you are. There's a big gap where your information might be. I'll show you. We'll go back to Swanny's house and I'll show you. Tell me about your murder."

"You mustn't think of it as an ordinary sordid case."

"I'm not thinking of it at all," I said. "I'd never heard of Roper till you mentioned him."

"It's not a series we're planning but a three-part serial. You see, the story's not so much sensational as tragic. I'm fictionalizing it but only to fill in a few details. There are huge gaps. There's a missing child. And then Anna mentioned Roper in the diaries."

By this time I had found it, a single mention. It was in the entry for June 2, 1913, when Anna speculates that Rasmus might think her as bad a woman as Mrs. Roper. "Only once," I said. "Who was he, this Roper?"

"He was a chemist, he lived in Hackney. I mean he was a pharmacist, I suppose you'd call it. He murdered his wife or they said he did. That was in 1905."

"And this happened near where my grandparents lived?"

"They found the body in a house in Navarino Road, Hackney, and brought Roper back, he was in Cambridge with his son. It was a terribly hot summer, a hundred and thirty degrees, so they said though I can hardly believe it, and there were a lot of murders brought on by the heat. There was a terrible lot of violence. I've been reading the newspapers for July and August that year. But you ought to read about it in Famous Trials, I've got a copy you can have. It's good as far as it goes, only it doesn't go as far as I want."

I said it was time to go to the house and see, but she wouldn't find anything in the diaries.

"Oh, but you can't be sure!"

"I'm sure."

It was dusk outside by then. The air is always clear up there and fresh like the country, in spite of the long line of cars that winds its slow way up Heath Street until past nightfall. We walked across Streatley Place and New End, under the gleaming lamps and through the dark spaces to Willow Road.

"Are you going to come and live here?" she said.

"I shouldn't think so, not for a moment. It's too big for one person on her own."

I sensed the discomfort this gave her. She said rather brightly, "It'll fetch a fortune."

"I know."

We went in and it struck me at once that I should have brought the diaries, or at least the relevant one, downstairs. Was it possible that I had been too in awe of the *Anna* originals to disturb them? I determined that this time that first volume at least should come down with me.

Cary puffed up the stairs behind me, growing more and more breathless and sounding her smoker's wheeze. She didn't exactly hold Anna in reverence as a good many of her readers did but still she wanted to pause at the third floor and look inside that room. I had left the door wide open, not sharing Swanny's passion for closing the door each time you leave a room and closing all of them before you leave the house.

What she saw inside seemed to disappoint her. She expected Anna's domain to "look more like the diaries," she said, without explaining what she meant. When we got to the top floor it seemed so dreary up there and so desolate among the trunks and boxes that I grabbed the bundle labeled 1905–1914 and handed it to Cary to take down while I carried 1915–1924 myself.

We sat in Swanny's drawing room and must have been there for a good five minutes before I realized we hadn't taken our coats off. This was a dwelling house, a home, and it was mine, though this was hard to realize, not a railway waiting room. I took off my coat and took hers and hung them up in the hall.

"D'you want something to drink?"

She said, "Is there anything?"

"I expect there's wine. In her last years Swanny never drank anything but champagne. I don't mean she drank much of that but when she drank it would have been champagne."

"Let's see if there's something to celebrate first."

She was poring over the first notebook, touching the yellowed sheets quite reverently. Her face went quite blank when she came to the stubs where the five pages had been torn out. I hadn't warned her, just let her find them for herself.

"Who's responsible for that?"

"Swanny, I suppose. There are five pages gone."

She said, "Was it at an interesting bit?"

"I can't help thinking they were torn out because it was getting too interesting."

She asked me what I meant.

"Too personal. Too near the bone, if you like." I wasn't going to tell her. "Nothing to do with your murder."

She shrugged. "Does it happen anywhere else? I mean, are there other places in the diaries, maybe in the other ten-year sets, where she's torn chunks out?"

"We could look."

So we went through the two bundles we had and found all the notebooks intact. Cary thought she was really on to something, had had a spectacular brainwave, when the idea came to her that the pages from the notebooks had been removed *after* the translations had been made.

"Sorry," I said. "I've thought of that. What you see there is what was translated."

"So what we're saying is that Swanny Kjaer tore out the pages in her mother's diary where reference was made to something personally unacceptable to *her.*"

"Wouldn't we all do the same? Most of us aren't put to the test. We don't have mothers who wrote bestselling diaries. Haven't you anything in your life you wouldn't want exposed in what amounts to someone else's autobiography?"

She wouldn't catch my eye. She must have known what I implied but she wouldn't look at me or give any sign.

"In most cases," I said, "I imagine you don't know you're mentioned until you read the autobiography and then it must come as a shock. Let's say Swanny was in the position to edit someone else's autobiography and she did edit it—to her advantage."

"She censored it, for Christ's sake," said Cary. "She'd no business to tamper with it like that."

I didn't like her finding fault with Swanny. It was because *she* was doing it, I would have overlooked it from anyone else. Gordon Westerby, for instance, he could have said it and I'd have let it pass. But this was Cary Oliver. I repeated what I'd said about there being nothing there on the Roper murder. Why would Swanny want to hide significant details of an ancient crime? What was it to her?

"Can we go through the other diaries?" Cary asked.

We went back up all those stairs and took out 1925–1934 and 1935–1944 and so on. In none of them were there any torn-out pages until we got to 1954 where a single sheet was missing. I struggled with the Danish and realized this must be where Anna was writing about Hansine's death.

"Let's have the champagne," I said.

She raised her glass and said, "Here's to the future editor of *Anna.*"

"I don't know if I shall be. The diaries aren't all translated, you know."

"Why would Swanny Kjaer tear out stuff in 1954? I mean, wasn't she already quite ancient by then? All passion spent and all that?"

I couldn't resist it. "She was the same age as you are now, Cary."

Cary didn't say anything for a moment or two. I thought how it was no concern of hers anyhow. She was interested in the Roper murders and by 1954 the last Roper had been long dead. She repeated what she'd said on the phone.

"Have you forgiven me?"

That made me laugh, though it wasn't funny. "Anna once said to me that she thought we ought to forgive people," I said, "but not too soon."

"It isn't too soon, is it? It's fifteen years. And I'm sorry, Ann."

"You're sorry because it didn't work out, not because you—how shall I put it?—intervened. Intervened and pinched my lover."

She said very softly, "I am sorry."

"I don't think I'd want Daniel now, anyway," I said carefully. "Not in any circumstances, not the way things are and not if he'd gone on living with me instead of you."

"You were going to marry him. That's what he said."

"I wonder if I ever would have. I've never been married." I looked hard at her, the jeans that were too tight, the stomach that stuck out, the double track of tendons that led from chin to throat to neck. I looked at her and was glad there was no mirror in the room for me to look at myself. "We're too old for lovers now," I said.

"Oh, Ann, what a terrible thing to say!"

"All passion spent. Your words, I think. Have some more champagne."

She giggled. It was from nervousness and understandable but it still seemed misplaced. I wished then that I was the sort of woman who could have reached out and touched her hand. Or even put my arms round her. But I no longer liked her, I had ceased to like her long ago, and I was sure she must dislike me, the way we do dislike people we have injured.

Instead of that gentle touch, I spoke to her. "You can borrow the diary translations if you want to. There may be something in them that never found its way into print."

She said, "Thanks," in a thick slurry voice.

I remembered then that she wasn't very good with wine and knew I shouldn't give her any more. Her face was puffed up and curiously shiny. There weren't enough lights on in Swanny's drawing room and the warm, golden, intimate atmosphere seemed terribly at odds with us and what we'd talked of. I switched on the central chandelier and set it blazing. Cary blinked and gave a shiver.

"I'll take the translations," she said, "and then I'll go. I'll give you the account of the Roper case and and one of the trial and some more stuff I've unearthed on separate sheets." She bent right over to take them out of her briefcase and I could hear—or I could sense—the strumming of the blood in her head. "Here." The hand she extended to me trembled a very little.

I knew then that had what had upset her wasn't my nonforgiveness or her memories of Daniel Blain or her embarrassment at the subject coming up at all, none of those things. She was upset because I'd said we were too old to have lovers. It wasn't true, of course, one is probably never too old and we were still in our forties, but I had said it and cut her to the quick. I couldn't help it, then I felt desperately sorry for her, something I'd thought I'd never feel.

"Let's forget it, Cary. We'll never talk of it again. All over, okay?"

"Please," she said and brightened almost at once, was all smiles, hugging the folders full of translations to her as if they were her lost love letters. She could always astound me with her changes of subject. "What do you think she did with the pages she tore out?"

"What?"

"Your aunt. We're saying she tore them out because there were things in them she didn't want people to see after she was dead."

I supposed we were. It just didn't sound like Swanny, the way I remembered her. "So?"

"Would she have thrown them away? I wouldn't think so. She'd have hidden them somewhere."

I could imagine being there all night while Cary and I searched Swanny's house for this kind of treasure trove. Or, rather, I couldn't imagine it. She and I weren't talking about the same people. But after she had gone, uttering promises to see me soon, after we had found a taxi for her, and I had retreated into the warm, shiny, empty house, I sat down with the last of the champagne and thought about what she'd said. No doubt I thought about it to stop thinking of Daniel Blain, who I used to describe to myself in a dramatic inner voice as the only man I'd ever loved.

Did I want to know who Swanny really was? Did I care? Not as she had done, of course, but, yes, I was curious. And by now there were more questions to be answered. Not only who was Swanny, but did she find out who she was before she died? Was it in those missing five pages for July and August 1905 and was there also included some vital fact relevant to the Roper case?

Too late I realized Cary hadn't told me if Roper was hanged or acquitted and I hadn't asked.

11

NOVEMBER 7, 1913

Igaar flyttede vi ind i vores nye Hus, Rasmus og jeg, Mogens, Knud, Swanny og Marie, Hansine og Emily. Aah ja, og selvfól-gelig Bjórn. Der er nok Sovevaerelser til Bórnene, saa de kan have hver sit, og Hansine og Emily oppe i Loftet, saa de behóver ikke mere at dele Vaerelse. Men Hansine er slet ikke tilfreds med det. Hun er bekymret for, at hendes Cropper ikke vil tage hele Turen fra Homerton, eller hvor det nu er, at han bor.

Yesterday we moved into our new house, Rasmus and I, Mogens, Knud, Swanny and Marie, Hansine and Emily. Oh, and Bjórn, of course. There are enough bedrooms for the children to have one each and Hansine and Emily, up in the attics, don't have to share anymore. Not that Hansine is at all pleased. She's worried that her Cropper won't want to make the journey all the way from Homerton, or wherever it is he lives.

Everywhere is a mess, the new carpets haven't come and our furniture looks very shabby in these fine rooms. I left it all and went out this morning, exploring my new terrain. The air is strong and fresh up here, breathing it is like tossing off a glass of very cold *snaps*. From our back windows you can look down over the whole of London and see the river Thames sparkling in the sun, but outdoors you really feel in the country with the woods here and the windy hilltops.

I walked through the woods to Muswell Hill and down to Hornsey, I walked for miles. I found Alexandra Palace like an enormous greenhouse and I found the station where the trains run that go up there and down to London. Since I've been in this country I haven't been in trains much but I shall go in them now and I shall walk on to Hampstead Heath.

When I got back Rasmus wanted to know where I'd been and how could I go out enjoying myself when there was so much to be done at home. Well, I'm back now, I said, what shall I do? So we went out in one of the motorcars to buy furniture and then he showed me the big shop he's taken in the Archway Road to sell his "automobiles."

DECEMBER 12, 1913

I have got my fur coat. Rasmus has given it to me for Christmas, two weeks in advance.

When I look back in these diaries, as I sometimes do, and read the things I've written I see myself as a thoroughly bad wife, a wife who seems to hate her husband. And I'm often sorry for myself, I'm a real self-pitier. They say—or someone said—that the important thing in life is to know yourself. Well, keeping a diary teaches you to know yourself. But does it teach you to improve? Probably not. One is oneself. People don't change except when they're very young. They make stupid New Year Resolutions to be different and keep to them for two days. The truth is they *can't*. Even a great tragedy coming into your life doesn't change you much, though it may make you harder.

When I got the fur coat I was bitterly disappointed. It reminded me of something that happened when I was a child. Someone had given me a paintbox, it may have been Tante Frederikke, and I was quite fond of painting pictures. My father promised to get me a palette and I formed a picture in my mind of what this thing was going to be. I'd seen one in a painting of an artist. The funny thing was that the artist in the painting was a woman, and that must be pretty well unheard of, a woman being a painter and getting well known for it. She was French, this one, and called Elisabeth Vigée Lebrun and with red hair like me. In the painting she was holding a brush in one hand and a big oval palette with holes for her thumb. Paint in all sorts of colors was daubed on it and I imagined myself holding something like it and looking like that. But when Far gave me his present it wasn't my idea of a palette at all but a little square sheet of metal with a handle sticking out.

I've never forgotten that and of course it came back when Rasmus gave me the coat. Dark brown skunk, a long way from that dream of mine of Persian lamb trimmed with white fox, as far removed as that bit of metal was from the beautiful oval palette. My face must have shown him how I felt. I put it on to please him and he said it was a good fit. "Don't you like it?" he said. "I thought you wanted a fur coat."

I didn't answer him. Instead I said, "Do you think I've been very unkind and ungrateful in all our years? Have I been too hard and sharp and critical for you, Rasmus?"

He didn't think I was sincere. He thought I was getting at him in some way. I could see his crafty look. "I don't try to understand women," he said. "They're a mystery. Any man will tell you."

"No, you tell me. Have you had enough of me? If you could, would you be rid of me?"

What was I hoping for? What could I hope for? And what on earth did I think he'd say?

"I don't know what you mean," he said.

"I thought we could talk about it."

"We are talking," he said, "and much good it'll do us. If all this is because you don't like the coat I can change it."

"No," I said, "don't bother. It'll be fine."

DECEMBER 18, 1913

It's a strange thing how, when a name comes into your mind and you think about it, that same name keeps coming up throughout the day. I hadn't thought of Vigée Lebrun for years until she came back to me when I remembered the affair of the palette. She was there in my head when I took the children to the National Gallery and suddenly I saw her self-portrait on the wall in front of us. There she was with her pale red hair and the dress and hat to match her hair, her thumb hooked through the famous palette, the kind *I* wanted, and a bunch of brushes in her hand.

Dear little Swanny looked up into my face and said, "That lady looks like you, *lille* Mor."

Of course the boys had to spoil it by saying it was *I* looked like the lady because the lady came first and Marie said Mor didn't have earrings like pink tears (her words), but I suppose I do look a bit like Madame Vigée.

Then, in the afternoon, I was in the library—I'm determined to read English books as well as my Danish favorites—when what should I see on the shelves but a book about Vigée Lebrun in the Masterpieces in Color series, this one by a man with the very fancy name of Haldane MacFall. Of course I took it out and I've been reading it and looking at the pictures of Marie Antoinette, sad pictures because the poor queen was executed. I was glad to discover that Madame Vigée escaped the guillotine by getting out of France before the worst of it started.

That led to another train of thought. One always thinks of France as being the only country to have a guillotine but this isn't so. The Swedes had one and have one now, but they've only used it once. My cousin Sigrid told me that in the street next to them in Stockholm there lived a man who was condemned to death for murdering a woman. It was a strange story. He was married but he and his wife had no children and they desperately wanted a child. It must have been the wife's fault because he had a child by his mistress who lived up in Sollentuna. The mistress refused to give up the child, she wanted him to divorce his wife and marry her, but he loved the wife, so he murdered the mistress and took the child for himself and his wife to adopt.

They were going to guillotine him. He would have been the first person the Swedes had ever used their guillotine on, in the old days they used an axe, but somehow he got reprieved and was sent to prison for life instead. I think I'd rather have my head chopped off!

Eventually they used their guillotine, once and once only, just three years ago. Who knows? There may be someone else who will one day get his head sliced off. If a man commits a murder he deserves death, say I.

DECEMBER 27, 1913

Our first Christmas in the new house. We had a Christmas tree six feet high and I decorated it all in white and silver, no colors, just the pure brightness of snow and frost. Rasmus has decreed that now we are in our own house that we own and are real "Britishers," we must have an English Christmas which means in fact that we have two: a dinner on Christmas Eve and another one on Christmas Day with presents in the morning.

He's always hated dressing up as Father Christmas, so Mogens did it for the first time this year and now he always will, he says. "You won't always be here," I said, "you'll have a home of your own and children of your own." That's something I can really believe when I see how tall he is and realize he'll be sixteen next month.

The girls of course wouldn't go to sleep, they'd eaten all that rich food and they were waiting for Father Christmas. Rasmus would never have had the patience to wait until they were asleep before filling their stockings, but Mogens did. He sat on the top of the stairs in his red coat and hood with cottonwool stuck all over his face and he had to wait for hours. He said it was two o'clock before they closed their eyes and he could creep in with his sack.

I believe he would do anything for his sister Swanny, he loves her so and always has. Marie is just the baby for him and a bit of a nuisance but he adores Swanny. And so do I.

She came downstairs on Christmas morning and said as cool as you please, "Why didn't you do Father Christmas this year, Far?" That was the first we knew that she didn't believe in him anymore. I forget how old she is, I forget she's eight and growing up and away from me. She put her arms round Mogens and kissed him and said he was her *Brother* Christmas.

Another present from Rasmus. Money this time for me to buy clothes. Following dear little Swanny's example, I went up to him and gave him a kiss. It's hard to say who was the more surprised, me at getting the money or him at being kissed. I am becoming quite a saint. It must be due to getting all these things I want—or more or less what I want—a nice house and furniture and now this money. Well, whatever they say, happiness makes you better and suffering makes you worse.

I am going to buy a French tricot cardigan I've seen and a motoring coat with raglan sleeves and maybe a pagoda-shaped costume that has a tricorne hat to go with it. I like extreme clothes that make people stare.

JANUARY 3, 1914

All the children made New Year Resolutions—well, Swanny made Marie's for her. She may suck her thumb but she is never again to suck that bit of blanket she carries about everywhere with her. Poor little Marie kept to that for a whole two hours! Swanny made a resolution not to cry anymore, Mogens to work harder at mathematics and Knud not to smoke cigarettes. When I said he didn't smoke cigarettes anyway, he was too young, he said you never could tell when the craving might start and it was as well to be prepared.

Rasmus, half in fun no doubt and to please the children (he says) made his resolution to be a millionaire! I think he's serious.

JUNE 30, 1914

Two days ago the Austrian Archduke Franz Ferdinand and his wife were assassinated in a place called Sarajevo by a Bosnian Serb. Why is it that important people, royalty and suchlike, get assassinated while other people are just murdered?

It is obvious that the poor man who did it had been driven mad by having his country taken over by Austria-Hungary. My father felt the same about Schleswig and Holstein though he didn't assassinate anybody, thank God. The fools are those people who say it was all a plot engineered by Serbian officials. Why do they want to *make* trouble?

I'm glad it's all happening such a long way from here.

I took the girls and Emily for a picnic in Highgate Woods but Marie got bitten by a mosquito, cried and cried and refused to be comforted. I was carrying her and not too happily because she is a big lump and must weigh three stone—Emily had the picnic basket—when who should we meet in the Muswell Hill Road but that Mrs. Gibbons who lived next door but two in Lavender Grove.

I don't think she'd have recognized me if I hadn't spoken first. She eyed me up and down, taking in all the details of my Bordeaux-red dress with the tricolor motifs and my white hat with red cockade. I've worn my wedding ring on my left hand ever since she told me people would think I wasn't respectable if I didn't, and now I wear Rasmus' emerald on top of it. I moved my hand up across Marie's back to show off the rings and I could see her looking.

"Did your husband ever come back, Mrs. Westerby?" she said, as if she hadn't seen him in Lavender Grove scores of times. I suppose it was her way of getting revenge for me being so obviously rich and having a maid with me. She looked pretty badly off herself, poor thing.

I made Marie say hallo to her, though her face was all puffy with crying.

"Children have been known to die of mosquito bites, you know," she said.

I'd been going to invite her back to Padanaram for tea but that stopped me. All the more reason to hurry back, I said, and get some arnica put on it. But it made me think about me and the women I know. Mrs. Bisgaard that I met at the Danish church and who lives in Hampstead is quite nice and I have been to tea with her and she to me, but she is so correct and well mannered, all her talk is small talk and she cares for nothing but children. I wish I had a friend!

JULY 29, 1914

Yesterday was Swanny's birthday. She was nine. We had a birthday party after school and ten of her friends came—well, ten girls from her class. I don't know if they were really friends. I'm not much of a cook but I wanted to make her birthday cake myself and it turned out quite well, a Victoria sponge with jam in the middle and Royal icing on top and nine candles. She blew them out in one go.

I made her party frock too, saxe blue and emerald shot silk with picot edges to all the flounces. When Hansine saw the material she said, "Blue and green should never be seen," but I think they can be a beautiful combination. Swanny's lovely fair hair reaches to her waist. She was quite the prettiest little girl at the party. The little Bisgaard girl, Dorte, had the most beautiful dress, real matelasse in a shade of old rose, but nothing can take away the plainness of her face. Rasmus didn't show himself at what he called the "jollification" but stayed outside in his workshop all the time. When I complained he said, didn't I want a wrought iron jardiniere for the hall? He thought I did (very sarcastic) and that was why he was laboring out there at all hours.

Much less important than the party was those Austrians declaring war on Serbia. Mr. Housman and his new wife, his bride really, came in much later in the evening and Mr. Housman said it will all be over in a week. He's a sensible man and I believe what he says. Russia, who thinks of herself as the protector of this small Slav state, will have to sink into the humiliating position of a beaten power. She dare not fight and must watch the Teuton Empire expanding in overwhelming might (his words—I don't think he intended a rhyme).

Mrs. Housman, who is a very big woman but quite good-looking and with hair so red that it must be hennaed, had a very smart dress on. She's tall so she can carry it off. It was green and white check, high-waisted and without a girdle but with huge hip pockets and a great black satin bow on the bosom. She has asked me to tea and to bring the girls.

AUGUST 2, 1914

How glad I am that my sons are too young to fight. By the time they are old enough to be soldiers it will certainly all be over—if it starts. But it looks as if it will start.

Germany has declared war. Her object, it seems, is to sweep down and conquer France, the ally of Russia, before Russia can make a counterstroke. These matters are always very complicated. The British Empire hasn't seemed much concerned in all of it but it may be different now, especially if Kaiser Wilhelm is going to challenge our sea power. Funny, I wrote "our," though I think of myself as every inch a Dane.

Rasmus talks of nothing but war. To distract myself I've started reading those books Tante Frederikke left me. I've had them for a year and never bothered to look into them till now. The one I've started is called *A Christmas Carol.*

SEPTEMBER 7, 1914

Hansine is in great distress of mind because her Cropper has joined the Army. He is a bit younger than she, no more than thirty-one or thirty-two, so by no means too old to enlist. In floods of tears, she told me they were engaged, were saving up to get married and had been planning to do so next year. I must say, I think she might have said something about this before.

He's a very handsome man. It will be a crying shame if he gets himself killed.

I meant to chronicle everything that happens in the war in this diary but it's impossible, there's so much of it, it's so complicated and happening in so many places. One thing is for certain, it isn't going to be quickly over. The wounded, coming back from Mons, all tell stories of German cowardice and treachery. One said, "If you stand up in the firing line they cannot hit you. They do not aim with the rifle and will not face the bayonet. They are afraid of cold steel." Well, who wouldn't be? I can believe any Teuton is treacherous but if they're such cowards and bad soldiers why couldn't we drive them out of Belgium?

It's once again a very good thing I write in Danish because if anyone here could read this I don't know what they'd do to me. One has to be very patriotic, say all the British are saintly heroes and the Germans cowardly rats. There's no middle way.

There was a photograph in *The War Illustrated* of a painting of Belgrade—as it used to be. "The beautiful white city," they called it. Since the Austrian bombardment it's become a desolate stretch of ruins. I'm glad I'm not Serbian and my children aren't. They say Belgium is full of beautiful age-old churches. I wonder how long they'll remain standing?

I took Marie to tea with Mrs. Housman at her house in Hampstead, at Frognal. Swanny was at school. There were six other ladies there and two more children, so no chance for conversation, only chat and small talk. You wouldn't have believed there was a war on.

JANUARY 21, 1915

Mogens was seventeen yesterday. We have to face the fact that he isn't clever, he's just a very kind nice boy. I wonder where he gets it from? I can't think of anybody you could call nice in my family that I've ever known. My mother was always ill throughout my childhood, so you can't count her. Who could be nice when they're always in pain? My father was very strict and stern, famous for his moral character, but that didn't stop him offering me to the first taker in need of hard cash. As to Tante Frederikke and her sons, they were a fault-finding, humorless, dour bunch of people. So there's no knowing where Mogens gets his niceness from. Happy, laughing, sweet-natured Rasmus maybe and his family of brutish peasants.

Mogens wants to leave school in the summer and Rasmus says in his sour way that there's no point in paying school fees for someone who can't pass exams or won't try. I don't know what Mogens will do, go into Rasmus' business perhaps, if that's possible. Rasmus says his only intellectual exercise is collecting numbers of *The War Illustrated* which he intends having bound into volumes. That will make depressing reading in the future.

Zeppelins crossed the North Sea last night and bombarded the coast of Norfolk. People were wounded in King's Lynn and Yarmouth and a woman was killed while her husband was away fighting at the front. What an irony! The newspaper called the Germans "loathsome blood-mad fiends" whose war methods are more savage than those of "the lowest races known to anthropology." That made me laugh. What would Mrs. Housman say if she could read Danish? The paper said we should be able to take reprisals. Up till now our airmen have flown over German cities but dropped no bombs.

Mrs. Housman's brother has joined the army.

MARCH 1, 1915

Mr. H. G. Wells must be much cleverer than I am, otherwise he wouldn't be in the position he is in, famous and listened to and honored by everyone. But sometimes when I read what he writes I can't help thinking, what a fool! Doesn't he know better than to think people change, that a whole nation can change more or less overnight? Here is an example, he is writing of what will happen to the Englishman when the war is over: "All the old prewar habits will have gone. He will, as chemists say, be 'nascent,' unsubmissive, critical . . . He will be impatient with a Government that 'fools about,' he will want to go on doing things. So that I do not see that the old forensic party game is likely to return to British political life with the ending of the war . . ." Ah, well.

Anyway, the war isn't over yet and not likely to be for a long time. I have taught Swanny to knit and she is really very good for a child not yet ten. She is making khaki socks for soldiers. Her kind father's comment: "I pity the poor fellow who has to feel all those lumps and knots in his boots."

She is growing very tall for her age. I try not to worry about it. If she were a boy I suppose I should be delighted. She is nearly as tall as Emily and Emily is a full-grown woman, though a small one. Rasmus never hesitates to rub it in and says very tall women don't find husbands.

"Would that be so bad if she didn't?" I said.

He laughed. "Where would you be without one, old girl?" he said, and he's right. A woman has to have a husband or be a useless laughing stock, but there's something wrong with that somewhere, it can't be the proper way for things to be organized.

I am reading *The Old Curiosity Shop*. I didn't know reading stories could be such a pleasure. It's funny but I seem to get right inside the characters and *be* them, which makes me care about what happens to them and get quite impatient to be back with my book.

MARCH 30, 1915

Mrs. Housman's brother has been killed in Flanders, three weeks after he joined up.

Of all the women I meet who've lost men at the front none ever seem to expect they might get killed. It's the others who will die, theirs have charmed lives. Does it make the shock and the pain worse, I wonder? Perhaps not, because I've noticed you can't prepare yourself for death. You may know it's inevitable and tell yourself so day after day but when it comes it's the same as if you never expected it but thought the person would live forever.

Mrs. Housman kept saying, why him? Why me? Why did it have to happen to him? As if it wasn't happening to hundreds, thousands. And what does she mean? That it should have happened to other men but not to this man because he was hers?

The French have published a list which shows *three million* German casualties but our list of *our* men lost at the Dardanelles shows just twenty-three dead, twenty-eight wounded and three missing. I don't believe in these figures, they can't be right.

JULY 28, 1915

Swanny's birthday and Mogens' last day at school. He is going to start straightaway in the motorcar sales business with Rasmus. I suppose he will do a clerk's job because I'm sure he knows nothing about motorcars. I'm never told much but I can tell business isn't good at present, I don't suppose it could be with this war going on. It's more than a year and a half since Rasmus made that New Year resolution and he's not a millionaire yet!

For her birthday we gave Swanny Greek dancing lessons, every Friday night from now till next spring. I found a wonderful word for her in my dictionary, we never have words like that in Danish: *terpsichorean.* I told her we should expect her to be proficient in the terpsichorean art.

Hansine's Cropper has been reported missing in the Dardanelles. She is hoping—we are all hoping—he is a prisoner of war. Because they aren't officially engaged, she is just his sweetheart not his fiancée, she had to hear the news from his sister who came round in secret yesterday to tell her. His mother is jealous as a tigress and won't acknowledge Hansine's position, calls her "that foreign slavey." Then today poor Hansine got a letter from Cropper, weeks old of course, dated before the evacuation of West Gallipoli. I don't think he knows she can't read or he wouldn't bother to write. He can't want me to read out all the private things he says to her, all the endearments and lovey-dovey bits. And really that's all there is because although he wrote more, most of it is slashed out by the censor. For all we know he's dead. Strange reading the cheerful and hopeful words of a dead man.

MARCH 14, 1916

Mrs. Evans, who lived next door to us in Ravensdale Road, came to tea and brought her brood of ugly children with her. This was supposed to be all in aid of her second son, a fat spotty boy called Arthur, playing with Marie on her birthday. Only one way and another it was put off, first because one child had a cold, then another, then Mrs. Evans herself got the shingles of all things. Today wasn't much of a success. The boy hit Marie who screamed so loudly that her father heard her from his workshop down the garden and came running in threatening to thrash Arthur and causing a fearful commotion. Somehow I don't think we'll be seeing Mrs. Evans again!

We were sitting in the drawing room this evening, Rasmus and I, I was reading *A Tale of Two Cities* and he was puffing away at a cigarette while devouring *The War Illustrated*, when suddenly he looked up and said he was going to make Marie a dollhouse.

"You're too late for her birthday," I said, not very interested "it'll have to be for Christmas."

"Oh, I won't finish by Christmas," he said, "this'll take me ye maybe two years. I'm going to make a copy of this house. I'm go to make her Padanaram."

"What, for a child of five?" I said.

"She'll be seven by the time I've finished. You might give a fe low a bit more encouragement, old girl. There are some wom who'd think themselves pretty lucky having a husband who can d what I can."

"Why Marie?" I said. "Why not Swanny? I thought you were supposed to love all your children equally."

"She's too old. The rate she's growing she'll be six feet tall by time it's finished."

"Well, don't think I'm going to help," I said. "If you want carpets and curtains and cushions and whatnot you can get Hansine to do them. You know what a magnificent needlewoman she is. Just don't come asking me."

MARCH 26, 1916

Swanny and Marie both have the chicken pox. Swanny came down with it yesterday and Marie was all over spots this morning. I've heard it said children can catch it from a grown-up with the shingles and though I don't usually believe tales like that, old wives' tales mostly, it certainly looks as if there's something in this one. We joke about it and call it Mrs. Evans' revenge for the way Rasmus shouted at Arthur, but I'm worried about their faces scarring. Swanny is good and obedient and has promised not to scratch but that little monkey Marie, I don't know what to do with her, I've threatened to tie her hands behind her back and I will too if I see her nails at her face again.

Sam Cropper is a prisoner in German hands. I don't know how they can be sure but his sister came round this afternoon to tell Hansine and she has been laughing and singing ever since.

Rasmus began the dollhouse this evening. That is, he began making drawings. I will say for him, he draws magnificently, the sketches he makes remind me of photographs I've seen of drawings by Leonardo. Swanny asked him, "Why are you drawing our house, Far?" and he said in his surly way, and in English, he's proud of sayings like this he knows in English, "Ask no questions and you'll get no lies."

I've bought a new dress, old-rose taffeta with white polka dots, and a matching turban in old rose embroidered with white beads.

MAY 7, 1916

I don't know how I can write it. Perhaps I can because I can't believe it's true. I want to wake up and have that wonderful feeling you do after a nightmare: it didn't happen, it wasn't real.

But this is real. Mogens came home this evening to tell us he has enlisted. He is now a private in the Third London Battalion, the Rifle Brigade.

12

On top of the papers Cary had given me were two photographs. I don't know why they interested me, for neither Lizzie Roper nor her husband was good-looking, nor if these pictures were anything to go by, intelligent or sensitive people. She looked coarse and he looked hag-ridden. But still there was something about each of them that caught my imagination. Besides, Anna had known them or at least known of them, she had seen Mrs. Roper in her fashionable clothes and big feathered hat.

Few of us much enjoy reading anything that isn't a book, a newspaper or a magazine. I've had to read too many photocopies of book pages, not to mention manuscripts, typed and handwritten, to want the experience again. I looked at the books first. One was a green Penguin paperback in the Famous Trials series, a shabby, much-thumbed copy, the other looked as if it had been privately published. It was a very slim volume. There was no jacket, no title on the front cover and that on the spine was no longer decipherable. Inside, on the flyleaf, was printed, *A Victorian Family* by Arthur Roper and the date in Roman numerals, MCMXXVI.

A piece of paper fell out. It was a note from Cary. "Read the Ward-Carpenter piece first, then the paperback. You can probably miss out on Arthur's memoir." The Ward-Carpenter turned out to be the stack of rather crooked, black-smudged photocopying. Still, by now I wanted to know more about Roper. But before beginning

I looked him up in an encyclopedia of true crime my historical detective writer had edited.

Not much space was devoted to him: Alfred Eighteen Roper b. 1872, Bury St. Edmunds, Suffolk; d. 1925, Cambridge. Charged with the murder of his wife Elizabeth Louisa Roper in Hackney, London, in July 1905. The trial was at the Central Criminal Court, London, in October 1905, and distinguished by the spectacular performance of Howard de Filippis K.C., for the Defense.

That was all. There was nothing to show on the photocopy where the extract had come from, but no doubt some collection of true crime. Handwritten across the top of the first page was the date 1934.

THE DECLINE AND FALL OF A PHARMACIST
By Francis Ward-Carpenter, M.A., J.P.

Much of the interest and terror induced by great crimes is due, not to their abnormal content, but to that in them which is normal. Huge things happen to little men and they happen, not in mansions or palaces, but in poor houses in mean streets. The trivial is aggrandized by them and the sordid given a horrific cast, so that the crime, albeit briefly, elevates the petty, the squalid and the base to heights of tragedy.

The Roper Case was no exception to this. Indeed, with its principal players teetering on the lowest edge of the lower middle class, its London suburban setting and the portrait its principal actors give of family life, it might be said to exemplify it. Here in the dismal backwater of a great city the men and women drawn together by typical circumstances reacted to them with atypical vice, violence and a flouting of civilization's rules.

Alfred Eighteen Roper was not, however, a London man by birth and upbringing. His singular second name derived from his mother, who bore it before her marriage to Thomas Edward Roper in 1868. Eighteen is a Suffolk surname and it was in Suffolk, in the pretty little town of Bury St. Edmunds on the River Lark, that Alfred was born four years later. By this time his parents already had two daughters, Beatrice and Maud, but Alfred was the firstborn son and heir. Two more sons were later born to the Ropers, Arthur and Joseph, and another daughter who seems to have lived only for a few weeks.

Thomas Roper was an assistant in Morley's, a druggist's shop in the Butter Market, or perhaps something more than that. It appears he had men under him and today we would call him the pharmacist or manager of the shop. He must have been in a fair way of doing, for he could afford to dispense with the labor of his sons, sending all three to the Free Grammar School, and although Thomas' mother and his own wife had both been sent out into service there never appears to have been any question of this in the case of the Roper girls. It was apparently a happy family, respectable and reasonably prosperous, the boys at least with ideas for the future above the station in which Providence had placed them.

Much of this came to an end when Thomas died of an apoplexy, probably a subarachnoid hemorrhage, at the age of forty-four, when Alfred was sixteen. The druggist made the family an offer it would have been highly imprudent to refuse. A position in the shop could be Alfred's if he so desired.

Alfred is said to have told his brother he hoped to win an Exhibition, of which the Grammar School appointed four each year to be held for four years, and which would send him to the University of Cambridge. However, this was not to be. He left school and went into the shop, starting there on the lowest rung of the ladder, but earning money, enough to support his mother and keep his brothers from the necessity of leaving school. One of his sisters was already married and the other due to marry in the following year.

Alfred remained at Morley's for some years, during which he rose to the position his father had formerly held, that of pharmacist. He was dutiful and industrious, a quiet home-loving young man who, according to his brother Arthur, had few friends and no acquaintance at all with the opposite sex.

In 1926 Arthur Roper, a schoolmaster in Beccles, wrote and privately published a memoir of the Ropers. Its title was *A Victo-*

rian Family but its only interest to us today lies in the information it gives about Arthur's brother Alfred. The sole claim to fame or notoriety the Roper family ever had derives from Alfred Roper's trial for the murder of his wife, the circumstances which led up to that trial, and its outcome, yet Arthur has not a word to say about any of it. His brother features prominently in this short book, has no fewer than 250 lines devoted exclusively to him; the illustrations include two photographs of him, one a studio portrait, the other with his wife and children, but that he was tried for murder is never mentioned. He is referred to as marrying Elizabeth Louisa Hyde in 1898, and as a son being born to them in 1899 and a daughter in 1904.

All Arthur's comments on his family members are so eulogistic that we are obliged to take what he says with a grain of salt. Some of this determination to aggrandize what was, after all, a very ordinary and on the whole respectable family, has led to obvious inaccuracies. He writes, for instance, of his grandfather Samuel Roper as superintendent of the Botanic Gardens in Bury St. Edmunds in 1830 while in fact N. S. H. Hodson, the Gardens' founder, held that office. Samuel was probably one of the gardeners employed there. Arthur's maternal grandfather, William Eighteen, may have been employed by the Post Office but was not the Bury St. Edmund's Postmaster in 1844. This position, at the Post Office in Hatter Street, according to White's Suffolk, was held at the date he mentions by John Deck.

His brother Alfred he describes as a thoughtful and enquiring man, even something of an intellectual, an enthusiastic member of the Public Library and also a user of the large library at the Bury Mechanics' Institute. While living with his mother and brother Joseph at the family home in Southgate Street, he spent his evenings reading, often reading aloud to his mother whose sight had begun to fail and who seems to have depended on him for this and many more attentions. Without formal training in his trade of pharmacist, he was interested, according to Arthur, in all forms of "chemistry" and in his own room in Southgate Street, conducted experiments of an exploratory nature. He also built model steam engines, which he set puffing furiously away on the burners of his mother's gas stove.

Arthur gives us no description of Alfred's appearance beyond stating that, like all the male members of his family, his brother was very tall, something over six feet. From the photographs we have of him it can be seen that he was correspondingly thin with narrow shoulders and a frame which does not appear robust. His hair was dark and already starting to recede from the forehead when the portrait photograph was taken in July 1898, just prior to his marriage. His features were regular, he was clean-shaven, and his eyes were dark, though of what color is not known. A faint darker mark on the bridge of his nose suggests that he may habitually have worn spectacles, which he removed for the purpose of having his picture taken.

It was some years after he became manager at Morley's in the Butter Market—Arthur does not say how many but we know it to have been about six—that Alfred encountered Robert Maddox, a visitor to the town putting up at the Angel Inn on Angel Hill. Mr. Maddox came into Morley's, asking for a specific for a bad finger, and was attended to by Alfred Roper. Instead of supplying a placebo, Alfred lanced the whitlow himself and dressed the finger so expertly that Maddox returned on the following day to thank him and to ask if the pharmacist could prescribe a remedy for the nasal catarrh from which he was a chronic sufferer. This Alfred did and Maddox expressed himself delighted with the results.

Exactly why these actions on Alfred's part should have fitted him to become under-manager of a patent medicine advertising company is not known. At least, Arthur does not say why and Arthur's account of these events is almost all we have on which to base our knowledge of his brother's early life. Probably Robert Maddox simply took a fancy to him. By their very quietness and serious demeanor, men of Alfred Roper's type very often make an impression which is quite at odds with their actual abilities. At any rate, the offer of this position with the Supreme Remedy Company in High Holborn, London, of which Maddox was part-owner, was made to him and was accepted.

Had old Mrs. Roper not died some four weeks previously, it is doubtful whether Alfred would have considered this post. He would not, indeed would have felt he could not, have left her. In the latter years he had been doing much of the work of the house as well as carrying his mother up and down stairs and often preparing her meals. Now his brother Joseph was about to be married and intended to bring his bride home to Southgate Street where Arthur was also living. Reading between the lines of Arthur's memoir, we may believe that Alfred was relieved to have the opportunity of making his escape and, perhaps, his fortune.

In London he appears to have put up temporarily at a commercial hotel in the Gray's Inn Road and to have set about immediately looking for more permanent lodgings. At his trial it was stated by a witness, John Smart, a fellow employee at the supreme Remedy Company, that he, Smart, suggested to Alfred over supper in a chophouse that Fulham might be a suitable place for him to seek accommodation. Indeed, Smart himself lived in Fulham and believed there was a vacancy in the house where he had rooms. Travel was easy, a fifteen-minute train journey from Walham Green to Charing Cross on the District Line of the Underground, followed by a walk across the Strand and through Covent Garden.

What prevented Alfred from taking this excellent advice is not known, but it can indisputably be said that if he had taken it he would never have been tried for murder nor passed the subsequent twenty years of his life as a virtual outcast. Arthur has nothing to tell us of what circumstances led his brother to Navarino Road, Hackney, in East London, nor why he chose Mrs. Hyde's house as his future abode. Instead, perhaps through lack of knowledge but more likely through general dismay at subsequent events, he has only the most meagre facts to state about Alfred's life until the dangerous period is past and the year 1906 has been reached.

It was in 1895, when Alfred was twenty-three, that he moved into Devon Villa, Navarino Road, where he took a bedroom and sitting room on the first floor. Devon Villa was four stories high, not including the basement, and Alfred's rooms were large and even handsome with high ceilings and long windows. For these he paid twenty-five shillings a week, this to include the provision of breakfast, tea and supper each day. In receipt of an annual salary of £150, he was well able to afford it. The rooms were adequately, if not luxuriously, furnished, the sitting room enjoyed a view across leafy gardens to London Fields, and his accommodation was cleaned and his meals cooked for him.

Hackney had been a village "anciently celebrated for the numerous seats of the nobility and gentry" which, by the eighteenth century, was said to number among its residents so many merchants and persons of distinction "that it excels all other villages in the Kingdom, and probably on earth, in the riches and opulence of its inhabitants, as may be judged from the great number of persons who keep coaches there."

Before the railways made swift travel possible, Hackney represented the greatest distance at which a man of business could live outside London and come comfortably to his work in the city. The district became a suburb of large houses surrounded by their gardens, these separated from each other by market gardens and meadows in which cattle grazed. It was the occupants of these houses who built the fine churches and chapels of Hackney and who left endowments for the benefit of the poorer classes.

For the poor, as we are told, are always with us and for a long time slums had existed round about Homerton High Street. During the second half of the nineteenth century the tendency was for Hackney to become poorer. By the time Alfred Roper arrived there in that century's last decade there was a good deal of poverty and considerable overcrowding. For instance, statistics show that in the twenty years between 1881 and 1901 the population had increased from 163,681 to 219,272. In 1891 more than three thousand people were living four or more persons to a room and nearly eight thousand were living three or more persons to a room.

Mare Street was one of the demarcations between a surviving middle class occupancy of the grand old mansions and the dwellings of an increasingly miserable working class. The neighborhood of London Fields was rough, while the indigenous poor of Hackney lived in the vicinity of Homerton High Street and Wells Street. In

the north by South Mill Fields, Hackney Wick and All Souls',
Clapton, unkempt poverty prevailed. It would seem that there had
been a general spreading outwards and the rejected from the center
had been sent to occupy the decaying jerry-built houses on the
ill-drained marshes of the River Lea.

Navarino Road lay just to the west or "wrong" side of Mare
Street, a flourishing shopping area with a market, and Mrs. Hyde's
house was the former dwelling of a city merchant who had moved
up to Stamford Hill. The railway station called London Fields
which transported workers into the city was but a stone's throw
away. There were horsedrawn trams and omnibuses. Hackney
Common was not far distant and Victoria Park with its cricket
ground, bowling green and boating lake no more than a good walk
away. Everything the heart could desire was obtainable in the big
department stores of Mare Street and Kingsland High Street and
the emporium of Matthew Rose and Sons provided a number of
services including a refreshment room.

Entertainment abounded in the form of music hall, plays and
music. The Hackney Empire was famous and had many top music
hall stars, including Marie Lloyd, Vesta Tilley and Little Tich.
Moving pictures were not to arrive until 1906 but there was drama
and comedy at the New Alexandra Theatre in Stoke Newington
Road, the Dalston Theatre and the Grand in Islington. Most put
on pantomimes at Christmas.

This then was the expanding London suburb into which Alfred
Roper moved, a place of poverty and hardship, comparative comfort and middle class values, a churchgoing society of burgesses and
their wives, a pagan huddle of poor dwellers four to a room. He was
to live there for the next ten years.

It is time to say something about Mrs. Hyde, her family, her lodgers
and the house in which Alfred Roper found himself settled, of their
history and character.

Maria Sarah Hyde was a widow, or called herself a widow, and
in 1895 she was somewhere about fifty-seven years of age. She never
spoke of a husband and no one seems to have known where she

came from when she moved into Devon Villa five years before. It was a large house, on four floors, which had seen better days. There were in all twelve rooms plus the usual offices. The two reception rooms on the ground floor were spacious and high-ceilinged, the drawing room divided into two when desired by folding doors. At its lower flights, at least, the staircase was handsome and the hall had a floor of brick-red marble. Another, narrower, staircase led down to the basement kitchen and scullery and the windowless hole where the maid had her being. A widely held belief was that Mrs. Hyde had come into this house as a gratuity for services rendered. In other words, the man who had been keeping her had paid her off by this means.

It was undoubtedly hers. She brought to it an elderly man called Joseph Dzerjinski, a Polish or Russian immigrant, who occupied the best part of the second floor, and her daughter Elizabeth Louisa, always known as Lizzie, who slept on the first floor. Mrs. Hyde had then taken two more lodgers, a Miss Beatrice Cottrell, an elderly lady describing herself as a former court dressmaker, and who occupied another room on the first floor, and George Ironsmith, a traveler in canned meat products, with two rooms above hers next door to Mr. Dzerjinski. Mrs. Hyde herself occupied the whole of the top floor.

Nearly all the work of the house fell to the lot of the maid, Florence Fisher. Having left school the previous year, she was a mere child when she came to work at Devon Villa a few months after Roper moved in. Prior to her arrival Maria Hyde had employed an older woman who left her service to get married. Only two percent of Hackney householders kept servants at all, so Florence Fisher, aged thirteen, very likely thought herself lucky to have acquired a good place not far from her mother's home near the Disinfecting Station at South Mill Field. It was her task to clean the rooms, carry coals upstairs, sweep the front steps and the yard, wash the dishes and often do the shopping. The cooking, at that time, was shared between Maria and Lizzie Hyde.

Maria Hyde claimed to have a serious heart condition which she made the excuse for doing very little apart from drinking with

Joseph Dzerjinski in the Dolphin Tavern in Mare Street. Gin seems to have been her preferred tipple but she possessed the ability to hold her liquor and no one could claim ever to have seen her the worse for it. According to Miss Cottrell, she often said spirits were good for her heart.

There were those who said that she was on the lookout for a husband for her daughter. Others averred that this daughter was, in the phrase current at the time, "no better than she should be" and that, though she had never been married, she had borne at least one child. What had become of this child or children was not known. George Ironsmith, the traveler in canned meat, with the rooms on Dzerjinski's floor, was said to have been engaged to Lizzie Hyde and there was talk of a marriage in the following year. But for some unknown reason the engagement was broken off and Ironsmith went to America where the company of meat exporters by whom he was employed had their main base. After his departure his rooms were let to a married couple called Upton.

Lizzie Hyde claimed to be twenty-four years old in 1895. She was probably at least six years older than that and therefore seven years Alfred Roper's senior. The few photographs of her which have come down to us show a woman of undoubted beauty, albeit a beauty somewhat coarsened by time and rough usage. She has a full oval face, regular features, a straight nose and small full-lipped mouth, large bright eyes and strong shapely eyebrows. Her hair is massy and light in color, her neck swanlike and her figure well developed without being stout. According to a newspaper article written by a neighbor and a memoir left by Miss Cottrell, she had held various situations in the locality, as an assistant in a draper's shop and later as a milliner, she having been apprenticed to a dressmaker in her youth. She certainly had no outside paid work in 1895 but remained at home to help keep the house.

It was into this household that Alfred Roper came as the most favored lodger. Each and every one of them recognized his respectability from the first and his desirability as tenant, and this seems, for a while at any rate, to have regulated their behavior. According to Miss Cottrell, meals became more regular and the cleanliness of the place improved. A "gentleman friend" of Lizzie Hyde's, who had been a frequent visitor and, Miss Cottrell said, had been known to stay overnight, though in what circumstances she could not say, was no longer seen.

However, Miss Cottrell did take it upon herself after Alfred had been resident in Navarino Road for about a week to advise him to stay no longer than he could help. In fact, she suggested he would be wise to look for other accommodation at once; this house might be good enough for an old woman like herself with no character to lose but was "no place for him." Needless to say, Alfred did not heed this warning. Whether this was because he was the innocent Mr. Howard de Filippis, defending him at his trial, suggested he was or whether his vanity got the better of him no one can say. Certainly, at this point, the women all waited on him in a way he had never previously been used to. He was allowed to conduct his chemistry experiments in his room and use the gas stove in the kitchen for his steam engines. No doubt, he also found something gratifying about living in a big house for the first time in his life, enjoyed the size of his rooms and his view, even though the house was not his.

Perhaps he had already learned to take pleasure in the society of Mrs. Hyde's daughter. As for Fulham, the train journey was just as easy from the nearby station at London Fields and the walk at the end of it a matter only of heading south rather than north.

We have little information on what happened to Alfred during the next three years. It is known that he rose to become manager of the Supreme Remedy Company with a consequent increase of a pound a week in his wages and known too that he returned only once to Suffolk in those years. This was for the funeral of his sister-in-law, Joseph's wife, who had died in childbirth. The next firm fact we have is the record of his marriage in August 1898 to Elizabeth Louisa Hyde, spinster, at St. John's Parish church, South Hackney.

More surprising is the date of his son's birth on February 19, 1899, six months after the wedding. This gives the appearance of Lizzie Hyde's having entrapped Alfred into marriage and certain it is that whatever happiness they may have enjoyed prior to their wedding and up to the birth of their son, their contentment with each other was not to be prolonged.

Beatrice Cottrell later wrote and had published a scurrilous account of her life at Devon Villa. It was very much biased in Alfred's favor. Alfred "doted" on his wife in those early days. Lizzie waited on him hand and foot and was often heard to call her husband pet names and to say that nothing she could do for him was too much trouble. But this devotion was short-lived. Alfred was an ideal husband and man superior to his associates. A neighbor, Cora Green, as a friend of Maria Hyde's was always in and out of the house. She told her "story" to a newspaper after Alfred's acquittal and said she sometimes found Lizzie Roper too demonstrative for her taste, always hanging on her husband's neck and kissing him in public. The two couples, Maria and Dzerjinski, Alfred and Lizzie, went to music halls together and often to the Hackney Empire. Alfred was also seen to be visiting the Dolphin with his wife and mother-in-law, surely another new departure for him.

All this seems to have come to an end with the birth of Edward Alfred, their first child. Cora Green averred that Lizzie lacked any maternal instinct and found herself incapable of caring for a baby. The child was dirty, inadequately fed and soon failed to thrive. Lizzie made terrible scenes, threatening to kill the child and herself, then took to her bed for days on end. Florence Fisher had too much on her hands to undertake the care of a baby as well as clean the house. Besides this, her mother was seriously ill and any free time the sixteen year old had was spent with Mrs. Fisher in her squalid rooms off the Lea Bridge Road. Beatrice Cottrell noticed that the house became progressively dirtier at this time. Alfred was obliged to engage a nurse. This he could ill afford, especially as Maria Hyde, now that she had, so to speak, a breadwinner in the family, could see ahead of her an end to lodging house–keeping and repeatedly said so in Miss Cottrell's hearing.

The baby's incessant crying was one of the factors which drove the Uptons to leave. They also complained of the decline in the quality of the meals provided, now that Lizzie was no longer available to do the cooking. Mrs. Upton told Cora Green there were bugs in the bedroom walls. After they had gone Mrs. Hyde made no move to find replacements for them. She moved Mr. Dzerjinski downstairs into what had been Alfred's rooms, Lizzie and Alfred into what had formerly been his rooms and moved herself next door to Dzerjinski, saying that her weak heart would no longer allow her to climb all those stairs. The top floor she closed off, insisting that it was uneconomical to keep it clean and free of damp.

Alfred had his wife and baby but in some ways, as far as accommodation went, he was worse off than before his marriage. He was obliged to share the downstairs rooms with the lodgers and to take all his meals with them. His mother-in-law had grudgingly allowed him a room on the top floor for his chemical experiments, but withdrew her permission when she closed up these rooms. Then there was the noise. Dzerjinski was something of a virtuoso on the accordian and had performed on various music hall stages. He practiced this instrument often long into the night as well as giving English lessons to Russian and German immigrants in his rooms. The noise of the accordian and the mutter of guttural speech penetrating the walls and ceiling was often appalling.

Miss Cottrell remained for a further four years. According to Cora Green, Lizzie Roper took no interest in her child but left him in the care first of the nurse and after the nurse's departure, when Maria would agree to this, of her mother. The "gentleman friend," mentioned by Miss Cottrell, who apparently visited the house before Alfred's arrival there, was seen to reappear—he or perhaps another. Certainly, during the next two or three years, there was more than one.

A man that Cora Green heard Lizzie refer to as "Bert" was in the habit of calling for her in a carriage. This seems to have been Herbert Cobb, whom Mrs. Green describes as a manager of a gentlemen's outfitters. He was well known to Miss Cottrell who was fortunate he did not sue her for libel when her book came out. She refers to him, with moral vigor, as a "home-breaker" and "fiend in human form," as a frequenter of loose women, dishonest, irreverent, foul-mouthed and one who uttered blasphemies.

Lizzie had another string to her bow. A businessman and frequent patron of the Plume of Feathers called Percy Middlemass, said to be in late middle age and very prosperous, also came to the house and remained inside alone with Lizzie for several hours. Ironsmith, the traveler in canned meats who had left his lodgings and gone back to Chicago, she also alleged had reappeared and sometimes visited Lizzie. One day in the late summer of 1903 Mrs. Green met him in the street, coming away from Devon Villa, and recognized him at once, though he pretended not to know her.

Alfred himself, of course, was out of the house for twelve hours each day, leaving Lizzie free to enjoy herself as she pleased. If he was aware of her activities at that time we have no knowledge of it but his general air of unhappiness and decline in health was noted by, among others, John Smart, the young man who had advocated Fulham as a suitable area in which to live. Alfred, he said, had grown thin and acquired a stoop as very tall men sometimes do. Smart said he sometimes complained of dyspepsia and said he no longer slept well.

In May 1904 Lizzie Roper was delivered of a daughter and two months later the child was christened Edith Elizabeth at St. John's Church. From the first, Lizzie's attitude towards the baby was quite different from that which she had adopted towards her son Edward. For one thing, she nursed the infant herself. She took Edith out in the perambulator and proudly showed her off to the neighbors. Visits from Cobb, Middlemass and the rest seem to have ceased, at least for the time being.

Alfred became happier, according to Smart, and was excitedly anticipating taking his family on holiday to Margate in August. He was proud of his daughter but it was his son Edward on whom he seems to have lavished most of his affection. While the boy was little, owing to his mother's defection, Alfred had been with him and tended on him more than is usual with fathers in our society. This may in part have contributed for the extravagant love he felt for his son. Letters from Alfred to his sister Maud, in the present writer's possession, are full of Edward, his good looks, prodigious behavior and learning abilities, as well as long quotations from the boy's precocious remarks. Indeed, several of them contain little else. Lizzie and the child Edith are mentioned only as joining with Alfred in the sending of love—a surely empty message when we consider that, as far as we know, they and Maud had never met.

Alfred told John Smart that he hoped there would be no increase to his family as he would need all he earned to educate Edward properly. There was to be, he averred, no elementary school and Free Grammar School for him. Nor was he to miss his chance of the university because his father had made inadequate provision for the rest of the family, as had happened in his own case. Alfred believed Edward to be an exceptional child and mentions in his letters to Maud the boy's ability to read and do simple sums at the age of four and a half. He also sees it as a sign of future intellect that Edward walked at nine months and was talking articulately at eighteen months.

The happily anticipated holiday may have taken place or it may not, we have no way of knowing, but in August two momentous events took place. Miss Cottrell moved out of Devon Villa after a scene with Mrs. Hyde in which she accused her landlady of keeping a house of call and of acting as a procuress for her own daughter, and Alfred Roper lost his job.

It is Cora Green's "journalism" that provides us with this insight into Miss Cottrell's relations with Maria Hyde. According to Mrs. Green, Miss Cottrell had for some time been making insinuations about Lizzie Roper's moral character, this in spite of the fact that the former "gentleman friends" seem to have ceased calling. Now, however, she was not only suggesting that Maria Hyde had acted as a go-between for her daughter, but that Edith Roper was not Alfred's child.

One day, again according to Mrs. Green, a violent quarrel took place in which Miss Cottrell said the house was dirty, there were bugs in the walls, Lizzie was no better than a street girl and Alfred Roper should know the truth. "For two pins" she would tell him everything. Maria told her to get out of the house and later had

Dzerjinski help her bring Miss Cottrell's property downstairs and put it out into the street. That then was the end of Maria Hyde's career as a lodging house–keeper, unless one counts Dzerjinski as a lodger, though he certainly paid no rent.

The Supreme Remedy Company abruptly ceased trading one morning in early August. Substantial sums of money were owed and the company's creditors appeared in the street outside, clamoring at the door for the settlement of its debts. It was believed that Robert Maddox had absconded to the Continent with the company's funds. However, there were no funds, or none was ever found. Maddox had not gone to France but, traveling no further than Dover, had taken a room in an hotel and there shot himself. The company's nine employees, including the manager, lost their jobs.

No doubt, this was a considerable blow to Alfred Roper. He had a large house to maintain and five adults and two children to support. There was no other source of income, if we discount, as we probably can, the most heinous of Miss Cottrell's allegations. Alfred set about looking for work and eventually found himself a situation as a clerk with a firm that manufactured lenses, Imperial Optics Limited. The salary was half what he had been earning before and the only advantage Imperial Optics seem to have had over the Supreme Remedy Company, if advantage it was, lay in the proximity of its situation to his home. Alfred could now walk to work, for his new employment was in Cambridge Heath Road, Bethnal Green.

Soon after this, Cora Green also left the district. She moved only as far as Stoke Newington and occasionally came back to visit her friend Maria Hyde but she was no longer a neighbor, able to keep an eye on the comings and goings at the house next door. Mystery shrouds Devon Villa for a period of almost a year. True, Florence Fisher was there, and Florence Fisher's was some of the most important evidence at Alfred's trial. But she was not an observant young woman, she spent the greater part of her time when she was not engaged in cleaning the upper rooms, in the kitchen, scullery and her own quarters, and at this period had outside interests. Her mother had died and there was no home to visit up on the Marshes, but she had begun "walking out" with a young man she later referred to as her fiancé. Ernest Henry Herzog, in good service with a family in Islington, and himself the grandson of immigrants, was a year younger than his sweetheart and socially a cut above her, but in the event they were never married and he need not concern us further here. Florence, however, at last had a life of her own. If there were scenes of recrimination, accusation and reproach up-stairs, she paid no attention to them.

In the spring of 1905 things began to change. John Smart, who had remained Alfred's friend, who was indeed his only friend, had a meeting with him in April. They met in an ABC teashop and Alfred was accompanied by his son, Edward. On this occasion he imparted to Smart two highly significant pieces of information. One was that he had come to believe he was not Edith's father. His wife had said as much during the course of one of their quarrels, though later retracted and said she had been "having him on." Nevertheless, Alfred said, he had for a long time doubted Edith's paternity, as he doubted the paternity of the child Lizzie was now expecting.

Smart was deeply shocked by these revelations. He even volun-teered his own opinion that Edith closely resembled Alfred but Alfred was not to be shaken in his beliefs. He told Smart he saw no reason why he should be expected to "keep his nose to the grindstone" to feed a whole family and its "by-blows" who were nothing to him. He had been a fool to marry, he knew that now, but at least out of his marriage he had got Edward.

The other news he gave Smart was that he had heard of a situation that would soon be vacant for a pharmacist in a large and flourishing shop in Cambridge. No, he had not found this job advertised in the situations vacant columns of a newspaper. A fellow clerk at Imperial Optics was cousin to the man who pres-ently held the post and who would shortly be retiring. The clerk, a man called Hodges, gave it as his opinion that the situation would be Alfred's for the asking if he made application within the next month. Moreover, Maud, the sister he had always felt closest to out of his four siblings, lived with her husband in the village of Fen Ditton just outside the city.

Smart said the idea was an excellent one and advised Alfred to apply immediately. By these means, Alfred could remove his wife and children from the possibly evil influence of her mother and start a new life. Ah, no, was Alfred's rejoinder. That was not at all what he had in mind. Rather he intended to leave Lizzie and her daughter and begin this job in Cambridge, always supposing he could secure it, describing himself as a widower with an only son. For, of course, he meant to take Edward with him.

Smart did his best to dissuade Alfred from this course, not only on this occasion but at later meetings. And Alfred did seem to relent a little. Lizzie would have to change her ways if she expected him to stay with her. Mysteriously, he told Smart he was "treating" Lizzie for an "illness," his experience as a pharmacist had taught him what to do. At a later meeting, when Smart again asked him the nature of this illness Roper called her a nymphomaniac. He said he was treating her with hyoscin hydrobromide, a sexual depressant, to quell the demands she made on him and her need for other men. The whole situation at Devon Villa wearied him utterly. He was at any rate resolved to cease supporting Maria Hyde and Joseph Dzerkinski as soon as this was possible.

One of these people was soon beyond requiring maintenance by him or anyone else. Joseph Dzerjinski, paying a visit to his sister in Highbury, was taken ill in the street on his way home to Navarino Road. He was found lying on the pavement in a serious condition and was carried to the nearby German Hospital but died before he reached there. The date was early July 1905 and at the end of that month, had he lived, Joseph Dzerjinski would have been seventy-eight years old. An inquest was held and a verdict of death by misadventure recorded. At postmortem a serious heart condition was discovered as well as advanced cirrhosis of the liver. It seems that Alfred was expected to pay for the funeral and that he did so.

The summer of 1905 was very hot. Sun temperatures of 130 degrees Fahrenheit were recorded. Newspapers were full of stories

of people driven mad by the heat and rates of murder and infanti-
cide notably increased. All the windows and the front and back
doors of Devon Villa remained open during the hours of daylight
but even so the heat was overpowering.

No other evidence of Lizzie's pregnancy, apart from that of John
Smart, ever emerged, unless we consider her repeated claims of
being tired, "feeling faint," morning vomiting and continual drows-
iness as evidence, though these symptoms could have derived from
her continuous intake of hyoscin hydrobromide. No pregnancy was
mentioned by Florence Fisher nor is there a word about it in the
letter Maria wrote at this time to the late Joseph Dzerjinski's sister,
Marta Boll. Cora Green did not know of it. No evidence of a
pregnancy discovered at postmortem was offered at Roper's trial.
Therefore, it seems likely that, due to some physical cause or
perhaps to the excessive heat, Lizzie lost the child she was expecting
by miscarriage sometime in the course of that summer. Or else
there never had been a child but this was an invention of Lizzie's
to keep her husband from leaving her.

To leave her may have been what he always intended. The letter
he wrote to Mrs. Maud Leeming in Fen Ditton on July 15 mentions
Lizzie only (again) as sending her love. There is not a word in it
about Edith. The situation at Jopling's in Cambridge was his from
August 1 and he asks his sister to receive himself and Edward at her
house from July 27 onwards until he can find alternative accommodation for them. On the other hand, in writing of these lodgings he
needs to find in the city of Cambridge, he talks of "setting up
home" and of a "return to family life."

At the beginning of the second week of that month he, not his
wife, gave Florence Fisher notice. Her services would not be required after July 31 as he, Mrs. Roper and the children would be
moving to Cambridge. Mrs. Hyde would be remaining there and
must make her own arrangements but as a woman on her own
would not be in need of a servant. Those, according to Florence,
were his words.

Florence appealed to Maria Hyde, who knew nothing of any of
this. She in turn spoke to her daughter who expressed a correspond-

ing ignorance. Why Florence was so determined to stay in what was hardly a sinecure, where she was ill-paid and overworked, is unclear. Her accommodation was cramped, dirty and insanitary. She was at this time a strong stout young woman of twenty-two, could certainly have found another situation and there is no doubt Alfred would have given her a good reference. Perhaps she did not wish to enter service elsewhere for what would necessarily be a short time with the marriage she still expected to take place arranged for the following spring.

Whatever the reason, she was determined to stay at Devon Villa and Roper appears to have said nothing further about her leaving. On the afternoon of July 27 Mrs. Hyde told Florence she was feeling unwell with pains down her left arm and in her chest. It was her heart "playing up," she said, and she must lie down. Then Alfred appeared, told her he and Edward were departing "shortly" for Cambridge and added that Mrs. Roper and Edith would be coming up to join him "very soon." Florence did not see him leave the house but supposed that he had done so.

Three-quarters of an hour later he was back, ringing the front door bell and declaring that he had left his sovereign case behind. This was of silver and had belonged to his father. Florence offered to help him look for it but this offer he refused, told her to get on with her own work and opened the door for her to go into the dining room where she had linen to collect for the wash. She heard him go upstairs where his wife, Edith and Maria Hyde were.

Some half-hour prior to Roper's return Maria Hyde had come down to the kitchen, saying she was better and asking Florence to make tea and prepare a light supper to be taken upstairs. Her daughter was ill, she said, and lying down in bed. This Florence did and Maria took the tray upstairs herself. On it, as well as tinned salmon and bread and butter, was a pot of tea, the sugar basin and milk for Edith. This sugar basin with its contents was to become an important exhibit at Roper's trial three months later. Roper himself did not take sugar in tea or prepared drinks and nor did his mother-in-law or Florence Fisher.

Roper was upstairs a long time, no doubt hunting for his sovereign case. According to his evidence at his own trial, he said he finally found it on the dining room mantelpiece. With the case in his pocket, he walked to the cab rank in Kingsland High Street, a considerable distance, and on the way claimed to have tripped over a loose curbstone and fallen, grazing his right hand. One person at least said he had seen blood on Roper's hand and on his coat sleeve but was later unable to identify him.

He reached Liverpool Street station at last, where he had left his small son and his luggage in the care of the porter. Originally, he had intended to catch the five-fifteen train for Cambridge and would have been in ample time to have done so if he had not returned to Navarino Road. However, the time was now almost six-thirty and though there was a train which ran as far as Bishops Stortford, none went all the way to Cambridge until the eight-twenty. Roper and his son had almost two hours to wait.

One of the mysteries in this case is why Roper deferred his journey to Cambridge until so late in the day. He had resigned from his employment in Bethnal Green, he had no work to go to and no particular duties in the house. According to the Great Eastern Railway's timetable for July 1905, there were many trains running to Cambridge throughout the day. He could, for instance, have caught the twelve noon, or if he had wanted a nonstopping train, gone to St. Pancras instead and caught the twelve-twenty, reaching Cambridge at one-thirty-one. He could have aimed for the two-thirty, which stopped only twice before reaching its destination at just before ten to four.

He had a small child with him, a child whose normal bedtime was six-thirty p.m., yet he chose a train which was not scheduled to reach its destination until four minutes after that time, and in the event caught one two hours later, necessitating an arrival in Cambridge at twenty to ten. No doubt, he had his reasons.

In the morning the child Edith came downstairs at eight and Florence gave her breakfast. This was not at all an unusual proceeding, though one which was not particularly pleasing to Florence who had the work of the house and the shopping to do. The

nonappearance of Mrs. Roper and Mrs. Hyde caused her no great
surprise as it was often their habit to lie in bed until noon, but after
she had washed Edith and dressed her she sent her upstairs. The
little fair-haired girl clambering up the first flight of stairs at Devon
Villa, Navarino Road, Hackney, was the last sight Florence Fisher
ever had of Edith Roper. Indeed, it was the last known sighting of
her in this world.

Florence went out shopping at about ten. It was warm and close,
though less hot than it had been. However, such heat as there was
seems to have affected her adversely, for when after about two
hours she returned, no doubt laden with groceries, she had begun
to feel ill.

There appeared to be no one in the house. She dragged herself
upstairs to the first-floor bedroom in which was the cot where
Edith slept. She found the room in some disarray—again a not
unusual event. Doubtless wearily, she stripped the cot of sheets and
blankets soaked in urine. It was perhaps natural to assume that in
her absence Mrs. Roper and Edith had left for Cambridge. If she
had not been ill herself at this time, Florence might have been more
curious about the whereabouts of Maria Hyde and suspicious of
circumstances in which Lizzie Roper and her daughter had gone
away, not for a holiday but permanently, without taking any of
Edith's clothes with them. But she was ill. Possibly she was suffering from a form of heatstroke. Whatever it was, she was obliged to
take to her bed in the basement at Devon Villa and to remain there
for the next two days.

Then followed a period of more than a week in which Florence
Fisher was alone in Navarino Road. During that time she continued to suppose that Mr. and Mrs. Roper and the children were
in Cambridge. If she worried at all, it would not have been about
them but her own future. Would one of them return to pay her
wages? Or was she expected to have left their employment and
therefore to receive no further wages? Then there was the question
of the absence of Mrs. Hyde. In all the ten years Florence had been
in this house Mrs. Hyde had never spent a night away from it. On

the other hand, since she and her daughter had always lived together, so far as Florence knew, the likeliest explanation was that she too had gone to Cambridge and was even now there with her daughter and son-in-law.

Florence went about her business. She was soon recovered and returned to her duties. July 28 was a Friday and it is known, from the agency's records, that on the following Thursday, August 3, she called at Miss Elizabeth Newman's Servants' Agency in Mare Street in quest of another situation. Probably she had some contact with the man to whom she was engaged. Tradesmen called. The knife grinder was due and no doubt he came. The baker made his daily delivery.

It was months since Florence had been up to the top floor at Devon Villa, but she was in the habit of giving a sweep and dust to the one below it every week. Mounting the first flight of stairs on the morning of Friday August 4 with mop and duster, the first time she had been up there since two days before Roper's departure, she smelled a powerful and terrible odor she had never smelled before. She went up the second flight. She paused on the landing, no doubt considerably daunted. The smell here was ten times worse than on the stairs. Florence tied her clean duster over her mouth and nose before she opened the door of the first bedroom.

This was the bedroom Lizzie Roper had shared with her husband. However, it was the body of Mrs. Hyde which lay spread out face-downwards on the floor between the bed and the door. It was fully clothed but the hair was partly in curl papers. Clad only in a thin white cotton nightgown, the body of Lizzie Roper lay on, rather than in, the bed, which was covered with a whitish counterpane. Both bodies, the bed and bedclothes and the women's nightclothes, the carpet and to some extent the walls, were splashed or soaked with blood. Lizzie Roper's throat had been cut from ear to ear.

On a table was the tray with the two cups that had contained tea as well as the half-empty sugar basin, a three-quarters empty bottle of gin and two glasses. A week had passed and the remains of the salmon had rotted. The curtains were closed, the air thick and fetid and the room full of flies which wheeled and buzzed about the bodies and the rancid food.

Florence touched nothing beyond closing the door she had opened. She went downstairs, put on her hat and walked to the police station in Kingsland Road where she saw Sub-Divisional Inspector Samuel Parlett and told him of her discovery. Two police officers accompanied her back to Navarino Road.

An account of Alfred Roper's trial appears in the next chapter. Suffice it to say here that at the inquest a verdict was returned of murder with malice aforethought and that on the following day Alfred Roper was arrested in Fen Ditton, Cambridgeshire, and charged with his wife's murder. He appeared on the following morning at the North London Police Court before the magistrate Edward Snow Fordham where he was committed for trial at the Central Criminal Court.

Astonishingly, no violence had been done to Maria Hyde. Cause of death was cardiac arrest, brought on by natural causes. Maria Hyde had for years complained of having a bad heart which might at any moment carry her off, and it seems she was right. The assumption was made—and it is difficult to find an alternative solution—that she was either a witness to her daughter's death or that she discovered the body and the effect on her was to stop her heart.

But had Maria Hyde also witnessed the killing of fourteen-month-old Edith? The child had disappeared. A search was mounted, residents of every house in an area bounded by Graham Road, Queensbridge Road, Richmond Road and Mare Street, were questioned, the boating lake in Victoria Park was dragged and part of the Grand Union Canal. Although there was no sign of disturbance of the soil, the garden at Devon Villa was dug over to a depth of four feet. Local people joined in the search of London Fields and Hackney Downs and the hunt for Edith spread to Hackney Marshes.

It was all in vain. Edith Roper had disappeared and was never to be found, alive or dead.

13

The promised succeeding chapter may have been written but it wasn't enclosed in Cary's package. Still, I was not to be obliged to forego the trial. It had been written about, perhaps because Roper's acquittal was one of the early triumphs of the K.C., Howard de Filippis, in the Penguin Famous Trials series. The green paperback which also contained accounts of the cases of Crippen, Oscar Slater, George Lamson, Madeleine Smith and Buck Ruxton, had no illustrations. But its cover was a collage of photographic images of the subjects, and there hovering like a medium's fabricated ghost between Crippen in his high stiff collar and pretty, relentless Madeleine, was Alfred Roper, dark and cadaverous, resembling more than anyone Abraham Lincoln. The book and Arthur Roper's memoir I put aside, not even sure if I ever intended reading them. I had my own work to do as well as answering all those letters of condolence.

Paul Sellway's was the first I replied to. It wasn't a long letter I wrote him but I did mention the diaries and, for something to say, that I now wished my mother had spoken Danish to me as a child so that I had some grasp of it and I added a question I intended as rhetorical: was it the same for him or had he been luckier and had either Hansine or his mother ensured he was bilingual? This letter was to have interesting consequences.

· · ·

Gordon Westerby, my first cousin once removed, took no more than a week before following up our conversation outside Hampstead Heath Station. He didn't phone, he wrote.

It was a beautifully executed formal letter, more the product of desktop publishing than a typewriter, and he signed himself "yours sincerely." He had read the diaries and much enjoyed them. They had convinced him, if he needed convincing, that all that was lacking was a family tree to be set among the endpapers. Did I think this idea would find favor (his words) with the publishers of the diaries?

Could I tell him the Christian names of Morfar's parents? Would it be too much to ask for their dates? Was Tante Frederikke Anna's mother's sister or her father's? Who was Onkel Holger? Would I come to dinner with him and Aubrey in Roderick Road? On the 5th, 6th, 7th, 12th, 14th or 15th?

He could have asked Swanny these questions and I wondered why he hadn't. She had been ignorant about the Westerby history while Mormor was alive but after she was dead and the diaries came into her hands she set out to solve puzzles herself, looked up records while she was in Denmark and met the pastor of the church where Anna and Rasmus had been married.

These were not matters which found their way into the diaries. Mormor had never been interested in her forebears. She hadn't bothered to label the photographs in the albums with names or dates. If she knew who Rasmus' grandmother was or why the members of her own family were scattered across Sweden as well as Denmark, she had forgotten. In her extreme old age she had forgotten almost everything.

For the last year of her life Mormor lived alone with Swanny in Willow Road. She was ninety-three and she seemed to have all her faculties. She still wore glasses only for reading, had no hearing difficulties and was as agile as ever. But she had lost her memory.

What often happens to very old people is that they have no memory of recent events but almost perfect recall of things that happened sixty or seventy years in the past. This wasn't true of Anna. In her mind the past was either lost or terribly distorted, so that she would confuse the stories she told, mixing up the one about going to the orphanage with the one about mushroom poisoning. The result was a garbled tale of her cousin going to the orphanage on her own and returning home to find her husband dead of fungus toxins.

Of course, Torben had been saying she was senile for years. It hadn't been true but it came true once he was dead. Anna talked nonsense and almost nothing but nonsense. This would have been less painful to watch and listen to if she had been physically decrepit. But she looked no more than seventy, she could still walk a mile without hardship and climb the stairs without stopping. She still read her Dickens, did her fine sewing, her drawn thread work and petit point and the task she had not long embarked on of embroidering Swanny's monogram on every piece of linen she possessed. From this work she would look up and come out with an anecdote that was a fabrication but in the heart of which was a tiny thread of fact. For example, the polar bear story which forms the first lines of the first diary had become fact to her and she would recount how she and her mother, while walking in Osterbrogade on a bitter winter's day, had seen one of these animals gazing in at the window of a butcher's shop.

Strangely, the last thing I remember her ever saying to me was quite lucid, a story I had never heard before. Swanny was there and I don't think Swanny had ever heard it either. I was making one of my evening visits—rarer since Daniel Blain had come to live with me—and Anna was, as usual, reclining on the sofa, reading. Something she read may have recalled this to her. It's possible she simply invented it.

She began laughing softly. She lifted her head, took off her glasses and said, "We had this maid called Emily. We had Hansine too and we also had this Emily who was English. She was a very stupid girl but she meant well. You remember Björn, don't you, *lille* Swanny?"

Swanny looked amazed. She said, yes, of course she did.

"When we gave Björn his food," Anna said, "we'd always say, *spis dit bród.*"

" 'Eat your food,' " Swanny said for my benefit, though my Danish was adequate for that.

"I came upon this silly girl feeding Björn and holding out the dish to him and saying, 'Beastly boy, beastly boy.' "

Anna chortled and Swanny managed a doubtful smile. I suppose *spis dit brod* does sound a bit, a very little bit, like "beastly boy." God knows it might have done if the girl took Morfar for her exemplar. Anna went off into a rambling tale of her childhood and I went home to Daniel. Only Daniel wasn't there, he was meeting Cary somewhere, and soon after that he had left me and gone to Cary.

I've said this isn't my story. The difficulty with that is that it's I who tell it and the things that happened to me affect it. Perhaps it's enough to say that Daniel was the only man I had actually ever lived with, as distinct from spending weekends with or going home with overnight. And that, while Anna before she grew senile had seemed to take this as normal behavior, Swanny had deeply disapproved. She wanted me to regularize things by marrying Daniel and I wanted that too. But Cary set out to take him away, set out with what seemed a planned campaign, deliberate, relentless, unscrupulous and when a woman does this and she's attractive she usually succeeds.

The result was to make me get out altogether. It isn't true that you can't run away from things. Putting three thousand miles between you and the lost love and his new love does soften the blow, it does begin the process of driving the pain into the past. An American novelist had asked me to research the town of Cirencester in the nineteenth century. Anticipating an almost inevitable refusal, she wanted me to come over, spend some months with her, talk of my finds and of Victorian Gloucestershire and help her with the American angle of the historical epic she was writing. She was astonished when I said yes.

Therefore, I was in Massachusetts when Anna died.

I knew, as well as anyone ever can know of a coming death, that she was going to die. I also knew how unhappy Swanny was, how lonely and increasingly despairing of her mother and her mother's ways. It was all in the many letters Swanny wrote to me. She would have liked me to come home. Perhaps she had no idea how I felt or even thought that because Daniel and I had never been married, things had not gone deep with me. Some women of her generation did think like this. But I was literally afraid to be in the same country, the same *island,* with Daniel and Cary. It wasn't that I expected to bump into them but rather that wherever I was in the British Isles there would be a sense of proximity absent on the other side of the Atlantic.

Swanny wrote to me that Anna had been taken into hospital with what the doctor said "wasn't exactly a stroke, more a sort of spasm." Maybe I should have offered to come home. I told myself cravenly that Anna was only my grandmother, that she was very very old, that she had other grandchildren and great-grandchildren. It was Swanny who needed me, of course, not Anna. As it turned out it may have been the best thing in the world for Swanny that I didn't come.

The saddest letter was the one in which she wrote that she realized now she would never know. The question would never be answered. She had asked it for the last time a few days before Anna had her "spasm," one evening when they were sitting together in the drawing room, the curtains drawn and a gas fire burning in the neat brass grate. Anna had seemed more lucid, more like her old self, all that day.

She lay on the sofa, which was drawn up in front of the fire, a piece of embroidery on the low table, *Martin Chuzzlewit* open and face downwards on the cushion beside her with her reading glasses resting on it. Her white hair, Swanny wrote, was blond in the golden lamplight and if you looked at her through half-closed eyes you might have fancied it was a young woman reclining there. And Swanny (who was more fanciful and discursive in her letters than in life) asked me if I'd ever read that Poe story about the short-sighted young man who, too vain to wear glasses, courts and nearly marries the sprightly and bedizened old woman he has mistaken for a girl, but who is really his own great-great-grandmother. Swanny said she had never swallowed that before but she could now.

She said to her mother, on an impulse and as if she had never asked it before, "Who am I, *moder*? Where did you get me from?"

Anna looked at her, and Swanny said her expression was the most tender and loving she had ever seen on her face, and the most lacking in understanding. "You're mine, *lille* Swanny, all mine. Do you want me to tell you where mothers get babies from? Don't you know?"

As if she were very young. As if she were a child the teacher had forgotten to include in the sex education class. Anna's eyes closed and she fell asleep, as she always did now in the evenings when she laid her book down and took off her glasses.

Swanny phoned to tell me Anna was dead. I didn't offer to come home and when she was sure I wasn't going to offer, she begged me not to come, it wasn't necessary. Anna had been very old, ninety-three, and her death long expected. It was a shock, of course, but death is always that.

A week later she wrote to me.

Moder put in her will that she didn't want a funeral. She'd once or twice told me this but I suppose I never believed her. Anyway, I thought you *had* to have a funeral, but evidently not. You can just tell the undertakers and ask for the person to be cremated, which is what I did with many misgivings but they weren't all that surprised and didn't seem to find it strange.

Moder was an out and out atheist. She often told me she stopped believing in God when her little boy Mads died. That was the end of it and she never said a prayer again. I remember her saying loudly at one of our parties that she was a Nietszchean and believed God was dead. I don't know where she picked that up but she knew a lot, she had educated herself extremely well. Anyway, it was right for her to get her wish about no funeral.

In her will she left me everything she had, which wasn't a great deal but more than I need. It was specifically left to me, "to my daughter, Swanhild Kjaer," and of course no questions were asked, I wasn't even asked for my birth certificate. If I had been, so what? It gives Mor and Far as my parents and names me as Swanhild. But I felt strange about it, it brought up all those old feelings, and I even wondered if I should have said, no, I can't take it, I've no right to it.

Anyway, I didn't. The point of making a will, after all, is that you leave your things to the people you want to have them and Mor certainly wanted me to have hers. I feel so lost without her. Did you know I'd never really been without her, I've never been away from her before this? Even when I first got married Torben and I only lived round the corner. The longest separation was those few weeks I spent in Denmark in 1924 when I was nineteen and I first met Torben. All the rest of my life I've either seen Mor every day or spoken on the phone to her, and mostly it was that I saw her. Since Far died we'd lived in the same house, twenty years in the same house. I can't really believe she's gone. She was so much a part of my life, she *was* my life. I hear her footstep on the stairs, I hear her voice calling me *lille* Swanny, I smell the L'Aimant she always wore. The other day I opened a drawer in her dressing table and a gust of her scent came out, it was full of her, and it was so terrible, it made me weep.

I shouldn't write to you like this, I know that. I should be more cheerful or more philosophical. Her death has set me free and there are all sorts of things I used to think I wanted to do when I was free that I can do now. But I don't want to do them, I'm too depressed to do anything. On the brighter side, the doctor has given me some pills and at least I can sleep. I think I shall sell this house eventually so that at least I don't have to live with the memories all round me. Write me a line to cheer me up, if you can.

> With much love, as always,
> Tante Swanny

I hadn't called her Tante for ages, not since I was fifteen and said pertly, the way teenagers do, that I was going to drop the "aunt" and she didn't mind, did she? I think she'd forgotten, she was so low and in such a bad way, she'd forgotten that for years and years I'd called her Swanny like everyone else.

Not that there were many left among that everyone else. Far away from her, in the United States, I found myself trying to work out just who remained to call her by her Christian name. John and Charles, but she hardly ever saw them. Those friends from embassy days, if any contact had been kept up and I doubted if it had.

Daniel's father, that my mother had been going to marry, had sometimes visited but she'd seen very little of him since she became a widow.

If I'd gone home then, as I sometimes thought I'd have to, I suppose I'd have moved in and lived with Swanny. After all, part of my dread of being near Daniel and Cary was a reluctance to go back to my flat where he and I had lived together for five years, where every room was imbued with him, would probably smell of him, the soap he always used and his cigarettes, the way Anna's room smelt of her L'Aimant. I seriously thought of never returning there, of getting someone to clear the flat and an agent to sell it, while I stayed at Willow Road.

I was considering it, knowing how happy it would make Swanny, going so far as to wonder if the house could be divided into two separate dwellings for her and me, when another letter came from her, saying she had decided to move.

I don't like to ask you, as you very likely have other plans, but it would be wonderful if you could be home for Christmas. Do you remember the lovely Christmases we used to have? Christmas means so much to a Dane, the house always so beautifully decorated, the dinner on the Eve. Even last year when poor Mor hardly knew where she was we kept up the tradition, had the almond hidden in the rice, the fruit soup, the goose and the *aeblekage*. I would try to do something like that if you came, even if it were just the two of us.

My news is that I've decided to move. This house suddenly seems enormous. I haven't yet put it into the hands of an agent but I have been going all over it, clearing things out. It is something to do, something to take my mind off my troubles. I didn't realize we had so much stuff.

I started at the top, in the attics which are crammed full of old books of Torben's and the sort of suitcases that are really hanging wardrobes and which no one would dream of carrying today but were all right when porters did all the lifting. Imagine taking one of those on a plane, made of hide and heavy as lead before you even put anything into it!

Poor Mor had so little of her own. Her room will be the easiest to clear when I reach there. I didn't actually realize how few clothes she had left. She must have taken her old dresses and coats one by one to sell at those antique dress places. I wonder what they thought of her. I wonder if they appreciated how wonderful she was or if they thought in their ignorance that she was just a stupid mad old woman.

You can tell how grim I'm feeling by that last sentence, that I can even suppose for a moment people would feel like that about my darling mother. My darling mother that I loved so dearly. For I did love her, Ann, I loved her much more I believe most old people love an aged parent. I wanted her to live, I *prayed* for that. How she would have laughed!

Well, it's no good going on like this. As I've said, I've worked my way through the attics and am making a start on the bedrooms. You must let me know if there's anything I've got that you would like to have. That sounds as if I thought I was going to die myself but I hope you know what I mean. I shall have to get rid of a great deal if I am going to buy a little house up on Holly Mount, which is what I intend.

How is your work going? Did you go to that Thanksgiving dinner you said you'd been invited to? Let me know if there's a chance you'll be home in the next three weeks.

With all my love,
Swanny

I didn't go home for Christmas. I kept thinking of Cary and her treachery. She was more on my mind than Daniel was. I remembered the way she was always telling me how good-looking Daniel was.

"He's so good-looking, Ann!" as if she was surprised such a man should have fallen to my lot. And later, when she was visiting us and he, perhaps, had left the room for a moment, "He's so good-looking," with a sigh, as if his good looks were too much for her, as indeed they proved to be.

But "He's so good-looking!" as if there was nothing else to him. Perhaps there wasn't, though during those years when we were together, he had seemed sensitive and thoughtful, a good listener, witty sometimes, a man who laughed a lot and made others laugh.

But Cary, who was nothing if not honest with me when she had succeeded, even explained her unforgiveable theft with the same excuse.

"He was so good-looking, Ann."

She used the past tense. I noticed this particularly. It was as if his looks had been used for the purpose of capturing her and now they were gone. He looked the same to me, I saw his familiar face with ineffable pain and intense jealousy, but she never mentioned his good looks again, at least not in my hearing.

They were living in a house he had bought in Putney. An old college friend who had kept in touch wrote and told me that. These days they'd have bought it jointly but it wasn't so easy to do that fifteen years ago if you weren't married. Then my friend told me their wedding had taken place and a weight was lifted from my shoulders. I was the reverse of Cleopatra when the messenger told her Antony had married Octavia. It wasn't that I was less unhappy, less jealous, but the finality of it made me accept. There seemed now no more hope and therefore no more fear, no more waking in the night and thinking, suppose he has left her, suppose he's trying to find out where I am. No more speculation as to what I'd do if I heard it hadn't worked out and he was free again. I've never been married so I suppose I take an old-fashioned view of marriage. Or else the ones I've seen in my own family have always endured. Whatever it is, I think of it as a permanent indissoluble tie and I saw Daniel and Cary (erroneously, as it happened) as bound to each other for life.

What was left to me was a dull misery, something not very different from the feeling Swanny had. Or so I supposed. It brought me closer to her, this sense of a shared wretchedness. Perhaps I should go home and share it properly. By then it was February and bitterly cold in the neighborhood of Boston. Snow lay deep and the airport was closed. There was still plenty of work for me to do but nothing I couldn't finish by the end of the month. I wrote to Swanny, suggesting I might come and stay with her "for a few days" before moving back into the flat. It was a further two weeks before I heard from her and when the letter came it was to welcome me whenever I chose to come, but in a preoccupied way, referring to my proposal with a vagueness quite unusual in her. She had found something to do in the meantime, something to distract her mind. There wasn't a word in the letter about moving.

It would be satisfying to say that when Swanny found the diaries she knew at once; she was aware at once that she had discovered something marvelous. And this, in fact, was what she said later on. The various journalists who interviewed her were regularly told how a tremendous excitement took hold of her when she opened the notebook and read the first page and she knew she had come upon a great work of literature.

The facts about her feelings were otherwise, if her letters to me are a true record, and I believe they are. Two of them came before I left for home and both mentioned the notebooks she had come upon while clearing out. She got to the one lying on the desk in Anna's room first, her progress being from the top downwards. This was the last diary, the final entry made in September six years before.

Swanny wrote at the end of a long letter:

> I went through Mor's room yesterday, turning things out. Did you know there was a "secret" drawer in that black oak table of hers? There's a sort of frieze of carving all along each side and I noticed one side seemed to stick out more than the other, so I pulled it and it turned out to be a drawer. Possibly Mor herself didn't know about it as there was nothing in it but a really ancient photograph, sepia of course, and looking as if it had been taken before Mor was even born. A remarkably ugly fat woman in a crinoline, scowling furiously at the camera!
>
> There was a notebook lying on her desk. Of course I looked inside and when I saw her handwriting hope sprang up quite wildly. I actually thought I might find something vital inside, something about who I was. At the same time I was rather reluctant to read it, it seemed like a private thing, but I did read one page and then I saw the date was 1967, so that was no use.
>
> Without exactly reading the rest, I could see it was a diary. It made me feel awfully guilty, Ann. I thought, poor darling, did we

make her feel out of things, Torben and I? We were so wrapped up in each other that perhaps we excluded her, so that she used to go upstairs and put her thoughts down in that notebook . . .

The second letter was much shorter. I had to wait until I got home for a full account of her tidying the coachhouse and her discovery there. In the letter she wrote only:

I have found a great mass of notebooks Mor seems to have used as diaries. Mor keeping a diary, who would have imagined it? I counted them and there are sixty-three. They are all written in Danish and the first one begins before I was born in 1905!

They were all damp and bent and spotted with mold. But there must be literally hundreds of thousands of words, great thick notebooks full of words on both sides of the page. Isn't it the most extraordinary thing?

The phone rang while I was getting ready to go to dine in Roderick Road. It was Paul Sellway. For a moment I had to think who this was. I said I hadn't expected him to answer my question.

He seemed taken aback, then said quite reasonably, "Why did you ask it then?"

"Something to say, I suppose. It's always rankled a bit with me, I mean that my mother didn't teach me Danish. There must be some unconscious resentment that has to find outlets. Anyway, did they?"

"Did they what?"

"Teach you Danish?"

"No, they didn't, I'm afraid. My mother couldn't speak it and my grandmother wasn't allowed to. My mother bullied her rather. She was always telling her that if you lived in England you should be English."

He was silent for a moment and I was trying to think of something to say when he said, "But I do speak it and—well, read and write it and all that. It's my job to, I mean it was what I studied at university."

"I thought you were a doctor."

"Not of medicine." He laughed. "That's my mother, telling people I'm a doctor when what she means is a D.Phil. She'd prefer me to be a G.P. I teach at London University. Scandinavian languages and literature. And that brings me to why I'm ringing you. I had a feeling you wanted help with those diaries, the ones that aren't yet published. The tone of your letter, it sounded wistful, I suppose that's what it was. But maybe I'm quite wrong."

"No," I said, "no, you're not wrong."

We made an arrangement to meet the following week. He said to come to dinner but I wouldn't do that. His wife would be there, or I guessed she would, and though I hadn't any wish to un-marry him, though I bore Mrs. Sellway no illwill, I had had too many experiences of being the unmarried third, the odd one out, at meals with married couples. In a way, I was about to play that role this evening. He said he would come to Willow Road where, after all, the diaries were.

I asked myself why I wanted him to look at the translations and compare them with the diaries, or rather, to check that the missing pages hadn't been torn out *after* the translation was made, and I decided it was because I wanted to do Cary's job for her. I wanted to cut the ground from under her feet. Not out of malice, never that, I was long over that, but simply to be able to present her (by post, if possible) with a fait accompli and thus avoid ever having to see her again.

Someone said that nothing ever happens to a man but that which is like him. He, whoever he was, was proved wrong that evening. Formal, correct, conventional Gordon lived in a flat with black and purple walls, hung with paintings in pink and purple acrylic of androgynous people that owed their musculature to the figures on the Medici tombs. Low divans were upholstered in silver lamé, the bathroom was full of phalluses faintly disguised as trees or towers or pointing fingers, we ate at a green glass table off black bone china and Aubrey draped over our laps black napkins printed with the face of Michelangelo's David.

The theme was continued in his clothes, black velvet ski pants, a T-shirt that was a collage of Pre-Raphaelite faces. But Gordon wore what I was sure must be his usual summer gear, gray flannels, a white shirt and dark tie, and a garment I hadn't seen on anyone for twenty years, a sleeveless V-necked knitted pullover. Dinner was wonderful and the wine spectacular. If I hadn't drunk rather a lot of it I probably wouldn't have asked a question that might have been taken as a reproach.

"Why did you never go to see her?"

I expected him to say she was only a great-aunt, they'd had no contact since his grandfather's death, perhaps even that he didn't know her precise address. He looked puzzled.

"But I did. Didn't you know?"

"You went to Willow Road? You saw Swanny?"

He looked at Aubrey and Aubrey just lifted his shoulders, smiling.

"I suppose I thought you must know, I mean that she'd have told you." If you had heard him speaking and not been able to see him you'd have thought from his pedantry, his precision and what Anna would have called his old-maidishness, that he was at least fifty. He gave a little dry cough. "Let me see, I called the first time about a year ago. It was the height of summer, wasn't it, Aubrey? A woman came to the door, I suppose it was the housekeeper, I saw her at the funeral, but she wouldn't let me in. She said Mrs. Kjaer wasn't well but she'd tell her I'd called."

"Wasn't well" was, no doubt, a euphemism. That would have been one of Swanny's days for being her other self, the shuffling carpet-slippered persona with the wrinkled stockings and the knitting bag. It was understandable that Mrs. Elkins hadn't let him in.

"I tried again the next week. Of course I was anxious to see her for herself, you can understand that, but I also wanted to ask her the questions I've asked you. But I was turned away again and I must confess—well, I wouldn't say I was offended, but I came to the inescapable conclusion I wasn't welcome. And then a very odd thing happened, didn't it, Aubrey?"

"I took the call. I was amazed."

"Aunt Swanny phoned me. I'd left my number with the housekeeper that first time. She said she was sorry she hadn't been able to see me on those previous occasions but she was better now and would I come to tea?"

"It seemed such an appropriate thing," Aubrey said, "a great-aunt inviting one to tea. What other meal could it *rightly* be?"

"Did you go?"

"Oh, yes, I went, and we had a splendid tea, very old-fashioned and with cress sandwiches. I had to work quite hard at concealing from her that I hadn't read the diaries. She said she'd made a kind of rough family tree herself and she'd look it out and send it to me."

"But she never did," said Aubrey.

"No, she never did. And now we come to the curious part." Gordon's eyes twinkled. I half-expected him to ask me if I was sitting comfortably. "She phoned and invited me to go with her on what she called a voyage of discovery. Of course I said yes and could I bring my friend? You see, Ann, if Aubrey were my girlfriend or my wife (or my boyfriend or my husband, depending on how you regard it) I would have asked. We like to take things for granted and make other people take things for granted, don't we, Aubrey?"

He nodded, but smilingly, very laid-back. All the earnestness was Gordon's.

"So I said I'd like to bring my friend who is a man and with whom I share my home and she said, fine or something like that, and on the appointed day we went round and called for her. She had said a taxi but we thought going in Aubrey's car would be much nicer."

"Going *where?*" I said.

"To this house in Hackney. It was something of an adventure, I can tell you. She said it was the house where she was born and her parents lived and I must say we were impressed because it was quite big. Of course it was divided into flats and very much—well, bedizened, wasn't it, Aubrey? We all went in and she talked to this man who had the ground floor and who seemed to be a sort of caretaker for upstairs as well. And there was some story about a ghost which none of us took very seriously. And she seemed satisfied and we went home again."

I felt disproportionately upset and shocked. "When was this, Gordon?"

"I can tell you the exact date. It was the day before Aubrey's birthday, August the twelfth, a Wednesday."

Swanny had had her first stroke in August. I would have to look up the date but I was sure it had been on the thirteenth because Mrs. Elkins had remarked on the ill luck associated with that date. Why hadn't Swanny asked me to go with her to Lavender Grove? What had made her turn to Gordon Westerby?

Aubrey offered me brandy and I accepted, something I seldom do. They had begun to talk about their summer holiday which they intended to spend in Denmark, rooting out Westerby and Kastrup ancestors. Would I see if I could find the family tree Swanny had made and spoken of? Meanwhile, I answered Gordon's questions as best I could.

It wasn't late when I phoned for a taxi to take me home, no more than a quarter to eleven. The wine and brandy I'd drunk sent me immediately into a deep sleep and awoke me again at three sharp, headachey but alert and with a drumming heart.

I put the light on, took three aspirins and, sitting up in bed, read Donald Mockridge's account of the trial at the Central Criminal Court of Alfred Eighteen Roper.

14

THE TRIAL OF ALFRED ROPER

The trial of Alfred Roper for the murder of his wife was one of the last in which Mr. Howard de Filippis, K.C., appeared at the old building of the palace of justice called the Old Bailey. On October 16, 1905, the court was presided over by Mr. Justice Edmondson with Mr. Richard Tate-Memling appearing for the prosecution. Roper was charged with murdering his wife, Elizabeth Louisa Roper, on or about July 27, 1905, by cutting her throat, to which charge he pleaded not guilty.

Mr. de Filippis, a huge man of exceptional height and with bright piercing eyes, strode into the court preceded as usual by three clerks: one carried a pile of handkerchiefs, one a carafe of water and two glasses and the third an air cushion. These "props" were to be used by the great advocate in tricks of the trade or distraction tactics and were seldom employed to greater effect than in the Roper case.

Mr. Tate-Memling was an altogether smaller man—physically smaller, that is, for so commanding was his presence and effective the power of his voice that those present in the court soon forgot the insignificance of his stature. His voice was particularly famous, mellifluous, almost seductive, the tones of an actor but one on the stage of life itself.

The judge, the former Queen's Counsel Lewis Wilford Edmondson, was well known for the silence he maintained throughout the trials over which he presided. Far from interrupting the proceedings with those enquiries and interpolations, witty or merely bothersome, that so often distinguish other members of the judiciary, he shed upon the court an oppressive coldness, listening intently, observing circumspectly, speechless for much of the process.

The jury was charged to try the case for the murder of Elizabeth Roper, and Mr. Tate-Memling, having paused and surveyed the court in utter silence, having once eyed the equally silent and glowering judge, opened his address.

He said that the case was a very serious one and one that would command the jury's serious attention. Upon the morning of Friday August 4 was discovered in a room on the second floor of Devon Villa, Navarino Road, Hackney, the body of a married woman, Mrs. Elizabeth Louisa Roper, and lying close by her the body of her mother, Mrs. Maria Sarah Hyde. However, Mrs. Hyde's death was a natural one and need not concern them at this time. Mrs. Roper's death was due to having had her throat cut from ear to ear and she had been dead for at least a week.

He spoke of the accused's life at Devon Villa with his wife, his mother-in-law, his children and the various other persons who inhabited the house. The accused, he said, had been a pharmacist and apparently hoped to follow that calling again. He had, therefore, a degree of specialized knowledge of certain drugs. The court would hear how, during the spring and summer of 1905, he had administered to his wife, regularly and over a period of some six months, a quantity of hyoscin hydrobromide, a substance highly toxic unless given in carefully controlled doses.

The aim had no doubt been to bring about Mrs. Roper's death. The marriage was not happy and Roper had expressed a wish to take his son to another part of the country and live there without his wife. However, in spite of the sustained administering of hyoscin, Mrs. Roper did not die. The day came for the accused's departure for Cambridge and still Mrs. Roper lived and throve.

Indeed, she expected to follow her husband within a week and to resume cohabitation with him in Cambridge.

It was the prosecution's contention that at about four-thirty on the afternoon of July 27, the accused and his son left Devon Villa in a hansom cab for Liverpool Street Station, there to take the five-fifteen train for Cambridge. However, when they reached the station, the accused told his son, a boy of six, that he had left a silver sovereign case, usually attached to his watch chain and containing four sovereigns, at home and must return for it. This same story he told to a porter whom he asked to look after his son till his return and to the cab driver who had brought him thither. The accused then returned to Navarino Road, Hackney, where he went upstairs to retrieve the sovereign case. In the bedroom he found his wife sleeping, under the influence of the drug he was administering to her. He cut her throat with a bread knife and returned to Liverpool Street, again by cab, having been gone for an hour and a half.

Father and son, having missed the five-fifteen train, caught the eight-twenty for Cambridge, arriving in that city at nine-forty p.m. No murder could be more demonstrative of the cool callousness of its perpetrator than this calculated planning and arranging of the crime, culminating as it did in a train journey to a new life accompanied by the murdered woman's own child.

EVIDENCE FOR THE CROWN

Dr. Thomas Toon said he was an M.D. and one of the official analysts to the Home Office. He examined the body of Elizabeth Roper at Devon Villa, Navarino Road, on the morning of Friday, August 4.

The position of the body (he said) was normal as during sleep. The head was on the pillow and the face calm and peaceful. Blood was everywhere; the bedding was soaked with blood, now perfectly dry.

The wound was very deep, extending from the lobe of the left ear to the lobe of the right ear, the head almost severed from the body, being only attached by the muscles. Everything had been cut through to the vertebrae. It was an incised cut, very deep, and once inflicted the deceased would have been unable to cry out. The carotid artery, the windpipe, the jugular vein and the pharynx down to the spine had all been severed.

From the condition of the stomach he concluded that the deceased had been murdered several hours after last partaking of food. Death must have been instantaneous. In his opinion, the weapon used was very sharp and used with great vigor. The wound could not have been self-inflicted. He could not, and cannot, form any accurate opinion of when the accused met her death beyond saying that it took place in something of the region of a week before the body came to his notice.

Later, at the mortuary at St. Bartholomew's Hospital, he further examined the deceased's body. (Here Dr. Toon described the condition of certain organs of the body as healthy and said that Mrs. Roper had borne at least one child. She had not been pregnant at the time of her death.) In the stomach, liver, spleen and kidneys, he found hyoscin hydrobromide present, to the extent of just under a grain. In his opinion, hyoscin had not contributed to Mrs. Roper's death.

The prosecution then called Dr. Clarence Pond, a pharmacologist, to tell the court the properties of hydrobromide of hyoscin. He gave its chemical formula and described the substance. It was toxic only in large doses. A lethal dose was five grains.

He was shown a sugar basin by the police. (The sugar basin was then put in as Exhibit A and Dr. Pond confirmed that this was the basin he had been shown and the contents of which he had analyzed.) He said that he found the contents of the basin to be made up of approximately seven ounces of sugar and something over five grains of hyoscin hydrobromide.

Mr. de Filippis had had no questions for Dr. Toon but he rose to cross-examine the pharmacologist.

"Dr. Pond, is not hyoscin used as a sexual depressant in cases of acute nymphomania, in inmates, for instance, of lunatic asylums?"

"That is so."

"Is not that its principal use?"

"It is one of its uses."

"I will put my question in simpler language and ask the jury to pardon a coarseness of terminology they will understand to be necessary. The principal use of hyoscin is to suppress strong sexual desires, is it not?"

"It is."

Detective Sergeant Arthur Hood said he went to Devon Villa as a result of information brought to Hackney Police Station on Friday August 4 by Miss Florence Fisher. He saw Mrs. Roper's body in a bedroom on the second floor. The bedroom windows overlooked the garden at the rear of Devon Villa. Later, accompanied by Detective Constable Dewhurst, he searched the garden and found in a flower bed a large bread knife, the blade of which was encrusted with dried blood. The knife was lying in a flower bed close to the house and up against the fence dividing that garden from the one next door, as if it had been thrown from an upper window.

The bread knife was put in as an exhibit and Detective Sergeant Hood identified it as the one he had found. He said that on Tuesday, August 8, he accompanied Detective Inspector Lawrence Poole to the village of Fen Ditton in Cambridgeshire where the accused was living. The accused accompanied the two officers back to London where he was charged with willful murder at Hackney Police Station. Detective Inspector Poole charged him and Detective Sergeant Hood was present while he dictated a statement and later signed it.

Samuel William Murphy, cab driver of Judd Street, King's Cross, said that at about 4:30 p.m. on Thursday July 27 he was waiting at the cab rank in Kingsland High Street when a boy employed as a cabbie's runner approached him. As a result of what the boy said to him he went to Devon Villa in Navarino Road to pick up a fare for Liverpool Street Station.

He could see the fare in court. It was the prisoner Alfred Roper. The prisoner had a boy with him. When they reached the station the accused recollected having forgotten his sovereign case and he asked Mr. Murphy to take him back to Navarino Road, having first handed the boy into the care of a porter. Mr. Murphy took the accused back and left him there. He was not asked to wait.

Robert Grantham, cab driver, of Dalston Lane, Hackney, said that at about 6 p.m. or somewhat after he was waiting at the cab rank in Kingsland High Street when a man approached him and asked to be taken to Liverpool Street Station. He took him there and last saw his fare entering the station precincts.

Mr. Tate-Memling: "Was there anything remarkable about this man?"

"He had cut his hand."

"Which hand?"

"I cannot say that."

"Did you see the cut?"

"No, he had wrapped his hand in a handkerchief. The blood had come through and there was blood on his coat sleeve."

Mr. Tate-Memling (who must already have known only too well the unpromising answer to this question): "Would you know the man who was your fare again, Mr. Grantham?"

"Not to say know. I could say who he was not. I could say he was not you or his Lordship."

Lord Justice Edmondson, making an uncharacteristic interruption: "You may refrain from such negative identifications, Mr. Grantham."

"I thank your Lordship. Can you see the man who was your fare on July 27 in court?"

"I might. I cannot be sure. He was not a young man but he was not old either. I did not take much notice of him. When you have as many fares as I do you do not take much notice of facial appearance."

Mr. de Filippis, in cross-examination: "But you take notice of their hands?"

"Sometimes I do."

"You cannot remember a man's face but you can remember he had a handkerchief tied round his hand?"

"I do remember that."

"Was your fare the accused man, Alfred Eighteen Roper?"

"I do not know. It is a long time ago now."

At this point Mr. de Filippis sneezed loudly. He asked sotto voce for a handkerchief and was given one from the top of the pile and water was poured from the carafe into one of the glasses for him.

"I beg your pardon, my Lord. Would you repeat that, Mr. Grantham?"

"Repeat what?"

"I asked you if your fare was the accused, Alfred Roper."

"I can only say that to the best of my recollection, I do not know but he may have been."

John Smart, described as a clerk of Lillie Road, Fulham, he who had been Alfred Roper's best friend, was the remaining witness for the prosecution. Smart's presence there caused something of a flurry in the public gallery and there were gasps of indignation when Mr. de Filippis asked him if he were not the closest friend the accused had. Were you not the friend, Mr. de Filippis asked, to whom he confided the innermost secrets of his heart?

Mr. Smart was obliged to admit that he was. Before that, in giving his evidence, he told how on the occasions when they had met Roper had several times told him of the unhappiness of his marriage. On a day in April 1905 they had met in an ABC teashop in the neighborhood of Leicester Square.

He said that on that occasion the accused told him of a situation vacant as manager of a pharmacy in Cambridge. Smart said the idea was an excellent one and advised the accused to apply immediately. By these means, Alfred could remove his family from the evil influence of his wife's mother and start a new life. But this was not in Alfred's mind. Rather he meant to leave his wife and her daughter and begin this job in Cambridge as a widower with an only son. He confided to Smart his belief that the child Edith was not his. Roper believed, Mr. Smart said, that his wife was unfaithful to him. He confided in Smart that she made demands on him he was unable to satisfy and this led, he concluded, to her need for other men.

Examined, Mr. Smart went on to say that on another occasion, again in April of 1905 he thought it was, they had met in order to pay a visit to some city churches, as was their habit. The laughter which greeted this remark was immediately suppressed by the judge who asked Mr. Smart to go on. The accused had told him, he said, it was his opinion that his wife Lizzie would go with anyone. It was an illness rather than a vice. He was treating her for it.

"Treating her in what way?"

"He would not tell me then."

"But he did tell you later?"

"Yes, my Lord. He said he was giving her hyoscin. He was giving her hyoscin in the sugar she took in her tea so that she should not know."

"Should not know what?"

"That he was giving her medicine, my Lord."

"Did you know the properties of hyoscin?"

"I knew it was a poison."

"Did you know it as a sexual depressant?"

"No, I did not. He said it was but I did not know it."

Rising slowly to his feet, taking another drink of water, Mr. de Filippis then asked his question about Mr. Smart's position as the prisoner's closest friend. The court no doubt expected a rigorous cross-examination with particular reference to the description of hyoscin as a poison but all Mr. de Filippis said was: "Were you acquainted with Mrs. Elizabeth Roper?"

"Yes, I was."

"You met her on several occasions?"

"Yes."

"Sometimes, no doubt, you found yourself alone with her?"

"Once or twice, yes, when I arrived early and the prisoner was not yet home."

"Did she—let me put this as delicately as I can—did she ever demonstrate to you, as a man, these amative tendencies alleged to be characteristic of her?"

"No, never."

The laughter which ensued was once more suppressed by the judge who threatened to clear the court if it were repeated. But Mr. de Filippis had made his point. The woman who "would go with anyone" had not found John Smart sufficiently attractive to make advances to him. He was a man scorned, which might as much as anything account for his presence as a prosecution witness.

That was the case for the prosecution in *Rex v. Alfred Eighteen Roper.*

OPENING SPEECH FOR THE DEFENSE

Mr. de Filippis: "My Lord, I submit that there is no case to go to the jury. The law is well established that the presumption of innocence is in favor of an accused person until his guilt is proved. In the first place there is an absolute and utter want of evidence that the weapon which perpetrated the deed was ever in the hands of the accused. Secondly, there is an absolute and utter want of evidence that this crime was committed during the early part of the evening of July 27. There was scarcely time for the commission of such a crime and, moreover, no signs about the person of the accused immediately after the alleged commission of this crime that he might have perpetrated it. Thirdly, there is not a suggestion of motive attributed to the accused. His point of contention with the deceased had been satisfactorily settled by the treatment he was administering to her. I ask Your Lordship to say that the accused ought not to be put in any further peril on such evidence as that which has been put before the court. It is a matter for Your Lordship to decide whether the jury is here for the purpose of trying mere suspicion."

Mr. Justice Edmondson: "I cannot say there is no case to go to the jury."

Here Mr. de Filippis was seen to move his lips soundlessly and bow his head a fraction. He took another clean handkerchief and put it to his mouth. After a few seconds he spoke.

"I will now call the accused and other witnesses. Roper shall speak for himself in the witness box and it will be for you, gentlemen of the jury, to judge his story. We will put that man into the witness box and you will see an injured man, a man who has suffered two of the worst blows fortune can inflict upon a breadwinner and father of a family in our degenerate days: the loss of his lucrative and satisfactory employment and the inconstancy of her who should be his loyal wife and helpmeet. You will see a man bowed down by care and well-nigh broken by the persecution and reverses of fate he has suffered—but you will see too an innocent man, prepared to tell you with absolute honesty the history of his recent life.

"I will now come to that life. For all of it Alfred Eighteen Roper has been an honest and industrious man. There is not a stain upon his character, not even the faintest adumbration of a stain, gentlemen. All that has reference to Alfred Roper is as limpid and decipherable as an open book. There are no encoded passages in it and no uncut pages. It is a work which any of you without fear or hesitation might put into the hands of your womenfolk. It is pure and unsullied. Let us therefore read some of its early chapters.

"From the premature death of his father when he was sixteen years old, Roper had been the support and mainstay of his family. It was with a woman's care that he tended upon his aged invalid mother and with a brother's manly duty that he saw to the welfare of his younger siblings. Only when his mother died did he leave the family house in Bury St. Edmunds and seek his fortune further afield. With the promise of an excellent situation before him as manager of a pharmaceutical advertising company, he left his native Suffolk and came to London. Who will be surprised to learn that there, after such early years as he had passed, he found himself an innocent abroad?

"In London he sought and found lodgings which he believed, innocent and trusting young man that he was, would supply him with a comfortable home and resting place when his day's labors were done. There, too, he sought and found, as man must sooner or later do, a wife. Is there one among you who would attach blame to him if the wife he found proved to be other than the spotless epitome of virtue an honest man has a right to mate with?

"Be that as it may, he married her and lived with her in her mother's house at Devon Villa in Navarino Road, Hackney. In the fullness of time a son was born to Mrs. Roper and later a daughter.

By now Roper, his innocence gravely bruised, had found his happiness to be alloyed. It was well known and a cause of scandal in the neighborhood that Mrs. Roper had so far forgotten her matrimonial duty as to have commerce with men other than her husband, so much so that Roper became convinced the second child was not his.

"However, rather than seek the remedy of divorce, which would unquestionably have been his, and realizing so far as he knew the cause of his wife's dereliction, he set about treating the condition he was magnanimous enough to describe as an illness. His remedy seems to some extent to have been successful, so much so that, rather than separating himself from his wife, he set in motion plans for a new life for all of them. He would move them from the outskirts of London to the healthier air and rural environs of Cambridge, where he had secured for himself a situation as that for which he was qualified, the manager of a pharmacy.

"I will now come to the events of Thursday, July 27.

"Roper had made arrangements to travel to Cambridge by train with his son and there stay with his sister in the nearby village of Fen Ditton until such time as he could secure more permanent accommodation for himself and his family in the city. Mrs. Roper was to follow him within a week or so when such an abode would surely be theirs. During the late afternoon of the day in question, he bade good-bye to his wife and her mother and with his son and some amount of luggage took a cab to Liverpool Street Station. However, on his arrival he realized to his annoyance that he had left behind a much valued possession, a silver sovereign case which had been the property of his father, and which moreover contained money he would be in need of. Leaving his son and the luggage in the care of a porter, he returned in the same cab to Navarino Road.

"Although he naturally possessed a key to the house, he did not let himself in with that key, gentlemen of the jury, as he must surely have done had he arrived there with guilty intent. No, he rang the doorbell. This man that you see before you on the most serious charge for which a man in our society may be arraigned, the wilful murder of a fellow mortal, far from attempting to conceal his presence, far from moving, as the bard tells us, towards his design like a ghost, boldly and publicly rings the doorbell. And the doorbell was answered.

"Miss Florence Fisher, the maid, answered the door and admitted Roper to his own home. He told her why he had come back, to retrieve his sovereign case, and he went upstairs. Did she thereupon hear cries, pleas of mercy, a commotion? She heard nothing. Peace reigned. Silence reigned, until some twenty minutes afterwards, Miss Fisher heard the front door quietly close.

"Roper walked to the cab rank in Kingsland High Street. On his way there he stumbled over a curbstone and fell, breaking his fall by putting out his hand to save himself. In such circumstances it is his right hand which a right-handed man puts out and it was Roper's right hand that was cut.

"He wrapped his wounded hand in his handkerchief and continued to the rank to summon a cab. He returned to Liverpool Street Station. This man who is here charged with brutally killing a woman by the heinous and hideous act of cutting her throat, returned to his son and the porter in whose charge he had placed him, in no greater state of agitation than might be expected of a man who had sustained an unpleasant fall and through his own absentmindedness had missed his train.

"But he finally arrived in Cambridge at twenty minutes to ten that night and made his way to his sister's house in Fen Ditton. His first intimation that anything untoward had taken place at Devon Villa, Navarino Road, was when two police officers arrived at his sister's house to speak to him on the forenoon of Tuesday, August 8.

"I cannot, for my part, understand the methods the police have adopted in this case. They have not looked elsewhere, they have gone no further afield in their search for the perpetrator of this terrible crime. No, members of the jury, they have merely concluded in a manner that sheds upon our society a shocking cast that the most probable murderer of a woman is that man who of all men should be her protector, her support and a steadfast rock to her—her husband.

"They have concluded it but they have not proved it. The prosecution has come nowhere near proving it. By editing certain evidence and excluding other, the prosecution has not even approached revealing Roper as the author of one of the most atrocious murders of modern times."

EVIDENCE FOR THE DEFENSE

The housemaid and cook general at Devon Villa was beyond a doubt the most important witness for the defense. Conversely, she might with equal appropriateness have appeared for the prosecution. Her evidence was unbiased. If she disliked Roper she did not show it, nor show the faintest sympathy for him. If she disapproved of Lizzie Roper and her mother she showed none of that either. She had an earnest straightforward manner and an obvious intention to tell the whole truth.

At the time of the trial Florence Fisher was twenty-three years old and had been in service with Maria Hyde since she was thirteen, her residence in the house just predating Roper's own. She was a tall well-built young woman with curly red hair and blue eyes. These details are known to us from the account of her knowledge of the Hyde-Roper household given to *The Star* newspaper by a neighbor in Navarino Road, Cora Green. She was healthy and strong, according to Mrs. Green, and a hard, willing worker. Mrs. Green also said—attempting perhaps to please the newspaper which liked romantic tales, though it was doubtless true—that Florence Fisher was engaged to be married.

Mr. de Filippis asked her how long she had been employed at Devon Villa and what her duties were. He then asked her to tell His Lordship and the jury what happened on the morning of Monday July 10.

"My master, Mr. Roper, told me he was giving me notice from the end of the month. He said the family would be moving to the north except for Mrs. Hyde. Mr. Roper said Mrs. Hyde would be on her own so would not need a servant."

"What did you do then?"

"I did not want to leave. I went to Mrs. Hyde and asked her to let me stay and she said—"

"You must not tell us what Mrs. Hyde said, only what you did. What did you do as a result of what Mrs. Hyde said to you?"

"I stayed at Devon Villa. I made no efforts to find a new place as I then hoped to be married in the New Year."

"Is it a fact that your marriage did not take place because your engagement was broken and you are now in service with Mr. and Mrs. Sumner at Stamford Hill to the north of London?"

"Yes, sir."

"You must address His Lordship, Miss Fisher. So you remained at Devon Villa and were there on July 27?"

"Yes, My Lord."

"Please tell the court what happened on Thursday, July 27."

"Mr. Roper came to me in the afternoon and gave me half a crown. He said we should not meet again as I would be leaving and he was going to Cambridge to take up a new position. He was taking Edward with him and going by train. Mrs. Roper and the baby would be coming to join him soon. He did not say when, he said soon."

"Did you see him leave the house?"

"No, I did not. I was in the kitchen with Mrs. Hyde. She said to me that Mrs. Roper was feeling unwell and she would take the baby as she usually did at this time so that Mrs. Roper—"

Mr. de Filippis waited rather a long time before reproving Miss Fisher. The jury may not have known why but Mr. Tate-Memling certainly did and was on his feet just as Defending Counsel said: "You must not tell us what Mrs. Hyde said to you unless the accused was present. Was he present?"

"No."

"What did you do as a result of what Mrs. Hyde said to you?"

"I cut some bread and butter. I opened a tin of salmon and put this and some other food on to a tray with milk for the baby and a pot of tea and the sugar basin."

"Did you carry this tray upstairs to Mrs. Roper?"

"No, Mrs. Hyde carried it up."

"What time was this, Miss Fisher?"

"It was sometime after five."

"You cut the bread for the bread and butter with the bread knife?"

"Yes, my Lord."

Here the bread knife with which Mrs. Roper's throat was cut was shown to Miss Fisher who looked at it and turned visibly pale. Mr. de Filippis filled his second glass from the water carafe. He asked the witness if she would like a drink of water and if she would like to sit down.

"No, thank you, I am quite all right."

"Then, Miss Fisher, will you tell his Lordship if the knife you have just been shown and to which, if I may say so, your reaction has been one of considerable fortitude, is the knife with which you cut the bread for Mrs. Hyde sometime after five o'clock that evening?"

"Yes, it is the one."

"What did you do with the knife after you had used it?"

"I put it under the tap, my Lord, and wiped it and put it in the drawer."

"The drawer where it was always kept?"

"Yes, along with the breadboard."

"What happened then?"

"The doorbell rang. I went to the door and Mr. Roper was there. He said he had forgotten his silver sovereign case."

"Did you know what he meant?"

"Yes, my Lord. He was very fond of that case. It had been his father's. He would not have wanted to go away without it."

"Did he go into the kitchen?"

"I do not think he did. There would not have been time for that. I went into the dining room to take away some linen for the wash. I heard Mr. Roper go upstairs while I was in the dining room. I took the linen to the kitchen."

"When did Mr. Roper leave the house?"

"After about fifteen or twenty minutes. I did not see him go but I heard the front door close."

Florence Fisher then described how that evening had passed and the following morning. She had neither heard nor seen anything of Lizzie Roper and Maria Hyde. During the evening it had been very warm and she had taken a chair outside and sat in the backyard. In the morning at about eight Edith had come downstairs on her own, a usual occurrence. Florence gave her her breakfast in the basement kitchen. Edith could not speak more than a few words so did not say where her mother and grandmother were.

The judge: "You must not say what the child said to you."

Florence Fisher: "She did not say anything."

Mr. de Filippis: "Thank you, my Lord. Miss Fisher, were you surprised not to see Mrs. Roper and Mrs. Hyde?"

Miss Fisher: "No, my Lord, I was not surprised. They often did not get up until late in the morning or at lunchtime."

"Did you in fact see them at all that day?"

"I did not see any of them that day. I sent the child back upstairs to her mother because I had to go out shopping. I did not see any of them ever again after that."

Mr. Tate-Memling began his cross-examination. It was only then perhaps that the jury and the public must have understood Mr. Justice Edmondson's decision that there was certainly a case here to go to a jury, for all Defending Counsel had submitted.

"Miss Fisher, you have told his Lordship and the jury that you prepared a tray of food with a teapot, milk jug and sugar basin on it, and doubtless with teacups too, at Mrs. Hyde's request."

"Yes, I did."

"Who carried that tray upstairs?"

"Mrs. Hyde did."

"Did you not know Mrs. Hyde suffered from a bad heart?"

"Yes, my Lord."

"You knew too, or you could see, that she was an elderly lady. How old are you, Miss Fisher?"

"I am twenty-three."

"Yes, you are twenty-three and Mrs. Hyde was sixty-seven, was she not? Miss Fisher, when you admitted the prisoner to the house at about five-thirty on July 27, was there any discussion between you on the subject of the missing sovereign case?"

"I said I would help him look for it."

"And what did he say to that?"

"That it would not be necessary. He said I must have work of my own to do and I said, yes, I had the linen to collect for the wash. You had better do it then, he said, and he opened the dining room door for me."

The long pause Mr. Tate-Memling then left was undoubtedly for this significant statement to register with the jury. He cleared his throat after a full half-minute and continued.

"Miss Fisher, do you take sugar in your tea?"

"I beg pardon, sir?"

"I will repeat the question. I assure you it is seriously meant. Do you or do you not take sugar in your tea?"

"No, I do not."

"Did the other members of the household at Devon Villa take sugar in their tea?"

"Only Mrs. Roper took sugar. Mr. Roper did not take it and nor did Mrs. Hyde. Edward did not drink tea."

"But the deceased, Mrs. Roper, always took sugar?"

"Oh, yes, my Lord, I have seen her take three heaped tea-spoonfuls."

"Very well, Miss Fisher, you do not take sugar in your tea. Does your encratism extend also to the eschewing of bread and butter?"

Mr. Tate-Memling, in being clever, in hoping to bring a smile to the lips of the better educated among the jurymen at this humble housemaid's expense, defeated his own object. She had not the faintest idea what he was talking about and turned on him a look of total blankness. Rousing himself from his lethargy, the judge was moved to a rare intervention.

"You had better put it in plain English, Mr. Tate-Memling. I for one have no idea what encratism may be and have not a dictionary about me."

Mr. de Filippis here made a sound like a bray, which may have been laughter, but which he turned into a loud sneeze that occasioned the handing over of yet another handkerchief. He picked the air cushion off the tray and began to blow it up, doing so in utter silence.

"I beg Your Lordship's pardon." (Mr Tate-Memling was very stiff.) "Miss Fisher, let me put it another way. It was five o'clock in the afternoon when you handed the tray with the bread and butter and other foodstuffs on it to Mrs. Hyde. No doubt you did not go to bed for some hours. Did you eat nothing yourself during the evening?"

"I ate some bread and butter. I cut bread and butter for myself while I was cutting it for Mrs. Hyde. Then I washed and wiped the knife and put it away.

"Did you eat bread in the morning for your breakfast?"

"No."

"Did you give the child bread?"

"No, she had porridge."

"Did you open the drawer where the bread knife was?"

"Not then."

"When did you next open it?"

"I do not know. I cannot say. Not that day."

"Not July 28?"

"No, I am sure of that. I was not well. I did not eat anything. I came back from the shops and I was ill. It was a hot day. There was no one in the house, or so I thought then. I went to bed."

"Eccentric as it may seem to you, the court is indifferent to your somnific arrangements, Miss Fisher."

"Mr. Tate-Memling!" the judge said—sharply for him.

"I am sorry, my Lord. Miss Fisher, when did you see the bread knife again?"

"I never saw it again, my Lord. The police found it. I think it was out in the garden."

Here Mr. de Filippis placed the air cushion on the seat behind him and sat upon it, heaving an audible sigh. Mr. Tate-Memling looked at him before continuing.

"When did you find the bread knife to be missing?"

"I do not know. I looked for it on the Sunday, that would be Sunday the 30th, and it was not there."

"But you had not looked for it before, had you? You had not looked for it since five o'clock on July 27?"

"No, I had not looked for it."

"Bread, as we all know, gentlemen of the jury, is man's staple diet. The Scriptures tell us that man cannot live by bread alone but by the spirit, thus implying that whatever sustenance his soul may crave, the only food required for his material needs is bread. You members of the jury might, most likely would, confess that you have never so long as you can remember gone *one* day without it. Yet Miss Fisher is asking you to believe that she passed three days without bread, that she went for three days from the evening of July 27 until July 30 without a morsel of bread passing her lips. Is that what you are saying, Miss Fisher?"

"I was not well. I was not hungry."

Mr. Tate-Memling paused significantly. He then said: "While you were in the dining room, fetching the linen for the wash, where was the prisoner?"

"In the hall, I suppose."

"You suppose. You could not see him, of course."

"I heard him go upstairs."

"How much time elapsed—er, passed, between the time you went into the dining room and the time you heard him go upstairs?"

"A very short while."

"How short a while, Miss Fisher? A minute? Half a minute? Fifteen seconds?"

"I cannot say."

"May I crave Your Lordship's indulgence and request that we all observe one minute's silence for Miss Fisher—and the jury—to make an assessment of how long that period is?"

"If you must."

"I thank Your Lordship."

The minute's silence was observed. Florence Fisher said that had been a longer time than that which passed between her entering the dining room and hearing Roper go upstairs.

"Was it more than half that time?"

"I think it was less than that time but more than half that time."

"It was not until Friday August 4 that you went upstairs to the second floor of Devon Villa, was it, Miss Fisher?"

"No, not until the Friday."

"You were employed at Devon Villa to clean the house, were you not?"

"And to cook and look after the baby."

"But you were employed to clean the house?"

"Yes."

"Yet you did not go above the first floor to clean anything for seven days?"

"I thought they had all gone to Cambridge."

There was some laughter in court but not enough for the languid Mr. Justice Edmondson to call for order. Mr. James Wood, a porter with the Great Eastern Railway, of Globe Road, Bow, came into the witness box. He said he was at Liverpool Street Station at about five minutes to five on the afternoon of Thursday July 27. A man he now knew to be the prisoner came up to him and asked him to take care of a boy aged about five or six and a quantity of luggage. He gave him sixpence. He said he had left something at home which he needed and would return when he had fetched it.

Mr. de Filippis: "Did he return?"

"Yes, he did. He was away about an hour or more. More like an hour and a half."

"When you saw him again, how did he seem?"

"He was a bit put out because he had missed his train. I would say he was agitated. He said he had had to walk a long way to find a cab. He had a bandage on his right hand."

"A bandage or a handkerchief?"

"A white cloth of some sort."

"What did you notice about his clothes?"

"To the best of my recollection his clothes were just as they had been when he asked me to look after the boy."

"There were no stains or marks on his clothes?"

"There was nothing on his clothes that I can remember."

Cross-examining, Mr. Tate-Memling asked: "Did you not think an hour and a half a very long time for a man to go by cab from Liverpool Street to Hackney and back? Why, he could have walked it in the time."

"My Lord, I must protest!"

Mr. de Filippis had sprung angrily to his feet. "My Lord, what qualification or knowledge has Prosecuting Counsel for making such an assessment? Has *he* walked it? I doubt if he could even tell the jury the distance involved. What possible function is it of his to estimate the athletic feats of which Mr. Roper may be capable?"

"Very well. That remark had better be expunged from the record. Go on, Mr. Tate-Memling, if you have anything more to ask. And you may omit the ambulatory calculations, to use the sort of language you are fond of."

But Mr. Tate-Memling had nothing more to ask the witness. No doubt he was confident that, for all the reproof he had received, he had made a strong and telling point in the matter of the distance from Navarino Road to Liverpool Street. He sat down well satisfied as Alfred Roper himself entered the witness box.

15

THE TRIAL OF ALFRED ROPER (CONTINUED)

A journalist, Robert Fitzroy, who attended the trial and was present throughout the whole proceedings, wrote his own account of it afterwards and included a meticulous description of Roper. "He was," he wrote,

> a man who appeared far older than his actual years, his hair already sprinkled with grey and receding to show a huge wrinkled brow. Over-tall [the inescapable conclusion here is that Mr. Fitzroy himself was a short man] and thin to the point of emaciation, he walked with a pronounced stoop, his shoulders bowed and his head hanging forward on his breast so that his chin pinned the lapels of his coat against him.
>
> He was dressed in black which seemed to increase the extreme pallor that made him appear a sick man. Dark rings encircled his eyes which themselves burned like coals. Under his high cheekbones were deep hollows of shadow. His mouth was wide but without firmness and his lips trembled so frequently that he needs must be constantly compressing them in a repeated nervous gesture.
>
> His voice, as he came to answer the questions put to him by Mr. Howard de Filippis, was a surprise, shrill and almost squeaky. From those tragic lips, gazing at that rugged countenance, we expected sonorous tones and elegant vowels but heard the accents of a rustic backwater uttered in an old woman's squawk.

It is easy to say now that Roper was his own worst enemy and that his appearance did not help his case. He never once addressed the judge by his title. Nor did he volunteer a particle of information apart from that which was specifically asked of him. It may have been that his life, his wife's death and the circumstances of his arrest and trial had broken his spirit, but he gave the impression of invincible dullness. This was a man, the public may have decided, with whom no woman could have lived without going mad or else taking up with other men.

His counsel asked him about his marriage and his manner of living and was answered in monosyllables. When he came to the matter of the hyoscin Roper was rather less taciturn. He was heard to give a heavy sigh.

"You obtained hyoscin hydrobromide, did you not?"

"I bought it. I signed the poisons book."

"Did you give hyoscin to your wife?"

"I mixed it with the sugar she took in her tea."

"How much did you give her?"

"I was careful not to use too much. I mixed ten grains with a pound of sugar."

"Will you tell his Lordship the purpose of administering hyoscin to your wife?"

"She had a disease called nymphomania. Hyoscin suppresses excessive sexual feeling."

"Did you at any time intend to bring about your wife's death?"

"No, I did not."

When Mr. de Filippis took him through the events leading up to his departure from Devon Villa on July 27, Roper again became monosyllabic. His chin sank upon his breast, he muttered with bowed head, and had to be asked to speak up.

"When you returned to the house you did not ask the cab to wait?"

"No."

"Why was that?"

"I thought I might be a long time."

"Why did you think you might be a long time?"

"I could not recall where the sovereign case was."

This was better. He had uttered a sentence of nine words. Mr. de Filippis asked: "Will you tell His Lordship why you did not let yourself in with your own key?"

"I had no key. I had left it behind. I did not expect to return there."

"You were leaving that part of your life behind you?"

"Yes."

"You were admitted to the house by Miss Florence Fisher. What did you do?"

"I went upstairs."

"Did you go straight upstairs?"

"No, I looked for the sovereign case in the hat stand drawer first."

"The hat stand in the hall?"

"Yes."

"That would have taken you a few seconds? Half a minute?"

"Yes."

"Then you went upstairs?"

"Yes."

"What did you do upstairs?"

Here Roper seems to have recollected that he was on trial for his life. Convicted of this crime, he would certainly have been hanged and the execution carried out a bare three weeks from this day or the next. To use a current phrase, he pulled himself together.

"What did you do upstairs?"

"I went up to the second floor and into my wife's bedroom—the bedroom I shared with my wife, that is. My wife was there and her daughter Edith and her mother. My wife was in her nightclothes but not in bed. There was a meal on a tray and tea things."

"Did you speak to them?"

"I asked my wife if she knew where my sovereign case was. She said that as far as she knew it was on my watch chain. Most of my clothes were in my luggage but there was a suit in the wardrobe that my wife meant to bring with her to Cambridge. I looked through the pockets of the suit but the sovereign case was not there."

"Did you look elsewhere?"

"I looked through the drawers of a tallboy. I remember that my wife said I must have missed my train. I said good-bye to them once more and as I was leaving the room remembered that I had put the sovereign case on the dining room mantelpiece that morning. I found it there and left the house."

"How long were you in the house?"

"About fifteen minutes or rather more."

"Did you go into the kitchen?"

"No, I did not."

"You never went into the kitchen and took a bread knife out of the drawer?"

"Certainly not."

"You proceeded to the cab rank in Kingsland High Street. What happened on the way?"

"I tripped over a loose stone at the curb in Forest Road. I put out my hand to break my fall and grazed it. My hand was bleeding so I wrapped it in my handkerchief. I found a cab and was driven to Liverpool Street Station where my son was waiting for me."

"Did you kill your wife?"

"Most certainly not."

"You did not kill your wife by cutting her throat with a bread knife?"

"I did not."

The court adjourned and on the fourth day of the trial Mr. Tate-Memling rose to cross-examine Roper. He too elicited mostly monosyllables from the accused man as he took him painstakingly through the early years of his marriage, his conviction that Edith was not his child and the confidences he made to John Smart. When he came to the purchase and administration of the hyoscin he asked Roper how he had come to know its properties and Roper told him without hesitation he had read about the substance while employed by the Supreme Remedy Company. Mr. Tate-Memling placed great emphasis on the toxic properties of hyoscin.

"Five grains is the lethal dose, is it not?"

"I believe so."

"You have heard Dr. Pond say so. I do not suppose you dispute his statement. You would agree with him that five grains is the lethal dose?"

"Yes."

"You have told the court you placed ten grains in the sugar basin in the sugar that only your wife took?"

"Yes, but mixed in a pound of sugar."

"Never mind the sugar. You placed twice the lethal dose of this toxic substance in a foodstuff that only your wife used?"

Here Roper showed his first sign of indignation. He said: "That is not the way I would put it."

"You are saying then that you are a more accurate authority on the subject of toxic substances than Dr. Pond?"

"No, but—"

"I think the point has been made. When you returned to Devon Villa at about five-thirty on July 27, why did you not use your own front door key?"

"I had not got it on me. It was in the house."

"With the sovereign case perhaps?"

"I do not know where it was."

"When she had let you in Miss Fisher went into the dining room?"

"I do not know where she went."

"She went into the dining room and you went into the kitchen to find the bread knife?"

"I did not. I looked for my sovereign case in the hat stand drawer. I could not find it so I went upstairs."

"I put it to you that when you went into your bedroom you found your wife alone and asleep in bed."

"She was not asleep."

"I put it to you that she was asleep, as she often was at this time of day, as a result of the somniferous effects of hyoscin?"

"She was not asleep and she was not in bed."

"Did you not find her a ready victim, deeply asleep, in a drugged sleep, alone and in bed?"

"No."

"She was so deeply asleep that she did not stir or cry out when you cut her throat from ear to ear?"

"I did not."

"Although you covered your body with the counterpane you could not keep the blood from your right hand and your coat sleeve?"

"The blood came from the graze on my hand."

Over and over Mr. Tate-Memling took Roper through those ten minutes which passed while he was in the house but Roper did not weaken or alter his replies. Mr. de Filippis blew his nose and drank some water. He had used up five of the clean handkerchiefs and only one remained. The final drama came when counsel for the prosecution asked the accused a question that was inevitably charged with emotion. A gasp went up from the public gallery, not at the question but at Roper's reply.

"Did you love your wife?"

"No, I no longer loved her."

CLOSING SPEECH FOR THE DEFENSE

Gentlemen of the jury, I thank you for the unbroken attention you have given to this case. I should just like to remind you that you must return your verdict—the responsibility of which is yours—not on the speeches of Counsel or the summing up of the learned judge, but on the evidence and the evidence alone.

The Crown has not yet set aside that presumption of innocence which is the groundwork of our criminal law. I had hoped that my friend, at the close of the case for the Crown, would have said he would carry the case no further, resting as it did solely on suspicion. But I do not know that I regret it, now that you have heard the defense. It is my submission that it will compel you to return a verdict of not guilty.

Is it possible that a man would carry out such a murder in broad daylight in a house also occupied by two other women and a child? Is it possible that he have himself admitted to the house, though in possession of a key of his own? And having blood upon him, make no attempt to conceal it by washing his hand or his coatsleeve but merely cover his bloodstained hand with a handkerchief?

Is it possible that, having planned a murder, he would leave the obtaining of a weapon to the merest chance, so that securing it depended upon the unlikely absence from her usual place of duty of his domestic servant?

I have listened carefully to some sort of suggestion of motive. There are two kinds of murders: those which are motiveless and those which have a motive. A motiveless murder is that done by a practically insane person. I ask you, gentlemen of the jury, where is the motive for this murder?

Does a man murder his wife merely because he has ceased to love her? If that were the case, so sorry have certain aspects of our society become and so negligent of the old-fashioned virtues many of its members, that wife murder would become a commonplace. No, such a man settles down to a life of duty and obligation or else has recourse to the law which, in this case particularly, would have swiftly granted him his freedom. If, indeed, his misery grows insupportable, inflamed perhaps by jealousy and passion, there have been instances in which he makes a spontaneous attack of violence upon his wife and thereby brings about her death. He does not plan it, down to the deliberate mislaying of keys and sovereign cases, to the prearranged drugging of his victim and the assuring that all witnesses to his crime be occupied in other parts of the house.

Where is the evidence of a condition of mind that would account for the perpetration of this crime? Has the prosecution called witnesses to testify that they overheard Roper make threats against the deceased? Have you heard evidence of quarrels between the accused and the deceased? Had there been a single act of violence perpetrated against the deceased by the accused prior to the act which brought about her death? No to all these. No, no and no again. We have solely Alfred Roper's own statement, which you as humane men, men experienced in life, may see as tragic, may even find yourselves moved near to tears by it. "No," he said, "I no longer loved her." That has been his sole comment, gentlemen, on the years of suffering and upon his own state of mind: "I no longer loved her."

Whether he, as a man who was not a medical man, should have taken it upon himself to treat his wife for what he diagnosed as an illness, is not for you or me to judge. But there is one thing we can say, one thing that all who heard his simple testimony might say. It was a better thing that he did, a kinder, more generous, more forbearing thing, than the action of a man who, on less evidence than he had, would have dragged his wife into the divorce court or separated himself and his children from her.

I must strongly impress upon you, members of the jury, that you are trying the accused for murder, not for making unsound judgments or usurping the function of medical doctors. Remember that. Though there may be evidence of folly here and of imprudence, there is none of murder, and upon what the Crown has put forward I defy you to hang this man.

I must remind you that the precise time of the death of Mrs. Roper is not known and now never will be known. It may have taken place on the evening of July 27 but on the other hand it may have taken place on the following day. There is no evidence, medical or circumstantial, to point either way. As far as I can see the only thing the prosecution has against my client is his having a bandage upon his hand when he arrived for the second time at Liverpool Street Station. Not blood, gentlemen of the jury, mark that. Not blood. The man Mr. Grantham took to Liverpool Street may have had blood upon his hand but you must remember that Mr. Grantham could not identify his fare. Though he could say his fare had blood upon one of his hands, he did not know which one, he could not identify that fare. He could not pick him out in this court.

Mr. Wood, the porter at Liverpool Street, saw a bandage upon Roper's right hand. He saw no blood. You have no more reason to believe the man Mr. Grantham saw with blood on his hand was Roper than that it was any other man he may have transported to Liverpool Street on that evening.

Apart from this, all that the prosecution has against the accused
is that he was a husband and is now a widower. He was a husband
whose wife was murdered—*ergo,* says the prosecution, he must be
guilty of that murder. Never mind those other men, very possibly
those many other men, who had passed through this unfortunate
woman's life over the years both before and, alas, after, her marriage to the accused. They have not been considered. They have not
been found. At the very least, they have not been looked for.

If you are satisfied beyond all reasonable doubt that the man
standing there, on the evening of July 27, murdered Elizabeth
Roper, although it breaks your hearts to do so, find him guilty and
send him to the scaffold. But if, under the guidance of a greater
power than any earthly power, making up your minds for yourselves on the evidence, if you feel you cannot honestly and conscien-
tiously say you are satisfied that the prosecution has proved this
man guilty, then I tell you it will be your duty as well as your
pleasure to say, as you are bound to say, that Alfred Roper is not
guilty of the murder of his wife.

CLOSING SPEECH FOR THE CROWN

I ask you, gentlemen of the jury, not to attach any importance to
an apparent absence of motive. Evidence of motive is of great
assistance to a jury in coming to a decision, but it is never absolutely necessary. There are some cynical men who would tell you
that any married man has a motive for murdering his wife, though
I would not be among them. I would, however, tell you that of all
those persons surrounding Elizabeth Roper, no one had a stronger
motive for wishing to disembarrass himself of her society than her
husband.

Whatever she may truly have been, to him she appeared—and
I am obliged to use strong language—a libidinous, licentious and
immoral woman, a woman of voracious sexual appetites. Can we
suppose that he thought it feasible to drug her for the rest of
her natural life? Without doing so, could he contemplate living
with her?

But proof of motive is not imperative, most particularly in a crime like this where the circumstances surrounding its commission are so singular. I would ask you, before we begin to look once more at those circumstances, if it is within the bounds of possibility, not to say the bounds of probability, that any other person, whatever his motive might be, would have had the means and the knowledge to commit this crime. Would some casual visitor to the house have known where the bread knife was kept? Would he have known that Mrs. Roper frequently fell into a drugged sleep at this hour, that being the time after which she had drunk her afternoon tea, liberally laced with hyoscin? Would he have been able to count on finding her alone and asleep? Would he have been aware that at this precise time the deceased's mother was in the habit of taking her granddaughter from the room so that the mother could rest undisturbed?

The prisoner, gentlemen of the jury, knew all these things. Knowing too exactly where the bread knife was kept, he calculated that to fetch it would be the work not of a minute or half a minute but a mere fifteen seconds. In order to accomplish that he took care, you will have noted, to send his servant into the dining room where she could not be a witness to his securing the bread knife. With a courtesy that we have no reason to suppose habitual with him, he opened the dining room door for her to pass into the room.

The defense has made much play with the word "suspicion." There has been an attempt which I can only call absurd to persuade you, members of the jury, that there is no case to go before you. It was not an attempt which succeeded with the learned judge.

Could any honest man looking at the facts before you dispute the seriousness of the evidence of the blood on the prisoner's hand and his deliberate sending of Miss Fisher out of the way in his ruthless quest of the knife with which to commit this deed? Could any man of perspicacity view the facts of the prisoner's long administration of a toxic substance to his wife and place upon it no more sinister interpretation than that of a desire to calm the unfortunate woman's passions?

Are these suspicions? One of the definitions of the word "suspicion," gentlemen of the jury, is the imagination or conjecture of the existence of something evil or wrong without proof. It does not apply here. This is not suspicion. There is suspicion in this case, suspicion of the prisoner's contriving of a plot, suspicion of his hoping for his wife's death from poison, suspicion that he deliberately left his sovereign case behind when he traveled that first time to Liverpool Street Station.

But there is no suspicion that he administered a toxic substance to his wife over many months, that he drugged his wife on the afternoon of July 27, that he sent Miss Fisher out of his way so that he might secure unobserved the weapon with which to kill his wife. All this is evidence.

I ask you to act not upon suspicion but upon evidence, the evidence which is before you now.

THE CHARGE TO THE JURY

A change generally came over the demeanor of Mr. Justice Edmondson when the time came for him to sum up. His lethargy was shed and those who suspected he had not been attending or that he was indifferent to the proceedings, understood that their suspicions were unfounded. It was not that he suddenly became alert. It was not that he began to speak in circumlocutory or mellifluous phrases but rather that he showed a grasp of what had gone before and a mastery of the facts, an absolute ability to distinguish between the subtle hints of the defense and the prosecution and the true hard evidence. He embarked slowly and with gravity upon his charge to the jury.

I am exceedingly glad that I am at last able to congratulate you, gentlemen of the jury, on the fact that your labors are approaching an end. I cannot say that it will be any reward to you, but it may be some satisfaction, to know that you have been engaged in one of the most remarkable trials that is to be found in the annals of the Criminal Courts of England for many years. That the unfortunate woman had been done to death there is no doubt. She was murdered in a most remarkable way. There is no doubt that the murder was committed by someone who knew well how to put a person quickly to death.

I have tried a great many murder cases but I have never before tried one in which a woman was apparently murdered in her sleep by a single blow delivered with great force and apparently without a struggle. This poor woman was murdered in her sleep, without ever waking again in this world, by one blow inflicted with great force and skill, with great coolness and determination.

A great deal has been said about the absence of any clear motive and no motive has been shown by the prosecution. It is my duty to tell you that in these cases it is not a safe test to ask what was the motive that induced a person to commit such an act as this. We none of us can control, we are not able to control, human thought or feeling or fathom the workings of the human heart. You know from the records in the past that many of the most brutal murders have been committed without any apparent motive which would be appreciated or have any effect upon the mind of an ordinary individual. Therefore, it must not be assumed that, because no motive has been shown on the part of the accused, he is not guilty.

It is your task to determine this case on the evidence and if the evidence be sufficiently strong to convince you that the accused did the deed, you must convict him. This case has been conducted on both sides in the best possible manner, in a way that is worthy of the best traditions of the English Bar. Mr. de Filippis has set forth his defense in the most able and masterly manner. He maintains that the accused is not only entitled to a verdict of Not Guilty but that there is no evidence against him. And if you believe implicitly the story told by the accused and on his behalf, then he did not commit the murder. There is not an atom of direct evidence against him, for we do not know and can never know when this murder was committed. You must keep in mind that it may have been committed at any time between half past five on the evening of Thursday July 27 and the hour of twelve noon or thereabouts on July 28.

The great difficulty of the prosecution in this case is the question of time. Looking at the evidence, I must say that we have no more reason to believe Elizabeth Roper died on the evening of the 27th of July than that she died during that night or on the following morning. We have no more reason to believe that the prisoner secured the weapon from the kitchen on the evening of the 27th than that someone else did so on the morning of the 28th. On the question of time again, you may discount the time the accused took traveling from Devon Villa to Liverpool Street Station a second time. He tripped on a curbstone and fell. He bound up his hand. He was delayed. You have no reason to dispute any of this.

The main evidence against the accused is his undoubted administration to his unfortunate wife of a toxic substance. He may or may not have intended by the means of this substance to bring about her death. He may or may not have intended it for a less sinister purpose, the suppression of her libidinous needs. The point is not what he intended but what he achieved and Mrs. Roper did not die of hyoscin poisoning but of having her throat cut. It is important that you remember this when you are considering your verdict.

Much play has been made by both sides on this question of the administration of hyoscin by an unqualified person. You must disregard the fact that ten grains is a fatal dose and that the prisoner on his own admission made an admixture for his wife's consumption of ten grains to a pound of sugar. He knew, as we know, that she would not consume something over a pound of sugar in one, I think I may say "fell swoop," but gradually, over many days, at perhaps the rate of an ounce per day.

Although undoubtedly it is my duty to do all I can to further the interests of justice so that criminals are brought to justice and properly convicted, it is also my duty to inform you, and to tell any jury, that however strongly animosity is felt against him, you must not find a verdict of guilty against the accused unless no loophole is left by which he can escape. In my judgment, strong though suspicion is, I do not think the prosecution has brought the case home near enough to the accused.

As it is, I do not think the evidence is sufficient to justify you in bringing in the accused man Guilty. Unless you place more weight than I think the facts warrant on Miss Fisher's statement about the opening of the dining room door, unless you see this as a purposeful diverting of Miss Fisher's attention from the kitchen, you have no evidence at all on which to connect the accused with the weapon that was undoubtedly used. Here too you must take account of the time involved and ask yourselves if a man in his position, intent upon the terrible deed he is alleged to have been intent on, would have taken the risk of emerging with the knife from the kitchen and meeting Miss Fisher in the passage. You must ask yourselves also if a man who had blood on his hand and his coatsleeve from so terrible an act would have bound up his hand to cover it rather than have washed it off.

In dealing with circumstantial evidence it behooves judges and juries to be most careful before they convict a man. It is therefore my duty to point out that unless the effect of the evidence is so conclusive that there can be no doubt in anyone's mind, you should give him the benefit of the doubt and say that he is Not Guilty. You are not bound to act on my views at all, but it behooves us to be most careful before we find a man guilty of such a charge. It is, of course, a matter for you and you alone, gentlemen.

I am now going to ask you to retire to consider your verdict. Weigh carefully in your minds the evidence heard from both sides. If you think the prosecution has proved the case against the accused your verdict will be one of Guilty; if, on the other hand, it has not done so, if there is any loophole, however small, your verdict must be one of Not Guilty.

Two officers were sworn to take charge of the members of the jury and they retired at 2:35 p.m. They were absent for two hours and a half. It was not easily nor without dispute that they had come to their decision.

Clerk of arraigns: "Gentlemen of the jury, have you agreed upon your verdict?"

The foreman: "We have."

Clerk of arraigns: "Do you find the prisoner at the bar Guilty or Not Guilty of the wilful murder of Elizabeth Louisa Roper?"

The foreman: "We find him Not Guilty."

Clerk: "Is that the verdict of you all?"

The foreman: "It is."

Mr. de Filippis: "I have to ask Your Lordship that the accused may be discharged."

The judge: "Yes, certainly.

"Gentlemen of the jury, you have been put to great inconvenience by being kept here so long. I am extremely obliged to you for the great care you have taken throughout the case. In recognition of the time and labor you have devoted to this case, I shall make an order exempting you from further service on juries for a period of ten years."

16

THE TRIAL OF ALFRED ROPER (CONCLUSION)

Roper was free to return to Cambridge or, if he chose, to Devon Villa. Because the law says that when two people die in circumstances where there is no witness or other confirmation of time of death, the younger shall be supposed to have survived the elder, Roper, as his wife's natural heir, inherited from her the house in Navarino Road. Without gainful employment, he attempted to live there with his son and to let out rooms as a means of livelihood. However, no lodgers came and he soon suffered from the active hostility of his neighbors.

Everyone knew who he was. Most believed he was guilty. His windows were repeatedly broken. One summer evening a man fired a shot at him from an air rifle while he was in his front garden. Children called out after him in the street and the best he could expect from their parents was to be pointedly ignored by them. He became a clerk with a firm in Shacklewell but when his employers found out who he was he lost his job.

Eventually he moved to Cambridge with his son. His sister's husband, Thomas Leeming, took pity on him and offered him a storekeeper's job. This position Roper held until his death fifteen years later.

Edward enlisted in 1915, advancing his age, actually sixteen, by two years, but he did not meet his death until the last days of the Great War, dying in action in the autumn of 1918 at Argonne. After his son's death Roper gave up the little house he was renting and went to live with his sister and her husband outside the city in the village of Fen Ditton. There he died seven years later of malignant kidney disease.

In the twenty years since his wife's murder he is said never to have enquired after the child who bore his name but whom he refused to acknowledge as his daughter. He knew, of course, that she was missing and that in those early days after the discovery of Lizzie's body a massive search had been mounted for her. The police subjected him to intensive questioning about the child which he called harassment and this continued sporadically even after he had gone to Cambridge.

He never once gave the slightest indication that he knew what her fate may have been. Perhaps, indeed, he was as ignorant as the rest of them.

She was a baby, fourteen months old, healthy and strong, not only able to walk but able to climb up and down stairs unaided. According to the Metropolitan Police records, she had fifteen teeth. Her hair was flaxen, her eyes blue. She had no scars but she did have the distinguishing mark of a rather large mole on the cheekbone under her left eye. In height she measured two feet three inches; her weight was twenty-six pounds, nine ounces.

No photograph of her exists or probably ever existed. She is described as plump and fair with a full face so the chances of her actually bearing the resemblance to Alfred Roper John Smart said she did seem remote. Florence Fisher said she could not speak but it seems she could utter a few words, such as "Mama," "Eddy" and "Fo" (for Florence). On the day she disappeared forever, July 28, 1905, she was dressed in a blue-and-white striped pinafore over a blue flannel dress or petticoat and had a red ribbon in her hair. Florence Fisher was the last person to see her or the last person to remain alive after seeing her. So far as is known. So very little is known.

Florence Fisher was her last link with the world. It was Florence, as we know, who gave her her breakfast that morning when Edith came downstairs on her own sometime around eight o'clock. That breakfast consisted of porridge but no bread was eaten, if Florence is to be believed. Mothers were nervous of milk in the early part of the century. They knew it might carry tuberculosis, also called "consumption" though that was fast going out. Cocoa was popular, so perhaps that is what Edith had.

It is unlikely she could feed herself adequately. Remember that her age was only one year and two months. But she was almost certainly able to drink from a cup. Florence would have had to feed her, wash her face and hands, take her to the privy (there was one outside) or set her on the chamber pot. It was she who dressed Edith in the blue flannel petticoat and striped pinafore. All the while she had her own work to do. Poor Florence!

She sent Edith back upstairs to her mother. Who can blame her? It was hot and she was unwell. Nevertheless, she had the rooms to clean and shopping to do. No refrigerators in those days and no icebox at Devon Villa, so in warm weather food supplies had to be renewed almost each day. Probably she stood in the hall at the foot of the stairs and watched the child go up. If she took a certain grim pleasure in imagining Edith waking her mother and perhaps her grandmother too, again who can blame her?

At ten she went out shopping. A local grocer delivered daily and it is not clear why Florence went to the shops. Perhaps she longed sometimes to be out of that house and this was the only way to make an occasional escape. It may have been to the Broadway market just south of London Fields that she went or to the market in Wells Street or the one in Mare Street where there were also food shops and department stores. In Kingsland High Street was a branch of Sainsbury's. Where she went we have no way of knowing but she was out for two hours.

What happened in her absence?

Lizzie and Maria were almost certainly already dead before Edith appeared that morning, the child's mother lying stiff and cold in her bed, her grandmother not in bed but prone on the floor where she had fallen when her heart stopped. There was no one else in the house. Roper, beyond a doubt, as a score of witnesses could testify, was in Cambridge. When Florence departed for the shops, the child Edith was the only living human being in Devon Villa.

We may picture her clambering up those stairs, a baby, a tiny child not much more than a year old, perhaps calling her mother, "Mama, Mama," though knowing from past experience where to find her. A hard passage, those two long flights of stairs, when one is only twenty-seven inches tall and the riser of each stair eight-inches deep. If an adult man were to undertake a climb of comparable arduousness, each stair would have to be two feet high. He would have to use his hands as she must have done, climbing, pulling, pausing, climbing again. Before she reached the top it is probable she was crying because the expected assistance was not forthcoming.

Did she find the bodies in that room? And if she did and they were cold, did she understand this was not sleep, this was something other than sleep, and was she afraid? Did she observe that blood splashed everywhere? Did she approach that dreadful bed and see the gaping wound where her mother's throat had been? No one knows.

Suppose she made her way downstairs again in search of Florence. By this time Florence had gone out but no doubt, believing Lizzie Roper and Maria Hyde to be in the house, she left the front door ajar as they often left it these hot days. Suppose Edith wandered out into the street in search of Florence and there met her death under the wheels of a cart. Suppose the carter, in terror of what he had done, an unwitnessed act, picked up the tiny body and disposed of it far away. Or imagine some madman or madwoman snatching her up, a child molester searching for prey.

But always we return to the question of what became of her body. It was a very small body, less than twenty-seven pounds in weight, and therefore far easier to dispose of than that of a woman weighing ten or eleven stone. Still, it had to be disposed of. The weather was too hot for domestic fires, furnaces and boilers to be lit. There was a good deal of industry in the district and factories have furnaces, but this solution presupposes Edith's killer having access to one of them.

He could have buried her. If he did so it was not in the garden of Devon Villa, for the police dug that down to a depth of four feet during the second week of August. But they could see there had been no recent interment; the ground was hard and dry. They searched the local parks and open spaces for signs of freshly turned earth and found nothing. Nothing suspicious was seen. No one living in the vicinity of Navarino Road, Richmond Road and Mare Street admitted to having seen Edith Roper on July 28 or ever afterwards. The mystery of her total disappearance remains and now, very likely, always will remain.

There has been no shortage of claimants. Over the years, their appearance triggered off by particular significant events, a sequence of children, young women and later on older women, have presented themselves as Edith Roper.

Edith's brother, Edward, dying at Argonne during the last weeks of the First World War, was the subject of a sentimental piece in a Cambridge newspaper, which at the same time resurrected the whole Roper case, the murder or accidental death of Lizzie Roper, the death of Maria Hyde, Roper's acquittal and Edith's disappearance. Among the results of this article was the arrival at Cambridge police station of a Mrs. Catchpole from King's Lynn with a girl in her early teens she declared to be Edith and whom she said she had brought up as her own, having bought her from a commercial traveler for seven pounds, two shillings and sixpence in September 1905. Mrs. Catchpole was later discovered to have spent the previous two years in a private lunatic asylum. The girl was undisputedly her own daughter.

At the same time a girl aged about fifteen was at Hackney Police Station declaring herself to be Edith. She was in service with a family in Hampstead and went by the name of Margaret Smith. Alfred Roper was asked if he would see her with a view to making an identification but this he refused to do, just as he refused to see all the other claimants.

He told a journalist, "I have no interest in her. She was not my child."

Now a couple of national newspapers took the opportunity to revive the whole Roper affair, there were articles by people prepared to swear that they had been at school with Edith or their children had, photographs of young girls said to be Edith and letters from would-be Ediths with all kinds of surnames and from places as distant as Edinburgh, Penzance and Belfast.

It died down at last. Margaret Smith was reported as saying she had tried it on because someone had told her a legacy of a hundred pounds would be Edith's and was at present awaiting its rightful possessor in a Lombard Street bank. No more was heard from other claimants until a novel was published in 1922, purportedly based on the Roper case. This was *For Pity's Sake* by Venetia Adams, in which the child heroine, whose name is Pity, sees her mother murdered by a jealous lover, herself escapes death and is brought up by an eccentric painter who finds her wandering in Tite Street, Chelsea, near his studio.

The publication of this book, though it was far from becoming a bestseller, fetched forth another crop of aspiring Ediths. This time, as was appropriate, they were older. All claimed to be the true age Edith would have been, eighteen. None was able to furnish a shred of proof of identity or even establish a likelihood of identity. One was a mulatto.

Two more presented themselves when Alfred Roper died in Fen Ditton in 1925. Money, again, seems to have been the motive. Roper had died intestate and the few hundreds he possessed been divided between his brothers and sisters. Neither claimant was able to produce any evidence of identity, one being seven or eight years older than Edith Roper would have been. The other had natural parents, both alive and anxious to deny their daughter's claim.

After that, with interest in Roper fast dying, no more claimants appeared for many years. During the 1940s a woman called Edith Robinson wrote an article for the *News of the World* in which she claimed to have been kidnapped from Navarino Road in July 1905 by a man called Robinson and brought up by him and his common law wife in Middlesborough for the express purpose of becoming their son's bride. She had been married to Harold Robinson for fifteen years, she said, and they had four sons. The article appeared as one in a series by people who had gone missing as children. Two weeks later Mrs. Robinson retracted and declared the whole thing to have been a hoax.

She was the last of them. No more Edith Ropers appeared and it is unlikely there will be more. The possibility exists, of course, that when the present writer's account of Roper's trial appears in book form, more claimants will assert their rights. But the odds are overwhelmingly against their being that lost child who was last seen ascending a staircase in search of her mother.

On that summer's day fifty-two years ago, Edith Roper vanished forever.

Donald Mockridge
Moreton-in-Marsh
1957

17

NOVEMBER 11, 1918

Her i Morgenavisen var der nyt om, at Kejseren var stukket af
til Holland. Det hedder sig, at da han blev fodt, blev hans Skulder
flaaet i Stykker af Laegerne, da de forsógte at hale ham i Land
fra Kejserinde Frederick. I den senere Tid har jeg undret mig over,
om det var Aarsagen til hans Ondskab, om det var det, der gjorde,
at han hadede Kvinder, fordi han gav sin Moder og Maend
Skylden for, at de havde beskadiget ham.

In this morning's newspaper was the news that the Kaiser has run
away to Holland. The story goes that when he was born the doctors
tore his shoulder to pieces trying to pull him out of the Empress
Frederick. Lately I've wondered if all his wickedness stemmed from
that, if it made him hate women because he blamed his mother and
men because they injured him.

Mogens' arm was a bit twisted when he was born but I had a
good doctor in Stockholm who taught me to exercise the arm every
day. It got all right. At any rate, they found nothing wrong when
they examined him to see if he was fit to fire a rifle! I've been
thinking a lot about Mogens again, mostly about when he was little,
my firstborn, a nice good boy, very different from his brother. I
could never think of him as Jack, though he became completely

English. Yesterday I reread the letter I had from his commanding officer, telling me how brave Rifleman "Jack" Westerby was and, more to the point when it's a mother reading it, how he died without pain.

You can bear your children dying. What is unbearable is to think of them suffering, to think of that particular person, the child you carried, bleeding and in agony. I did think of that a lot before Colonel Perry's letter came and even now I have doubts, I ask myself, can it be true? Can it be possible that one moment Mogens was alive and well and brave, perhaps pointing his gun at the enemy or charging at their lines, and the next moment that he fell asleep? Being me, I'd like to know the truth. Writing about it helps me, writing about things always helps and I suppose that's why I do it.

Knud will be all right now. I'm sure of that, though I haven't the least idea where he is. Rasmus claims to know this because in the letter which came yesterday Knud put in a codeword. He wrote, apropos this ridiculous dollhouse, "I wonder if you got the Venetian glass you wanted for Marie's windows?" If Rasmus is right that means the Italian Front where everything came to an end when the Austrians got their Armistice last week. But Rasmus wasn't right last time when he thought Knud was in Palestine because he wrote something about a friend being a Good Samaritan. We shall see.

The Allies are meeting in a railway carriage somewhere in France to present their Armistice terms. Why a railway carriage, I wonder. If I wanted to meet an enemy and discuss putting an end to a war I'd do it in a really grand hotel with French cooking and plenty of champagne (of which there is lots in Paris), especially if someone else was paying, as no doubt they are. It appears that I say this because I am only a woman and know no better, as my dear husband told me when I suggested the idea in a cozy marital conversation.

He works on the dollhouse all the evening, and now it's too cold to be outside in his workshop he has brought it into my dining room. Laboriously, before he goes to bed he lugs it all out again so that Marie doesn't see it when she gets up in the morning. Joking apart (I've written this expression in English because I like it so

much, "joking apart") I think working on the dollhouse saved his
sanity after Mogens was killed. I haven't written about this before,
I don't know why not. One day I went out to the workshop for
something and there he was with the plane in his hand, working
away at smoothing a piece of wood, and the tears were pouring
down his cheeks.

I didn't let him see me but went quietly away. It's different for
me, I didn't cry when we first heard and I haven't cried since.
I don't.

FEBRUARY 10, 1919

When we gave Marie the dollhouse this morning she couldn't
speak, she was stunned, she went pale and I thought she was going
to cry. She was afraid to touch it but after a while she stuck out one
finger and gave it a little poke, pulling away as if she'd burned
herself.

She turned away and threw herself into my arms. Rasmus was
mortified, really hurt. He couldn't stop himself, I felt quite sorry
for him.

"What about me? Don't I get a kiss? Who made the thing, I
should like to know?"

He doesn't understand she's only a baby—she was eight today—
and that it was all too much for her, such a grand palace, more an
idealization than a copy of this house. I'm used to it and besides I've
always thought the idea silly, so I suppose I can't see any longer
how wonderful the finished work is.

Marie soon recovered. She's not sensitive like Swanny. Five
minutes later and she was hugging Rasmus, kissing him, opening all
the doors, fetching cushions and pictures out, putting them back all
wrong and shouting for Swanny to come and see. Swanny of course
had seen already and may well have been wondering—I would
have—why Far hadn't made one for her.

She was sweetness itself to Marie. Not a sign of envy or resentment. She had dressed two tiny dolls for her sister, for a birthday

present. They are a bit big for the house but they just fit in, and are supposed to represent Mor and Far, me in a splendid copy of my gas blue mousseline dress and Rasmus in a black suit and with a very lifelike brown beard.

There was no envy but I hate to see her so sad. Mogens' dying has made her sad like a grown-up, grave and quiet and with such a look of suffering on her sweet face. I've asked Rasmus to be especially kind to her—well, just *kind,* for a change—but all he says is, what about him? Who is there to pity him for losing his son? And then he says, what do children know about pain?

MAY 9, 1919

We dined last evening with Mr. and Mrs. Housman. Her brother's widow was there too, though no longer a widow, having married again before her husband was cold in his grave (as Mrs. Housman puts it, though not in her hearing). He and she are called Mr. and Mrs. Cline, which of course comes from the German Klein. His great-grandfather was a German who came here a hundred years ago but people still shouted after him in the street when the war was on. They broke his windows and someone wrote on his house in red paint: "The blood of British Tommies is on your head."

The funny thing is that he was hotter against the Germans than anyone else there last night. He kept saying we had to crush and destroy Germany so that what happened could never happen again. Then everyone started talking about what's going on in Versailles and Mr. Cline said Germany should lose all her possessions over-seas, have her army taken away and the Kaiser should be caught and executed. Mrs. Cline clapped her hands and cheered—she'd had too much to drink—and said she'd laughed out loud when she heard the Germans were protesting about the conditions of the treaty.

I wore my new Quaker-style dress of oyster-white charmeuse and old rose crepe de chine. It's the shortest I've ever worn, showing a lot of leg. Well, I'm not forty yet!

AUGUST 3, 1919

I see I haven't yet noted in this diary the return of Cropper. He has been back two months now and is as handsome as ever, no doubt the result of spending the war as a prisoner instead of in the trenches.

Supposedly, he was never allowed near any of those frauleins or mademoiselles. Anyway, he seems to have kept the faith with his Hansine and they have named the day. "Why next February?" I said. "Why not tomorrow? You're not getting any younger."

She's a few months older than me, so she'll be forty before the wedding.

"You don't have to be young to get married," she said.

"That depends on what you want out of it," I said.

She took my meaning. "I don't want children."

That made me laugh. As if wanting has anything much to do with it. She doesn't know much if she thinks it all stops at forty. But she did give me a surprise when she said, "I've had enough of children."

She no longer bothers to show me any respect. She's barely polite to Rasmus, whom she used to fear so much. I suppose she thinks she has nothing to be afraid of anymore. Cropper is back on the railway, earning a good wage and seems even keener to marry her than she is to marry him. I shall never understand people.

OCTOBER 1, 1919

I've just read, for the third time, a letter which has come from the man who carried Mogens out of no-man's-land. It was July 1, 1916, and he was the sergeant who went looking for one of his officers and before he found this man's body, carried five wounded men to the comparative safety of the British lines. One of them was Mogens. Sergeant E. H. Duke got the VC for what he did. Most VCs didn't survive, so he was lucky.

The Sergeant, which is how I've begun thinking of him, has

invited himself here to tell me about Mogens. That's what the letter is about. His address is Leyton, not too far from here. Of course I can't really judge with English, but it seems a very good, well-written letter for someone who is, after all, a common working man. A far cry, for instance, from the letters the lovelorn Cropper used to send Hansine. When I showed it to him Rasmus said, "I don't want to see him."

"Why not?" I said.

"It would have been another thing if he'd saved Jack's life."

I said he'd done his best but Rasmus, with typical lack of logic or even common sense just said, "His best wasn't good enough."

Once, when I was young, I'd have written back at once and told the Sergeant to come but I'm not young anymore and have learned the value of sleeping on things. Sleep on it and see how you feel in the morning, is what I tell myself. If need be, he can wait a week, it won't hurt him.

NOVEMBER 15, 1919

I wonder if I'm so bitter toward Hansine because she is going to have a love affair and I have never had one.

It took some effort to write that. Being honest isn't easy and it's just as hard on paper. When it's written down it's not over like some remark you make may be. You can reread it and feel the sting again.

Marriage can be a love affair, the only kind indeed respectable women are allowed. Once I thought mine would be but it never was, it was only a swift disillusionment and a long slow winding down.

It's strange really, writing in Danish, knowing as I write this language which is closer to me than any other, is *my* language, the first I ever uttered—I still read my Dickens in Danish—that it is as secret as the writing Mogens used to do when he was a child. He and Knud found that if you dipped a pen in lemon juice and wrote something the words would be invisible until you heated the paper.

Mine is more secret than that in a way because no matter how much the English held my diary in front of the fire they would never be able to read the words.

So I feel I can write without risk that sometimes when I look at a man like Cropper or at Mr. Cline (who at least is a gentleman), handsome men, I feel a curious longing I can't—or daren't—define. I think to myself, if I lived in another world or at another time or in a dream, I might have you or you for my lover. But in this world I never can and never would.

Poor little Swanny has the German measles. When Rasmus heard he said he thought the war was over but apparently they'd started a counterattack.

NOVEMBER 30, 1919

Sergeant Duke came to see me today.

I expected him in time for tea but he was early. Swanny is still away from school with the German measles, so she answered the door when the bell rang. It was Hansine's afternoon off. I was upstairs, getting dressed. Although I haven't worn mourning for Mogens, I put on my black crepe de chine with the satin bands, it seemed more suitable and dignified. But then I asked myself what I was doing, making a false image of myself for this man, this ordinary working man who happened to be braver than most men. So I got back into my navy skirt and crocheted blouse. The only ornament I had was that butterfly brooch.

He is even better-looking than Cropper. Fair haired, tall, a truly military figure. Why on earth had I expected him to be in uniform? The war is *over*. He was wearing a dark suit with a very high stiff collar and black tie. My first thought—it *would* be—was that I should have kept the black dress on.

I walked toward him and held out my hand. He took it in both his and that, for some reason, amazed me. I don't usually notice the color of people's eyes, I can have known them for years and not be able to say what color their eyes are, but I saw his. They're not likely to be as highly colored as mine! The color of his registered with me before I even spoke. They are gray, not a uniform gray but full of tiny gleaming sparks, like granite.

He called me "madam." He said, "Madam, it's very good of you to ask me here," and then, "This dear young lady and I have been talking about her brother."

I sent Swanny away. I had this premonition I'd be hearing things she shouldn't hear. He wouldn't sit down until I asked him to, he was very respectful, yet at the same time I felt this wasn't a man with the soul of a servant. He belongs to himself, he's no one else's, just as I belong to myself.

Emily brought the tea things but I made the tea myself, using the brass spirit kettle. I usually only do this for special guests. He said I must excuse him for staring, he had expected an older lady, and he called me "madam" again.

"You must say 'Mrs. Westerby,' " I said. "You've made yourself an important man, you have the highest honor any man can have. Will you show me your Victoria Cross?"

Imagine, he hadn't it with him. He never wears it. I asked him if he'd known Mogens before the battle.

"Moans?" he said.

I suppose that was the first time I realized how absurd the name must sound to English ears. "Jack," I said. "Everyone called him Jack but his mother," and I explained about names in our family and the language differences and how hard it is to adjust when you come to a new country. He listened as if he really cared, I'm not used to men like that, most of them never listen to what women say. It was distracting us from the real business of the afternoon, all this conversation about names, and I had to bring it back.

I said, "Did you know him at all? I'd like to know how he was beforehand."

"Quite cheerful," he said. "He was a brave boy," and then he went on to say they'd known each other well and talked together a lot. It was finding out they lived so near each other in London that gave them a sort of bond. Mogens told him he'd lived in Hackney, and said precisely where, when we first came to this country in 1905 and the Sergeant said that was a coincidence too because he knew the district well and had had friends nearby at the same time.

I asked him to tell me about that day, July the first on the Somme, and he said, how much did I know? Colonel Perry wrote to me, I said, and told me Mogens had died instantly, not that I believed it.

"I'd like you to tell me the truth about what happened that night."

"War's not the way the people at home believed it was," he said. "If they knew there'd never be any more wars. It wouldn't suit the politicians to let them know."

"What did you do?" I said.

He'd been looking at me with those granite eyes but he turned them away. It was as if he were saying, I can face you when we talk of polite fictions but it's not fitting for our eyes to meet when I tell you these truths. He said he went out into no-man's-land to look for a young officer, a second lieutenant called Quigley, whose soldier servant while searching for him had been killed by stepping on a live grenade. But before he found Quigley he came upon one wounded man after another and each time he managed to bring them in. All this he told with absolute modesty and self-effacement, speaking of it as lightly as another man might of retrieving dead birds after a shoot.

Quigley, when he came upon him at dawn, was dead right up by the German wire, so he left him there and returned in full view of the enemy.

"They never fired on me," he said, "I don't know why not. Perhaps they couldn't believe their eyes. I was looking at them and that's why I nearly stumbled over Jack. I gave him a drink from my water bottle and then I picked him up in my arms but that was too much for them and they started firing on me and got me in the arm. It was another fellow a lot braver than me dragged us both in on a groundsheet."

I would have given ten years of my life to have been able not to ask. But bargains like that can't be made. Either you're the sort of person who can hide from things or else you're not. I'd rather be so unhappy I want to die, and see the facts and look them in the face, than delude myself. What Rasmus wants is his business, he can deceive himself if he chooses, I won't even judge, but I'm responsible for what I am and what I do.

I asked, feeling so sick I could taste the tea I swallowed come up in my throat mixed up with bile. "Mogens was alive then, he was still alive?"

He said, "I could tell you what Colonel Perry told you."

"You tell me the truth."

So he did. I can't write it. I wanted to know and I got what I thought I wanted. Better get on quickly and not write that part. Mogens died two days later in the hospital on the Quai d'Escale in Le Havre.

The Sergeant expected me to cry. I didn't. I don't. I was thinking, this man tried to save my son's life. Why? He wasn't a relative, he hadn't even known him long, yet he risked his own life to save Mogens. I will never understand people.

"Will you come again?" I said. "When we could talk about it together?"

He said he would. I didn't really want to talk about it again, not ever again, but I want to talk to *him*. Am I mad? When he left I gave him my hand. He took it and brought it to his lips. No man has ever kissed my hand before.

18

Swanny wiped their covers with a damp cloth, stacked them in sets of ten, weighted these down with telephone directories and kept them in a warm place. Whether this is suitable treatment for old books that the damp has got to I don't know but it seemed to work fairly well. By the time I got to them, when I went straight to Swanny on my return from America, she had read all the diaries, made a tentative translation of the early ones and had some inkling of their value.

I remember looking at those which she put into my hands as objects rather than books. They smelled of mildew, in spite of being dried out. Their covers were spotted like a mosaic with ineradicable mold marks, a soft pinkish-gray marbling. Anna's writing was clear enough if you read Danish and didn't find her apparent dislike of starting new paragraphs an obstacle to decipherment. I picked up no more than a word here and there. Now I no longer remember which years I looked at, though I saw no stubs of torn-out pages. In any case, the first notebook wasn't among them.

"They were in the coach house," Swanny said, "on the shelves beside Torben's *National Geographic.* I can see exactly what happened. It was that day when the gardener told me she tried to burn some books but his fire had gone out. She wouldn't have wanted to take them all the way upstairs again, so she put them on the shelves down here and forgot about them."

The copy in my hands looked so uninviting I wondered why Swanny had read them.

She looked a little shamefaced. "I caught sight of my own name."

"And you had to see what she said about you?"

"I started reading, Ann, and I got caught up in it. It was like reading a novel. And not just like that, it was like reading *the* novel you've always wanted to read but have never been able to find. Does that make sense?"

It made more sense, though I didn't say so, that having seen her name, Swanny wanted to find out if her own origins were mentioned in this early diary. I could imagine a sick excitement possessing her as she saw that date, July 1905. She blushed. Perhaps I was looking at her too penetratingly.

"I wasn't sure if I ought to read them. I said to myself, if Mor intended to burn them it must have been because she didn't want anyone else to read them. But that's not certain, is it? There could be other motives. I'm sure there *were* other motives. In the first pages she says she doesn't want Far to read them. Hansine couldn't read. Jack and Ken and I used to be very tactful about that. But Mor says very little about not wanting people to know what she was writing, only that Danish is like a code. I thought, suppose she meant to burn them because she thought people might laugh at her? Suppose she thought they'd be found after she was dead and people—I mean, well, you and me, I suppose—would just find them ridiculous."

It didn't sound like Mormor, who had never much cared what anyone thought of her. A more likely reason for an intention to destroy the diaries seemed that she simply had no more use for them, they were finished, done with, actually as well as metaphorically a closed book. She had always hated clutter. Acquisitiveness bored her and so did sentimentality. She kept her diaries because she was a natural writer, she set down her days' events for the reason I suppose most diarists do, for therapy, for the unburdening of the soul. Every day such writers are on the analyst's couch. They are indifferent to the verdict of posterity.

"I'm sure you're right," Swanny said, mightily relieved. She had to justify her behavior, she had to excuse what might be an intrusion into her dead mother's privacy. "That would have been just like her. You remember how she used to get rid of her clothes. When she moved here she sold nearly all her furniture, though God knows we had room for it. She just dumped the diaries because they cluttered the place up. She can't have dreamed of possible future publication."

"Publication?" I said.

"Oh, yes, Ann, why not?"

"All sorts of reasons. It's not easy to get things published."

"Oh, I meant privately. I'm quite well-off, you know. I could afford it." She looked at me wistfully. "A few hundred copies, say?"

I began to tell her how expensive it would be, how publishing a book doesn't just mean printing it and putting a jacket on finished copies but sales, distribution, publicity, promotion, advertising. She interrupted me, she hadn't been listening.

"I've found a real translator. It was really rather clever of me. I went to the High Hill Bookshop and looked at all the novels they had until I found one translated from the Danish. They only had one. The translator was a woman called Margrethe Cooper and I guessed she must be a Dane married to an Englishman which in fact turned out to be the case. I wrote to her care of the publishers and asked her to translate the first diary for me and she said she would and she's doing it now. That's why the first one's not there, the one that starts before I was born."

Not a word about revelations. She was looking limpidly at me, her face open and frank, the way in fact the Westerby women did look when they had most to hide. There was no anxiety in her face, no stress. She looked happier than she had before I went away. She looked younger. It was then that I understood I shouldn't discourage her in this apparently extravagant venture. It was doing her good, it was giving her an interest. Perhaps too she thought it would give her the answer.

I stayed with her for two weeks. Whatever clearing out she had done, by then everything was back in place. When I asked her if she had thought any more about selling the house she looked at me incredulously. She seemed almost affronted and I realized that the idea had passed from her mind as if it had never been. She talked a lot about Anna, said she still fancied she heard her footstep on the stair and heard her voice saying, "Do I smell the good coffee?" I was invited to put my face inside a drawer in her room and experience the Anna scent. But not a word did she say about her own origins or that quest to know which at one time had been an obsession.

If it cost a lot to publish the diaries, she said one day, it would be the money Anna herself left that she'd be spending. But she smiled as if entirely comforted and no more was said about doubting if she had a right to inherit from her mother.

I went home to the place I had then in West Hampstead, bracing myself to face up to ghosts of Daniel's presence. Resolving to sell it and move, to do what Swanny had decided not to do, helped to exorcise them. I could tell myself, I shan't be here long, I don't have to get used to it.

I didn't buy the flat in Camden Town only because there was room in it for the dollhouse but it was a selling point the vendors can't have foreseen. When the time came it took up the whole of that room. Now that Anna was dead and, because of the diaries, the sheer bulk of them, had taken on a further dimension and become a woman with a secret life, the things she had made for the dollhouse also grew more interesting. Up till then they had just been miniature curtains and tiny cushions and tablecloths sewn with small exquisite stitches; now they were invested with her life. As I took them from the rooms and put them in the boxes and bags for removal they looked and felt different, for they were the work of a woman who between the times she sewed them was engaged in a totally disparate task, the committing of her daily life to innumerable pages.

It made her not quite the Anna, the Mormor I'd known, no longer the dollhouse-maker's wife, but someone quite other, someone apart. It was rather as if I had come upon her in a room in Swanny's house, sitting with her back to me, reading her Dickens perhaps, and when she turned round it was another woman's face that she showed me. I asked myself what or whose that face might be but came up with no answers.

Paul Sellway was due to come to Willow Road at six-thirty. I got to the house much earlier, worried in case it wasn't warm or Mrs. Elkins hadn't been in to clean it. But as soon as I stepped into the hall and began putting lights on, I saw that it was perfect, it was as it always had been, a serene and lovely place, the temperature that of a fine summer's day, smelling fresh but, as all houses should be, smelling of nothing. It gleamed as it had always done and everywhere were edges, surfaces, strands and facets of captured light.

On the hall table the Chelsea clock had stopped. No doubt, Swanny had wound it every evening. Now the gilt hands (two of those gleaming objects) on the small round face stood still at ten past twelve. As a child I had loved this clock for the two porcelain people who adorned it, sitting on top of a bank of porcelain flowers, the turbaned sultan in his yellow coat and his odalisque who lifts her veil for him alone. The last Bing and Grøndahl Christmas wallplate was dated 1987. The first one, with two crows sitting on a branch, looking at the prospect of a city, had *juleaften 1899* round its border. There would be a new one coming in time for Christmas. I went to the study, deciding to take Paul Sellway straight into there, and turned up the radiator, though it was as warm as the summery hall.

It occurred to me then that the diaries should be here, not upstairs, and I determined to bring them down before he arrived. They were heavier than I expected and there were more of them than I remembered, or rather I had forgotten how weighty each one of the sixty-three was. Four trips up and down stairs were needed to move the lot. When I'd finished I wondered where to put them. There was no vacant drawer in the desk, no empty bookshelf. Besides, I felt they should be put away somewhere, out of sight, out of dust. Probably, considering their past and potential value, they should be on safe deposit in a bank. But who would steal them? What use would they be to anyone who did?

Swanny had taken over the study, not when Torben died, she would have had no use for it then, but as soon as she began to translate the diaries. His desk became hers. Feeling quite daring, she told me, she bought a typewriter and set about teaching herself to type with three fingers, which after all is often the best and fastest way. Once she could handle the typewriter, translating became fun. She found herself sitting down every morning sharp at ten with Anna's diary beside her, rendering it into English on the Olivetti.

I sat down at the desk, trying to put myself into Swanny's shoes, turning the pages of the first diary and coming, inevitably, to the revelation. Or had she? Or was that discovery made before she bought the typewriter and while she was still painstakingly writing it all down by hand? It must have been early on, that was certain, before I came back from America. She had sat here and it had burst upon her, the solution she had been seeking for ten years, or else it wasn't like that at all, it was an anticlimax, a disappointment or a relief. It struck me then that she might have found out it was as Torben had always said; Anna was senile, Anna was wandering or hoaxing, she had made it up. On the page for July 28 (or 29 or 30 or sometime about then) she read that she was indeed Anna's own daughter, born of her own body, delivered on July 28 in Lavender Grove, Anna's own child by her husband Rasmus.

But in that case why had she torn out the five pages?

I looked up at the bookshelves that faced me, wondering if I could put the paperbacks that were on them elsewhere and use the resulting space for the diaries, when I noticed among them the green spine that denotes Penguin crime. There was only one. I sensed before I took it down what it would be.

This copy was in better condition than the one Cary had given me. The corners weren't dog-eared and a faint gloss still remained on the faces, shadowy or clear, that composed the collage: Madeleine Smith, Hawley Harvey Crippen, Oscar Slater, Dr. Lamson, Buck Ruxton and Alfred Eighteen Roper. Swanny and Torben always wrote their names and the date on the flyleaf of every book they owned. It's an old-fashioned habit and no one seems to do it anymore. I looked inside the Penguin with the green spine and there on the top of the title page Anna had written: A. B. Westerby, July 1966.

The only other crime books Swanny had were two Agatha Christies in paperback and *The House of the Arrow* by A. E. W. Mason. Or, rather, the only ones Torben had had, for it was his name written inside them. So Swanny must have found this copy among Anna's things, glanced through it and, finding Navarino Road mentioned and the name of Roper, begun to read. This was a name she had previously read in Anna's diary. Soon she came upon the missing Edith.

And yet I was sure the name Roper occurred only once in the diary. I'd read that first volume of diaries three times, once the translation in manuscript, once the proof, then the finished copy, yet when Cary had mentioned the name it had meant nothing. Then it came to me. The passages which alerted Swanny must have been in the missing pages. Cary was right. Somewhere in there Swanny had found a great deal more about Alfred and Lizzie Roper, an account of some aspect of their lives written by her mother in August 1905, and it had to be something pertinent to her.

I was looking through the green paperback, hoping to find in the piece on Roper a page turned down or better still a pencil marking or even an underlining, when the doorbell rang. Paul Sellway. I expected a big fair man, a man with one of those smooth Danish faces, mild blue eyes and the long upper lip that also seems characteristic. Although I'd never seen Hansine I'd seen photographs, notably the one in which she wears an apron and frilly cap, and Swanny had told me Joan Sellway was a tall blond woman. I expected him to look like my impressions, mostly imaginary, of Hansine and her daughter.

He was thin and dark. If I'd been asked to identify his nationality I'd have said he was Irish. He had the Irishman's upturned mouth and wild eye and sharp jaw and copious black curly hair.

"I'm a bit early," he said. "I've been getting excited about the prospect of seeing the diaries."

Even so, it seemed a bit brusque to take him straight into the study. "Come and have a drink," I said.

For the first time in my life I was experiencing the pleasure of being proud of my own home. For it *was* my home, something that hadn't quite sunk in when I brought Cary there, or perhaps I'd been distracted by the variety of emotions the sight of her aroused. When Paul Sellway followed me into the drawing room I felt a small childish unexpected glow of pride. The only color in Swanny's house was in the ornaments and the pictures. Otherwise all was pallor or darkness with everywhere the glint of gold and the shine of silver. I saw him look at the Larsson, move closer to study it.

"There's one very like it in the Stockholm art museum," he said. "I thought it was the same one at first but it's not. The other hasn't got the dog and it's got a second birch tree."

I didn't tell him that Swanny's couldn't be the Stockholm painting because it was an original. Torben had been heard to say he wouldn't have a reproduction on his walls. I'd thought it snobbish and elitist at the time and did so the more now.

I gave him a drink, said, "I thought while you're here you might like to see some photographs too. There are lots of your grandmother."

"In maid's uniform?"

I was a little taken aback. "One is. But I truly think it was more like fancy dress. I mean, *my* grandmother got your grandmother to wear it just to make a good picture."

He burst out laughing. It was very hearty infectious laughter. I couldn't help joining in, then saying ridiculously, "What makes you laugh?"

"I did my doctoral thesis on Strindberg, with particular attention to his autobiography that's called *The Son of a Servant*. He was, you know, and it rankled. My mother wasn't pleased at my choice of subject."

I asked him why.

"My grandmother was in service for a long time, at least twenty years, and she liked talking about it. After all, it was her whole youth. But my mother hated it, she was deeply ashamed of a mother who'd been a servant, and I'm afraid my grandmother played up to it. I mean, she teased her. I was very young but I can just remember that. My grandmother used to go on about having this lovely uniform and starching her caps and putting on a fresh apron to answer the door—all that sort of thing, you can imagine."

That reminded me of Swanny's visit to Joan Sellway, the denials, the cold response. I asked him how he remembered Hansine. Had he been fond of her? Was she the warm motherly creature I pictured and that the diaries seem to confirm?

"I don't think she was particularly," he said. "Hindsight tells me she didn't like children. She lived with us and she and my mother sparred a lot. My grandmother seemed to take pleasure in rubbing my mother up the wrong way, and the reverse was true too. I much preferred my other grandmother. I think I sensed that she treated me more as a person in my own right, not a pawn to be used in grown-ups' games. I suppose, when you say that about her being warm and motherly, you're thinking of her playing with Mogens and Knud?"

I was so surprised I came straight out with it. "You've read the diaries then?"

"Of course. I thought you knew that."

"Most men when you ask them say, 'No, but my wife has.'"

"I haven't got a wife. I did once but I haven't since the first volume of Anna's diaries was published. Now, please, can we go and look at them?"

Paul took the diary in both hands and held it in a way that was both reverential and delighted. He was rather like a child clutching the Christmas present he's long been waiting for. The stains puzzled him and the brown marks on the pages and he shook his head in wonder when I explained where Anna had hidden her books and where they'd been found.

I brought him a copy of *Anna,* a pristine first edition. He compared it with the original, confirmed of course that the missing five pages were missing in the printed book and in the translated manuscript, and said that if I wanted a closer and more accurate comparison that would take him a while. He didn't suppose I'd let him take the diary away with him? Just the notebook for 1905?

An hour earlier I'd have said that was the last thing I'd consider. Now I found myself saying of course he must, there was no other way, I knew the diary would be safe with him. A sensation of Swanny turning in her grave I chose to ignore.

"Does the name Roper mean anything to you?" I said.

"Brides in the Bath," he said promptly. Then, doubting himself, "No, arsenic. A poisoner, anyway, a sort of Crippen character."

I explained. Or I explained what Cary wanted if not quite what *I* wanted. Not that I was exactly sure then what that was. I gave him Anna's Famous Trials paperback. After all, I had two copies now.

"May I take the diaries that cover the next two years as well?"

In refusing, I knew very well that I was inviting him back to collect them when he had done with volume one. And, looking at me with a smile, not a smile of resignation, I guessed he knew it too. It's at this point that I should say he took me out to dinner. But it wasn't like that, it was a recognition on both our parts that we were hungry, it was past the time at which we usually ate and that there are several restaurants at South End Green. I suppose it would be true to say he suggested it but in the way very old friends might suggest dining together.

"Shall we go out and eat?"

"I'll get my coat," I said.

Much later that night I sat down to reread the first part of volume one of *Anna* and I was surprised to find how much it dismayed me. All Anna's digs at Hansine, her scornful comments, almost a subtext to her narrative, leapt out of the page and pinched me so that I winced. This was the first time I had given any thought as to how Hansine's descendants might feel about Anna's unkind remarks. What must Joan Sellway have felt when she saw her mother described as stupid, "like a farm animal," "fat and red-faced," greedy, lazy and less than fit company for her employer?

If Paul hadn't told me he had already read the book, I thought how much worse I would be feeling, and I sent up a silent prayer of thanks to whoever might be listening that I'd asked him that clumsy question about his wife reading the diaries. Even so, he would soon come to Anna's spiteful judgments in the original as well as in Margrethe Cooper's translation. Somehow that seemed to me to compound the unpleasantness of it. I knew I'd hear from him again because he was a conscientious man but, on the other hand, I wouldn't have been surprised if he'd sent all the papers back with a curt note.

I sat up a long time that night, browsing about in the diaries, looking for references to Roper, looking for clues to Swanny's identity and finding only that Anna dwelt rather a longer time than she might have done if she'd had nothing to hide, on Rasmus' questions about the new baby and his remarks on that baby's appearance. It disquieted me, though. I've said I've never been married and know nothing much about marriage, but just the same I was almost shocked by the idea of a relationship in which one party could keep such a secret as that from the other. These had been my grandparents, married to each other for more than fifty years, sharing a bed all that time, progenitors of many children. Thinking about it brought me close to the conclusion Swanny had herself perhaps reached towards the end of her life, that Anna had been telling the truth when she recanted and said she made up the story of the adoption.

So what of the anonymous letter? Torben obviously believed Anna herself had sent it. Anna had snatched the letter when Swanny showed it to her and quickly torn it into pieces which she burned. So that no one could identify the printing as hers?

To write such a letter would be a way, albeit a very devious way, of enlightening Swanny as to the truth of her origins. Anna may have decided she wanted Swanny to know before she died and by sending the letter she would avoid the first, impossibly difficult, breaking of the news, and precipitate the two of them immediately into the necessary argument and discussion—a controversy which would give her, Anna, a further chance to view her options: to confess or retract.

She had, of course, done both.

19

Translating the diaries cost Swanny a lot of money. Once she had started she felt she had to go on and she asked Margrethe Cooper to translate all the ten notebooks Anna wrote between 1905 and 1914.

Mrs. Cooper must have been a busy woman, she was in demand as a translator for three of the Scandinavian languages, not just Danish, and she was that rare linguist who is considered capable of translating both ways. That is, she put English into Danish for Danish publishers and Danish into English for English ones. A Dane married to an Englishman, she had grown up as Swanny herself had, with two cradle tongues, and was equally proficient in both of them. Unlike Swanny—as Swanny would have been the first to admit—she had a real feeling for literature and for the rhythms of the languages from which and into which she translated.

But I hardly suppose she wanted to devote many months of her life, perhaps years, to working on something for what must have seemed like a wealthy woman's whim. When she began she can't have dreamed that the translation she made would ever be published or publication be considered. She wasn't in it only, or even primarily, for the money. However, it wasn't long before she saw that there was nothing commonplace about the diaries, their style and content was far from that of Torben's St. Petersburg cousin. She went on working on them, she told Swanny, partly because she was fascinated by what Anna had to say and partly because she thought there was a very real chance of their being published.

This gave Swanny encouragement. She grew excited when she saw the first drafts Margrethe Cooper had made. How she also must have felt when she read Anna's words at the time of my mother's birth about Morfar's rejection of his elder daughter, she said nothing about. Perhaps she was resigned to it after so long. By then, of course, she had already removed the five pages that gave a clue to her own origins.

Did she ask herself if Morfar knew? There is nothing in the diaries to show that he did and Anna herself seems mystified by his dislike of Swanny. It's possible, of course, that he sensed somehow, or strongly suspected, she wasn't his child while finding it impossible to believe Anna could be unfaithful. Swanny's beautiful looks, that very fairness and height and whiteness of skin, were against her. Where did it come from? Not his brown-skinned, brown-haired family of thickset peasants, not Anna's ginger-headed, freckled, stocky forebears, none of them ever attaining even his own height of five feet ten, while Swanny at seventeen was nearly six feet tall. But Anna wouldn't be untrue to him, Anna wouldn't deceive him.

Whether Swanny asked herself all this or not I can't tell, for she never again spoke to me about her birth and her adoption. There was evidence in her later behavior that speculation about her origins was still a very important part of her life, but she talked of it no longer. And if she didn't talk about it to me I doubt if she did so to anyone. Besides, at this time, in the mid-seventies, she was beginning to set up for herself a role and a position that had to be utterly inviolable, that of Anna Westerby's daughter.

All her future success was to depend on her being Anna Westerby's daughter. She was to be the guardian of the diaries and their editor, the keeper of the shrine, the confidante of the living and the spokeswoman for the dead.

She tried part one of what became *Anna,* that is the year 1905, on two English publishers. Both sent rejections, the second one keeping the copy rather longer than the first, that was all. The year was

1976 and *The Country Diary of an Edwardian Lady* had not yet been published, was not to be published for another year. It was by the merest coincidence that Swanny gave her manuscript the title of *The Diary of a Danish Lady.*

She didn't seem upset by these rejections. From the first she had enormous confidence in the diaries and Margrethe Cooper, who had become a friend, supported her. It was she who persuaded the Danish publisher Gyldendal to look at the original, painstakingly photocopied by her on an old Roneo copier, and thus it happened that the diary Anna had written in Danish was first brought to the notice of the public in her native land. Gyldendal published their edition, in a large format and exquisitely illustrated, in 1978. They called it *Annas Bog.*

These illustrations were later used in the English edition when Swanny found a London publisher that same year. Nearly half of them were line drawings and watercolors, a Hackney market in the first decade of the century, a fashion plate of a lady in motoring clothes and many others. The rest were family photographs. The cover design was of a medallion containing a photograph of the very young Anna, taken in Stockholm, in Nackstromsgatan, by a photographer called Berzelius. She is in a V-necked dress with a silk patterned insertion and mandarin collar, her hair is tightly drawn back but for a little curly fringe, but the picture isn't really appropriate for that first diary. Anna may look grown-up but in fact the photograph was taken when she was fourteen, staying in Stockholm with her mother's cousin and his children, Bodil and Sigrid.

There's no need for me to describe *Anna* further. Those who haven't read it have at least seen it. Those who haven't seen it have seen its cover picture in newspapers and magazines and the windows of department stores. Swanny, though not a particularly shrewd woman, had the common sense to insist on exclusion from the contract she had with her publishers, the clause that attempted to provide for the use of this image and others from the book on calendars, tea towels, jampots, bedlinen, oven mits, notelets, and crockery.

No doubt they were amenable because it hardly crossed their

minds that the book would sell more than two thousand copies, still less inspire a cult. It was to come out in October, in good time for Christmas. Meanwhile, Swanny was in Copenhagen, the guest of Gyldendal, promoting their edition of *Annas Bog*. She stayed in a hotel which was a converted warehouse in the newly respectable Nyhavn where, all those years ago, according to one of Anna's stories, a drunken relative of hers had thrown a beer bottle at someone in a bar and spent the night in a police cell.

Swanny had a good time in Denmark. In the two or three letters she wrote to me she said she felt as if she had come home, although the truth was that before this the longest time she had ever spent there was that three months during which she met Torben. Since then she and Torben had been back a few times but never for more than two weeks at a stretch. They had scarcely been outside Copenhagen while now she was traveling all over the country, from Aarhus to Odense to Helsingór. Her publisher's publicity department must have loved her. She was a foreigner but she spoke Danish, she knew Danes and she was willing to go anywhere and do anything. They could put her on television without dubbing or translation. No local paper was too insignificant for her to grant it an interview.

She visited her cousins or, rather, Torben's cousins, for her great-aunt Frederikke's sons had both died childless. She spent a weekend with Torben's niece and her husband in Roskilde. She went to the theatre and the opera, she visited the castles of Frederiksborg and Fredensborg and Andersen's house in Odense. She was photographed in Copenhagen, standing beside the statue of Andersen's Little Mermaid, and it is this picture which has since appeared on the back jacket of every edition of the diaries. Swanny is in a tweed suit and the kind of small felt hat the Queen wears, the inevitable handbag hooked over her left arm. Because of her height and her upright slenderness, because of her good legs and fine ankles and feet in the punishing high-heeled shoes, she looks less than her age. Certainly she looks less than the age she was shortly to tell people she was.

The letters she sent me were those of a happy woman enjoying herself. That's a slight exaggeration: a woman learning to be contented, a woman discovering a new potential. Perhaps she realized, as I did, that until now, at the end of it, she had always lived her life in someone else's shadow. First she was Anna's, then Torben's, then Anna's again. To them she had deferred, she had been obedient and even submissive, the favorite daughter, the good wife, her personal life ruled by them. If they were benevolent despots, they had still kept her in a kind of subjugation. Her mother treated her like a child. Her husband put her on a pedestal and adored her, gave her everything she wanted and expected nothing from her, only that she should be there, but he never consulted her about anything. He never asked her opinion. Even her parties were to entertain his friends and diplomatic contacts. Would Swanny, left to herself, have wanted to spend time with Aase Jórgensen, the professor of Maritime History?

But now she was doing something by herself for herself, of her own free will. Because she wanted to. And she was being honored for it, deferred to, sought after. She was earning money, something she hadn't done since before she married Torben and for a while had a job as companion to an old lady in Highgate, arranging flowers and taking the papillon out for walks.

The remarkable thing was that she never seemed fazed by any of it. Journalists who interviewed her after *Anna* first came out persistently asked—and went on asking over the years—if she hadn't been astounded by the success of the diaries. Could she have imagined such a thing happening "in her wildest dreams"?

"As soon as I read the first page I knew this was something special," she told the *Observer*.

With the Sunday *Times* she was sharper. "What I do find strange is that I knew from the start the diaries would be a bestseller and those publishers I sent the manuscript to didn't. You'd think their experience would have taught them, wouldn't you?"

"Do you think you'd have been a good publisher yourself then?"

"Women didn't go into publishing when I was young," Swanny said.

The young women who interviewed her couldn't believe Swanny

had never been to a university. Why wasn't she illiterate? How did she come to read Danish? And so on. Swanny took it in her stride. She told me that the first time she went on radio in this country it was live and she was nervous, but once the interview began everything came right and she enjoyed herself. Then the interviewer asked her the price of the book. She didn't know. There was a copy lying on the table between them and she picked it up to look in the front jacket flap, but it was a book club edition and there was no price inside.

"I said, 'I'm afraid I don't know but whatever it is it's worth it,' and he laughed and I laughed and it was all right."

She was a changed woman. She'd become a professional. Daily she worked on the diaries, the fifty-three notebooks as yet unpublished. She had frequent conferences with Margrethe Cooper and lunches with her publishers. She bought an electronic typewriter with a memory. Her reading matter, which had formerly been the better kind of romantic fiction and the so-called quality magazines, now became famous diaries: Pepys, *The Paston Letters,* Fanny Burney, Kilvert, Evelyn and *The Journal of a Disappointed Man.*

Two afternoons a week a trained secretary came to deal with the post. Swanny was getting two letters a week from readers in the spring of 1979 but an average of four a day by the end of that year. Sandra, her secretary, kept a complicated filing system for *Anna* alone: a section for Swanny's agent—she had acquired an agent that year—and one for film and television approaches and option agreements, a section for foreign publishers, a whole section to itself for her American publisher, others for readers' letters, artists' illustrations, paperback cover designs, newspaper and magazine reviews, engagements.

She began to be invited to open events, present prizes, judge competitions, give talks, speak at literary luncheons. But that was in the future. In 1979, with *Anna* looking very pretty in all the bookshop windows and whizzing up the nonfiction bestseller list until in April it stood at number one, most invitations that came to her were from newspapers and magazines asking for interviews. At that time, I believe, she never said no. After a lifetime of seldom talking about herself, she relished the opportunity of telling the world, as well as how she found the diaries and realized what they were, what she liked to eat, to drink, to wear, where she went on holiday, what she did in the evenings, what she read, watched on television and who was her favorite media personality. And, of course, she talked about Anna.

There was never a word in any of these "profiles" to indicate that she might have been anything other than the daughter, and the favorite daughter, of the author of the diaries. While for quite a long time she'd been in the habit of referring to Anna by her Christian name or, when talking to me, as "Mormor" or "your grandmother," it was now always "my mother" to the newspapers and on the television. Of course, a lot of these feature articles were about Westerby family life, which magazine readers were supposed to find perpetually interesting, and perhaps did, and Swanny complied enthusiastically with all demands for reminiscence and anecdote. Her stories were full of "my mother this" and "my father that" and "my brothers went to so-and-so" and "when my sister was born." When volume two, *A Live Thing in a Dead Room*, was published, the one that began with the diary of 1915, she talked on radio about the dollhouse that her father had made for her sister, giving the explanation that she was by then much too old for such a toy.

The result of that was that *Woman's Own* sent a photographer round to my flat where Padanaram by then was housed in the room on the mezzanine floor. She took pictures of the inside and outside of it and alongside them the magazine ran an interview with Swanny (dressed in blue tweed with a blue felt hat) talking about Anna in the First World War and the death of Mogens a.k.a. Jack on the Somme. Or, rather, in a hospital in Le Havre, two days after being carried off the battlefield by Uncle Harry.

It was at about this time that Swanny's way of talking about herself and her family subtly changed. Whether this had anything to do with the publication of the second set of diaries I didn't know. Certainly no connection was apparent. But there seemed no explanation for this new oddity of behavior.

She was seventy-six. I don't mention this because I think what was happening to her was anything like what Torben alleged happened to Anna, I don't think she was growing senile. She was seventy-six but she began saying she was seventy-seven. Whenever there was something in the paper about the diaries, and there constantly was, her age would be given as seventy-seven—and this, moreover, in the summer before her seventy-sixth birthday at the end of July.

There was another thing. Swanny was by now in *Who's Who* where her parents were given, of course, as Rasmus Westerby and Anna Kastrup, her place of birth as London and her date of birth as July 28. But when she gave an interview to an astrologer for a women's magazine she said she had been born under the zodiacal sign of Taurus, which spans the end of April to three-quarters of the way through May.

At first I put all this down to journalistic inaccuracy. They had got it wrong, as they often do. Then I was shown the jacket copy—a potted biography plus sample quotes from past reviews— for the paperback edition of *A Live Thing in a Dead Room*. It said that Swanny had been born in 1904.

"No, I don't want to correct it," she said when I asked her. It could be easily done, I said. That was why they sent her the copy, for her approval or otherwise.

"I don't suppose they'd change it." She had a shifty look which I couldn't remember seeing there before.

"Swanny, of course they would."

"I said to myself when I started all this with Mor's diaries, I said, never lie about your age. It's so terribly undignified pretending to be younger than you are and I never have."

"No, you're pretending to be older than you are. That's not undignified, that's absurd."

"It doesn't matter very much when you get to my age, does it?" Swanny said with a sublime lack of logic. "It's just that one tries to be honest. Honest and open in all one's dealings, that's the way Mor brought us up and I've tried to live by it."

I didn't even try to stop myself laughing. She looked injured. "Saying you were born in May 1904 is honest, is it?"

"They twist things, these newspapers."

I couldn't think what she was up to. A few weeks later I saw she had told the *Sunday Express* that the brother she lost in the First World War had died at Argonne in 1918. If the journalist interviewing her had bothered to look this up in *Anna* he would have seen she had got it wrong by a couple of hundred miles and two years.

The explanation most readily available was, in my cousin John's phrase, that she was losing her marbles. He rang up to tell me so. He and his brother, perhaps envious of Swanny's distinguished place in popular letters, had appointed themselves guardians of our Uncle Mogens/Jack's memory. At some point, perhaps when she was moving in with Swanny after Morfar's death, they had got hold of the letters Jack wrote to Anna from France. Very likely she just handed them over. She was the last person to be sentimental about a dead son's letters home. With an introduction by John and some bits of prose to link them, John and Charles had tried to get these letters published. They were climbing, so to speak, on the rollicking wagon first set in motion by Swanny. But their efforts were in vain. No publisher wanted them and considering poor Jack wrote on the lines of "I am well and hope things at home are still tip-top," I can't say I was surprised.

John wrote to the *Sunday Express,* asking for a correction, but they didn't print one and they didn't use his letter. The journalist had recorded her interview with Swanny and I've no doubt when she played it back she got her subject's clear voice uttering in no uncertain terms that her brother had died at Argonne in the last months of the Great War.

For once, I agreed with John about something. I agreed that Swanny was—well, the word I used to him was "confused." She had been doing too much, swept up as she had been into the promotional machine that publishers insist is required even to sell a bestseller. Her arthritis had begun once more to trouble her. I was relieved when she told me she felt in need of a rest and would be going away on a cruise with the relatives from Roskilde.

20

Paul phoned to say he had made his comparisons between Anna's original notebook, Margrethe Cooper's translation and the published *Anna* and could we meet to discuss his findings.

I wasn't really disappointed that these were practically nonexistent. It pleased me that he had done it all so fast, in four days, and I knew that he must have worked on the diaries every evening. There was no sign in his face or manner of having been offended by what he'd read but I didn't postpone what I felt I had to say. "I wish my grandmother had been less harsh and insulting about yours. When I think of the things she wrote it makes me wince. I feel I ought to apologize to you on her behalf."

"Then I'll apologize to you for all the times my grandmother was intrusive and awkward and broke the china."

I said it couldn't happen to many people, to find out precisely what one of their forebears thought about the other's forebear, an exact contemporary.

"Do people write more frankly in a diary than they speak?"

"Yes, if they think no one's going to see it."

"You believe a woman writes down her whole life and hopes no one will ever read it?"

"Anna did. She not only did that, she threw away what she'd written."

"There are ways and ways of throwing things away," Paul said.

"If you really want to destroy something it's not too difficult. Are you sure she didn't want it found?"

We were in Willow Road. I'd gone home once to fetch some clothes and come back again. Like Swanny, after she had found the diaries, I was forgetting about selling the house. Perhaps the diaries had that effect. They changed one's tastes; one wanted to be where they were, under the same roof with them.

Paul laid the notebook, the manuscript and his own copy of *Anna* on the table in front of us. There were markers inserted between the pages but they were there only to point up a line here and a line there he thought interesting or significant. The translation Margrethe Cooper had made was the notebook word for word, the notebook with the five pages gone. *Anna* in first edition was the Cooper translation in print, in no way cut, in no way augmented.

His first marker was at the entry for November 2, 1905, the day Morfar came home from his travels in Denmark. It could have nothing to do with Roper, he said, but it interested him that Anna had set down her husband's remarks on the new baby looking like neither of her parents. There was more too, in the following February. Paul had marked that as well. Why did Anna protest so much about her fidelity and go on for a whole page about what she thought of women who were false to their marriage vows? Presumably, she wasn't, so why labor the point?

That was the cue for me to tell him about Swanny and the question which had haunted her last years, which hadn't stopped or become quiescent, as I now believed, with the discovery and publication of the diaries but persisted until a few years before she died when, after reading a "famous trial," she came to her curious conclusion.

Paul listened attentively to all this. He has a remarkable way of listening. He gives you his whole attention but without eye contact, his head resting on one hand, a small frown of concentration on his face, and he attends in absolute silence. It's interesting to watch someone who is so thin and even athletic, a vigorous man, with at the same time a capacity for keeping entirely still for long periods of time, still, silent, listening.

I told him the whole Swanny tale. Sometimes, when you're telling a very long story, you have the feeling you should hurry, gloss over some bits, synopsize others, but with Paul it's not like that. If he wants to know he'll listen—if necessary for hours. It didn't take me hours, no more than fifteen minutes. He asked one question.

"What put her on to doubting she was Anna's child in the first place?"

"Didn't I say? She got an anonymous letter, one of those things with the words printed."

It's hindsight that makes me say his face changed, that he turned pale or became very still or something. I noticed nothing at the time. I went on with my story and when I came to the end I told him who I thought Swanny believed she was.

Swanny made a lot of money out of the diaries. They had world-wide sales and by 1985 were published in twenty languages, not including English and Danish. A film was made, rather awful but lucrative, and of course the adaptation of *Anna* in five parts, beginning with Rasmus' courtship of Anna and his learning of the existence of the dowry and ending with Anna and Uncle Harry meeting soon after Jack's death (Anthony Andrews with a beard, Lindsay Duncan in a red wig and Christopher Ravenscroft in army uniform) won an award as best television serial of the year 1984. It was shown on PBS in the United States as well as all over Europe.

She made a lot of money and she spent it prudently, as she had always spent money. Torben might as well have still been alive, it might as well have been his earnings. But she was sensible in the way she used some of it to make sure she was properly looked after. Mrs. Elkins, who for a long while after Torben died had come in for a few hours three times a week, was now appointed housekeeper and though she didn't sleep at Willow Road, was there all day and every day except Sundays from nine till five. A girl from Kilburn came over twice a week to help. However, her wisest move was in taking on a nurse-companion to be with her every night from nine in the evening until Mrs. Elkins came in the morning.

Not that she was aware how strange she had become. There was never a sign that she was conscious of a growing mental disturbance. The nurse was there because Swanny's arthritis, apparently in remission for several years, had returned and with particular sharpness and agony in her neck, back and hands. Also she slept badly, lying wakeful for long hours of every night. If she had to get up, and she usually had to, she was afraid of falling as she crossed the few yards of floor between her bed and the bathroom.

She had rapidly declined from her position as busy, distinguished editor of the diaries. Before Christmas she was still touring, still speaking at literary lunches and giving interviews. By the following June she had grown old, in mind as well as body.

The contrast between her old age and Anna's was marked but she never pointed this out. She never said (as she might once have done), "Look at me, and just think what Mor was like at my age." She had ceased entirely to refer to Anna as Mor or mother. It was now always "Anna." The people in the diaries were no longer "my brother," "my great-aunt," but spoken of by their first names. And she herself was not a Dane anymore but English. She had become someone else.

Privately, at home, that is. With me. With the various people who worked for her. To her agent, her publisher, the world out there to whom she was Anna's daughter she remained just that. It was as if she had, late in life, mastered the handling of a split personality. It took its toll, of course, it drove her further down the slope into madness.

It wouldn't be putting it too strongly to say Anna had driven her mad. Our need to know our own origins is deep-seated, is at the root of personality. Most of us have no difficulty about this. We grow up knowing, taking for granted, in an absolute unshakable certainty that this man was our father, this woman our mother, and these other people, therefore, our ancestors. Swanny did that too and lived with this certain knowledge until she was almost an old woman. Then this part of her life, its foundation in fact, was cut away, as a spade swiftly digs a pit and makes an abyss. Anna built the foundations and Anna dug the hole she fell into. No doubt, she didn't know what she was doing. If her own mother had told her she was adopted and refused to say more Anna would have snapped her fingers at her and got on with her life.

When Swanny was her other self she spoke differently. Her normal voice was that of her Hampstead neighbors, cultivated, so-called educated English. But Danish had been her first language, the language Anna spoke to her from babyhood, and like all Danes, those great polyglots, there were one or two English words she pronounced in a way that revealed her cradle tongue. All Danes say "lidd'l" for "little" and Swanny was no exception. But in her alter ego she didn't pronounce it like that. Her smooth rounded vowel sounds became flat and she dropped the ultimate *g* from present participles. "Everything" and "nothing" had a *k* added to their final syllable. She was speaking with a working class north London accent and it sounded, embarrassingly, as if some of her remarks were a deliberate send-up of Mrs. Elkins.

Fortunately, none of the people with whom she was associated in the publishing, marketing and publicizing of the diaries ever saw or heard her when she was like this. Sandra quickly took on the role of buffer between Swanny and the world outside. She became adept at watching Swanny's moods and if the other self was in the ascendant, canceled interviews, book signings, meetings with publishers, or whatever it might be. Swanny, after all, was by now a very old woman. In 1985 (or 1984, depending from which viewpoint you looked at it) she had become eighty. Saying she was tired or "not so well today" was a perfect excuse and one nobody was likely to argue about it.

So her other self was shown to me, to Sandra, to Mrs. Elkins, and to the two nurses, Carol and Clare, and only to us. Perhaps we were all naturally discreet. For my part, I told no one of Swanny's personality split. If the others talked, it never reached the press. As far as the rest of the world knew, Swanny Kjaer continued to be the "remarkable," "wonderful," "amazing"—and all the other adjectives newspapers use about an old person who isn't bedridden and gaga—custodian of the diaries she had always been. When Jane Asher recorded *Anna* on audiotape, the picture of Swanny on the promotional pamphlet was the photograph beside the Little Mermaid in Copenhagen, the last one she was ever to have taken.

At home, increasingly often, even her appearance was changed. She had always been fastidiously clean and sleek and groomed, taking a shower or a bath twice a day—to Anna's derision—dressing with formal care, paying great attention to her hair and going to the hairdresser twice a week. Like my mother, she had devoted part of each day to the care of her clothes, and buying new ones was one of the pleasures of her life. Now, on the days when she became her other self, she refused to bathe and resisted the attempts of Carol or Clare to get her to do so. She insisted on putting on an old tweed skirt and woolen jersey, though jumpers and skirts were the kind of clothes she had once condemned as sloppy dressing. Her hair was thick and short, the naturally tidy kind, so she untidied it by simply leaving it as it was when she got out of bed. She went bare-legged, her feet thrust into bedroom slippers, and succeeded in looking like the bag lady who pushed her box barrow up Heath Street.

Swanny had always had, as long as I had known her, a tiny red mark on her left cheekbone under the eye. It was a broken blood vessel, not a mole, but she began to turn it into one. I thought she had a dirty mark on her face and told her so but she only gave one of her mysterious smiles and next time I saw her the mark was bigger, a perfect circle about the size of a shirt button and put on with eyebrow pencil. It was always there after that, whether she was Swanny or the other one.

One day she asked me to buy her some knitting wool and a pair of needles. Anna, of course, had been a fine needlewoman and my mother was good at sewing. There had been a phase when she made all my clothes and her own. But although Anna mentions buying wool to make baby clothes in the early part of the first diary, she must have stopped knitting when she became more prosperous and I'd never seen Swanny with any kind of needle in her hand.

"I didn't know you could knit," I said.

"I've had to," she said in Mrs. Elkins' voice. "There was a time when I made everything I wore—that is, in the woollies line."

"What color would you like? And come to that what weight? It does come in weights, doesn't it?"

"Lilac or pink, a nice pastel shade. And it'd better be doubleknit with the needles number eight. It'll keep me busy when I'm watching the telly in the evenings. I've never cared to sit about idle."

"I'll get you some pink or mauve wool this afternoon," I said, "so that you can make a start tonight."

Humor the mad and go along with everything they say used to be advice given to those having to do with them. Yet advocating it is unnecessary, for this is our natural, or at any rate our easiest, response. It is the normal reaction. To challenge them, which is what Daniel used sometimes to do as a part of therapy, is such a frightening thing that we balk at it and fall back on placebos and smiling acquiescence. Better humor the madwoman than face the unknown but potentially terrifying results of saying: "Why do you talk like that, act like that, dress like that? Who is this person you've become? Where is yourself?"

I'd lived with a psychotherapist and knew his methods. I knew what he would advise, yet I did otherwise. I didn't even ask her who she thought she was. She had become a working class grandmother, knitting baby clothes, and I behaved as if this were entirely normal, just what I expected, and even pretended to admire the tangled mess she made as the pink wool was transformed into a cat's cradle of infinite complexity suspended from needles awkwardly gripped in her arthritic hands.

There were, of course, the other days, the days when she was Swanny Kjaer again. The knitting was put away—where, I wonder, and with what thoughts and resolutions?—the clothes were back to normal, her hair was brushed and her face discreetly painted, though the mole was painted on as well. Like this, speaking like a Hampstead lady, with a tweed suit on and stockings and high-heeled shoes, she took a taxi down to Covent Garden or Kensington to sign books in a bookshop or have lunch with her agent. Nor did Sandra have to cancel when the day came for her to go out live on *Woman's Hour*.

But the other one was taking over. The other one, the nameless unspecified separate persona, was slowly absorbing the Swanny I had known. The occasions when she was herself became fewer and fewer. I don't mean to give the impression, when I say I and all of us humored her, that we took no action. Her doctor had kept a watchful eye on Swanny from the start of all this. Since she went to him privately, in other words she paid him, he visited every week.

"I could ask the psychiatrist to come to see her," he said to me. "That would mean explaining to her who and what he is and why he's coming. In other words, it's bringing out into the open that we think she's mentally disturbed."

He too belonged to the humoring school, it seemed.

"She seems happy enough," he said.

I wasn't sure of that but I was a coward too. I didn't say to him that sometimes, when she was herself and when she was the other, I saw in her face a blank waste of despair.

"At her age do we want to cause upheavals in her equilibrium? She's a very old lady." I didn't say that her mother, at Swanny's age, had been walking for miles across Hampstead Heath, going to parties, selling her antique clothes, reading Dickens and writing her diary. What was the use? People are different. "It may be the best thing," he said, "for me to give her something to calm her down."

So Swanny went on the doctor's tranquilizers, though she had never been anything but tranquil. If I had to find one single adjective that most exemplified her that's what it would be. She was tranquil. She always had been and I suspect it was her reposefulness and quiescence, her gentle calm, which originally attracted Torben as much as her Norse goddess looks. To say that someone is tranquil doesn't, after all, imply contentment, only perhaps a peaceful acceptance of or yielding to an unhappy fate.

I have said I never asked her who she was when she wasn't herself. As far as I know, no one asked her. The rest, Sandra and Mrs. Elkins and the nurses, tended to shun her when the other took over from Swanny Kjaer, that is they spoke to her when they had to, they performed their duties, but it was obvious they were growing afraid. They were simply afraid, as people are with the mad, of what she would do.

Probably, they didn't want to know who it was she became. All of us fear the manifestations of madness because its vagaries and its revelations show us what may lurk under the surface of our own minds. I was sometimes as frightened as they but I did want to know. I nearly asked. It was on the tip of my tongue to ask and I felt on these occasions much, I'm sure, as Swanny must have felt when she screwed herself up to ask Anna for the truth. But each time I drew back. And perhaps she would never have told me but have taken refuge in cunning and invented a name and an identity for the old knitting woman in the bedroom slippers.

My understanding of who this woman was came to me six months after Swanny was dead. She was Edith Roper. Swanny thought she was Edith Roper.

I reread the Donald Mockridge coda Swanny had read. Edith had been born in May 1904. Edith was a blond blue-eyed child, tall for her age. She had a mole on her left cheek. By some twisted reasoning Swanny must have worked it out that if Edith hadn't been adopted by Anna, if she had grown up in the milieu from which she had come, at eighty-one she would very probably have been like Mrs. Elkins' own mother, living in Walthamstow, many times a great-grandmother, a television-watching knitter and member of the local senior citizens' club.

So she became her. Because, perhaps, she or her unconscious thought it the proper thing, the right thing. Destiny had been cheated and it was for her to put things right. Or, believing herself to be Edith Roper, she *wanted* to be her, she had found an identity at last, and if it wasn't the one she would have chosen, it was all she was going to get.

Her imagination, the limited imagination of a sheltered woman whose contact with a working class had been as an employer of domestic help, made her place Edith among the unwashed. Her reaction to the occasional sight of the Heath Street bag woman was to put Edith's bare feet into slippers and leave Edith's hair uncombed. The sound of Mrs. Elkins' speech patterns her unconscious mimicked for Edith's utterances.

"Yet she was wrong," Paul said.

"Oh, yes, she was wrong. Anna adopted a baby around the twenty-eighth of July 1905. At that time Edith was fourteen months old and walking."

"And, as I remember it, she was writing about nursing the baby three months later. Besides, she could hardly have passed off an eighteen-month-old child, as Edith would then have been, as a new baby to Rasmus when he came home in November."

"How well you know the diary," I said.

"I've just gone through it. I may not be such a wizard in a week's time. Your aunt very obviously wanted to believe, she wanted an identity and she latched on to the one that was a possibility. Perhaps it was the only possibility she could see. She may have found others in the past but none of them fitted as closely as this did."

"It really isn't possible, is it?"

"That she was Edith? Not unless Anna falsified all the entries about her daughter Swanhild for the next three or four years, not unless she lied about what she said to Rasmus and he said to her, not unless she persuaded Rasmus to take on a child he would certainly have seen as the daughter of a murderer and a woman who was more or less a prostitute. I think we can discount all that. Besides, what are we saying? That Anna, who certainly did give birth on or around July 28, was walking about the streets on that same day, ready to pick up and carry home someone else's wandering infant?"

"I wonder what happened. I mean, was her own child born dead? Or did it die soon after birth? Was it another boy or a girl at last? We'll never know, will we?"

"Oh, I don't know," Paul said. "It's going to be in those five missing pages from the first diary. Your aunt tore them out but she may not have thrown them away."

"You mean I should search the house?"

"That depends on how much you want to know."

I said I supposed I did want to know. Yet if I did come to know I'd never be able to tell Swanny who was dead, who had died the victim of a gross delusion, believing herself to have been someone she could not by the wildest stretch of facts have ever been. Swanny hadn't looked like the Westerbys, but plenty of people look different from the rest of their family members. Anna had told Swanny she was adopted but there had never been proof. They had all been born a century or many decades too soon for genetic fingerprinting.

She was Anna's own daughter and Anna had invented the story. Torben had been right all along. Anna had written and sent the anonymous letter herself. Hadn't it been posted in Hampstead? Hadn't she burned it? Yes, in spite of her protestations of disgust, Anna wrote it.

"I'm afraid I don't believe that," Paul said.

"Why 'afraid'?"

"Just a figure of speech."

With that I had to be content but I wasn't. Not altogether. He has such an open face, as those with Irish looks do have, eyes that are mirrors of the soul and a mobile mouth. His expression had become rather blank and fixed, a look that lifted gradually while I talked, wondering and speculating as one does when a complex revelation has been made, of Swanny's references to her brother's death at Argonne where Edith's own brother had died and of Swanny's insistence on adding that year to her age.

It didn't strike me particularly then that he didn't want to talk any more about the anonymous letter. I supposed, quite wrongly as it happened, that he was growing bored with the whole subject and I changed it as soon as I could without obviousness.

Nor did any searching of the house take place. Instead, we went back to his house in Hackney which was so near to where Anna had once lived. He wanted to show it to me and nothing more was said that night about the diaries or Swanny's strange misapprehension.

21

JANUARY 17, 1920

Det er maerkeligt, men sidste Gang Sergeanten kom paa Besóg,
var det igen Hansines Frieftermiddag. Jeg kan svaerge paa, at jeg
ikke arrangerede det med Vilje, men det var bare helt tilfaeldigt.

It's strange but last time the Sergeant came to see me it was again
Hansine's afternoon off. I swear I didn't arrange it that way, it just
happened. Of course, I'm happier with her out of the way when he
calls. I don't want her flapping her apron and saying how handsome
he is or even making snide remarks, and now she's left there's no
risk of that.

She has gone to stay with Cropper's mother and father until the
wedding next month. I don't envy her, I must say. Unless she's been
exaggerating, old Mrs. Cropper never misses a chance to cast up to
her the fact that she's a foreigner, criticizes her English and has
found out she's *a whole six months older* than Cropper. An awful
crime, this one. What bosh it all is!

Poor Hansine's biggest dread is that her future mother-in-law
will find out she can't read and write. I don't know how she thinks
she's going to keep that dark.

FEBRUARY 12, 1920

Hansine is married. Rasmus and I were invited to the wedding but of course we didn't go. I gave the happy couple a Royal Copenhagen vase which I've had for years, given me originally by Onkel Holger's sister for my own wedding. I never liked it and it's been shut up in a cupboard for years, so closely hidden away that I was sure Hansine had never seen it before. However, from the look she gave me when I presented it to her, I'm not so sure. I hope she won't drop it like she has so many of my nicest pieces.

The new maid who takes over from her is called Elsie. Emily and Elsie, how confusing! Mrs. Cropper as she now is will be living with her husband in Leytonstone. One of these fine days, if I'm invited, I shall get the Sergeant to drive me over to her house. Or, on second thought, perhaps not. I'll have more interesting places to go to.

Who would have thought Rasmus would agree to the Sergeant driving me about? (I must make a note here to remember to call him Harry.) The fact is I was sure he would fly into one of his rages, as he does more and more these days. I imagined him saying, "If *my* wife goes out in *my* motor *I* am going to drive her." But all he said was that in that case it would have to be the Mercedes, which I know is the motor he's least fond of.

Harry was very pleased. He said he'd take me out every Saturday if I liked and in the evenings in the week when his work is done. His job is with the Metropolitan Water Board, though he started life as a coachman. We'd best stick to Saturdays for the time being, I said. What about your wife and your daughters? Won't they want you to be with them? He only smiled and said he'd never neglect his family, he knew better than that, and we went out for our first drive, up into Hertfordshire to see the country and some pretty villages.

I felt rather strange and awkward for a while. I thought he would take advantage, I'd been brought up to believe people of his class do take advantage if you let yourself relax with them, but he didn't. He is always perfectly respectful. I had brought a picnic with me. We found a lovely place under some trees down a quiet country lane. Harry brought the picnic basket out to me and spread the cloth on the grass, he laid a blanket down for me and put the cushions just so, but I could see he wasn't going to sit down with me and share it, he was going off for a walk.

Of course I wasn't going to have that. I made him sit down opposite me and though he was awkward at first he soon got over that. It was a strange feeling, the sense I had that at last, at my advanced age, I'd found someone I could talk to. I felt I had to grasp at it before it flew away and my chance of it was gone forever.

He asked me about Denmark and how it had felt to be an exile and then I saw that the trees above us were beech trees. There came to me then such a yearning for my home and my country that it was like a sharp pain in my heart. I believe he could tell but instead of changing the subject he got me talking on and on about Denmark and this free talking and remembering helped me so that I felt stronger and I could laugh again.

He knows a lot. I was going to write "for a working man" but that wouldn't be right. He knows a lot for *any* man. A lot of history, for one thing. He told me which members of the English royal family had married Danish princesses, for instance. It wasn't possible for me to confirm this but I looked it up in an encyclopedia when I got home and he was right. Then he is very knowledgeable about the countryside and talked about an English painter I'd never heard of, not knowing the English had any painters. This one was called John Constable who painted woods and fields in Suffolk and Essex but lived in Hampstead and is buried in the churchyard there. I said we might go there and look at his grave.

Next week we are going to take the children with us. Harry is very fond of Swanny, is always saying how lovely and charming she is. In one way I like this, I love to see Swanny admired as she deserves, but in another it makes me uncomfortable. I think I'm a bit jealous—jealous of my own daughter!

JULY 29, 1920

Yesterday Swanny was fifteen. She didn't want a party, she says none of the girls at school is close enough to her for her to want to invite friends to her home. She has no real friends. Like me, she doesn't make friends easily. Parents are always saying of their child, "Where does so-and-so get that from? Not from me or her father. There's none of that in our family," as if everything about you must be inherited. I don't think it happens quite like that, I think children copy their parents and behave the way they've seen them behave, though it's not a view that's fashionable.

Swanny said she might have felt differently about having a party if Mogens had been alive, if Mogens could have been there. I might have said to her that he'd be twenty-two if he'd lived and probably not even living at home with us, but I didn't. I said that though we'd always be sad about Mogens dying, life had to go on and we'd have to learn to remember him without being unhappy. It didn't have much effect. I don't want her young life spoiled by mooning and brooding on a dead brother.

I am reading *Bleak House* for the third time.

SEPTEMBER 4, 1920

We are off to Denmark, Rasmus and I. It's strange, I've been on holiday to Paris and to Vienna but I've never been back to my own country and I'm very excited. We'll have to spend a day or two with his horrible sister in Aarhus but the rest of the time will be with Ejnar and Benedicte in Copenhagen. From what I've seen of her, which isn't much, just when they stayed a night with us two years ago, I rather like Benedicte. On the face of it, she didn't seem bitter and mean-spirited and prudish and cold and snobbish and high and mighty like the rest of them. The Danes are supposed to be merry folk, drinking beer and laughing and having a jolly time, but I can't say I've seen much sign of it.

The girls will stay with Mrs. Housman. It wouldn't be right to keep them away from school. I should have written, the girls will stay with Mrs. Housman if Rasmus hasn't quarreled with her husband by that time. He goes about telling everyone he has swindled him and I just hope it won't reach Mr. Housman's ears before the twelfth when we go away.

I've bought two new dresses for the trip, a Chanel two-piece in blue and black charmeuse and a blue and violet tea gown with lilac and black velvet scarf sleeves. Everything is blue and black this year and luckily those colors look good on me. I have a new pair of shoes in black patent with Louis heels and a double instep strap, a style I like better than any other. Both dresses are very short. I never thought the day would come when I would wear skirts that show eight inches of leg.

This morning when Emily went downstairs she found Björn lying dead and cold in the scullery. Poor old dog, he had a good life and a long one for his breed. Rasmus actually wept when I told him, he who hardly ever shows feeling for anyone—except, of course, for Mogens—cried real big wet tears for a dog.

"No one would call you a Great Dane, that's for sure," I said to him.

MARCH 20, 1921

Harry has told me a surprising thing. We had intended to go for a drive to Kew Gardens but it was pouring with rain, so instead we went to a theatre matinee. It wasn't a good play and I remember scarcely anything of it these few days later. The remarkable thing was that I was able to persuade Harry to take a ticket for himself and sit with me. We found we had exactly the same feelings about this terrible play, wanting to laugh at the sentimental parts and yawn at the long speeches. Most plays seem to be about the war or about what happened afterwards, bereaved parents and crippled men and girls left to be old maids because there are no young men to marry them.

I did a bit more persuading and got Harry to come and have tea with me in a tea shop. We talked about Swanny and the girl in the play whose fiancé had been killed and I opened my heart and said, wouldn't it be terrible if there was no suitable young man to marry Swanny. The fact is, you don't see many young men, just middle-aged ones and little boys. The fine young men have all been killed.

I look back to the top of this page and see I wrote that Harry told me a surprising thing. I seem to be a long time getting round to what he did say. We'd got on to the subject of the English hating foreigners and he said that we were lucky having a name which sounded English even though it was Danish. Harry said he'd had a German name, his grandfather was a German who came here back in the 1850s, and though his father was born in London and he was too, he had this premonition of what it would be like having that name if war came. I thought that was clever of him and I said so, remembering Mr. and Mrs. Cline, who hadn't changed their name enough and still had trouble.

Calling himself Duke was very clever. He said he didn't know any German but he could read, had looked up his name in a German dictionary and found it meant Duke. This was just before he met his wife and when he began courting her he'd changed his name by deed poll.

Talking of people who can or can't read, Hansine has had a baby girl. She is to be called Joan. So much for not wanting children!

Swanny surprised me by asking to see the new baby, so Harry is to drive us over there. We are good friends, Harry and I, and each week that passes the class barrier between us seems to grow a little thinner and weaker. The barrier of sex is another matter. I feel very strongly that even though we strictly speaking are mistress and servant—still, we pay him nothing—he is a man and a strikingly handsome one while I am a woman who, I think I can say, am more aware than most women of the nuances and *frissons* of sexual tension. If I am frank, I'll say I am aware of love all around me, in other people and between other people, I know I have never had it and, yes, I long for it. Even at my advanced age, I long for love.

Well, ungratified, it will soon pass, I suppose. I shall be forty-one this summer but have not a single gray hair. This morning I examined my head very closely, noting that every hair remains the same sandy color. Poor Rasmus's beard is quite gray, though the hair on his head is still brown.

JUNE 23, 1923

Rasmus and I got back from Paris last night. I never write my diary when I'm away on holiday and I miss it. Holidays are strange things. You are supposed to have a change and a rest but what do you *do?* If you are with someone you can't talk to because you aren't interested in the same things the days are very long and pass very slowly. We went to the Louvre and up the Eiffel Tower, we went to Versailles and promenaded in the Champs Elysées, but all Rasmus cares about is motorcars.

There are, of course, plenty of these in Paris and practically each one he sees has him craning his neck and staring and pointing out to me all sorts of things about it I don't understand and don't want to. Oddly, the only thing we seem to enjoy doing together is shopping for clothes for me. I will say for him, he doesn't mind how much money he spends.

Paris has decreed that the chemise is gone and the straight silhouette is in. The waist has gone right down to the hips and belts have disappeared. We went to Patou to get me a straight pleated dress in black and white with a cape and to Chanel for a printed foulard costume. A lot of fashion is based on Indo-Chinese national costume but I don't like it, I don't want to look like a Cambodian peasant. I bought a dress for Swanny in crepe de chine with floating panels, a very pale shade of *eau-de-nil,* which Rasmus thought was for me. He must have some strange ideas if he thinks I'd wear something down to my ankles!

I missed my diary and I also—oh, how much more!—missed Harry. All the time I was out with Rasmus I kept thinking how different it would be if Harry were my companion, how we would talk and laugh and share things. I thought how we would want to see the same things, for we are both fond of paintings, especially paintings of people, and how we would enjoy the wonderful food. We both like large delicious meals that go on and on. Rasmus eats to live.

Still, I shall see Harry tomorrow and I shall ask his advice. Rasmus is the proper person to ask but I know he'll only say to suit myself, he won't care. A letter was awaiting me from Benedicte, asking if I would spare Swanny to go and stay with them. She isn't talking about weeks but months and suggests six months. I'm not sure I can bear to be parted from her for so long but I shall ask Harry what he thinks.

APRIL 12, 1924

Rasmus is jubilant. Today he heard that he had been granted something called the Cadillac concession for the British Isles. This means apparently that he and only he can sell Cadillac motors in this country. Well, he and Mr. Cline, who he's gone into partnership with, can sell them. Rasmus has fallen out thoroughly with Mr. Housman, who he says has swindled him out of thousands.

They intend to open a large showroom in the King's Road at Chelsea. The next thing I suppose will be that I'll be asked to leave Padanaram and move to Cheyne Walk or some such place, which I shall certainly refuse to do. I've learned to stick up for myself a bit more since those days before the war when he could announce we were moving in a month's time and I had to make the best of it.

One instance of how I've asserted myself happened yesterday when he informed me of the summer holidays we'd be taking. Two weeks at Bognor Regis, wherever that may be, with the girls and two weeks in Brussels for us. I don't want to go to Brussels, whatever would I do there for a whole fortnight alone with him? We had a terrible quarrel, one of our worst, and of course Marie had to overhear it and start crying.

I could have killed Rasmus. He sat her on his knee and hugged her—and her a great girl of thirteen—and said that if he couldn't stand life with Mor any longer would she come and live with him and be his little housekeeper. I screamed at him not to talk like that to the children. The worst was when Marie said if that happened would Mor go and be married to Uncle Harry.

She is much too old to say things of that sort. You could understand it if she were six. Rasmus had her on his lap and her cheek pressed against his beard and I could see him smirking over the top of her head.

"So Mor's going to marry the chauffeur, is she?" he said, and then, to me, "You see what you've done, going about alone with that man."

He doesn't mean it, though. He knows I wouldn't misbehave myself. I wish I could, I want to, but it's no use. Perhaps Harry wants to and feels the same, that it's no use, that we aren't those sorts of people. He kisses my hand sometimes, that's all. But I won't go away alone with Rasmus anymore, not to be abroad somewhere thinking of Harry all day long and how if the world was ordered differently it might be he walking by my side.

Mrs. Duke, Harry's wife, has had another child, another girl. That makes four girls they have. When he told me I felt myself grow pale, I felt a shiver as the color was drawn out of my face, but I nodded and smiled and said congratulations and how nice. The truth is I am jealous, I am jealous of the woman who has Harry's children. I would like Harry's child myself but to write that down makes me faint and sick with longing.

JUNE 2, 1924

Swanny has gone to Denmark. She left this morning on the boat in the care of Mrs. Bisgaard. Dorte Bisgaard is going to be married to some very rich aristocratic Danish boy, so of course the wedding can't take place from the Bisgaards' common ordinary house in West Heath Road. What nonsense it all is! Still, I'm glad to let Swanny go in the keeping of a thoroughly trustworthy person.

This will be Swanny's first time as a bridesmaid. There are to be six of them, all dressed in duck's egg blue silk jersey with overskirts of turquoise satin. I had to persuade Swanny to agree, she insisted she would be so much taller than the other girls she would look ridiculous. Of course, she never could, but she is so modest, *too* modest.

Mrs. Bisgaard will take her straight to Ejnar and Benedicte and she will leave for the wedding from there. I don't want her staying in different houses, I want to know where she is. The fact is, I wish it were she getting married to a rich young handsome man who would look after her.

This house feels dead without her, all the rooms lifeless and stale. But I'm alive all right. I'm a live thing in a dead room.

MARCH 16, 1925

We are all recovering from Knud's wedding. This was Swanny's second time as a bridesmaid and I don't want there to be a third. Superstition is very foolish and I'm not superstitious but just the same I can't help thinking of those words, three times a bridesmaid, never a bride.

Maureen threw her bouquet for Swanny to catch, a custom I've never come across before but which apparently means that the girl who catches it will be the next to marry. Of course she is only twenty and she has her admirers. That young man who was so keen on her in Denmark, the one she met at the party after Dorte's wedding, bombards her with letters. He's a Dane and very suitable but the one big drawback is he wants her to go to some place in South America with him. They are to marry and set sail immediately for Santiago or Asunción, I forget which. Swanny sensibly says to wait and see. She writes back but not very often and not at great length.

APRIL 16, 1927

I am a grandmother. I don't feel or look any different and I certainly don't feel anything for the baby. We went to see him and his mother this morning. He is exactly like Maureen, a pudgy-faced plain child, but Knud is no beauty either. They are going to call him John Kenneth.

The men went downstairs to celebrate by drinking, what Knud calls "wetting the baby's head," and the moment they were gone Maureen began telling me every detail of the birth, how terrible it was and how long it went on. I cut her short. I said there was nothing new in that, we all had babies—except those unfortunate "surplus" women, of course, whose fiancés died in the war—and we all went through much the same. I reminded her I'd had five, not to mention the two I'd lost by miscarriage, and she couldn't tell me anything I didn't know.

The awful flat they live in must be her choice. But perhaps not. Knud has nothing in common with me or his father, for that matter. The funny thing is that he is more English than the English and it's a well known fact they all love to live in houses while Europeans prefer apartments. Still, people aren't consistent, I ought to know that.

Now the evenings are light Harry has begun taking me out again after dinner. There is something wrong with the Mercedes, so Rasmus said we could take the Cadillac. I don't sit in the back anymore but up in the front next to Harry. It's odd how this began. I used to start in the back and then, once we'd stopped to look at something or go for a walk somewhere, I'd get back into the front seat. But the day before yesterday I was about to get into the back when I realized I was only doing this for fear of the neighbors seeing and talking. Well, I was ashamed of myself. When have I ever cared what people thought? So I shook my head and Harry seemed to know at once, to read my thoughts as he often does, and immediately he opened the passenger door for me. We have never done anything wrong and never will. Evil to him who evil thinks, is what I say.

He laughed when I said I didn't much care for being a grandmother and surprised me by telling me his eldest wants to get
married, so it may not be long before he catches up with me. She
is only sixteen, born in 1911 and born a bit sooner than she should
have been, I think. For some reason I like the idea of our being
grandparents together.

We went to see Somerset Maugham's *The Letter* at the Play-
house. Gladys Cooper is in it and I always like her, so beautiful, as
actresses should be, but a silly story about a woman who shot a
man who was trying to rape her. Only he was really her lover and
she killed him because she found out he had a Chinese mistress.

Afterwards, though it was late and dark, we drove to Hampstead
and walked about on the Heath. These days our drives get shorter
and our walks or expeditions or meals together or visits to theatres
and concerts get longer. I know what has happened and he knows,
though we never say. He is courting me and I am courting him but
with no possibility of kisses or even an arm round a waist, no
eventual coming together, nothing beyond what we have, the meeting of eyes across a table, a shared burst of laughter and my hand
tightly held in his.

NOVEMBER 2, 1929

Swanny started her job today, very much against my wishes. But I
have set down my feelings exhaustively and mean to say very little
more about it. Torben Kjaer would marry her tomorrow if she
would have him. Then there is that young man who is some sort
of cousin of Maureen's. He's mad about her, he is always on the
telephone. If she prefers walking to Hampstead every morning to
take an old lady's dog out and read trashy novels to her, I suppose
she must do it. She is grown-up. Rasmus, of course, doesn't care
what she does except that he is rather pleased not to have to pay
for her clothes anymore. The pitiful amount she earns will just
about cover that.

Looking back, I see I have forgotten to set down that Knud and

Maureen have another child. A boy called Charles was born last Monday. And Harry's eldest is expecting a baby. She's the same age as I was when I had Mogens but perhaps more to the point, the same age as Marie and I see Marie as a child still.

The New York market crash will affect Rasmus' business, he says. I don't understand how but I suppose he knows. All sorts of dire things are threatened, the loss of this concession of his, the possibility of our moving out of this house to somewhere smaller. He told me this evening that Mr. Cline had swindled him out of thousands.

I am going to write it once and never again. I will write it and never even read it again—but when do I reread this diary?

I am in love with Harry. I shall be fifty next year and I am in love for the first time. What will become of us, he and I? The sad thing is that nothing will. We shall go on just the same.

22

If this were my story I should chronicle in some detail the progress of my love. Our conversations would be recorded, but those concerned with *Anna* left out. I would note our first kiss and our first lovemaking. Instead, a precis of all that must suffice. It will have to be enough to say that I soon discovered, if I didn't know it already, how wrong I'd been to tell Cary I was too old to have a lover and how foolish to tell myself that my capacity for love had been burned out in the years with Daniel.

Cary herself I realized I must no longer neglect. It was two weeks since I had slept at my flat, for I had been dividing my time between Willow Road and Paul's house in Hackney, but I'd gone back there several times to retrieve messages from the answering machine. Cary's voice issued from it every time, on increasing levels of hysteria. She sounded extremely relieved when at last I called her back.

"Oh, it's wonderful to be actually speaking to you and not that bloody machine! I kept thinking I must have done something, I mean something *more* than what I've done, if you see what I mean. Listen, will you come with me to see Roper's house?"

A strange thing had happened. I found that I no longer disliked her. She came to Willow Road on a Saturday morning, dressed up defiantly, as if it were important to prove to me more than to any other that her youthfulness had survived the years. And perhaps, in the light of what I'd said to her, it *was* important.

She had leggings on, the kind that were first designed for skiing with an instep strap, a bright blue tunic tightly belted and a kind of tasseled poncho. But her expression was anxious. Her eyes were strained. I understood that when I said I'd forgiven her I was lying but I wouldn't be lying now. We'd been friends once. Then, into our late youth Daniel had intervened. It seemed to me that something had happened to wipe away those years and this was the old Cary and, come to that, the old me, in a way made young again as she would wish.

I kissed her. She drew back as if in recoil but then, as we walked into Swanny's sitting room, she caught up with me and kissed my cheek. I must have been slow on the uptake that day, for it took me quite a long time to realize what had happened, why I liked her again and no longer resented her. We were in Hackney, Cary and I, exploring the Ropers' house, walking through the rooms where Lizzie had lived and died, when, quite suddenly, I understood.

The question was whether, when the Roper film came to be made, the indoor scenes should be shot inside Devon Villa, Navarino Road, itself or in some other house chosen for the purpose. Devon Villa is still standing, as I'd been told Anna's house in Lavender Grove still stands, though I'd never seen it. The obvious and best thing surely, as I said to Cary, would be to use the real house and consider it a piece of luck it hadn't been demolished. Ah, she said, you say that because you don't know television production companies like I do. It's possible another place might be more suitable even though they didn't live in it.

"You mean you're rearranging history?"

"History could sometimes be tidier than it is," she said. "Think of all the unlikely things that happen. I want to eliminate unlikely things from this production."

"And Devon Villa's unlikely?"

"I don't know yet. I haven't seen it. But it's a big house, I know that, and quite grand, though it had seen better days even when

Maria Hyde first came there. Somehow it's not quite the sort of place you'd expect people like that to have lived in."

She was on her way over there. I said on an impulse that I'd go with her, though up till then I'd held out and said I wasn't interested. But things had changed. My feelings for her had changed. I'd no objection to being with her and thought I might enjoy a day in her company. Now that I knew too whose identity Swanny had assumed in her last years, though there was no possibility of that identification being correct, I wanted to see the house where the child Edith had lived.

Cary, as the producer of the proposed serial, had an appointment with the owner of the ground floor and basement at Devon Villa and the owner of the flat on the first floor. The second and third floors were currently empty, the owners being away in Morocco, but the people downstairs had a key and would show us over the rooms where the bodies of Lizzie and Maria had been found.

She had been right about the house being grand. In Hampstead it would have been a stately residence but here the shabby neighborhood detracted from its snob appeal. The whole terrace was more the kind of thing you see in Bayswater, Victorian classical, long sash windows, a flat stuccoed front, steps up to a front door inside a pillared porch. Devon Villa had been renamed Devon Court and there were three bells alongside the front door. I began to understand what Cary meant about unlikely things as soon as the woman who introduced herself as Brenda Curtis had let us into her flat. Once the sights and sounds of the neighborhood were excluded and the front door closed, we might just as well have been inside one of the flat conversions next door in Willow Road.

The entrance hall had seemed promising, for the red marble floor mentioned by Ward-Carpenter was still there and unchanged, as were the carved balusters of the staircase. The chair rail that traversed the walls was surely a hundred years old and the lincrusta with its pattern of stylized leaves and flowers in relief. Now, of course, it was painted white, which Maria Hyde would probably have associated only with bathrooms, and the woodwork was white but for those mahogany banisters. But in here, where Brenda Curtis and her husband had the two, now three, rooms on the ground floor and the three more in the basement, we might have been in a house built last year, though built of course in a neo-Georgian way with arches and alcoves and recesses and, incongruously, an open-tread staircase descending to the basement.

"I don't know that I should care to live in the second-floor flat," she said as she took us down to where Florence Fisher had had her domain. "The Mannerings are away a lot, so perhaps it doesn't worry them. And they've got quite an obsession about keeping things in period, so of course it's clean up there but not really changed much. They sleep in that room, you know." She gave us a sidelong look. "The one where they found the bodies, I mean. I shouldn't like that myself."

We murmured, no, no indeed, we shouldn't like it either.

"When we came seven years ago nothing had been done down here. The place was just the way it must have been when Roper lived here. A very old woman had the basement, she'd lived here alone since she was thirty and she died here, and I don't think she ever put a coat of paint on it. It didn't look like it, anyhow. She kept the kitchen just the way it had been when Maria Hyde had it and when we came it was infested with black beetles. There was a room over there no bigger than a large cupboard where the poor little maid-of-all-work slept. The scullery was in this part, nearest to the outside, and would you believe it the old copper was still there, a dreadful old stone and plaster thing with a wooden lid. The estate agent said it was a collector's piece like the kitchen range but we had it out. We altered everything and made it all spacious and airy, so you can't really imagine how it was."

A French window gave off the Poggenpohl kitchen onto a paved and walled garden. A tabby cat was sitting on the rim of a fish pond between stone tubs of bay trees. Only the garden walls themselves looked as if they might be the originals, ten feet high and of brown brick blackened by ancient, long-forbidden smoke. Where the police had found the bread knife stood a raised bed, built up with a stone wall, and filled with dwarf conifers.

My head was full of Edith, but as this woman had said, it was impossible to imagine her in this kitchen, seated at a table, eating her porridge while the maid bustled about. By gaslight perhaps it had been, for little daylight could have penetrated down here even on a July morning. There had very likely been a window or two giving onto an area but that too was hard to re-create in the mind.

Before we went up to the first floor we stood at the foot of the staircase, glad to leave Mrs. Curtis behind her own front door, and thought of Edith climbing those stairs that last time she was seen, mounting them on legs that were too short, vanishing from view round the curve at the top. We were halfway up ourselves when the owner of this floor heard us and came out onto the landing.

"You won't see her at this hour," he said.

Cary asked who it was we wouldn't see.

"Edith."

He seemed to enjoy the effect this had on us, the widening of our eyes perhaps.

"Only a joke, ladies. Don't look so worried. I've never seen her and I've been here ten years."

"A ghost?"

"So they say. The woman upstairs, Mrs. Mannering, swears she saw her once. You want to take more water with it, I said. Don't be daft, she said, you know I don't drink. I saw her on the stairs. It was when I came in last night just before midnight." He had plainly told the story many times before and made himself word perfect. An elderly man who lived alone, he had perhaps made this retelling of his own domestic ghost story the high spots in an otherwise dull life. "I was at the foot of the stairs, she said, and I looked up and saw this child climbing them."

"What happened next?" Cary said.

"Not a lot. She disappeared round the bend and that was the last of her. Round the bend is right, if you ask me. Mrs. Mannering saw her again on another occasion and then that Mrs. Curtis downstairs saw something. Anyway, she screamed out, though she wouldn't say why but she won't go out in the entrance after dark on her own anymore."

This was all very gratifying to Cary. I could see it was giving her all sorts of ideas for the program. It made me feel warmly towards her and pleased for her and it was then that I knew why friendship had returned. I didn't care about Daniel anymore or the memory of Daniel or that she had taken him away from me. He had grown dim, he was just someone I'd once known. Her part in all of it no longer mattered, "it" no longer mattered, because now I had Paul.

I put my hand in Cary's arm. She didn't seem surprised but she made that warm and pleasant gesture that is the way people reciprocate when they're pleased to be arm-in-arm with you. She gave her elbow, and my hand in it, a squeeze against her waist. I believe she thought the ghost story had sent a shiver down my spine. We walked together into the old man's flat, into the bedroom that had been Edith's. Mr. Wagstaff stood proudly by, gratified I think that nothing remained here of that past. The windows were hidden under double glazing and the walls under paper encrusted with peach velvet roses.

Upstairs, another floor up, it was different. Mrs. Curtis had been right when she said things had not changed much. They had been very deliberately and self-consciously retained or the originals copied. For instance, all the lighting was made to look as if the power which came through was from late-nineteenth-century sources. The table lamps were converted oil lamps and the overhead lights had the kind of fluted shades of etched glass that used to be over gas mantels. The picture rails were still there but I doubt if the ceilings on this level of a house would have had fruit and flower moldings. They had them now because the Mannerings had put them there.

A thin layer of dust lay over everything. Mr. Wagstaff's stewardship scarcely extended, Cary whispered to me, to keeping the place clean. It was stuffy and smelled as such places do when shut up over long periods, of dusty fabrics never shaken out, of old paper and airlessness.

The Mannerings had filled it up with turn-of-the-century junk and a few good Edwardian pieces. There was one of those black horsehair sofas that remind you of old railway waiting rooms and must be impossible to sit on without gripping the arms or sliding off. The crimson velvet which proliferated looked as if it needed a

Florence Fisher to come and beat it with one of those cane flails. Everywhere, on the walls, hung old sepia portrait photographs in arts and crafts frames, the kind you see in pubs where the landlord thinks they are trendy. I'm sure these weren't the Mannerings' ancestors but no one in particular, just photographs they had picked up in junk shops. But it's curious to think that, unlike paintings, they must of necessity have been of real people, these people were alive once, someone's lovers, husbands, wives, mothers and fathers, who went to sit for their likeness and hated or loved or were indifferent to the result. And here they were, nearly a hundred years later, brought to this, an immortality of a kind, but a suspect one. For those who have bought and framed your likeness and hung it up have done so not because you were beautiful or good or clever or arresting but merely because you amuse. You provoke visitors to ask, whoever is that extraordinary woman or that peculiar man? Look at their clothes, their hair! Do you suppose they ever thought they looked nice?

Cary said to me afterwards that she felt a deep distrust of people who made a joke of their environment. What kind of a person can it be who surrounds himself with "fun" objects, who purposely discards beauty in favor of the amusing and comfort in favor of the grotesque? Doesn't he or she tire of it? And if so what happens then?

The Mannerings had apparently not tired of it. On the other hand, they were away a lot. Perhaps the freshness of the joke was renewed each time they came back. It was hard to escape the idea that they had made their bedroom the "funniest" place because it was there that the murder had happened. What other reason could there be for the upside-downness of the flat? Their living rooms were on that top floor that Maria Hyde had closed off.

Cary and I looked at each other. She made a face. Roper's portrait was up on the wall with Lizzie's beside it, the photographs from the Ward-Carpenter account, hugely enlarged and framed in ornate gilt. It was a brass bed the Mannerings shared, no doubt a copy of the one on which Lizzie's body had been found. A white cotton counterpane covered it. The window curtains were of dark pink rep with lace half-curtains. On each of the marble-topped bedside cabinets stood a lily-shaped art nouveau lamp, not the genuine article but the kind of thing most chain stores have in their lighting department.

"You'll know who those two are."

Mr. Wagstaff pointed at the framed portraits. He began to chuckle. He too found them amusing. It made me wonder if the majority of humanity would find this kind of thing entertaining. What he said next put it all out of my head. "An old lady and two young fellows came to look at this flat a couple of years back. She was very taken with the photos. She wanted to buy them but I had to say it wasn't up to me. Would I ask Mr. and Mrs. Mannering, she said, and I said I would, yes, next time they were home but I never did. I didn't feel like I could take it seriously, she was a little bit—" he tapped the side of his head, "—if you know what I mean."

"What was she like?"

He looked at me rather suspiciously, as well he might. "Tall, very thin. She had a hat on, which ladies don't so much these days. You know her, do you?"

So it was here that they had come, Swanny and Gordon and Aubrey, not to Lavender Grove as I had taken for granted. They had come here, to where the Ropers had lived.

"How did she get on to you?"

"Came to the front door, I reckon, and Mrs. Curtis sent her up to me. Can I see upstairs, she said, and I said I didn't see why not. She wasn't the first, you know. Folks do come from time to time and Mr. and Mrs. Mannering have got no objection. The stairs bothered her, she said she had arthritis, one of the young chaps had to take her arm."

Swanny had taken those photographs for pictures of her parents. No wonder she had wanted them. I felt a rush of pity for her, standing here where we stood, trying to match her features, as they had been and as they now were, to a mouth, a nose, an eye, a head of hair, in the faded grainy brownish faces that looked down unsmiling. And, in the event, she had never acquired them. Mr. Wagstaff hadn't taken her seriously.

A thought struck me that seemed terrible. "Did you tell her your ghost story?"

He smiled. "I certainly did, thought she'd like it." It was obviously something he regularly told to the "folks who come from time to time," in the tradition of the guide in Holyrood Palace who used to point out a brown stain on the floor as the remains of blood shed by Rizzio when he died.

"Did she like it?"

"She didn't believe it. She said it couldn't be because the living don't have ghosts and Edith was alive."

We went down the long staircase that Edith had climbed and climbed. No one knew how far she had reached. Perhaps no further than the first floor, had gone into her own bedroom—and then what? Could she have fallen from the open window? But if someone had found her wouldn't an alarm have been raised?

Or perhaps she had gone on upstairs. I tried to construct some story of her grandmother still being alive then, of the old woman struggling with her from that place to a safer one, giving her into someone's care before she herself died.

Mr. Wagstaff seemed disappointed that Cary didn't immediately make him an offer of five hundred pounds a week for the use of his flat over an indefinite period. I rather admired her firmness, her refusal to commit herself or her company to anything, and it made me understand how little we know of our friends as professionals, what they are like as working people. That side of her I had never seen before, that smiling, polite yet adamant side.

"Nothing has been decided. If we want to take it further we'll be sure to be in touch."

She said to me, when the door was shut and we were going down the steps, "It won't do at all. It's too tarted up. That bedroom's right in the wrong sort of way."

"Where's the other house?"

It was in the street where Paul lived, Middleton Road. I didn't tell her so and felt a sudden unwillingness to go there. It was Saturday, he would be home and might see us. We were due to meet that night, he and I, but still I felt a ridiculous reluctance to be seen by him on his street with her.

"We can go there, if you like. I can't very well take you inside, I haven't an appointment, but you can tell me what you think from the outside."

"Oh, no, we don't have to."

"Yes, really, I think we will. I quite like the idea. After all, we're here. One doesn't exactly pass through Hackney on one's way anywhere, does one? We should take advantage of the opportunity. It's not very far. One can walk it. I mean, even *I* can walk it."

"Cary," I said, "they were all supposed to be ill, Maria Hyde, Lizzie Roper and Florence Fisher. Lizzie took to her bed at five in the evening with whatever her illness was. Next day Florence was taken ill. What was the matter with them? Was it something infectious and has anyone ever thought to ask?"

"We know what was wrong with Maria. She died of cardiac arrest. Lizzie, of course, was being doped up by Roper with that bromide stuff. Apparently it makes you feel sick and it sedates you if you have too much of it. And he could never calculate how much she took, could he? Florence says she sometimes took three teaspoonfuls of sugar in a cup of tea. Well, suppose she sometimes had two or three cups?"

I said that Florence didn't take sugar. Florence wasn't doped up with hyoscin hydrobromide.

"I've often thought that Florence exaggerated all that about being so ill. Tate-Memling got to the heart of it when he wanted to know what she was doing as one employed to clean the house and in fact not going up to the second floor until a week had passed. The truth probably is that as soon as her employers were out of the way she just skived off but she wasn't going to tell the court that. If you were a domestic servant in 1905 and you skimped on your work or admitted to hating it, that was tantamount to immoral behavior."

"It was odd she didn't carry up the tray but left Maria to do it. Maria'd obviously had a heart attack earlier in the day."

"She was better by then. I don't know all the answers, Ann."

"Did the police ever suspect Florence Fisher of making away with Edith? Was she questioned much? She never seems to have been a suspect, yet she was the last known person to have seen her alive."

"I did think of that myself but as far as I can discover they never for a moment suspected her. Perhaps she gave a great impression of honesty and probity and all that and it may be that she had absolutely no motive for killing the child. She seems to have been fond of Edith. Why kill her? Even after all this great long time, she does impress one as a strong honest sort of person."

"I wonder what became of her."

"Of Florence Fisher? I can tell you something of that. We've had a whole team of people researching. She never married that chap she was engaged to, no one seems to know why not. When she gave evidence at the trial she was a housemaid with a family called Sumner at Stamford Hill. She never married at all. We've got a whole dossier on Florence, you can have a look at it if you like, but it doesn't tell one much."

I asked if she was still alive.

"Well, hardly, Ann. She'd be well over a hundred. She died in 1971 if I remember rightly and I probably don't, my memory's like a sieve these days. There's a great-niece, a sister's granddaughter, but most of what she said was the old eulogistic stuff, you can imagine, how wonderful auntie was and good and unselfish, all that. She wasn't always in service. Somehow or other she got the money together to open a tobacconist's shop and she ran that for years. She did get to be something high up in the Women's Voluntary Service and had her photograph taken with the Marchioness of Clovenford. The niece insisted on showing me that. The only interesting thing about that, as far as I'm concerned, was that Lady Clovenford's father-in-law was the first Marquis of Clovenford and the first Marquis of Clovenford was that Attorney General who had been Richard Tate-Memling who prosecuted Roper."

"I wonder if Florence knew," I said and, drawing a deep breath, pointed to the house on the corner. "That's where my friend Paul lives."

Cary gave a little scream. "Oh, Ann, what a dark horse you are! Why didn't you say? Can we go and see him? Shall we go and ask him to give us coffee? I could do with some, couldn't you?"

Like schoolgirls. Is that where your boyfriend lives? Can I sneak a look at him?

"Where's this house?" I said.

She led me to it reluctantly. We stood on the opposite pavement and I wondered if Paul was watching us. The house had three floors and a basement but otherwise was quite unlike Devon Villa. It was newer, dating from a less gracious time, when dwellings had begun to be mass produced. The proportions had the characteristic wrongness of many buildings put up in the 1890s. It was cheap and ugly, brown brick with heavy plaster trimmings, a front with a double panel of red and green stained glass. But I could see it was more the sort of house Maria Hyde ought to have lived in than the one in which she actually did live. We turned back. Paul had seen us and come out into his front garden.

"Isn't he good-looking!" Cary said.

I burst out laughing.

"What's the matter with you?"

"You can't have this one," I said and I introduced her to Paul and we went into his house.

23

In the event, there was no danger of another theft on Cary's part. Paul told me, rather diffidently, that he hoped I didn't think it unreasonable but he hadn't much liked her. What was less gratifying to me was his refusal to concern himself any further with the diaries.

"Refusal" is too strong a word. It would be better to say that he was reluctant. He seemed quite happy to talk about the Roper case, read the Ward-Carpenter and Mockridge accounts and he even got the whole uncut trial for me, in the Notable British Trials series. The Senate Library had it so of course it was available to him. He seemed interested in speculating about Edith's fate too, what might have become of her and if she had survived. But the diaries, that he had at first been so enthusiastic about, he seemed to have finished with, to have put aside. I had the strange feeling that talking about them had begun to embarrass him. The notebooks he had borrowed he returned to me without a word and when I suggested he might like to look at those for the 1920s and '30s he only shook his head and changed the subject. If the diaries had been no more than records left in my possession by an ancestor, this would scarcely have mattered. Falling in love with someone and entering into a new relationship need not mean you must share everything. Paul himself, after all, played golf, Paul played chess, neither of which activities interested me in the least. But the diaries were more than just a family possession to me, more than an heirloom living in a cupboard. I had become their editor, the mantle of Swanny had to a great extent fallen onto my shoulders. I was doing less and less author research and when almost a year had gone by after Swanny's death, I gave it up altogether.

The diaries wouldn't become my whole life, as they had been Swanny's, but they must inevitably take an important part in it. All those things Swanny had done were now for me to do, discussing new editions with publishers, approving paperback formats, studying illustrations, assessing foreign sales and a host of other matters. It was proposed to issue the diaries that spanned 1935–1944 during the following year, in a simultaneous enterprise by the English publishers and Gyldendal. There was plenty for me to do and, naturally, as one does, I sometimes wanted to talk about what I was doing with the man who was closest to me.

Paul, who is so warm, so enthusiastic, so generous in spirit, gave me, every time, the gentle brush-off. He was always polite, he was always considerate, but he didn't intend to talk about those diaries, come what might. I concluded they must bore him. And this, I thought, was maybe quite natural. Wouldn't they have bored me if they hadn't been by a person I had known well and about people I knew well? On the other hand, they didn't bore the millions who bought and read them.

I ceased to speak of them to him, a difficult prohibition since he would often ask me what I'd done that day and since I wasn't a housewife or much of a shopper and didn't see my friends in the daytime, I was often hard put to answer him. I'd been, after all, all day involved with the next set of diaries.

I didn't just let it go, I asked him. He hesitated and said he didn't suppose I wanted to know how he had got on teaching Danish literature to nineteen year olds.

"Oh, I don't know, I might, if it was funny or different."

"It's seldom different and it's never funny."

"Yes, well, lots of different and sometimes amazing things happen when I'm talking to Margrethe or Swanny's editor about the diaries."

"Tell me," he said, but he said it only because he was kind.

I stopped telling him when his expression became, not so much glazed or bored, as sad. Yes, sad, and I never guessed why. I should have done, it was staring me in the face but I never did. I might have done if I'd ever met his mother. Still, I wasn't the kind of woman who expects her man to take her home to meet his family, especially at my age, with my fiftieth birthday approaching. And Paul never suggested it. He went to see his mother and told me he'd been there and made some comment about her, how she was and what she had been doing, but he never once asked me if I'd feel like coming along too.

We weren't exactly living together. I often think that in our society there is a bar to steady relationships sociologists never seem to think about; people own their homes, they have spent a lot of money on them, often they love them: which one in a partnership is to give up the beloved home? It's not just a matter of money. One may love living in Dulwich and loathe the prospect of Brondesbury while the other couldn't consider the idea of living south of the river. Paul was very fond of his house in Hackney, I had two homes in and around Hampstead. Which of us was to make the sacrifice?

At any rate I'd gone so far as to put my flat on the market, though moving none of my furnishings out of it but for the dollhouse. Padanaram now had a room of its own at Willow Road. The removal van came and it was transported up to Hampstead on the very day that Margrethe Cooper showed me her new translation and I read how the original Padanaram had been sold in the early thirties. I was living in Swanny's house most of the time and, though we stayed with each other and always spent our weekends in one or the other's home, Paul was still living in Hackney.

The solution would have been for each of us to sell our house and buy one jointly, but I had grown to love Willow Road. He loved his house but sometimes talked of selling it. If I stopped him, or didn't encourage him, it was because I wondered what it would be like living with a man who was clearly bored (or somehow distressed or upset) by what occupied me for the greater part of every day.

. . .

Cary found someone to write a script for her, liked what she got, appointed a director and set about casting the production which was simply to be called, in the currently fashionable way, "Roper." It was to be in three parts, to be transmitted on a Monday, Tuesday and Wednesday or else weekly. No one had decided that yet.

The house in Paul's street was to be the venue and she told me that six people worked on it for three months, getting the appearance and all the period detail right. The lucky householders, who would get everything put back as they had left it or else a house interestingly decorated in the style of 1905, had gone on an extended trip to see their son in New South Wales. Paul and I saw them shooting the scene where Roper comes back for his sovereign case. It was a Sunday morning, very early, and I was staying the weekend with him. Middleton Road, which was usually lined with cars, had been cleared and a hansom cab stood outside the house, drawn by a horse that was too fat and sleek. They hadn't been able to find a thin spavined one.

A little crowd had gathered on the opposite side and we all stood gazing before Paul and I decided we could see it just as well from one of his bedroom windows. The actor playing Roper looked quite like his photograph and even more like Abraham Lincoln than Alfred himself had. When we'd seen him get out of the cab and run up the steps fifteen times and still the director wasn't satisfied, we gave up and had our breakfast.

It took the company eight weeks to make the film and when it was done, though not I think before it was edited, Cary produced some very handsome promotional material. This consisted mainly of a large glossy four-page brochure in full color, mostly showing stills from the production but with a blurb on the back page about the cast and who they were and what they'd done and a lot of acclaim for Cary herself and her director, Miles Sinclair. There was a photograph of Roper with Lizzie and one of Lizzie with Maria Hyde. One showed the baby Edith climbing those stairs and another Florence in her kitchen. There was a cast list and I mention it because it was of importance to what happened later.

Principally, it was used for the purpose of drumming up foreign sales. It went to Australia and New Zealand, Canada and America, and one of the results was that Cary did sell the production all over the place. Another was a more personal reaction.

She told me she had had a letter, then a phone call, from an American woman called Lisa Waring. She worked for a television company in Los Angeles and it was her business or the business of her department to select from those on offer foreign (principally British) productions to be transmitted on a cable network. At present she was still in California but would soon be coming to this country.

The name Lisa Waring had seen in the promotional material for "Roper" was that of one of her great-grandfathers on her father's side but she had never come across it elsewhere. The few attempts she had made to establish her ancestry on this side of the family had come to nothing because she was never able to trace this man's origins.

"Which man?" I said.

"She doesn't say. It's all a mystery but then again it's probably not very important."

"What does she expect you to do about it?"

"She wants to come and see me and show me various papers she's got."

Paul said this sort of thing was bound to happen, wasn't it, when a drama that had really happened was adapted for television. There would be more of it when "Roper" went out on the network.

"I don't suppose I can help her," Cary said. "If her great-grandfather was a Roper he could only be Arthur because the other brothers either had no children or their children died, like Edward who was killed in the First World War. Arthur had two daughters and one of them could be her grandmother, I suppose. They were born in 1912 and 1914, he says in the memoir."

"It can hardly be a Roper," Paul said. "Roper's quite a common name."

I know Cary very well. She shows everything she feels in her face, and I could see in a sudden gravity and an accompanying abstraction that she was afraid for the fate of her production. She was afraid this woman was about to tell her something that would put it in jeopardy.

She told me a few days later that she had always wondered if something lay in Roper's past that would explain the nature and the method of Lizzie's murder. It isn't everyone who can cut someone's throat with a single clean blow of a sharp knife. What was there in Roper to negate the normal inhibition that restrains most men from such an act? Where, too, and how had he acquired the skill to do it? If he had done it. If it was Roper.

Lisa Waring wanted to meet Cary, at her home, at her office, wherever was most convenient. In her usual effusive way Cary begged me to *be there*. I said I would but since she hadn't heard any more from Lisa Waring it might be that she had changed her mind. It might even be that all along it was a hoax or a ploy to attract attention to herself. There was even a possibility she didn't work for this company at all but had been shown the promotional material by someone who did. Had Cary checked up on that? It wouldn't be difficult.

Cary confessed that she hadn't. I could see she was worried but she brightened at my suggestion that Lisa Waring—if there was such a person—might be doing this out of malice or amusement and said she would phone the company and ask to speak to her. I reminded Cary that to many the mere thought of being in even tenuous contact with television people seemed exciting.

Meanwhile, my flat was finally sold and Willow Road became my home. Gordon and Aubrey were frequent visitors. They had been on their records-searching trip to Denmark and Gordon had filled in most of the gaps in his genealogical table. He had been able to take the Westerbys back to 1780 and the Kastrups a further fifty years. Gyldendal liked the idea of a family tree as frontispiece to their new edition and the British publishers were nearly as enthusiastic. At this time all that was left for Gordon to do was find who it was Anna's great grandfather and Tante Frederikke's grandfather had married in the 1790s and if, as he suspected, Rasmus' maternal grandmother had been illegitimate.

Of course I'd questioned him about that visit to Devon Villa but he knew no more than he had originally told me. Swanny had been mysterious about it. She had been secretive, he'd thought so at the time.

"You couldn't say she led us to believe this was Anna's home she was taking us to," Aubrey said. "Not exactly. She never said whose home it had been."

"But she did imply her own family—well, *my* own family—had lived there. She said, 'my mother and father.'" Gordon remembered the ghost story and he remembered Swanny's dislike of it. The second floor had appalled him as it had me but he had no recollection of the pictures nor of Swanny's offer to buy them. "I didn't ask who they were, I wasn't interested. I knew they weren't Anna and Rasmus."

Then I told him, I told them both, of Swanny's ignorance of who she was. At first Gordon was concerned only for his genealogical table. He wanted to know if he should put "adopt" in brackets after Swanny's name, but agreed not to when I explained what difficulties something like that would incur for future, and indeed past, editions of the diaries.

He said in his earnest way, nodding a little, giving me that Westerby look, right into the eyes, "I shall find out who she was."

"Well, good luck," I said.

The next set of diaries were in print and I, along with a dozen other people, had the task of reading the proofs. It's true what a lot of writers say, that you never really know what a work is like until you see it in print. A typed manuscript or even one that is a word processor print-out isn't the same. Reading them for typographical errors and errors of fact and sense, I nevertheless aimed at reading them for pleasure too.

I knew, from having seen Margrethe Cooper's translation in manuscript, that there was nothing here to give a clue to Swanny's origins. But that was what I was on the lookout for. It hadn't much concerned me while Swanny was alive but since her death, since Roper, since learning of the identity she'd assumed, my own need to know had grown and grown. It would never in the nature of things be as great as hers had been but it was strong enough for me. Cary longed to know who was Edith Roper and I to know who Swanny was. Practically the only thing we did know was that they were not each other.

I had never read Arthur Roper's memoir and I gave the copy back to Cary. She suggested I might like to look at the piece Cora Green wrote for the *Star* in the autumn of 1905.

I took a break from the diary proofs and read it. Of course, Cora Green hadn't written it herself, it had been "ghosted," though no doubt the facts, if facts they were, came from her. The ghostwriter had a flowery, precious and pompous style, and one that was old-fashioned even then. Lizzie Roper was dead and therefore couldn't, in law, be libeled, so Mrs. Green had gone to town on her lovers and her behavior in their company. Maria Hyde was dead too and the fact that she and Cora Green had once been bosom friends conveniently forgotten.

Our street had been a respectable place until that notorious family, whose doings have lately formed the subject matter of so much scandal, took up their abode at Devon Villa. As one of those inclined to believe the best of people until proved otherwise, as a trusting and perhaps overly innocent woman, I confess I soon formed a friendship with my new neighbor, Mrs. Maria Hyde.

Was that honorable title hers by right? Naturally, I did not enquire. She was known as "Mrs." and so I called her. We were Mrs. Hyde and Mrs. Green until the intimacy of friendship dictated a change to Maria and Cora.

In those early days, the final decade of the last century, Maria Hyde had three lodgers, Mr. Dzerjinski, Miss Cottrell and Mr. Ironsmith. The little maid, not much more than a child but required to do most of the work of the house, was called Florence and she hailed from that wretched part of Hackney that is an acknowledged disgrace, the marshes of the River Lea.

Mr. Dzerjinski, a foreigner as his name evinces, was more Mrs. Hyde's friend than her lodger. What their relationship truly was, what degree of intimacy of a possibly criminal kind they had reached, I cannot say. My tendency is to seek out the good in my fellow creatures, not the evil. However, even a saint or angel would have been hard-pressed to take a charitable view of the activities of Mrs. Hyde's daughter, the ill-fated Elizabeth, or Lizzie, and the gentlemen (for want of a better word) who called at Devon Villa.

Mr. George Ironsmith did not have to call. He was resident in the house. One day Mrs. Hyde told me he was engaged to be married to her daughter and Miss Lizzie herself showed me a ring he had given her, a poor thing made of some base metal and paste or glass, I adjudged it, but nevertheless a pledge of his intent to make their association legal. The promise she had given him did not, however, hinder her from receiving the visits of others. Her betrothed was, after all, away from the house at business for the greater part of each day. Mrs. Hyde herself introduced me to a Mr. Middlemass, a gentleman of quite advanced years, as "Lizzie's friend."

We happened to meet one afternoon when she was showing him off the premises and I emerged quite by chance from my front door. Mr. Middlemass was at least fifty years old and appeared prosperous with a fur collar to his overcoat and carrying a gold-topped cane. I saw him several times after that and it is my belief, albeit reluctantly entertained, that Miss Lizzie's engagement was broken off as a result of his visits. Soon after this the luckless Mr. Ironsmith moved out.

His place in the house was taken by a couple of irreproachable respectability, Mr. and Mrs. Upton. Mrs. Upton and I were soon to recognize a mutuality of tastes and general philosophy of life and became firm friends. Indeed, our friendship was to outlast our sojourn in the neighborhood and persists staunchly to this day. It was Mrs. Upton who told me of the disgraceful condition into which the house was sinking, "livestock" in the walls and even mattresses, black beetles in the kitchen regions as well as other unwelcome denizens of the insect kingdom.

There was a good deal more description here, written in the same unctuous style and high moral tone, of the conditions prevailing at Devon Villa. Cora Green also gave detailed descriptions of the personal appearance of all the occupants of the house. Miss Cottrell's departure was referred to and Mrs. Upton's version given of the quarrel between her and Maria Hyde which led to her departure.

I remembered Cary saying how that other document of value in establishing the true state of affairs at Devon Villa, Beatrice Cottrell's memoir, had disappeared. Like certain classical literature which perished, for example, in the great fire that consumed the library of Alexandria, its existence and nature were known only through quotations from it in other works. Cary had applied to the British Museum but in vain. I can't say I was sorry. I read on.

I was deeply relieved when Miss Lizzie married the new lodger, Mr. Roper. At first I had, unfortunately but perhaps with justification, seeing what had gone before, believed that Mr. Roper was merely another string to her bow and the "friendship" was not calculated to lead to any lasting relationship, sanctioned by church and law. But Miss Lizzie was intent this time upon matrimony and the other "gentlemen" disappeared from Devon Villa.

Rumor in the neighborhood of our street had it that Miss Lizzie, or Mrs. Roper as she became, was in a certain condition at the time of her wedding and it is true that Mr. Roper's son and heir was born a mere six months after that interesting event.

How happy I would be to be able to say that Mrs. Roper settled down after these events and became a loyal and devoted wife and mother! Unfortunately, that would be an untruth. Unnatural though it seems, she hated the fine healthy boy to whom she had given birth. To save him from a pitiful death from neglect, malnutrition and perhaps even wanton cruelty, Mr. Roper was obliged to engage a nurse.

Florence had too heavy a load of domestic labor in that household to undertake in addition the care of a child. I had always pitied *her,* burdened as she was with an unfair load of menial tasks. She was often moved to confide in me and reveal the innermost secrets of her young heart. She had engaged herself to be married to another servant, a young man whose employers enjoyed the benefits of a handsome house in Canonbury. I was greatly relieved to hear it and relieved too that the man I had seen come to Devon Villa and be admitted through the basement area was Florence's beau and not, as I had feared, yet another admirer of Mrs. Roper's.

These, however, were not few and far between. Mrs. Roper had restrained herself while her son was an infant but it was not long before I saw Mr. Middlemass arrive at the front door of Devon Villa in a cab. Another visitor at this time was a young man of the name of Cobb or Hobb. My astonishment may be imagined when I encountered Mrs. Roper walking arm-in-arm with this person in London Fields. Mrs. Roper had always been demonstrative in a way acceptable to no refined taste, but when her husband was the object of these transports only the most particular would have found fault. It was a different matter to see her putting her face close to that of Mr. Cobb (or Hobb) and allowing him to place an arm round her waist.

No doubt, on this occasion she would have preferred *not* to see me but since we were approaching each other along the same path, there was no help for it. She put a brave face on things and introduced the young man to me as "Bert," whom she called a friend of Mr. Roper's.

It was shortly after this that I saw another old friend of Mrs. Roper's in our street. This was none other than Mr. Ironsmith, who had moved away some years before. I recognized him at once but he pretended not to know *me.* Where he had been in the meantime I cannot pretend to say. He was very gaudily dressed in a checked coat and wide-brimmed hat and was smoking a cigar and later, while coming down my front steps to speak to a tradesman, I was unable to help overhearing him in conversation with Mrs. Roper on the doorstep of Devon Villa. If I had only heard him and not previously *seen* him I might have doubted who this was, for he spoke with a strong Colonial accent.

I came to the reluctant conclusion that Mrs. Hyde herself played a part in these transactions. In short, at Devon Villa she was keeping a certain kind of house in which her own daughter was put to work. Whatever excuses may have been made, I have no doubt that it was a similar inference to my own which led to Miss Cottrell's leaving. On this occasion a terrible altercation took place in the house next door, leading I believe to physical as well as verbal violence and culminating in poor Miss Cottrell's furniture being put out into the street.

Mr. Roper was in no doubt that he was not the father of the daughter born to his wife in May 1904. Whose was the paternity I cannot pretend to say. The shocking situation at Devon Villa became too much for me and I was fortunately able to discover alternative accommodation in Stoke Newington in the November of that year, whereupon I moved away. I heard no more of the Ropers and Mrs. Hyde until I was confronted, through the pages of a newspaper, with the appalling revelations of Mrs. Roper's murder in the house next to the one in which I had lived for so long.

Anna's diaries for the war years and those which preceded the war were full of herself and her feelings, more so than the ten notebooks for 1925–1934. There was less domesticity in them, less of interiors and furnishings and more of independence, politics, international events and physical fear. A bomb had fallen nearly opposite number Ninety-eight. A family friend in Denmark had been shot by the Nazis for harboring a Jew.

Middle age engrossed her, though she was funny and philosophical about it. She seems to have managed to ignore her husband totally for long hours or even days, though they shared that house and that bed, the one with the sphinxes, for the past six months occupied by me and often by Paul too. A great deal of time, more than ever, was passed in the company of Uncle Harry. Page after page was concerned with what Harry did and what Harry said and sometimes what Harry ate, drank and wore. She loved him, she said so, and there was no doubt he loved her, but the relationship never became sexual.

Anna would have considered herself, in her fifties and sixties, far too old. But she hadn't always been too old, she hadn't been too old when she met Harry in 1919. There was a class barrier, of course, erected by both of them. But neither their ages nor social differences seemed to have been enough to keep them from going for walks together, going to tea with each other, visiting the zoo, the parks, the British Museum, the cinema and theatre matinees together. The answer, of course, is that there was a moral prohibition, a taboo on both of them as married people. They were companions, they were friends, they could never be lovers.

But Harry, except in this aspect, didn't much interest me. I wanted the solution to a mystery, not the chronology of a friendship. I was Swanny's heir in more ways than one. Like her, I wanted to know, though being far less emotionally involved was not liable to clutch at impossible straws. And as I thought about it, about how subtly and insidiously this desire to know had grown in me, I realized that it had permeated my attempts to talk to Paul about the diaries. In fact, I hadn't tried to talk to him about the diaries in general but only and invariably in connection with Swanny's origins. Whatever I had begun to say about them I had always returned to this one thing.

So it was this he didn't want to talk about. Once I understood that I wanted to ring him up at work and apologize and tell him I'd been obtuse and ask him why. Why? But I never, or very seldom, have phoned him at work. He isn't a man to hang about the Senior Common Room, is either teaching or holding a tutorial in his own room where he refuses to have a phone at all. We weren't planning to see each other that evening. His mother was very ill, had had a severe heart attack a week before and lay in intensive care in a big heart hospital on the other side of London. Paul went to see her every day and that evening he had an appointment for a talk about her condition with the consultant in charge of the case.

Of course, in the absence of a chance of finding out for sure, I speculated. I laid the proofs aside and began asking myself why on earth Paul, who had seemed quite intrigued by the whole thing at first, should have set his face against discussing who Swanny might have been. One answer was that he knew. That was tantalizing but impossible. How could he have known and if he did, by some extraordinary chance, surely he would have wanted to tell me.

The last diaries, those written between 1955 and 1967, hadn't yet been translated. That is, Margrethe Cooper hadn't translated them. Paul had, or had been in the process of doing so when he took against the diaries and lost interest in them. I asked myself if he had found something that not only put him off further translating but also stopped him telling me.

His grandmother, something about his grandmother. Inevitably I came back to Hansine. She had died in 1954 but Anna says very little about her death in *Peace and War*. Perhaps she had saved her comments for the following year and Paul had discovered them. Or else his grandmother herself had told him. There had always been a strong possibility that Hansine knew, Hansine had been living with Anna in Lavender Grove and, unless something very strange was going on, must have known. But would she have passed this knowledge on to her grandson who was only a boy of eleven when she died?

No, but she may have passed it on to her daughter. I had got no further than this, had come to a dead end with this, though turning it over and over in my mind, when Paul phoned. It was evening by then and I was back with the proofs, laboriously inking in the proofreader's marks from the guide in the *Encyclopedia Britannica.*

He phoned to tell me his mother had died. She died a few minutes before he arrived at the hospital.

24

Det er nójagtig femten Aar siden idag, at vi maatte tage fra Padanaram og komme hertil. Jeg skrev ikke Datoen ned nogen Steder, men jeg kan huske den. Hvis jeg var den Slags Kvinde, der er dramatisk anlagt, saa vilde jeg sige, at den var skrevet i mit Hjerte.

It is exactly fifteen years today since we had to leave Padanaram and come here. I didn't write the date down anywhere but I remember it. If I was the kind of woman who went in for drama, I'd say it was written on my heart.

It's quite a strange coincidence that when Marie came to tea this afternoon she told me she intends to give her Padanaram to Ann for a seventh birthday present. I think her birthday's in December, I must look it up. I loved that house, the big one I mean, not the silly thing Rasmus made and which made me so angry that it wasn't for Swanny. "Ninety-eight" isn't so bad but the district is shabby and it reminds me more and more of those days long gone by in Lavender Grove.

I was glad Marie didn't mention *her* Padanaram in front of Swanny but got all that out of the way before Swanny arrived.

Perhaps I'm wrong but I still have this feeling she was hurt by the way Rasmus rejected her. The funny thing is he's charming to her now and spends as much time in her house boring Torben with his tales of being swindled as he does in Marie's. Silly old man! No doubt, it would be a different story if Swanny had married a poor man and lived down the road in Hornsey.

All those years since the business failed and Westerby Autos was no more and still he goes on every day, day after day, about who stole this and that from him, who did him down and where he might be today if people hadn't treated him so basely. I wonder if he knows what he looks like, setting off in a stiff collar and a homburg hat, still wearing spats, sitting high up there in that old Fiat, the old black box. Yet, can even a woman as hard as I am escape the curse of tenderness? If he's an old fool, I'm a sentimental old woman. I look at him and remember—one or two things. A hundred years ago. I remember that night he came back, though not what I wrote. I know it wasn't quite true what I wrote, it wasn't quite like that. But it's no use pretending I care for him. I don't.

The girls came to talk about this Golden Wedding party they are giving us at Frascati's. What a lot of bosh it all is! For one thing, there will be no nice food, there isn't any. I think it's worse now than when the war was on. All that restaurants can find to serve is vol-au-vents and blancmange. Vol-au-vents filled up with vegetables in tinned soup is what it tastes like and probably what it is. But never mind the meal, we know that will be bad. The guest list is going to cause trouble, I can see it coming.

I will *not* have Hansine invited. What an idea! It comes from Marie, of course. "All those snobbish ideas have gone since the war, Mor," she says to me. It isn't snobbery, though I don't tell her that. Anyway, Joan Cropper married a man with a good job and a good salary, they live in a much better house than Ninety-eight and Hansine's been living with them since Sam died. You could say she'd come up in the world more than she can ever have dreamed of and we've gone down. But the fact is that I don't like her. I never have. It's not just that she reminds me too much of those early days, though she does, but when I see that big raw red face of hers and those flat eyes and silly smile I feel something quite unlike me, I feel afraid.

Well, I shall have who I want to my party. I won't have Hansine but I'll insist on Harry and, of course, his wife. I can't avoid that. If Marie doesn't like it—Swanny will, she loves Harry—she's welcome to give up the idea of a party altogether. Isn't it ridiculous celebrating the fact that my husband and I, who haven't even liked each other for forty-nine years, have been together for fifty?

SEPTEMBER 15, 1954

I never complained to anyone about Rasmus while he was alive. I didn't need to, I had my diary to complain to. Not even to Harry, though I could have told him and it would have gone no further.

When you keep a diary as a regular thing over many years it's not just a record of your life and your thoughts, it becomes a person. Your diary is the one person you can say everything to, you need keep nothing back, you can put down the whole contents of your mind, however bad. Or what the world calls bad. There's no living human being I could do that to, not even Harry. No, when I come to think of it there are a thousand things I've felt but never dared to say to Harry. On the other hand, I've put everything down in this diary but one thing.

While I never complained about Rasmus that didn't stop people telling me how I'd miss him when he was gone. Perhaps they could see I never cared much for him. Even Marie, who ought to know better, was always saying in those last months when he was so ill, that I'd feel his loss more than I could calculate. Well, he's gone and I don't. I don't miss him. I'm free at last and I like it.

When Harry's wife died, it must be three years ago, he seemed to miss her bitterly. I remembered what he said about not really wanting to marry her and sometimes I wanted to remind him of those words, but I never did. Saying a thing like that can make a person hate you, one or two words are enough, they last forever.

She died and he mourned and I was jealous. I wrote of it at the time but I won't look back in the diaries, I never do that. I no longer remember what I wrote but I remember the jealousy for a dead woman.

Which one of my children shall I live with? Swanny, of course. There was never any real doubt and they all know it. We were just playing games when we talked about it after the funeral. I shall be a little further away from Harry, that's all, but that's of no consequence since he got a car of his own.

NOVEMBER 23, 1954

Everyone dies, one after another. Hansine now. Joan Sellway née Cropper sent me a very vulgar card with a black border round it.

I shan't go to the funeral. There have been too many funerals in my life. Besides, the day they are going to have it Harry and I have tickets for a matinee. I am rereading *Hard Times*, I think for the fifth time.

APRIL 3, 1957

I've only had two proposals of marriage in my life and they came sixty years apart. The first one I said yes to, more fool me, and the second one was today.

I didn't expect it. After all, I'm seventy-seven and he must be seventy-five, I'm not absolutely sure but something like that. He'd asked me to have lunch with him and he drove me down to London, to a very nice French place in Charlotte Street. We've always enjoyed sharing meals, we both like the same food and a lot of it.

We were having our coffee and a brandy each. Harry's taken to smoking cigars and I like to see a man with a cigar, though not smoking them myself the way so many Danish women do. He lit his cigar and he said without anything to lead up to it and not a bit nervous, "Anna, will you marry me?"

I didn't know what to say, which is unusual with me. I didn't blush either. Perhaps you get too old to be able to blush. I think I went pale instead, I know I shivered.

He said, "I love you and I know you love me."

"Oh, yes," I said. "Oh, yes, that goes without saying."

"Nothing goes without saying, Anna." He said it very gently and sweetly.

"I love you then," I said.

And there was a long silence in which we looked at each other and looked away and looked at each other again. In that time I was thinking furiously, I was thinking like I've never thought before. Or so I suppose. In a long life like mine you forget what you've felt in the past and what you've thought before, there's no use pretending. But I thought how I'd longed for him when we were young and how handsome he was and longing for me, and now I'm a dried-up old woman, really dried up, though no one ever writes things like that down. Except me. I write them. I don't think I could do those things in bed with a man now, it wouldn't be possible physically. I am dried and closed like a husk. And my naked body looks as if it needs ironing, nothing else will get the creases out. I'd be ashamed to let a man see me and touch me now.

No doubt, he didn't mean a marriage with that in it. What's the point then? That was the only thing in marriage I wanted and never had. The rest is the part I don't like, the familiarity, the getting to know someone's worst side, the increasing contempt. That would never happen with us, I could hear him saying if I told him. So I didn't. I just said no.

"No, Harry, I won't marry you," I said.

"Funny, I was afraid you wouldn't, almost knew you wouldn't."

"I would have once," I said, "when we couldn't."

"I wonder what good it's done us," he said, "being so good and moral. Sticking with the people we were married to, I mean. Honorable behavior, they'd have called it when we were young."

"You couldn't have left Mrs. Duke," I said. It's funny but I couldn't remember her name. I'd always just called her Mrs. Duke. "I always knew that. And I wouldn't have left my husband. I'm too stubborn, I suppose. You make a bargain and you stick with it but it's all bosh really, isn't it?"

He said he didn't know. He didn't know the answers, only that it was too late, it would have been too late even if he'd met me when I lived in Lavender Grove and he was single with a job in Islington. "But we'll never leave each other, will we? We'll be friends till one of us dies?"

I nodded. For a moment I couldn't speak, so I just kept nodding my head, on and on, like a toy or a doll. He took my hand and kissed it, the way he does sometimes.

JUNE 16, 1963

I have bought two dozen cards to send out for the chocolate party we shall have for my eighty-third birthday next month. Swanny and Marie will be there, of course, and I shall ask Ann, though no one knows where young people get to these days. Does anyone know where she actually lives? Not with her mother, I'm sure.

Knud and Maureen will have to be invited but I doubt if they'll come all this way. Knud is supposed to have something wrong with his prostate gland, whatever it is men have. I'm not asking John and his wife, I hardly know them, I don't suppose I've seen John since Rasmus' funeral. Mrs. Evans, of course, and Mrs. Cline and Margaret Hammond who's married now but whose surname I can't remember. I don't think women keep up these long-term quarrels like men do. If Mr. Housman hadn't died I'm sure Rasmus would have gone on hating him till *he* died but the flu carried him off by a piece of luck for everyone, to be frank, so that Mrs. Housman who I always liked could be free to marry Mr. Hammond. I can't help feeling I've written all this before. You do get to repeat yourself at my age. I must remember to ask Swanny for Margaret's married name and where she lives.

Someone I'd really like to invite is that Mrs. Jörgensen I had such an interesting talk with at Swanny's luncheon party. But I'm told she's gone back to Denmark. I wonder if she'll keep her promise and send me a copy of the book she's writing when it comes out, the one with the chapter in it about the *Georg Stage*?

Harry hasn't gone anywhere, I'm glad to say. A chocolate party would be no celebration without him there. I'd better ask his eldest girl as well and she can drive him. He's been nervous about driving since he started getting those tremors in his hands.

I've left writing about this to the end. In fact, I nearly didn't write about it at all. Swanny showed me an anonymous letter she had had. Poor thing, she was in an awful state, hardly able to speak, shaking all over, I can't imagine why. It was just as I was getting ready to go out and buy the cards and I was thinking about that and the people I'd invite and I wasn't really paying attention. But when she waved the wretched thing at me and I could see she was working herself up, I took it from her, tore it up and burnt it. The best thing to do. I went out immediately afterwards, to be on my own really. Shock doesn't affect you straightaway, it takes a few minutes. I was shaking a bit as I walked down Willow Road and then I said to myself, who cares? Who cares now?

OCTOBER 5, 1964

Ann didn't phone but came to us this afternoon to tell us Marie had died. We expected it, we were waiting for it, but the shock is still there.

It is a terrible thing to lose one's children, perhaps the worst thing in the world. But long ago I decided it was for the best not to show my feelings, to keep calm, to carry on. Soldier on, as Torben says. Grief is best kept in the heart—or written down. Nowadays I pretend I have no feelings left and I find people believe it, I think they like to believe it, it removes their responsibility for me. I pretend that my heart has been made hard by the many blows it has taken over all these years.

This diary sometimes looks like a chronicle of death, as one after another die, but I didn't expect to lose my youngest, only fifty-three and still young to me.

APRIL 21, 1966

The papers are full of a murder trial, a man called Ian Brady and a woman called Myra Hindley charged with killing children up in Lancashire. It's fascinating but horrible. From her photographs the woman looks much older than she is, only twenty-something, and the man looks just a thug. To me she looks just like a German, I'm sure she must have German ancestry.

Not many people have known a murderer. It would be strange to find out afterwards that a person you knew had murdered someone. This case has made me remember that business in Navarino Road when we first came to London. My memory is falling to bits because I can't remember the name of the house or the name of the people, only that I saw the woman once and wished her house was mine.

JUNE 4, 1966

I hate this forgetfulness. Whole decades of my life have slipped away from me and only a dim impression of a whole ten years remains, like a picture painted on glass that's nearly faded away. I remember my childhood and going up to the cottage in Strandvej for the summer, that holiday on Bornholm when I was seven, my mother always ill in bed and having to creep about so as not to disturb her. Tante Frederikke used to make me walk with a book on my head for my posture and give me buttermilk soup, which I hated so much and had to sit at the table until I'd finished it. I can remember whole days from that time in the greatest detail. It is the middle years which are gone.

I wish Swanny wouldn't keep asking me. She refuses to believe me when I say I can't remember. Some, of course, I remember, the fact of it, but not who and when and how. I resolved once never to write of it but I could laugh when I think how little that resolution matters now. I couldn't write of it if I chose because I've forgotten nearly everything.

OCTOBER 2, 1966

I get very tired in the evenings now, quite early in the evening, which never used to be the case, and I think the bits I write are getting shorter and shorter. What I've started doing instead is writing to Harry. We do see each other a couple of times a week but that's not so easy now he is housebound and never drives and I'm dependant on Swanny for taxis.

Taxis are *extremely* expensive. I pay for mine out of the sales of all those old clothes. I've been back to the woman in St. John's Wood High Street and sold the blue and black Chanel two-piece and the pleated Patou dress. Did I buy them in Paris or in London? I can't remember. She got quite excited, said she never expected to see anything so beautiful and in such good condition.

I'm going to stop now and write to Harry. I still write English very badly but he doesn't mind. He calls them his love letters and he says I'm the only woman who has ever written him any.

"What about that girl you were in love with when you were twenty-five?"

"Twenty-four," he said. "I was twenty-four. It's true I was in love and I meant to marry her but when it came to it she wouldn't have me, she said something had happened to put her off men and marriage. But she said all that, she didn't put it in a letter."

"Your wife must have written to you when you were in France in the first war," I said.

"Oh, she did, and regularly," he said, "good letters full of home and the girls and how they all missed me, but they weren't love letters. They weren't like yours, Anna. Yours are great love letters like—well, like Robert Browning's."

"Don't you mean like *Mrs.* Browning's?" I said. I said it to cover up how pleased I felt. No one else has ever told me I write well. I suppose no one else has had the chance.

We read those Browning letters together—well, not together. I got them from the library and then I passed them on to him.

SEPTEMBER 2, 1967

It is all over. I feel that life is, but it won't stop, it has to go on. I will never cease to be grateful to that kind good girl that she sent for me to be with her father when he was dying. Not when he died, not that, for he died after we had all gone, in the night, in his sleep, but while he lay there waiting for the end. He had pneumonia and the drugs they gave him couldn't fight it any longer, it was too strong for them. One of the girls said he always had such bad bronchitis, winter after winter, because he'd been gassed in the Great War but I never heard that before. I didn't say, though, I let her think it. All I could think of was how he coughed over those cigars.

He was eighty-five and that's a good age. Long enough for anyone, you'd think, but not long enough for me. I'd have kept him alive until after I was dead myself, I'm selfish. He didn't say any wonderful things to me as he lay there in the hospital, not about loving me forever or any of that. He just held my hand and looked into my eyes but he was too weak to kiss my hand.

Well, he's gone. Swanny had driven me to the hospital and she brought me home just as Torben was coming in. I didn't say anything, I had dinner with them as usual and went to bed at the usual time. We got a phone call this morning to say he didn't last the night. Swanny was good to me but I wouldn't let her hug me, I was embarrassed, after all Harry wasn't my husband, he was just my best friend. I went up to my room and stayed there all day and all night and thought about him and wrote this down. Not a very brilliant diary entry. Not some of my best prose! But at least I didn't cry. I don't.

SEPTEMBER 9, 1967

I am dead tired. I've been to Harry's funeral. Swanny wanted to take me but I wouldn't let her, I had to go there alone. She looked at my flowers as if it was a bunch of rhubarb I was carrying, but if my memory's as bad as can be at least I remember how Harry loved canna lilies. When we went for walks in parks he'd always stop by the flower beds with the cannas and say that was what he really called a flower.

There's nothing else to say. I'll never stop thinking about him but I've no wish to write it down. I'm too tired. This is the last entry I shall ever make in this diary. It's pointless trying to keep any sort of record when you can't remember what's happened five minutes ago. I may burn all these notebooks, we'll see. I burned the ones I made when I was very young, I can remember that as if it were yesterday.

No, not as if it were yesterday, for that's just what I always forget.

25

Joan Sellway is too close to me, or would have been had she lived, for me to judge her. But Paul, who never said a word against her while she was alive, is no advocate of that adage about *de mortuis* and quite right too, I think. It's wiser and kinder to say the good things about people while they're alive and leave the condemnation for later. Not that there was much of that. But there was an explanation.

I'd said nothing to him of my thought processes on the afternoon of his mother's death. It was he who spoke of it first.

"Do you remember telling me about an anonymous letter your Aunt Swanny had? The letter that started all the trouble?"

As if I could forget. It had started trouble not only for Swanny. I could date the beginning of our own difficulties from my mention of that letter. I could see his face now as it had closed and his eyes grown dull, I could see him as he had withdrawn into himself and slowly become uncharacteristically cold.

"My mother sent it."

I looked at him. I looked at him in simple wonder.

"I don't know it absolutely, that is I couldn't prove it. But of course I do know it. As soon as you told me I knew and it was like a blow. I was horrified. I could hardly speak." He said miserably but with an attempt at shrugging it off, "You must have noticed. I know you noticed but I couldn't do anything about that. I was too full of disgust and I was too frightened."

"How did you know?"

"That she had sent it? I won't say 'written' it because she didn't write them, she printed them in block capitals."

"She'd done others?"

"Lots. No, that's an exaggeration. Four or five before the one to your aunt. There was one to a woman whose husband was having an affair and another to someone who didn't know her son was homosexual. One day she was in a rage about something and she told my father. It was her duty to enlighten people, she said. I expect something like that is always used as justification. My father left her when they were both middle-aged, they'd been married for twenty-five years. He gave me a long explanation of why and those letters came into it."

"She never told you herself?"

"No, but I think you could say I never gave her the chance. Conversations with my mother were conducted on a very superficial level. I didn't want to go below the surface. I suppose I was afraid to do that."

I thought about it, we were both silent, eyeing one another. Then I asked him why he was filled with fear: why had he been afraid when I first mentioned the letter?

"Of losing you." He said it with transparent simplicity.

"Over that?" I said.

"People expect sons and daughters to be like their parents, they expect them to have the same faults. They blame people for their parents, though they shouldn't. I'm not proud of being the son of an anonymous letter writer. Can you honestly tell me that if I'd told you then it would have made no difference?"

The odd thing was that I couldn't. I couldn't have told him that. It would have made some difference, a small difference, though perhaps not so small. But did it make a difference now?

"What a good psychologist you are," I said and I got up and went to him and put my arms round him. I kissed him and felt that all was well, all was well enough.

. . .

That letter had damaged the last twenty years of Swanny's life. It had occupied her life with its repercussions and isolated her from all the good enjoyable things that might have been hers. From its arrival could be dated the beginning of that fruitless quest and the ultimate madness and destruction of everything she had once been. It could be argued, of course, and this I put to Paul to make him feel better, that without the letter the diaries would very likely never have come to light, never been published to become bestsellers and make a fortune. Swanny would very likely not have bothered to read them, still less have had them professionally translated and set in motion the publication process.

But I remembered her deathbed at which I had been present. She had died at home, in the very early hours of one dark winter morning.

We were to move her to hospital that very day, the doctor had recommended, then urged, it. Since the big stroke that took away the use of her left side and drew down the corner of her mouth, she had withdrawn into herself, into a dull silence and immobility. The attentions of the physiotherapist and all the jollying-along that is part of postthrombosis therapy she had rejected by her simple apathy. She refused to relearn to walk or make attempts at recapturing the use of her arm. She lay in her bed by night and sat in a wheelchair during the hours of daylight. I came to see her most days and sometimes I stayed in the house over a weekend.

It was during one of these periods that the doctor's recommendation to move her was made. One of the nurses had left and there was difficulty in finding a replacement. Swanny needed a day nurse and a night nurse and substitute day and night nurses when these women took their time off. A private room in a nursing home would make things easier for everyone, including, the doctor said, Swanny herself, who refused to be brought downstairs and was necessarily left alone for long dreary hours at a time.

The duration of the dual personality was over, the reign of Edith Roper was over. I didn't know it then but I'm pretty sure now that Swanny had her first stroke on the day, or a little while after the day, she went to Hackney with Gordon and Aubrey, was shown the Roper rooms and told the story of the haunted stairs. It was too much for her, it was too much for her blood and her brain.

With that stroke Edith was sent away or else subsumed in the real Swanny, whoever and whatever that real woman was. She gave the impression of a great fear and a great horror just contained. As she lifted her head and attempted to compress her distorted lips, I would sometimes see in her eyes not that old tranquility or newer despair, but straight simple fear. And there was nothing I could do about it, nothing I could say, no action I could take to change it.

On that morning the night nurse came and woke me and I went in to Swanny. She could speak, she had always been able to speak, though she seldom did. Her lips worked constantly as if she were trying to say something. Her right hand, the mobile one, fluttered along the edge of the sheet, plucking at it, sometimes rubbing it between finger and thumb. A sign that "they were going," the nurse had whispered to me.

She was the first person I had seen die. The dead I had seen but I'd never been present when someone passed from life to death. I held her hand, the good hand that had feeling in it, and she squeezed my fingers very hard in her own. It must have been for about an hour that I held her hand and during that time the pressure on my fingers grew gradually weaker.

Clare, the night nurse, was due to go but she stayed on after the day nurse arrived. They waited in the room, sitting in silence. We all knew Swanny was dying. Her lips continued to work, as if she were chewing bread, but the motion began to grow more feeble. The hand that held mine slowly relaxed its hold. She spoke and behind me I heard one of the nurses make a little sound, an indrawn breath.

"Nobody," Swanny said, and again, "nobody."

That was all. Nothing else. Did it mean anything? Did it mean, nobody understands, nobody knows, nobody can go with me now? Or was she referring to herself? Was she nobody? Was she like Melchizedek, without father, without mother, and without descent? I shall never know. She didn't speak again. Her throat rattled as the last breath was expelled from her lungs, her hand slackened, her mouth closed and grew still. The light went out of her eyes.

Carol, the day nurse, came over and touched her forehead. She felt for a pulse, shook her head and closed Swanny's eyes. I saw the youth come back into Swanny's face, the lines fade, the cheeks and forehead grow smooth. It always happens, Carol told me later, they always get to look young like that.

Clare and Carol said they would leave me alone with her but I only waited there a moment. Already I could feel the heat of life withdrawing itself and I didn't want to touch Swanny grown cold.

"Why do you think your mother waited so long?" I asked Paul. "She was over forty and Swanny was fifty-eight."

"Something must have happened to set her off. It was usually some jealousy or resentment. Or a slight or the man or woman in question had done something to offend her. I wish I didn't have to say that but I do. In the case of the man who was gay all he'd done was pass her by in the street without speaking to her."

"I always thought the person who sent the letter must have seen Swanny's picture in the *Tatler*."

"That would have been enough to do it. Did she look happy and prosperous and well-dressed and beautiful?"

I nodded. And then he laughed and I laughed. It wasn't funny but who can claim we laugh because we're amused?

How did his mother know Swanny wasn't Anna's child? I asked him that and he said he supposed his grandmother had told her. His grandmother must have known. Anna and she were living in the same house. Anna couldn't have given birth to a dead baby, somehow found a substitute live one, gone out in the street to find one or had one brought to her, without Hansine knowing at least something of it. Somewhere in the diaries Anna refers to her and Hansine having been through so much together. It's clear she has a special relationship with Hansine, though not a very warm or sympathetic one.

"Why would she have told?"

"People find secrets a burden and as they get older they seem to weigh more heavily on them. Also, I suppose, my mother and grandmother scarcely ever saw your family. My grandmother would have thought them quite remote from my mother—she didn't know her or she didn't know her in that respect. You can imagine it coming up in a discussion about adopting babies and my grandmother saying it used to be easier than it is now, all you had to do was find an unwanted baby and take it on the way Mrs. Westerby did."

"I wonder if that was the reason Anna kept away from your family," I said. "In the diaries there's a bit about Anna refusing to ask your grandmother to her Golden Wedding dinner. I thought it was plain snobbery but now I'm not so sure."

"It all goes to show," Paul said, "that the way babies are adopted these days is better. Better do it through the courts all ship-shape and Bristol fashion. Still, we shan't be adopting any babies, shall we?"

"No, thank you," I said.

Paul and I went together to a private screening of "Roper." The press weren't there, it was mostly BAFTA members, but Cary was present of course and Miles Sinclair and the actor who played Roper and the actress who played Florence Fisher.

We had a drink in the bar with Cary first. She was looking very handsome and pleased with herself, wearing a Chanel suit she mysteriously said had been bought for her in the January sales but had still cost over a thousand pounds. I asked her if she was pleased with the production.

"I'm very pleased, absolutely thrilled in fact. But, you know, it turned into an investigation too—well, you know it did, Ann. I thought I was going to find out whodunnit and I haven't done that."

"Did you expect to after eighty-five years?" Paul asked her.

"Oh, I don't know, I'm such a fool sometimes. I suppose I thought the truth would emerge."

She gave us each a leaflet with a cast list and a photograph of Clara Salaman as Lizzie standing under a gas lamp. It was quite a

big cast, the Roper family and Florence, the lovers, various police-
men, the judge and counsel, Florence's boyfriend, cabdrivers, shop-
keepers, the railway porter and Roper's sister and brother-in-law. I
was curious about Edith and saw she was played by twin sisters.
They have to do that because of the law about the short periods of
time very young children are permitted to act.

We went into the auditorium and it started promptly at half-past
six but first Cary got up on the stage and said she'd like the
audience to see the two people who had made this possible, the
scriptwriter and the director. She asked them to stand up, which
they did a bit sheepishly. Miles Sinclair was a huge man with a
bushy gray beard. He was sitting next to Cary, very closely next to
her, and when the lights went down he slid his arm along the back
of her seat. I wondered if he was the purchaser of the Chanel suit.

What can I say of "Roper"?

It was very good, it was entertaining, in fact it was enthralling.
It wasn't cheaply or sensationally made but subtly, almost intellec-
tually and with real feeling for the time in which it was set. I'm sure
there were no anachronisms. Anyway, just as they have read Anna's
diaries, so many people reading this will have seen "Roper." I need
not describe it. The difficulty with it was, for me, that it came
nowhere near the pictures of life in Devon Villa, Navarino Road,
that I had involuntarily formed for myself from what I'd read. The
actors didn't look like the Ropers and the house wasn't like Maria
Hyde's house. There hung over it, I felt all the time I was watching,
the ghosts of the many and various television productions concerned with Jack the Ripper which must haunt all producers of
crime drama set in London at the end of the last century and the
beginning of this one.

We never saw the murder committed, only dead Lizzie with her
throat cut. No doubt it was my own fault that I constantly expected
to see a dreadful figure with a bloody knife appear out of an alley.
Needless to say, nothing like that happened. Cary and her scriptwriter had had no solution to offer, though we were left feeling, as
readers of Ward-Carpenter and Mockridge must be left feeling, that
Roper probably did kill his wife and got away with it.

Cary had read Arthur Roper's memoir and the letters between Roper and his sister from the Ward-Carpenter collection as well as the contemporary newspaper accounts of the trial. The information she had got enabled her to bring in a few more characters but scarcely more enlightenment. Still, I'd enjoyed it and I told her so. Paul said he hoped it would put up the price of his house when he came to sell it. I was about to say that was the first I'd heard of his selling his house but by then Cary was introducing us to Miles Sinclair and in a way that left no doubt of their relationship.

I was glad for her. Two or three years ago, if anyone had told me I'd be pleased to see Cary Oliver happy I'd have thought them mad, but I was glad. We made an arrangement to meet and all have dinner together. Miles Sinclair wrote his phone number down on one of the leaflets with the cast list—I gathered that Cary was more often to be found at his place than her own—and I folded it up and put it in my pocket.

"You never said anything to me about selling your house," I said on the way back to Hampstead.

"It was a spontaneous decision."

"Where are you going?" I was for a moment breathless with terror.

"It'll take a long time to sell. It'll take a year."

"But where are you going?"

"I thought Willow Road in Hampstead. If you'll have me."

I had forgotten about Lisa Waring. When Cary mentioned the name I had to ask who she meant. The planned dinner with her and Miles had taken place and we were all having our coffee when, quite suddenly, she said Lisa Waring had phoned her. She was here, staying "just round the corner" from Cary's office in Frith Street. Cary spoke as if this made it worse, as if it confirmed her as some sort of spy or nemesis figure, though she still knew no more than she had of what Lisa Waring had to show.

"When are you seeing her?" I said.

"Wednesday morning. You'll be there, won't you? You promised to be there."

Miles gave her an indulgent look, as at an excitable child, but I wasn't very pleased. Wednesday wasn't particularly convenient. Still, it's always easier not to cross Cary, something on which she has built a successful career. Crossing her leads to public scenes, wild accusations, tears and other dramas. She took hold of my hand.

"I have to have you there in case she destroys me."

Lisa Waring didn't look capable of destroying anything larger than a beetle. One of these creatures, scuttling across the floor of Cary's ancient dirty Soho office, she trod on with precise deliberation as she was shown in. She trod on it, pushed the resulting squashed mess aside with the toe of a black running shoe and asked if it was true Mozart had stayed in the house next door when he came to London as a child.

Having stopped smoking a week or so before, Cary had taken it up again, lighting a fresh cigarette as the girl came in to announce her visitor. The atmosphere in the little room was blue with smoke. Cary's voice came out very hoarsely, she had to cough to clear her throat and then she couldn't stop coughing. At last she managed to say that where Mozart had lived was now the entrance to the London Casino. Lisa Waring nodded in a sage way.

It was obvious she had no documents with her. She didn't even have a handbag, only a coat with pockets over her jeans and sweater. She looked to be in her late twenties, small, sallow, black-haired and with enough of a tilt to the eyes to show that one of those ancestors had been an Oriental. I remembered, in that moment, that it was she who wanted something from Cary, not that she had something to impart to Cary or even threaten her with. Somehow we'd overlooked that, or Cary had, seeing her as a menace, almost as a blackmailer.

And now she sat in silence, looking from one to the other of us as Cary introduced me, then casting down her eyes.

"What exactly do you want to know?" Cary said.

"About my ancestor. My father's grandfather. Where he came from, who he was."

I'm sure Cary was thinking as I was then, that it was easy enough to find out. Alfred Roper's life was well documented, as we both knew. This girl was probably like one of those students that were Paul's despair, the kind that in spite of training, teaching and advice, have no idea about research, where to find a source, how to go about it, where to look anything up, and anyway always prefer to get others to do it for them.

She dispelled that fast. "I can't. I've done my best. I've never come across the name anywhere until I saw it in your cast list."

I suppose that's what gave me a hint we were talking at cross-purposes. "You're not thinking about Roper at all, are you?"

Of course I'd put that badly. She looked puzzled. "That's the name of your production, yes. I know that. It's my great-grand-father I'm interested in. His name was George Ironsmith and I want to know if it's the same one."

26

I tried to remember who George Ironsmith was. The name was in the cast list on Cary's leaflets, one of which lay on her desk. I looked at it and—ah, yes, Lizzie's erstwhile fiancé, the one who gave her the ring with a glass stone. Cary produced photocopies of the Ward-Carpenter account and of Arthur Roper's memoir and Cora Green's story for the *Star*. She passed them across the desk and Lisa Waring looked at them, took a pen, said "May I?" and started underlining words or names.

"A George Ironsmith was this lady's lover, right?"

"Apparently," Cary said. "He was engaged to her in 1895 but the engagement was broken and he went away."

"Away where?"

"I've no idea. Cora Green says he had a 'colonial' accent, whatever that means."

Whatever it did, Lisa Waring didn't look too pleased. "How old was he?"

"At the time of the murder? Maybe between thirty and forty. For the production we made him about that. The actor who plays him is thirty-six."

"My great-grandfather George Ironsmith was forty-nine when he died in 1920, I've seen his tombstone. He was born in 1871 and that would have made him thirty-four in 1905."

Cary was immensely relieved. "It looks as if it's him, doesn't it?"

"How can I find where he came from?"

Cary suggested looking through phone books for the whole country. Each of us recommended the records at St. Catherine's House. I told her how to go about this kind of research and that she could probably pursue her ancestors back through *The Mormon's World* listing of parish baptismal records. I suppose I was disappointed. What I'd wanted was a revelation that was exciting but not calculated to upset Cary's reconstruction.

But Cary was relieved. Like many people, when a burden is lifted off her back she becomes expansive. If Lisa Waring had told her, for instance (I'm fantasizing) that her great-grandfather was Arthur Roper, that he had once worked as a surgeon's assistant and had been in London on July 28, 1905, the last thing she would have done was agree to her request to "see the movie." She hadn't told her that, but rather that she was probably descended from a minor character in the drama, so Cary promised to send her the three "Roper" cassettes.

Cary expressed her relief after Lisa Waring had gone by leaping up and hugging me and offering to take me for "a wonderful lunch somewhere." It was over this lunch, which became protracted and swallowed half the afternoon, that she asked me something she said she had been wanting to ask me about for some time. What made me connect Anna's household with the Ropers at all?

"You connected them," I said. "That was what put you in touch with me in the first place. You wanted to know if there were any more references to Roper in the diaries and then we found Swanny had torn out those pages. It was you, not me."

"Yes, but I stopped making the connection when we found those pages were missing. Without any further references, which may or may not have been there, we don't know and never shall. All you have is the link of Hansine coming across Dzerjinski dying on the pavement and the two or three references Anna makes."

"Six," I said. "There are six. And I know them by heart. The first one is when she writes about Hansine and Dzerjinski, the second when Hansine asks if she can have Florence Fisher to tea and the third when Anna goes to Navarino Road and by chance sees Lizzie

Roper come out of the house with Edith. That's when she says Edith is pretty and fairylike and she has that odd experience of sensing that Edith makes some sort of telepathic contact with her unborn child. Then she refers to 'the man who murdered his wife in Navarino Road' without naming him. The fourth one is just what anyone might say, that is anyone who happened to be keeping a diary and lived nearby. It would have been odder if she'd left it out. The only reference that's a bit strange is the fifth one because she makes it eight years later in 1913. It's when Rasmus thinks Sam Cropper is an admirer of hers and she goes on to say that he 'thought I was following in the footsteps of Mrs. Roper.' Then, in one of the last notebooks, she records reading about the Moors Murders and it reminds her of 'that business in Navarino Road.' "

"You mean it indicates that she had Lizzie Roper on her mind?"

"In a way. Of course it could be no more than that Anna had never come across any other woman that she'd have called a 'bad' woman."

"Lizzie could have been the only one she knew and we have to remember she'd actually seen Lizzie. Doesn't she refer to her big showy hat? Women like Anna, that is 'good' women, were often fascinated by the other sort and that could account for her thinking of Lizzie after so long. But all this goes to show that there's no real connection between Anna's family and Devon Villa. *I* put it in your mind and it didn't go away after we'd found those pages were lost."

"Surely because whatever it is may have been in those pages."

"But we don't know it was. All we know is that Swanny Kjaer found a clue to her own origins in those pages and the truth, whatever it was, wasn't acceptable to her, so she tore them out. Oh, Ann, I'm so happy that horrid little girl—she was horrid, wasn't she, so cold?—I'm so happy she didn't come to tell me her great-grandfather was Arthur Roper and he'd written a murder confession on his deathbed!"

Although I'd promised myself to do so I had never searched the house that was now mine for those missing pages from the first diary. It was after Cary pointed out that the Roper connection was mostly in my imagination that I began my search. The only way to do it was systematically, starting at the top and working downwards, neglecting nothing, lifting carpets, looking for false backs to cupboards.

I was about halfway through when something struck me. If the pages Swanny had torn out of the diary told her who she was, why had she persuaded herself she was Edith? She cannot in reality have been Edith, the missing pages can't have told her she was, so what did they tell her? Something much worse, something entirely horrible, so that Edith was by far the better option?

It suddenly looked to me as if Swanny had made herself into Edith because the alternative, the true identity she had discovered, was too appalling to live with. Yet it was quite a long time after she had torn out the pages that she took on an imaginary Edith personality. To imagine what she might have found defeated me but I went on looking.

The fourth volume of the diaries was soon to be published. We hadn't been able to decide whether this one should have Swanny's photograph on the back jacket. All the previous volumes had carried it but Swanny had been alive then. She hadn't been the author of the diaries, only their editor, and now she was dead and dead before she had had time to edit the notebooks spanning 1935–1945, wouldn't it be better to do without her picture?

There was no question of a picture of me replacing it. No reader would care much about Anna's granddaughter who was only four at the end of this volume. But the idea of having nothing there but snippets from favorable reviews of past editions was vaguely unsatisfying. Anna's own face dominated the front cover illustration, or, rather, four of her faces at various stages of her life, staring levelly from oval cutouts.

Swanny's publishers—I still thought of them like that—kept sending me suggested versions. We could keep to the old format, we could have the photograph reduced in size and on the back flap instead of the back jacket or we could use a different photograph of Swanny, perhaps one taken when she was a child or a young girl.

Plenty of these were available. I had only to look through Anna's albums. She had had Swanny photographed more than her other children, perhaps only because she was better-looking than the rest. There was a studio portrait done for each birthday and many snapshots taken between times. I thought I'd seen every one of Anna's albums but soon found I hadn't or else I'd forgotten. They filled drawers in the room that had been hers. As I lifted them out the idea came to me that Swanny might have hidden the missing pages among them but of course she hadn't.

It was in the study that Swanny had first examined the note-books. Still not quite convinced that she would have destroyed those missing pages, I looked through every book on the shelves for papers inserted among its pages. I found plenty, one always does: a thank-you letter of no interest, recipes, postcards from friends at seaside resorts, newspaper cuttings, nearly all of this in Danish, but not of course the missing pages. They had hurt too much to be kept, I thought, they were smoke dissolved, the sound of Swanny tearing them to bits lost somewhere in the spheres.

If you want to destroy something you destroy it at once. You don't keep it for posterity. It's a bit like those thrillers on film where the villain has the hero at his mercy but instead of shooting him as anyone would settles down to boast of his triumphs and taunt his victim. By the time he's finished rescue has arrived. Swanny wouldn't have waited for rescue to arrive but have burned the sheets at once.

There was a half-column in the newspaper about a VC coming up for sale at Sotheby's. The vendor was a Richard Clark, grandson of the man who had won it. His name meant nothing to me but his grandfather's did.

Of course, much less space would have been devoted to this story if the original VC hadn't achieved a kind of fame elsewhere. It wasn't for his conspicuous gallantry on the Somme on July 1, 1916, that readers wanted to know about the late Sergeant Harry Duke, but because of the important place he had in Anna's diaries. This was the brave soldier who had done his best to save Anna's son's life and later been Anna's platonic lover.

I was reading the piece aloud to Paul, including a not very

accurate synopsis of the relevant diary passages, when Gordon arrived. He came up the front steps and seeing us, tapped on the window.

He was dressed like an undertaker. His suit was dark and formal, his tie not black but gray with a black design. If there had been anyone I dearly loved elsewhere I would have feared he had come to tell me of a death or dreadful accident.

It must all have shown in my face for he said in his earnest way, "Don't look so alarmed. You're not really going to *mind* this. You may even quite like it."

Paul must have thought he was referring to this unexpected visit, for he simply said we were delighted to see him and went on to talk about the sale of the Harry Duke VC. Gordon listened politely but at the first opportunity said to him, "I want to see a photograph of your mother."

"Of *my* mother?"

"Ann says you've got photographs. Just to confirm something."

She was in her garden in a flowered silk dress. It was a windy day and her hair was blown about, one hand holding down her skirt to stop it flapping up over her knees. You couldn't see much of what she looked like, only that she was tall and thin and fair-haired. Paul had it among the small stack of photographs and papers he had brought away from her house after she was dead. Gordon had his own copy of *Anna* with him and he opened it to show Swanny's picture on the back jacket flap. Blue tweed suit, blue felt hat, a tall thin fair woman standing beside the Little Mermaid.

"What do you see?"

He had paused before speaking, spoke in measured dramatic tones. I've sometimes thought Gordon has considerable acting ability.

"They both look like Danes," I said.

"Is that all?"

I asked him what he wanted me to see.

"Don't they look like—sisters, half-sisters?"

"If we take it for granted that sisters, especially half-sisters, often don't look very much alike."

I turned to Paul and saw his uneasiness. He said, making an effort to keep his voice light, "What are you saying, Gordon?"

"I don't want to give you a shock. But you probably won't be, you'll be pleased. It'll sort of make you and Ann cousins."

"Are you telling us," I said, "that Hansine was Swanny's mother?"

"It explains a lot of things," Gordon said. "Anna says in the diaries how fat Hansine is and we've taken this as spitefulness or a typical attitude of the thin woman to one a little heavier. She's not fat in the famous photograph of the family having tea on the lawn and Hansine waiting on them. Anna never refers to her being fat in later years. She was fat in 1905 because she was pregnant.

"Anna may not have known she was pregnant for quite a long while. Clothes were a good disguise for a pregnancy in those days. Authorities on the history of fashion say that the shape of women's clothes for hundreds of years was designed that way because women were always pregnant. The sort of clothes that became fashionable in the twenties, narrow and clinging, and remained more or less like that, did so partly because women were pregnant much less often. Hansine might not have had to admit her pregnancy until she was seven or eight months and then it would have been too late to turn her out. Besides, we get the impression Anna wouldn't have been all that intolerant about something like that. Rasmus might have been but Rasmus wasn't there."

"So Anna and Hansine were pregnant at exactly the same time? Isn't that too much like coincidence?"

"Not necessarily. Hansine's baby could have been born a month or even six weeks after Anna lost hers. We don't know that Swanny's birthday was July 28, only that Anna says it was because that was the day she gave birth to a dead child."

"Who was the father?"

"The obvious candidate is Rasmus himself but it's just as obviously wrong. He comes out of the diaries as strict and straitlaced, not a philanderer, not much interested in Anna but not interested in other women either. Not at all the sort of man to tumble the maid while his wife was out. Much more likely to be out tinkering with a car engine."

"Besides," I said, "he didn't like Swanny, he liked her least of all his children. If he didn't know it, he sensed she wasn't his."

"We know Hansine had an earlier lover. Anna says so when Hansine asks permission to have Paul's grandfather to tea. She says some uncomplimentary things about Hansine's appearance and then reflects that Sam Cropper isn't the first man to come courting her."

"I wonder who it was."

"Some Dane," Gordon said. "Someone in Copenhagen, a working man or another servant. She had to leave him when your grandparents emigrated to England."

"She didn't have to go with them."

"Perhaps she did. Perhaps he wouldn't or couldn't marry her. He may have been married already or unable to support her."

I said that Hansine had always loved Swanny best of the Westerby children. The truth began to come clear. Anna lost her own child but no doctor had been present at the birth. She says frequently how much she dislikes being attended by a doctor, a man being witness to these intimate and, in her eyes, degrading things. Somewhere she says she wishes there could be women doctors. She never registered the death because she looked to Hansine's coming child as a replacement for hers. Perhaps she stipulated that she would only take it if it was a girl. That would be like Anna.

"They must have been on tenterhooks lest Rasmus came back early," Gordon said.

There was no way of knowing when the child was born. What would have become of it if it had been a boy? I couldn't imagine Anna actually harming a baby but I could easily picture her going out at night with a bundle in her arms and dumping it on the doorstep of, say, the German Hospital.

But Hansine's child had been a girl and she had gladly given it up to Anna. What else could she do? Apart from being able to claim Swanny as hers and be called her mother, she had for years most of the pleasures and pains of motherhood. She saw the child every day, looked after her, put her to bed and bathed her, sat her on her lap, enjoyed her affection. Indeed, it could be said that it was she who had deserted Swanny, not the other way about, when in 1920 a few months before Swanny's fifteenth birthday she left the household to marry Paul's grandfather.

"Sometime or other she must have told your mother," I said to Paul.

He said nothing. He had hardly spoken since Gordon began his explanation. I thought of his mother, the unhappy author of anonymous letters. Probably Hansine had not told her until she was grown-up. It would have had a bad effect, it may have been responsible for the way Joan Sellway reacted to so many things. For instance, that hatred of her mother's references to being in service. She would have seen her position as a servant as responsible for her having to give up her child. A servant is totally in the power of employers and has no rights or choice. That's how it would have appeared to her. The irony of it made things worse, that the illegitimate unwanted child had a more privileged life than the legitimate presumably wanted one.

She had never met Swanny but she saw that picture in the *Tatler*. Her resentment and bitterness came to a head and she composed the anonymous letter. I remembered how Swanny had later gone to her and asked her if she could throw any light on her origins but Joan Sellway had pretended not to understand.

I could say none of this in Gordon's presence. I felt a sudden terrible embarrassment for Paul, an awkwardness that might never be erased. Then I saw him smile.

"We can't be cousins, Gordon," he said. "If Swanny was my grandmother's daughter she was certainly my aunt but she was only Ann's if she was Ann's mother's sister. All that's happened is we've swapped aunts."

Sensitive enough to have realized Paul's temporary dismay, Gordon was delighted to see him laughing and making jokes about the relationship. He was naturally proud of himself for his successful detective work and insisted on going through the earliest part of the diary with us. Here, in June 1905, Anna notes that Hansine was "so fat and getting fatter," later on, in July, she refers to Hansine holding "her hands over her stomach, which is nearly as big as mine," and then, again of Hansine, to "the man she was going about with in Copenhagen."

To refer back to the time of her birth, wasn't this the easiest and indeed the only way a baby might have been found to replace Anna's dead child? Anna, having just given birth, wouldn't have been able to go out and secure for herself someone's unwanted child. Hansine was there, Hansine was under the same roof. Just as Hansine had played the midwife to Anna on July 28, 1905, so Anna had assisted at Hansine's delivery a few days or a week or two weeks later.

So we accepted it. Details were most likely in the missing diary pages and those we were never going to find. There would be no records left by Hansine because Hansine couldn't write. But this was the answer Swanny had sought for twenty-five years. If Anna never told her, this was because Anna had always despised Hansine and balked at admitting her favorite child was the daughter of a servant and of some tradesman or artisan in Copenhagen.

No doubt it happened all the time. Grandparents brought up their daughters' illegitimate children as their own and childless householders took on their servants' secretly delivered babies. It was a kind of underground or unofficial adoption society. Why did Hansine keep silent? Because, doubtless, it was infinitely to her advantage to see her baby, who would otherwise have gone to an orphanage, brought up in comfort and love as part of a secure middle-class family. It wasn't as if she was separated from her child, but saw her every day, as a mother in a fairy story, deprived of the title of mother, condemned to servitude and the name of a servant, to a life of menial tasks, watched her daughter grow up as a princess, remote yet close at hand.

Such women figure in mythology because once this was the reality. Children were less precious and less valued than today. The laws governing their lives were more lax. Paul and I accepted Gordon's explanation, as I've said, or I accepted it.

The only flaw in it was that it wasn't true.

27

I had forgotten Lisa Waring and I believe Cary had too. If she ever came into Cary's mind she must have thought Lisa had returned to the United States long ago. A mild uneasiness was all she felt when a parcel came, a padded bag containing all the material she had given Lisa, including the three cassettes, and with the sender's name and address on the back in the American fashion. The address, however, wasn't America but Battersea. Lisa Waring had moved but not more than a mile or two.

Television productions are seldom transmitted on the expected dates. There are nearly always delays and postponements. "Roper" was to have gone out in February but was put off till April and finally scheduled for May, just over two years after Cary began her project, exactly two years after I discovered the stubs in Anna's notebook where the pages had been torn out.

The press screening in early April was at BAFTA where Paul and I had been to the private showing. It was over by nine and at half-past Miles Sinclair was on the phone to tell me that Lisa Waring had turned up at it, had walked in at the last moment before the lights dimmed and stood surveying the audience before proceeding slowly—and, he said, menacingly—all the way down the aisle to take the only vacant seat in the front row. Miles has nearly as exaggerated a way of talking as Cary and when he described Lisa's appearance as being like the wicked witch turning up uninvited to the christening or Ate throwing the golden apple into the midst of the guests, I didn't take him very seriously.

Afterwards, when they were all in the bar and he was in the middle of an interview with some journalist, Lisa came up to Cary and said to her quite baldly that she could tell the press a few things that would make her production look pretty silly. Cary was astounded because Lisa had been perfectly pleasant on that day we had all met and the covering note that came with the returned papers was friendly, saying mostly that she was still in London because she had found freelance work here. Now Lisa was antagonistic. She resented the portrait of her great-grandfather, felt even more angry now she had seen the production on the big screen.

During the past weeks she had been searching for George Ironsmith's origins. He had been born in Whitehaven in 1871, apprenticed to a tradesman in Carlisle at the age of fourteen, emigrated to America in 1897 and married her great-grandmother in the autumn of 1904. The substance of her complaint was that Cary should have called her in as an adviser before she went ahead with more screenings of "Roper" and hadn't done so.

According to Miles, Cary did have the presence of mind to ask her what on earth any of this had to do with the validity of her production. Ironsmith, Lisa said, shouldn't have been consigned to an insignificant role, he was the most important figure in the drama. She and Cary should talk about it, she was prepared to do this before she spoke to the press. This last remark was uttered in ringing tones but no one took much notice because all the journalists were concerned with was the fate of Edith Roper.

Children are always of interest, girl children for some reason more so, and missing girl children consumingly so. This may have happened eighty-six years before but the press were still fascinated by Edith's disappearance, the claimants to her identity and all the possibilities of what may have happened to her. They didn't much care, Miles said, about who might or might not have killed Lizzie, that was water under the bridge, ancient history. So a wild girl with Chinese eyes dressed all in black, shouting about her great-grandfather's rights, was only a momentary diversion.

Cary didn't want to know any more. She would have liked Lisa to fall under a bus in Piccadilly and her production to go out unchallenged. But she had to have a meeting with Ironsmith's great-granddaughter, there was no escape. And I had to be there. I didn't ask to speak to Cary myself, knowing of old that as soon as she had a man on the premises she would always get him to make her awkward or difficult phone calls for her. She had even managed to use Daniel in this way.

A few days had gone by since Gordon came to tell us Swanny was Hansine's child. As soon as he had gone Paul said quite adamantly that he knew this solution was the wrong one. He *felt* it was wrong and he thought feelings, intuition, meant a lot in these matters. Without being able to prove it, he knew Hansine had never had a child before his mother's birth, he knew his mother wasn't Swanny Kjaer's half-sister. But he thought he could prove it by recourse to the diaries, by examining the original Danish in Anna's first notebook.

I said nothing to anyone of Gordon's revelation. Who was there who would care? Gordon's own father perhaps and his uncle Charles. If he wanted to, Gordon could tell them himself. More important were the diaries themselves. As things were, much of the interest in the diaries rested on a huge deception. Swanny, the beloved daughter of a woman whose name was almost a household word, was not that woman's daughter but the illegitimate child of a servant who figured prominently in the diaries. You will see by this that I had very little faith in Paul's intuition. I don't trust it, in men or women, and in this case I thought it was a defense he put up against a curiously painful disclosure.

Sometime, I supposed, I would have to decide, I and Swanny's editor would have to decide, whether the next set of diaries to be published should carry a note to the effect that Swanny wasn't Anna's daughter. It would be awkward. It would deprive the existing diaries, those previously published, of a good deal of verisimilitude and it would look like a calculated deception. While Swanny knew, or almost for certain knew, she wasn't Anna's child but could only fantasize about whose she might be, it seemed all right for concealment to go on. Things changed when the truth was established. Could we really go ahead and publish *Peace and War, 1935–1944*, while aware that the woman written about on nearly every page, the woman figuring in Gordon's genealogical table as the elder daughter of Anna and Rasmus, had an entirely different origin?

Time was left to me before I need take any steps. There were a few weeks to go before it would be too late to insert a page of explanation into each of the twenty thousand copies the diaries' publishers knew they could sell in hardcover. I had, in fact, much less than that to wait. Paul soon found his proof. It came in the early part of the first notebook. First he asked me to read the passage in the published version:

> Hansine takes Mogens to the school which is two streets away in Gayhurst Road. He wants to go alone and soon I'll let him but not quite yet. She grumbles under her breath because when her visitor is in the house she gets fearful pains in her stomach. I stay at home with Knud and take him on my lap and tell him a story. It used to be H. C. Andersen for both the boys but when I left Denmark I left Andersen behind too. I suddenly realized how cruel some of his stories were.

"There's a bit I don't understand," I said, "but there are bits like that all through the diaries."

"You mean the 'visitor in the house,'" Paul said. "I don't suppose Gordon understood it either. You're too young."

I said I was older than he and he laughed and said maybe it wasn't a matter of age, more of being interested in euphemism. Because he was, he had noticed that phrase when he first read the diaries and it must have remained in his mind. That was the real source of his intuition.

"I went back to the Danish. The Danes don't have anywhere like as many euphemisms as we do but they have some. Anna may have been frank about a lot of things but not about menstruation. That's the last bastion of prudery, you could say it's only gone down in the past twenty years. Margrethe Cooper translated what Anna originally wrote as 'visitor in the house' because in spite of English having more euphemisms than Danish there was no idiomatic translation for Anna's *den rode blomst,* which actually means 'her red flower.' "

If Anna had written *"hun har det maanedlige"* (she has her monthly) or even *"hun har sit skidt"* (she has her dirt) it could have been literally translated and there would have been no difficulty. Even Gordon, presumably no expert in female physiology, would have known what that meant. Margrethe Cooper had had to find a matching English expression and had come up with one used by very old women still alive in the 1970s, "she has a visitor in the house."

"Swanny must have known," I said.

"She knew from her first reading of the first notebook, so from the start she could dismiss Hansine as a possible mother. Hansine menstruating on July 5 couldn't have given birth to a child on July 28, or even a month later."

It would have been different, as Cary said later, if this had happened a year before. Then with what delight and excitement she would have welcomed Lisa Waring and her revelations from the past. Lisa would have been taken on as her adviser—that she hadn't was a principal cause of present and ridiculous resentment—and Cary would have enjoyed the distinction of solving a murder nearly a century after it had been committed.

That resentment had another, and very peculiar, cause. Few of us would relish discovering that even a remote ancestor was a probable murderer. A father cast in such a role would be terrible, a grandfather disquieting and a great-grandfather quite bad enough. But that was Lisa's Waring contention. George Ironsmith, otherwise undistinguished, was, she insisted, the killer of Lizzie Roper and she wanted his rights, she wanted recognition for him, fame or infamy, celebrity or notoriety, whatever you chose to call it.

I had that sensation of watching psychological disturbance actively at work that you have when someone presents the irrational as rational and the absurd as entirely serious. Lisa's face was pale and heart-shaped, her nose rather long. Only the hair, black and straight and worn pageboy fashion, and her eyes, nipped at the corner by the epicanthic fold, were Oriental. As she talked her eyes grew glazed and fixed themselves on a distant point. She had done her homework on the texts given her by Cary and quoted Mr. Justice Edmondson verbatim.

" 'You have been engaged in one of the most remarkable trials that is to be found in the annals of the criminal courts of England for many years.' That's what the judge said. I'm quoting from the transcript of the trial in the Mockridge account. He goes on, 'That the unfortunate woman had been done to death there is no doubt. She was murdered in a most remarkable way. There is no doubt that the murder was committed by someone who knew well how to put a person quickly to death.' It sounds like he admired the perpetrator of that murder, doesn't it? Well, doesn't it?"

We were in Cary's flat this time and Miles was with us. He said, "Okay, so you're looking for some posthumous glory for your great-grandad. It's weird but it's well known some people want the limelight no matter how it comes."

"There's no need to be insulting," she said.

I could see Miles was thinking that, in the light of her recent claims, what others would take for an insult would be flattery to her. He didn't say it.

"I was going to say," he said, "that that's all very well but have you any evidence that George Ironsmith cut Lizzie Roper's throat?"

She had. If you could believe her. Watching her strange eyes that were dull yet continually shifting, her otherwise concentrated stillness, I had difficulty in believing anything she said. Evidence should be provable and this was hardly that.

"There's a family tradition that he killed someone. He couldn't go back to Britain for that reason. Everyone in our family knew it. His wife knew it and he told his daughter, who was my grandmother, he told her when she was sixteen. That was just before he died."

She had made a rough genealogical table, just a direct family line of descendants of George Ironsmith, nothing like the complicated structure of Gordon's Westerby tree. It was passed round and I spent a minute or two looking at it. Ironsmith had married a woman called Mary Schaffer in 1904 and they had one daughter, also Mary, born that same year. Mary Ironsmith married Clarence Waring in 1922 and the youngest of their four children, Spencer Waring, born in 1933, married Betty Wong Feldman in 1959. These two were Lisa's parents.

A "family tradition" wasn't of course proof that Ironsmith had killed anyone. Lisa had been in touch with her father since she first saw Cary's video and he had sent her a bundle of papers that had come down to him from his own mother. As far as I could see, the only item of any relevance was a postcard Ironsmith had sent to his wife from England in 1904. There was no address on it beyond "London" but it was dated and the date was July 28. Another interesting thing about this postcard was the picture. Visitors to London mostly send home picture postcards of Buckingham Palace or the Houses of Parliament but this one was of the boating lake in Victoria Park, a sepia photograph of the only scenic part of Hackney.

Ironsmith's message to his wife was that he would be leaving for home on the following day, that is Saturday, July 29. That was all there was on the card apart from "Dearest Mary," a line about the weather being hotter than at home, "my best love, Georgie," and at the top, above the address, a curious mark like an asterisk or a multiplication mark drawn on top of a plus sign. It proved Ironsmith had been in London and probably in Hackney around the time of Lizzie's death but not that he had killed her.

"What's the significance of that mark?" Cary asked.

"It's to tell my great-grandmother he'd killed Lizzie."

This was so patently ridiculous we had nothing to say to it. Lisa gave us her explanation just the same. Mary Schaffer Ironsmith was jealous of the woman she saw as a rival and could only be satisfied when she knew she was dead and out of the way. Lisa's father remembered his mother saying what a devoted couple her parents were. Ironsmith "adored" his wife, he would have done anything for her.

Cary wanted to know what was in the rest of the papers but Lisa said there was nothing significant, they were just letters between her great-grandparents and irrelevant documents. Still, it would be wrong not to look, Cary said, and began going through them. Lisa got up, rubbed her back as if sitting in an armchair was unfamiliar and uncomfortable, and dropped cross-legged onto the floor.

The "irrelevant documents" included Mary Schaffer's birth certificate but not, of course, George Ironsmith's.

"If I'd had that I'd have known where he came from," Lisa said in her rather surly way.

The Ironsmiths' marriage certificate, issued at Chicago in February 1904, gave Mary Schaffer's age as thirty-eight and her status as a widow. George Ironsmith was himself thirty-four, his profession described as "commercial traveler." The letters that had passed between them, mostly during their engagement, were as dull and uninformative as those which poor Mogens had written home from France and my cousins had tried in vain to publish. Lisa had been right and they told us nothing beyond the fact that Mary Schaffer had been married to her first husband for fifteen years and the marriage had been childless.

The bombshell wasn't in the letters at all but in a copy of George Ironsmith's indentures. These showed that for seven years from 1885 he had been apprenticed to a butcher and slaughterman in Carlisle.

"My dad found that," Lisa said from her Buddha-like pose on the floor. "I'd never seen it before."

We all looked at the document, yellowed and faded with age. She watched us, pleased with the effect it had.

"You know what the judge said. 'She was murdered in a most remarkable way.' He said she was murdered by someone who knew well how to put a person quickly to death. He would, wouldn't he? He'd been putting all those poor cows and sheep to death for years and years." Lisa squeezed her eyelids together. "Personally, I'm a vegetarian."

"But why would he do it?" said poor Cary.

"I told you, to please his wife. To get rid of Lizzie forever."

"He'd put his own life in jeopardy for that? Murder a woman his wife had never seen and scarcely heard of? Murderers got hanged then, you know. They weren't sent to do community service for a couple of years."

"For love," Lisa said coldly. "It was a great passion with my great-grandmother. People do these things for love. I know what ship he went back to the States on, if that helps you." She gave Cary an unpleasant smile when she spoke those last four words. "It was the *Lusitania* from Plymouth, England, to New York, and it called in somewhere, Boston, I think."

Miles said perhaps passenger lists still existed.

"You mean you don't believe me," said Lisa. "You do really though, don't you? You'd never have made that movie if you'd known what you know now. So what are you going to do about it?"

Not lose touch, Cary promised.

"Oh, I'll call you," said Lisa. "You don't need to worry about that."

After she had gone Cary went into hysterics. That's easily said but Cary really did. She howled, she laughed, she banged her fists against the wall, she ran her fingers through her hair, stared wild-eyed at Miles and said she was going to start smoking again. This was it. She needed a very large drink and twenty cigarettes.

We went down to the pub.

"What shall I do?"

"A bit of checking before you commit yourself," I said. "That boat for a start."

The two of us are inveterate researchers. We both knew where to find things and how to go about it. Not even for a couple of days, let alone years, would we have remained in ignorance of our great-grandparents' provenance, we would have found out.

Of course, when doing research, in most cases one wants to find out. The truth may not fit a theory but then the theory must be sacrificed and one possibility after another eliminated. Cary, this time, didn't just not want to know; she was emphatically, almost neurotically, against knowing. She would have liked to be able to forget it and simply get on with her next project. Not only did she not dare do this for fear of Lisa's disclosures spoiling the effect of her production, but the way she had been trained made it not a feasible solution. She would get no pleasure out of the transmission of "Roper," no possible satisfaction out of presenting to the public an erroneous account. She had to know but she was wretched as she went about it.

The first thing she discovered was that Lisa Waring—or, more probably, Spencer Waring—had been wrong about the ship in which George Ironsmith returned to the United States and his wife Mary on July 29, 1905. Very likely the name *Lusitania* came into his mind because this was the British liner almost as famous in the history of sea tragedies as the *Titanic.* It was the sinking of the *Lusitania* by a German submarine in 1915 which contributed to the entry of the United States into the First World War.

What had plied between Great Britain and the United States, across the Atlantic, in the early years of the century?

Cary got hold of a Cunard passengers log book. A formidable number of vessels went back and forth, the *Hibernia,* the *Arabia,* the *Servia,* the *Umbria* and *Etruria* among others. The *Cephalonia, Pavonia, Catalonia, Bothnia* and *Scythia* provided the weekly Boston service, from Liverpool on Thursdays and back from Boston on Saturdays, calling at Queenstown. It obviously wasn't on one of these liners that Ironsmith had traveled.

Nor, if the postcard was to be relied on, had he used the fortnightly Tuesday service, plied by the *Aurania, Servia* and *Gallia.* None of these ships left from Plymouth but all from Liverpool, disembarking their passengers at the company's centrally situated wharves, 51 and 52 (North River) New York City, and at the New Pier, foot of Clyde Street, East Boston.

Cary decided to forget Plymouth. This was obviously a mistake on Spencer Waring's part. In her view the New York Saturday mail service from Liverpool was the most likely option and that Ironsmith had traveled on the *Campania,* the *Lucania,* the *Etruria* or the *Umbria.* Second class, she hazarded, on a return ticket which would have cost him between $75 and $110. She applied to the Cunard Steamship Company and found to her astonishment that passenger lists existed. These, however, were kept in the country of destination, in this case in the National Archives in Washington, D.C. It took her a little while but she found what she wanted—or what she needed to know.

George Ironsmith had traveled to Liverpool from New York on Saturday July 15, 1905, and returned from Liverpool to New York on July 29.

He had made the journey from the United States alone but he had not gone back unaccompanied.

28

It was all so long ago.

The *Lucania*'s passenger list showed only that among the second-class passengers on Saturday July 29, 1905, had been George Ironsmith and Mary Ironsmith, the latter traveling at half fare and so therefore a child between the ages of two and twelve.

If Ironsmith had a child there was no evidence for it. He had been a bachelor when he married in February 1904. The Waring family had never heard a whisper or rumor of some child born to him and his wife before they were married. Letters which had passed between him and Mary Schaffer made it clear she had no children of her first marriage.

Questioned by Cary, Lisa said she had no idea who this child was, had never before heard mention of a child in this connection. Plainly, this digression made her impatient. All she wanted was for Cary to recognize her great-grandfather as the murderer of Lizzie. Probably this child was just someone Ironsmith had been asked to take to America in his charge, had Cary thought of that?

That would hardly explain that child being called Mary Ironsmith, Cary said. Besides, what parents or guardians would place their little girl in the care of an unknown young man on a six-day sea voyage?

It was Cary herself who at last expressed what we had both been thinking and had both half-dismissed as impossible. She had been rereading the first volume of the diaries in the hope of finding a positive Roper clue. What she did find wasn't a statement of contemporary fact at all but only one of Anna's famous stories.

She rang me up to tell me. The date was years after the Roper affair, December 18, 1913.

> My cousin Sigrid told me that in the street next to them in Stockholm there lived a man who was condemned to death for murdering a woman. It was a strange story. He was married but he and his wife had no children and they desperately wanted a child. It must have been the wife's fault because he had a child by his mistress who lived up in Sollentuna. The mistress refused to give up the child, she wanted him to divorce his wife and marry her, but he loved the wife, so he murdered the mistress and took the child for himself and his wife to adopt.

It was just a story, I said. Hadn't Anna been writing about guillotines, of all things?

"I know it's a story. I'm not saying Anna is doing anything more than referring to something she was told by someone else possibly ten or more years before. But it's a scenario, isn't it? It's something that happens. It happened in Sweden in 1900 or whatever and it could have happened in England in 1905."

I said the child called Mary Ironsmith who accompanied George Ironsmith on the *Lucania* couldn't have been Edith Roper. She was too old. Unless she was over two he wouldn't have had to pay a fare for her.

"Edith was too old to be Swanny Kjaer," Cary said, "and now you're saying she was too young to have been Mary Ironsmith. But look at it this way. He would have wanted to avoid too many questions being asked, wouldn't he? Edith was a big child and she was walking. She probably looked two years old. Ironsmith had no way of knowing when Lizzie's body would be found. He didn't know Maria Hyde wasn't alive and asking questions. It was a piece of luck for him they weren't found for a week. By then he'd arrived in New York and no doubt was on his way in the train to Chicago."

"You're saying that if he hadn't bought her a ticket he might have been questioned about her age and he wouldn't have been able to prove she was under two?"

"More than that. He wouldn't have wanted to be even suspected of traveling with a girl child of fourteen months. According to the passengers log book, Marconi's Wireless Telegraphy was installed on all Cunard passenger boats. I'll read you what it says: 'The world's news and weather reports are circulated by this means between isolated liners crossing the Atlantic, and passengers' messages are accurately transmitted to the shore, even while many hundreds of miles from land.' "

Hadn't I read, I said, that Crippen in 1910 had been the first murderer apprehended at sea by the means of wireless?

"Ironsmith didn't want to precede him by five years, did he?" said Cary.

The unwritten script we made, verbally, among ourselves, Cary and Miles, Paul and I, had Ironsmith asking Lizzie to give their daughter up to him as soon as he married. He had married a woman that he knew could never have children and who wanted a child. Cary suggested he made a trip to this country specifically for the purpose of gaining possession of Edith, that he asked for her, offered to buy her, and when his efforts failed began making threats. Had it been in dread of Roper's finding out from her former lover himself, that Lizzie confessed to her husband Edith wasn't his? Did she preempt an uglier revelation?

Miles believed Lizzie half-yielded. After all, it looked as if she would lose her husband if she persisted in his bringing up her child. As it was, he had gone to Cambridge without her and taken her son with him. He had already told her (Miles thought) that when she joined him in Cambridge after a week or so she was to come alone. The child could be left with Maria Hyde. Miles said he had never understood that arrangement whereby Roper and his son went to Cambridge and Lizzie was left behind. It would have been another matter if it had been a permanent separation but it wasn't. Roper had evidently expected her the following Saturday. However, all was explained if Lizzie was left behind to spend the next few days finding a home for Edith or persuading her mother to keep her.

But Lizzie loved the child, Cary objected. Lizzie wouldn't have considered giving her up. Ah, but she might have done at the prospect of being a deserted wife and without means of support. No alimony in those days, no maintenance, for a woman who was a "guilty party." Better to join Roper in Cambridge and maintain an outward respectability, especially if she knew Edith was being well-cared for, was wanted and loved and getting a better chance in life than she could give her.

"That's all very well but she didn't give her up to Ironsmith," Paul said.

"Suppose she promised to do so and reneged at the last minute?"

We considered this suggestion of Cary's. No one had any information about the week preceding the murder. Ironsmith might have been at Devon Villa every day for all we knew, arguing with Lizzie, cajoling, persuading, threatening. At some point she gave in. It could have been the Tuesday or the Wednesday before Roper left. An arrangement was made for Ironsmith to come for Edith on the evening of Thursday July 27 after Roper had gone.

When he got to Devon Villa, letting himself in with the key he had kept since he was lodger in the house, Lizzie told him she had changed her mind. She was keeping Edith and staying in Hackney with her mother. They would survive as they had in the past before Roper came on the scene. No doubt he tried to make her see reason but she was adamant. She hated Roper, she had no feeling for her son. Her little girl was all she had to live for.

Ironsmith had a passage booked on the SS *Lucania* for Saturday July 29, two days off. He had told his wife he would be bringing the child. I kept thinking of Anna's story and the man who had wanted his mistress's child for his wife, had murdered her and just escaped being guillotined. Perhaps such stories proliferated, apocryphal tales founded on a single real instance, and then sometimes they came true. Ironsmith might even have heard such a story himself and made it true.

He went back to Devon Villa next morning. It was Friday

July 28. Florence Fisher had gone out to the shops at ten o'clock. Did he mean to kill Lizzie then or did he only mean to threaten her with the knife he took from the kitchen drawer?

There was no sign of Maria Hyde. Edith lay asleep in her mother's room, worn out perhaps with trying to awaken Lizzie who lay in a deep sleep induced by repeated doses of hyoscin. Why not just take Edith, then? She was Lizzie's child and ostensibly Roper's child, a child born in wedlock. If he had left her alive, Lizzie would have told the police he had abducted Edith and taken her to Liverpool en route for the United States.

So he wrapped himself in the counterpane and cut Lizzie's throat. She knew nothing about it, she never woke. He was a slaughterman, trained to put living creatures swiftly to death. He took Edith with him to Euston Station and caught a train to Liverpool where he bought a one-way passage to America for a child over the age of two but under twelve. He sent a postcard he'd bought in Hackney to his wife and put an asterisk on it to indicate he'd got the child and would be bringing her home. They spent the night in Liverpool and on the following day boarded the SS *Lucania.*

At first Lisa Waring was disproportionately angry. She wanted her great-grandfather vindicated as the true butcher he was; it was another matter altogether having her grandmother revealed as other than the Ironsmiths' legitimate daughter. Cary and I were accused of romancing, of inventing and elaborating. She spent a lot of time on the transatlantic phone to her father and eventually got out of him that as far as he knew his mother had no birth certificate, he had never seen it and none was found among her effects when she was dead. Mary Ironsmith Waring had passed her childhood in Chicago, had married a New Jersey man and spent her entire married life in the pretty little coastal town of Cape May.

A photograph among a number of photographs Spencer Waring sent Lisa was the best evidence. It showed Mary Waring in her wedding dress in 1922 and it might have been Lizzie Roper at her own wedding in 1898. Only the fashions were different.

In this picture it is impossible to see much of the left side of Mary Waring's face. For the pose is turned three-quarters away as Lizzie's is in her photograph. But Lizzie, as far as is known, had no mole on her cheek under the left eye while her daughter did. Lisa had never really known her grandmother, she died in 1970 when Lisa was seven. The many other photographs we saw showed no mole on Mary Waring's face but Spencer Waring wrote to say he remembered such a mole well and the cosmetic steps his mother had taken daily to cover it.

It could never absolutely be proved that George Ironsmith had killed Lizzie Roper, but Edith was found.

Though the worst panic was long past, Cary worried a good deal about her production. But since it offered no solution and made no claims to discovering Edith, "Roper" was transmitted as planned. Before the first episode was shown, Cary and Miles were already setting in train a kind of documentary about the making of "Roper" and the Waring revelations.

Lisa Waring became their consultant. This was what she had wanted in the first place. She was highly excited by the whole thing and would have liked to see a semifictional series made with Roper exonerated and Ironsmith exposed. Cary balked a bit at that, especially as Lisa's father and two of his siblings were still alive and likely to live for years. What they did show in the production was how when "Roper" was finished Lisa had come on the scene and revealed the identity of Edith. There were clips from "Roper," notably Edith as a little child climbing those stairs and disappearing into the darkness at the top. This was followed by a reconstruction of Edith's life, her time with her adoptive parents, Ironsmith's death, her own marriage and her years in Cape May.

Making this seemed to give Cary more pleasure than all her work on "Roper." Her worries, after all, were over. No more truths would appear. The answers were there and it seemed, so she told me, that whenever a problem arose or an unanswered query, Lisa was there with the solution. Lisa was invaluable and Cary was determined to take her on as her assistant for future productions.

They went to the United States for the shooting of the American scenes. The last day of filming was Lisa's twenty-seventh birthday and at the party they had for her she announced she was pregnant. Cary wasn't too pleased because she could see herself losing her assistant, though she suspected nothing, was quite innocent.

Next day Lisa flew back to Los Angeles. Cary didn't go to the airport to see her off and it was some hours before she realized Miles had gone with her.

After Paul had shown me the flaw in Gordon's theory about Swanny's parentage I stopped thinking I should ever find out the truth of it. It was all too long ago, it was too late, too much had been destroyed or never committed to paper.

Cary and I, two childless women, had each adopted a little girl. That, at any rate, was one way of looking at it. She had found who hers was and in the process had lost her lover. I kept mine and abandoned all chance of discovering the infant Swanny's identity. If anything at all had changed it was that the only person we had always known Swanny could scarcely be, we now knew she positively was not.

I have searched this house, I have opened every book and shaken its pages, I have scrutinized the diaries, looking always for tiny pointers and infinitesimal clues. Where else is there to search?

Over the years Anna wrote few letters. What writing she did was for that million-word long novel, her diaries. Uncle Harry's eldest daughter had returned to me the few letters she wrote to him towards the end of his life, the love letters he said were like Robert Browning's. When the diaries began to be published Swanny's second cousin had returned to her the letters Anna had written to his father Ejnar. There is nothing in any of these letters to show that Swanny was not Anna's own child.

Photographs may have pointed the way to identifying Edith Roper; they tell us nothing about Swanny's origins. When I look at the photograph on the book jacket, the studio portrait I chose for this latest set of diaries, replacing the full-length picture with the

Little Mermaid, when I gaze into the familiar face, the strong handsome Nordic face, I fancy sometimes that I see some other one I once knew. Long ago, when I was very young.

But perhaps it is only my grandfather Rasmus that I see. Or my mother who for years Swanny believed was her sister. I don't know.

It is an unsatisfactory way to end, I know that.

1 9 9 1

29

The pages came in a package from Copenhagen. It was just three weeks ago. I didn't even open it on the day of its arrival but put it aside for that hour in the afternoon I keep for dealing with the larger items that come by post.

When Swanny's mantle settled on my shoulders and I took over the task of becoming editor of the diaries, I didn't suppose it would be a full-time task. With the publication of the fourth volume of the diaries I expected, after the initial hype, a long lull in Anna attentions. I hadn't anticipated the huge increase this new book would bring about in the mail I received and the requests for interviews, public appearances and, from newspapers, comments on practically every conceivable subject.

Sandra's successor, whose mind was a filing cabinet of Anna-lore, was to marry a fiancé on the other side of the world. It was a choice between training a new assistant or doing it myself. The compromise I made still left me with a dozen enquiries to respond to each day and a pile of letters that only someone who knew the diaries as I did could answer. It may be true that authors of detective stories have outlines of murder plots sent to them, writers of romance love themes and those who produce travel books accounts by a reader's ancestor of rowing up the Zambesi in 1852. I've heard that it's so. Certainly, I regularly received copies of other people's diaries; old manuscripts, new ones, barely decipherable exercise books, even journals kept by children as a project while on a school trip. They come from all over the world and a good many of them aren't even in English.

One percent of these I send to my publisher. The rest go back where they came from, though I wish they would include return postage or an international money order. When the padded bag came from Denmark, forwarded to me by Gyldendals, I thought it was another one. A sample only, perhaps, a few pages to whet my appetite, because it was thin and it didn't weigh much.

I opened five parcels and two quarto-size envelopes before I came to it. Inside was a diary or part of one. But I didn't notice this at first because that part of the contents of the bag was inside a cardboard folder. Attached to this with a paper clip was a letter and the publisher's usual compliments slip. The letter was in English, the very correct English of the well-educated Dane. Her address was a district of Copenhagen, the date two weeks before. She appeared not to know Swanny was dead, nor that she had been a Danish speaker.

Dear Mrs. Kjaer,

I regret to tell you that my mother, Aase Jórgensen, died in November. I believe you knew her a long time ago and she was a visitor at your home.

When going through her papers I made this interesting discovery. Of course, like everyone, I have read the famous diaries! I saw at once that these pages must be from *Annas Bog*. You have copies but I felt it right to send them to you as I believe these are the originals and they are of historic interest.

My mother, as you know, was a maritime historian and for many years professor at the university. I have tried to account for these pages being in her possession and think Mrs. Anna Westerby must have given them to her because of the references in them to the *Georg Stage*. In 1963, the date of her English visit, my mother researched that happening to prepare for the book she was writing on Danish naval history. No doubt she mentioned the subject to Mrs. Westerby who then provided her with this data.

I enclose the pages and hope they will be of interest.

Yours sincerely,
Christiane Neergaard

It wouldn't be an exaggeration to say I opened the folder with trembling hands. We had looked for those missing pages for so long and always on the premise that it was Swanny who had torn them out. Never once had it occurred to us that Anna herself had removed them. It seemed impossible because we could never imagine a diarist defacing her own records.

And yet it was so like Anna. I could imagine her, at that luncheon party Swanny gave in Aase Jórgensen's honor on the very day the anonymous letter came, I could imagine her talking to Mrs. Jórgensen, saying that she might have something to interest her, running upstairs to find the relevant diary while the desperate Swanny searched everywhere for her in vain. In her room she hunted quickly through the notebooks to find the first one. She didn't want to be long, there was too much fun and food going on downstairs. Here it was, just where she thought, July and August 1905, and here the comments on Tante Frederikke's letter. She found the passages she needed and tore out the pages. What use were they to her? What did she care? The writing had been all, now they were so much dead paper.

Swanny, I remembered, had found Anna and the historian together in the dining room, looking at Royal Copenhagen china. The sheets of paper had been handed over by then, folded and tucked into Aase Jórgensen's handbag. So lightly and casually are great wrongs set in motion and tragedies precipitated.

The pages were all there inside the folder, well-preserved, cared for as by a scholar, untouched by staple or paper clip. The date on the top of the first one was the day after Swanny's birthday, or the day after the day Swanny had been told was her birthday. But there were a few sentences before that, the final words for the entry for July 26 that had seemed to end, "they must ask their father, a sure way of postponing things for months." And the entry for August 2 was incomplete, the continuation of it missing.

I gave the pages to my husband and he translated them into English, reading them aloud to me.

. . .

The baby hasn't moved much today. They don't in the last days before birth. I've been thinking about a story I read from one of the sagas, the one with Swanhild in it.

I'm going to call my daughter Swanhild.

JULY 29, 1905

I'm still waiting, still without pain.

Meanwhile, I do my best to keep occupied, to think of anything except what's going on—or isn't going on—inside me. School has finished for the long summer holiday, so the boys are at home, running about and making a terrible noise. Thank God it never seems to rain anymore and they can be outside in the street.

Hansine asked for the evening off yesterday and I said yes, not wanting her fussing about me. As it was, she was out half the night. I couldn't sleep, of course, and heard her come in at two. Can she have a lover? Anyway, I had the boys in here in the drawing room with me in the evening and told them they were to have a baby sister. I wasn't taking a risk saying that. This time I feel so different from what I've ever felt before that I know it's a girl, there's no other explanation.

It isn't right to let them know all the horrible details at their ages. They have to be shielded from that for a few more years. But instead of that nonsense about storks and gooseberry bushes, I told them Hansine would go out and fetch the baby home when the time came. Of course they asked a lot of questions about where she would find her, would she have to buy her et cetera. I said they'd hear more about that when they were older. Then Knud said he didn't want a girl, he wanted a boy to play with. Girls were no good. They lost interest when I gave them the bag full of cigarette cards Mrs. Gibbons brought round this morning. Her husband must be smoking from morn till night!

The place is alive with mosquitos. I used to think you only got them in the country but they are everywhere. I hate it when you get one in your bedroom and are afraid to go to sleep lest the beastly thing bites you in the night. Mogens has got bites all over his legs. I've told Hansine to rub his legs with rock camphor and then bathe them in cold water.

I know what is wrong. I thought this baby was a girl because I feel different, she, he, feels different. But I've realized, and I felt sick when I did, that it feels different because it's upside down. The baby's head isn't down where it should be but still pressing up against my ribs and its bottom or feet are down where it will have to come out.

JULY 31, 1905

Hansine says she can turn the baby when labor starts. She did it for her sister. Do it now, I said, and she did try, massaging me with her great beefy hands. The baby shifted about and squirmed a bit but she wouldn't turn over and the only result was that I was all over bruises. According to Hansine, it will be easy to turn her once birth starts and she gets moving. I don't want a doctor, I don't want a man doing it, that's for sure. I must think of other things to take my mind off it.

According to the paper, there are lots of people in hospital with mosquito bites. There's a yellow fever epidemic in New Orleans but we don't get that from mosquitos in Europe.

A letter has come from Tante Frederikke all about her friend Mrs. Holst whose son, aged sixteen, was a cadet on the *Georg Stage* but who miraculously escaped when the ship went down. Not miraculously, I suppose. Fifty-eight of them were saved.

The captain of the British ship, Captain Mitchell, seems to have done everything in his power to save the boys. They say he wept when he was a witness at the enquiry before the Danish naval court. The president of the court was very cruel in his attitude to him, blaming him for everything, which earned him a reprimand from counsel for the defense for not being impartial. Anyway, Mrs. Holst told Tante Frederikke that there was another English vessel only 150 yards distant, which steamed away without offering any assistance. The Swedish steamer *Irene*, on the other hand, immediately responded to the signals and saved forty lives. I'm glad because I'm a bit Swedish myself and my favorite cousin Sigrid is a Swede.

Erik's best friend was drowned. He was a year younger, only fifteen, a boy called Oluf Thorvaldsen. The Thorvaldsens live up on Strandvejen, near where my father took that cottage once for a holiday. It's all very dreadful, he was his parents' only child and a brilliant cadet, top of his year. You can't imagine how the collision came to happen. It was a bright starry night and the *Georg Stage* was only three miles outside Copenhagen harbor, on her way to Stockholm. The *Ancona*, out of Leith, was carrying a cargo of coal from Alloa in Scotland to Königsberg in Prussia, steaming twelve knots, whatever that means. The *Georg Stage* crossed her bows and drove nearly fifteen feet of her stem into the steamer's side.

But this did a lot more harm to the training ship than it did to the steamer. It went down in less than a minute and a half. Most of the cadets on board were asleep! There was no time to launch the lifeboats. The papers here and in Denmark said there was no panic, it was all conducted very coolly, but not according to Erik, Tante Frederikke says. The screams and terror were frightful. Boys were clinging to the wreckage and calling out to the sailors to come and save them. They were calling for their mothers, which they say men always do at the point of death. The *Georg Stage* now lies six fathoms under the sea.

AUGUST 1, 1905

I said I wouldn't write in this diary every day but I do it because there is nothing else. Hansine has taken over, looking after the house, caring for the boys. I am waiting. Today is the day I calculated she would be born but everything is still, expectant, waiting. I no longer go out, I haven't been out since last Thursday.

Hansine brings me the newspapers. The Kaiser has gone to Bernstorff Castle as the guest of King Christian. He's calling himself once again a son of the Danish House, though on what grounds

I can't think. It would be monstrous if a Hohenzollern prince became King of Norway when there are Swedish and Danish candidates. But they say they are going to let the Norwegian people choose, which everyone must see is the proper thing.

More on the *Georg Stage*. Not in the newspapers but a letter from Mrs. Holst. I *was* surprised because I hardly know her, have met her only a few times and she wasn't invited to our wedding, which displeased Tante Frederikke a good deal. I suppose Tante gave her my address.

She must have a very strange idea of geography if she thinks, as she seems to, that Leith is near London. She doesn't want much, I must say! Only that I should find out Captain Mitchell's address so that she can get in touch with him and thank him for saving her son's life.

Why couldn't she have thanked him while he was in Copenhagen at the enquiry? Anyway, I should think there was considerable doubt as to how much saving Mitchell did and how much he was to blame. He *said* the *Georg Stage* abruptly changed course and he heard no bells from her, while Captain Malte Brun of the training ship said that the two vessels were almost parallel until the *Ancona* changed *her* course and he knew a collision had to happen. The president of the Court believed Captain Brun, there's not much doubt about that, even though Captain Mitchell said he'd been following a line he'd previously taken with a pilot to guide him.

AUGUST 2, 1905

Such a lot has happened! I am writing this in bed with my baby beside me. Things have worked out well. Once I had fed her and seen her fall happily asleep, I had this great urge to write and just record her arrival and my happiness. Is there anything to compare with the happiness that follows great grief, when all is made good, like waking after a bad dream you thought was real? My girl, my daughter, at last I

. . .

Here a page was missing. This was the page with too many intima-
cies or confessions on it to be given to Mrs. Jórgensen.

AUGUST 4, 1905

On Wednesday afternoon Hansine left Knud with me and went to
fetch Mogens home from his friend John's house in Malvern Road
where he'd been playing since the morning. Mogens wasn't surprised to see her coming along Richmond Road with a baby in her
arms, it was what he had been expecting. "Hansine's a stork, Mor,"
he said when he came running into my bedroom. Knud didn't say
a word, just stared. I sent them away and put the baby to my breast,
which I must say was a relief to me and I daresay to her.

The Princess of Wales' baby has been christened John Charles
Francis and Prince Charles of Denmark was among his godfathers.
I expect they had him because they're hoping he's going to be King
of Norway. I shan't have my baby christened. What's the point? It's
all a lot of bosh, anyway. She's a very pretty baby, fairer than the
others were. All babies have dark blue eyes but I think hers will stay
that color. Her features are very well-formed and regular and she
has a beautiful mouth.

AUGUST 18, 1905

This afternoon Hansine and I and the boys and Swanhild all went
to Wembley Park to see a man try to fly. Isn't it strange how all
people want to fly? That's what the nicest dreams one has are about.
This man's name is Mr. Wilson and he thought he had over-
come the problems of flying, but he hadn't. His machine fell into
the water.

I would have liked to see the pygmies at the Hippodrome. They
come from a forest in Central Africa and before they were brought
here only four explorers had ever seen them. Apparently, they are

tiny people but normal, not like dwarfs. Anyway, I couldn't go alone and Hansine couldn't come with me because of the children. This, as far as I can see, is the only reason for having a man about.

I've written to Mrs. Holst. I had the brilliant idea of looking in back numbers of newspapers. We never throw them away in the summer, but are saving them for winter fires. There I found what she could have found if she'd thought of looking in the Danish paper's account of the enquiry. So I told her that I couldn't find Captain Mitchell's address but she should write to him care of the company that owns the *Ancona*, James Currie and Company, of Leith, *Scotland*.

Next week I must go up to Sandringham Road where the registrar is and register Swanhild's birth.

We looked at each other, Paul and I. I took the pages and his translation from him. There is a kind of disappointment so intense that it expresses itself as indignation.

I had always *known* those pages, no matter who had torn them out, contained the answer. The answer would be there for us to see and that was why they had been destroyed. But I should have known, as soon as I had read Christiane Neergaard's letter, that the answer couldn't come to light in these circumstances. Anna might be careless, Anna might have little interest in what became of her diary once it was written, but she wouldn't have given a stranger the account of an adoption that her husband hadn't known about, that her daughter, the subject of that adoption, hadn't known about.

"There's absolutely nothing," I said. "Nothing at all. I feel angry. It's ridiculous but I feel angry. Not a clue, not a hint. Swanny might have been Anna's own daughter. I'm beginning to think she *was* Anna's daughter."

"You're wrong about there being no hints," Paul said. "Of course I've seen more of these pages than you have. I translated them, and I can find clues. The child hasn't been born by the time she's writing on August the first, though we know Swanhild Kjaer celebrated her birthday on July the twenty-eighth. Have a look at the entry for August the second. 'Things have worked out well.' An odd thing to say, isn't it, to indicate you've had a baby?"

I thought it was, even for Anna, so cold-blooded sometimes, at others so passionate.

" 'On Wednesday afternoon Hansine left Knud with me and went to fetch Mogens home from his friend John's house in Malvern Road.' That means his friend's mother's been looking after him, the school being on holiday. Then Anna says he's not surprised to see Hansine with a baby in her arms. That must mean there was no baby when he left home that morning. 'Knud didn't say a word, just stared.' So it's pretty evident Knud hadn't seen the baby before either. Indeed, Mogens says that Hansine is the stork who brought her. So what's happened? Sometime between the evening of Tuesday, August the first, and the morning of Wednesday, the second, Anna's had a baby."

"A dead baby?"

"I'd say yes."

I began trying my hand at this sort of reconstruction. "Hansine tried to turn the baby during labor, as Anna says she will. She fails and it's a breech birth, during which the child asphyxiates? Why doesn't she say anything about it? She couldn't have known in 1905 that fifty-eight years later she'd want to give those pages to a historian because they had stuff in them about the *Georg Stage*."

"She does say something about it. In the page that isn't there. When she went upstairs to get those pages for the historian she took that one out and destroyed it. Probably she screwed it up and put it in her wastepaper basket."

"And that page told who Swanny was?"

"Perhaps. Perhaps it told only of Anna's sufferings and loss. She writes of a 'great grief.' That must refer to the death of her own baby."

"Then we're no closer to finding out who Swanny was."

"I wouldn't say that," said Paul.

. . .

Next day Gordon came round in a hired van to take the dollhouse away. He had offered to transport it across London when there was an idea of giving it to his niece, Gail's daughter, Alexandra Digby. But Alexandra, never having been much for dolls, announced at the age of eight that she intended to be an engineer and didn't want Padanaram, so we had to find someone who did, someone preferably who would love it. Even before we were married Paul and I had decided it was a wicked waste, hiding it away on an upper floor at Willow Road, the possession of people who never looked at it from one year's end to another.

Uncle Harry's youngest, the one whose birth in the twenties had brought Anna such pangs of jealousy, had long been a grandmother. Her granddaughter was called Emma and, on some occasion, probably the only occasion any members of that family visited us, had seen the dollhouse and been lost in wonder and awe and, we later learned, desire. After finding out that her parents had room for it, we decided to give the dollhouse to Emma, and Gordon was as willing to take it to her as if his own niece had been the recipient.

Anna would have liked it to go to Harry Duke's descendant, I thought as we carried it downstairs. Swanny would have liked it. My mother, for whom it was made, certainly wouldn't have minded. Before he left on his journey to Chingford, we showed him the yellowed sheets we had begun calling the Neergaard pages and the translation.

It was Paul, of the three of us, who knew most about Hackney but he hadn't spotted what Gordon pointed out. He found the relevant page in the *London A-Z Guide.*

"What was Hansine doing in Richmond Road?"

"Malvern Road, where Mogens was with his friend, runs south at right angles from Richmond Road," Paul said. "It's still there, it's all much the same."

"Yes, but Malvern Road crosses Lavender Grove. You wouldn't go there by way of Richmond Road. It would mean a great detour. You'd go along Lavender Grove and turn right or left. You might just step into Richmond Road if the friend's house was on the corner but you wouldn't 'come along' it which is what Anna says Hansine did."

I asked him if we were to infer that Hansine had brought the baby she was holding in her arms from somewhere in Richmond Road, had been to fetch the baby from its natural mother and was on her way home to Anna when she picked Mogens up from Malvern Road.

"Something like that. But not necessarily in Richmond Road. In some place that could only be easily reached by going along Richmond Road."

He drank up his tea and went off in the van, taking the dollhouse to where it would be appreciated. Paul and I waited five minutes before getting into his car and going up to Hackney.

The area is supposed to be dangerous, people get mugged around there by night. Paul had never let me go alone to his house, he had always come to meet me. But in daylight it looks pleasant, quite elegant Victorian, a good deal cleaner I should think than in Anna's day. No horse dung, for instance, no smoke, no yellow fog.

I'd last been there when Cary and I went prospecting for locations and came finally to the street where Paul had lived. That was south of Richmond Road. Across here Cary and I had walked after inspecting Devon Villa as a potential setting for the film and gone on to Middleton Road. We had walked down here from Navarino Road, across Graham Road, turned right into Richmond Road, and leaving Gayhurst Road school on our right, turned down Lansdowne Road, its name changed over the years to Lansdowne Drive.

This time we started in Malvern Road, which runs parallel to Lansdowne Road on the west side of it. Mogens' friend's house must have been at the top on the corner and he watching from a window or standing in the front garden for him to have seen Hansine coming. If he saw her walking along Richmond Road she must have been coming from Navarino Road and in Navarino Road was Devon Villa.

Paul and I turned right at the top and walked up there. It was a warm almost sultry afternoon. The trees were in heavy leaf, shading the place, sequestering it. In the afternoon sunshine it had a serene and gracious look. Those porticoed entrances at the top of steps, those gracefully proportioned windows, might have belonged to a terrace in Belgravia. Or nearly so, almost so, if you narrowed your eyes.

We stood on the pavement and contemplated Devon Villa. The face of Brenda Curtis, occupant of the ground-floor flat, looked out at us from the window to the right of the steps, looked, failed to recognize me and turned away indifferently.

On just such an afternoon as this, a warm August afternoon Hansine came here and came by prearrangement. You could say she had an appointment. She had an appointment to collect a baby from this house sometime in the afternoon of August 2. Upstairs in Devon Villa lay the bodies of Lizzie Roper and Maria Hyde but that fact was still unknown. It was not to be known for two more days. Roper himself was in Cambridge and his son, Edward, with him.

"Florence Fisher was alone in the house," Paul said. "It must have been Florence that my grandmother went to see. Florence was her friend. Florence was the only person she knew at Devon Villa."

"Are we saying then that, in spite of the medical evidence and all the other evidence against, what Roper told John Smart was true, and Lizzie had been pregnant? Lizzie had given birth at some time before she was killed?"

"Why Lizzie?"

"There was only Lizzie."

"There was Florence."

30

In a moment options were gone and it became the only thing, the inevitable thing. The pieces began to drop into place. We turned away and walked down Navarino Road in silence while I thought of the implications.

Florence Fisher was engaged to be married but she hadn't married, not then or ever. She had kept a tobacconist's shop and had her photograph taken in WVS uniform with the Marchioness of Clovenford.

Did she relate the fact of her pregnancy to Hansine when the two women first met in early July? That pregnancy may not have shown much, especially if Florence was a big woman, as we have been told she was. But perhaps she told Hansine, or admitted to Hansine what was too evident to be concealed.

"Was it known, d'you think? Did the Ropers know?"

"I think so. Roper gave her the sack but Maria Hyde reinstated her," Paul said. "We've never really known why. It gets a lot clearer if she was pregnant. Employers sacked their servants for getting pregnant. It would have horrified the straitlaced Roper but wouldn't have much affected old Maria, whose own daughter was supposed to have had a baby before Roper met her. She'd have had to go when the baby was born. No householder in those days would have let a maid keep a child with her."

I hardly noticed where we were going, Paul and I. I went with him, walking beside him as he led me southwards, and we were in Lavender Grove before I realized it. This was the way Hansine had come with the baby in her arms and the little boy running along by her side. It had been a hot day probably, hotter than today, and the newborn child, Florence's child, ran no risks.

For the first time I looked at that house where Anna lived when she came to London.

The little faces are still there, the young women's faces in stone with stone crowns on their heads, one above the porch and one under each of the upstairs windows. Anna sat inside that window, waiting for her baby to be born and watched the boys playing with their hoops. Outside here, where someone had parked a Land Rover, Rasmus had once left that car called a Hammel in the days when almost no one had cars. In the big bay window hung the lace curtains Anna refused to have.

We had slipped into the way of asking each other questions.

"Why did Swanny celebrate her birthday on July the twenty-eighth?" Paul asked me.

"Probably because she was born on that day and Anna knew it. She was born on Friday, July 28, and perhaps for a time Florence thought she could keep her. The Ropers weren't there, after all. Or perhaps she didn't know what to do about the baby. She wouldn't have known how she was going to live, who would employ her, if her boyfriend would still marry her. In some ways Anna losing her own baby was a godsend. Here was someone—a lady—who actually wanted her little girl."

"Did Florence deliver the baby on her own? In that hole off the kitchen where she had her bedroom?"

I said we'd have another look at the diaries and the Ward-Carpenter piece on Roper. We'd go home now and have recourse to our documents. Back in Willow Road we spread the lot out on the table in front of us, the diaries, the originals of the diaries, the Ward-Carpenter account, the trial transcript, the Neergaard pages and Paul's translation.

Quoting Ward-Carpenter, Paul said, " 'Why Florence was so determined to stay in what was hardly a sinecure, where she was

ill-paid and overworked is unclear.' It's not unclear, is it, if you
know she was seven-and-a-half months pregnant and had nowhere
else to go. At least at Devon Villa she had a roof over her head.

"A few pages on he says of Florence that when she came back
from shopping on the morning of July 28, 'she had begun to feel
ill.' We've always wondered what that illness was. We could account for Lizzie's as the result of taking hyoscin and Maria's
because her heart was bad, but not Florence's. Florence was going
into labor.

"And all this accounts, of course, for Florence's lack of curiosity
as to what was going on upstairs or what had gone on. She had
troubles of her own to think about. At the trial Tate-Memling made
a lot of Florence not using the bread knife for three days. 'She went
for three days from the evening of July 27 until July 30 without a
morsel of bread passing her lips.' That's less surprising if you know
she was having a baby during that time and was possibly quite ill.
The court was amused by those digs he had at Florence because she
didn't go upstairs to clean until August 4, although she was employed to clean the house. I'd say the last thing she was interested
in was the state of the rooms on the second floor.

"Her pregnancy and imminent delivery is also a reason for her
not carrying that tray upstairs for Maria. We now know why she
didn't. Even Ward-Carpenter says she had to 'take to her bed and
remain there for the next two days.' "

"Was she quite alone?" I found the thought appalling. After
eighty-six years it was still unbearable.

"I don't think she was," Paul said. "Have a look at the Neergaard
pages. Look at the entry for July 29. Anna writes, "Hansine asked
for the evening off yesterday and I said yes, not wanting her fussing
about me. As it was, she was out half the night . . . I heard her come
in at two," and then she speculates as to whether my grandmother
has a lover. But we know where she was. Apparently, she had some
reputation as an amateur midwife. She was round at Devon Villa,
helping to deliver Florence's baby."

"Swanny," I said.

"Swanny. My grandmother knew who she was better than anyone because she delivered her. And we know Swanny was indeed born on July 28, probably just before midnight, if Hansine got home to Lavender Grove at two."

"Did Anna know?"

"Not then. I think my grandmother told her about Florence's baby after her own baby was born dead. Perhaps some few hours after that."

There was something it had never occurred to me to ask him. "What did you call her?" I said.

"Who?"

"Hansine. Your grandmother."

"My mother wouldn't let me call her Mormor. I called her Gran. Why?"

"It was a daring thing she did. She must have been a woman of character. I wonder if Anna's baby was a boy or a girl. And I wonder what they did with him or her, what they did with the body. Buried it in the garden?"

"Probably. I don't think we're going to suggest someone should dig and see, do you?"

"Anna never said a word about it. Not a word. I suppose she forgot, she made herself forget. They only lived in that house till the summer of 1906."

"So when was Anna's dead child born?"

"On the night of August 1. Hansine went to fetch Florence's baby on the afternoon of August 2."

It was no wonder Anna so much disliked—and feared—Hansine. Hansine had done so much for her and knew so much. Only once does she say an even moderately generous thing about Hansine and that's when she considers sacking her for telling Swanny her mother can be unkind—"We've been through so much together . . ."

"Who was Swanny's father?" I said. "It can't have been Roper, can it? Swanny thought Roper was her father."

"But that was only when she thought Lizzie was her mother."

"True. Anyway, she may have appeared for his defense but she didn't like Roper. She was engaged, the father was the man she was engaged to. What do we know about him?"

"Not much and what there is is all in Ward-Carpenter."

"And a bit in Cora Green," I said. "He wasn't mentioned by name at the trial."

Paul found the relevant piece in Ward-Carpenter and there certainly wasn't much. The fiancé's name was Ernest Henry Herzog, "himself the grandson of immigrants." This presumably refers to the fact that Joseph Dzerjinski was an immigrant. Ward-Carpenter says Herzog was in service with a family in Islington and describes him for some reason as "socially a cut above her." No explanation is given for why they never married. Perhaps no one knew but Florence and Herzog. Ward-Carpenter says that at the time Roper sacked her, in early July, she still expected to be married the following spring.

So why didn't they marry? It can't have been the reason Anna used to give for why a girl should preserve her virginity, that no man would want a bride who had lost hers. Florence was over seven months pregnant when Roper gave her notice, yet she still expected to be married. Therefore, her fiancé must have known of the pregnancy. Why did he leave her to give birth alone, in that empty house?

Because she wouldn't be alone. She'd have Hansine. For all he knew, she would also have Maria Hyde and Lizzie Roper. Because his own duties as a domestic servant prevented him being there. Did he perhaps still intend to marry her even after the baby was born, Paul asked. Possibly, he stipulated for some reason—he was too young? he would lose his job?—that he would marry her but wouldn't take the baby.

"But he didn't marry her," I said.

"It's possible, you know, that when it came to it she wouldn't have him. If he'd married her before the child was born that would have been all right. But the child was born and given away and she was free again. We tend to think of women at that particular time as all longing to be married, of having to get married, there was nothing else. Suppose Florence was different and she simply ceased to care for him, even ceased to fancy him. It's possible that something may have happened to put her off marriage, now she didn't need it for her personal safety."

I could hear a distant bell ringing, the way one does. It was very much the feeling I'd had when I looked analytically at the book jacket photograph of Swanny and saw in that strong Nordic face the shadowy features of someone I knew long ago. Someone, I thought now, I had seen, and last seen, at Morfar's funeral when I was fourteen. But the bell rang on, the bell that Paul's tentative explanation had set ringing.

"I wonder if what put her off," Paul said, "could have been finding those bodies, Maria Hyde dead on the floor, Lizzie on the bed with her throat cut. No one seems to have considered what she thought. No one really treated her like a human being at all, they didn't seem to think of her as having feelings. For instance, she must have had her own ideas about who killed Lizzie. No one cared about her ideas so no one asked. She was a witness for the defense. But, in spite of that, did she take it for granted as everyone did, as the police certainly did, that Roper had killed his wife? She had seen enough of marriage in that house to make her think seriously about embarking on it. Was finding Lizzie with her throat cut the last straw? She had no child to bring up now, Mrs. Westerby round the corner had adopted her child, she felt differently about her fiancé anyway now the birth was behind her. Was this what marriage came to, the ultimate assault, this violence done to a wife? She had already taken steps to get new employment. She would take the job, move up to Stamford Hill and never see her fiancé again."

I said slowly, "There's something in the diaries about it."

"Something in the diaries about what?"

"About a girl throwing her boyfriend over. I can't remember where or even in which volume. It may have been Anna's cousin Sigrid, it may have been the daughter of some friend."

"Is it relevant?"

"Oh, yes," I said, "I'm sure it's relevant."

We set about looking. There was nothing in the Neergaard

pages, which was where we looked first. I even thought I might have remembered it because those bits of the diaries were the latest I'd read. Then Paul began working through Anna's originals and I read the volume from 1905 to 1914 that is called *Anna.*

I don't know how many thousand words there are but the Neergaard pages alone contain over seventeen hundred. Paul wanted to know if I was sure that what had sparked off that vague memory was definitely in the diaries. Or might it have been in the Ward-Carpenter account or even in the trial transcript? It was the next day and we'd been reading for hours before he asked. By that time I wasn't even sure anymore.

"It's more likely not to have been in the diaries," he said, "because Anna probably didn't know who Swanny's father was."

"I'm not saying it's as direct as that." I wasn't. That seemed almost presumptuous. "It may be no more than one of Anna's stories. After all, if we'd attended to Anna's stories earlier we might have guessed the motive for Ironsmith's killing Lizzie and even that it was Ironsmith who did it."

So we read out every Anna story we came to but none was appropriate. I finished *Anna* a bit sooner than he did and moved on to volume two, *A Live Thing in a Dead Room, 1915–1924.* Paul remained doubtful about the source of my flash of recognition and returned to Ward-Carpenter. He wondered where Ward-Carpenter got his information from. How did he know Florence's fiancé was called Ernest Henry Herzog? There was no mention of the man's name at the trial, none of course in Arthur Roper's memoir. It must have come from Cora Green's story for the *Star.*

"It didn't," I said. "I've read that and the man's not mentioned by name. I suppose Florence could have told him herself."

"When did Florence die?"

"Cary told me she thought 1971. The Ward-Carpenter piece was written in the thirties. I think he must have interviewed her. There are facts he couldn't have got otherwise. How would he have known the names of Lizzie's lovers? They weren't mentioned at the trial. Cora Green writes about Middlemass but only by his surname and she doesn't know if another man was Hobb or Cobb, but

Ward-Carpenter does. He must have got Middlemass' first name as Percy from Florence."

"So Florence told him she'd been engaged to a man called Herzog and he must have said that was an unusual name for an Englishman. It would have been a good deal more unusual in 1934 or whenever this was."

"And she said his grandfather was an immigrant as Mr. Dzerjinski had been. She also told Ward-Carpenter he was in service with a family in Islington. Where does he get the information that Herzog was a year younger than Florence?"

"Not from Cora Green, so from Florence herself."

Paul said, "Is there any more we're going to know? Is there any more *to* know? This is who Swanny's father was, Ernest Henry Herzog, a servant, aged twenty-four."

"I wonder what he looked like," I said.

"Tall and fair and handsome, I should think. North German—looking possibly. Herzog is a German name. That can't have been very pleasant for him when the war came nine years later. There was enormous prejudice against anything German. Orchestras even stopped playing Mozart and Beethoven." Paul looked at me. "What have I said?"

"Oh, Paul."

"What have I said?"

I hadn't been able to find the piece I wanted about the man whose girl jilted him but I knew where to find this one. For some reason I remembered. It was the entry for March 20, 1921, and I suppose I remembered it because in there was the first mention of Hansine's baby, who was Paul's mother. I found what I wanted and read it.

" 'His grandfather was a German who came here back in the 1850s and though his father was born in London and he was too, he had this premonition of what it would be like having that name if war came.' Paul, the translation you made for the last diaries, where is it? It's 1966 I want, I think, or 1967, nearly at the end."

He went to find it. Margrethe Cooper had the last thirteen notebooks and was translating them. It won't be a longer or a thicker volume, though, for Anna wrote less and less often in the last years of the diaries. When Paul put his own typescript in front of me, I found what I wanted in October 2, 1966.

" 'I was twenty-four. It's true I was in love and I meant to marry her but when it came to it she wouldn't have me, she said something had happened to put her off men and marriage' "

"Who are you quoting? Who's speaking?"

"Paul," I said, "you know German. What does Herzog mean? Does it mean anything or is it just a name?"

"It means Duke," he said, and I could see he didn't know. The diaries seldom mention the name. Why should he know?

"Swanny's father was Uncle Harry," I said. "He was Harry Duke."

We sat, digesting it in silence. He had been twenty-two in 1905, a year younger than Florence. What happened to put her off marriage was the murder of Lizzie Roper, the death of Maria Hyde, the disappearance of Edith. Did he know he had a daughter somewhere or did Florence tell him the child was born dead? I was certain he never knew and Anna never knew. He told Swanny you could always see the parents in a child's face but he couldn't see his own in hers. Yet I could. His was the face her photograph dimly recalled to me, though I had seen him for the last time in the fifties.

"I wish she'd known," I said. "She always loved him, she'd have liked him for her father. And Anna loved him. How strange to think of Anna saying she'd like Harry's child when she had her all the time."

The first time Harry came to Padanaram, Swanny had answered the door to him. He called her "this dear young lady." He'd got to know Mogens in the first place because they came from the same part of London and Mogens had once lived in an area of Hackney he knew well. So there weren't even many elements of coincidence in it, after all.

I thought I'd dream of it that night and I wanted to. I even did the reverse of what Anna recommends for avoiding a subject to dream of—think about it before you fall asleep. Deliberately, I didn't think about it, I thought of Paul and our life together and my happiness, but still I failed and I had to imagine the kind of dream I might have had.

The sun is shining, the dull, half-obscured dusty sun of late summer in a city. There is a great deal of dust but no litter, no paper wrappings in the gutter, and there is no smell of fuel oil. Hansine comes down the steps of Devon Villa, with Swanny in her arms. She has closed the door behind her, for Florence can't bring herself to see her off, to watch the child carried away to her new life. Florence is alone in the depths of the house, bereft. Tomorrow she will go to Miss Newman's agency to find a new employer and the day after she will at last betake herself upstairs where an unimagined horror awaits her, where the only living things are the flies that feed on death. But that is to come. In the meantime she is a childless woman again, a woman who has yet to resolve what her future will be.

Mogens is waiting excitedly for Hansine, watching from the window of John's house. Along Richmond Road she comes and she is carrying what he expects to see. He runs to tell his friend and his friend's mother and so it is that when Hansine arrives at the door it is John's mother who is the first to see Swanny in her new guise as a member of the Westerby family.

Women wore such unsuitable clothes then, cumbersome and grotesque for summer's heat. Hansine's long skirt trails in the dust. Her collar comes high and tight up under her chin and she sweats. The big hat is anchored by a hat pin but still it slips and wisps of fair hair come loose from the cottage loaf. The five-day-old baby is better off in her thin lawn gown and Florence's old shawl that wraps her. Mogens is better off in his sailor suit as he runs ahead of Hansine, to get there first, to be the first to tell Mor.

Already he loves this new sister that Hansine has been out to fetch from some mysterious source of babies. No one knows, of course, that he has just eleven years in which to love her, and it is as well they don't. Who would wish to read the book of fate?

There has been little point in his getting to the front door five minutes ahead of Hansine, for only she has a key. But at least he can be the first to reach Mor's bedroom with his news and by the time Hansine comes in she knows and has given a sigh of relief, as if she weren't sure Hansine would find a baby or that the baby would consent to come.

All smiles, all pride, Hansine puts the child into Anna's arms. Then Knud comes to see her. He who has changed his name wants to know the name of this sister.

"Swanhild, but we shall call her Swanny."

She looks up at Hansine and says thank you, a rather cold thank you, and then she says that things have worked out well. Are they going to stay here in her room forever, all of them? Can't they see she wants to be alone with her daughter?

"Take the boys away, will you, Hansine, and dispose of this old shawl while you're about it."

When the door has closed she puts Swanny to the breast, a living child, a girl, a strong child that sucks strongly. Anna could cry with happiness but she doesn't cry. She never does. For a long time she holds Swanny in her arms, feeding her and watching her fall asleep, touching the cheek that is like a plum and stroking the fine fair hair.

But after a while she lays her daughter gently in the bed beside her and does what she has to do. The most important thing, the stuff of life. She takes the notebook and the pen and the ink bottle from the bedside cabinet and begins writing it all down. There in her strong forward-sloping hand go her pain and loss and joy, those profound emotions set down on a page destined for no one's eyes but her own, never to be known and never to be read.